MONICA'S WAR

BUCKET LINE BOOKS LLC

A complete life may be one ending in so full an identification with the nonself that there is no self left to die.
— Bernard Berenson

JO HORNE

MONICA'S WAR ★ ★ ★

BUCKET LINE BOOKS
copyright © 2021 Jo Horne

Book design by Nate Voellm
Typeset in *Maiola*, designed by Veronika Burian

ISBN 979-8-5454405-9-7

★ ★ ★

With deepest gratitude and appreciation to
Ellen B; Meg; Ellen M;
  Bill A.; Bill C.; Bob; Harold; Seab and Tom.

Your love of this story brought Monica
to life with truth and authenticity.

PROLOGUE

January 1944
Occupied Denmark

THEY ARRIVED IN THE BLACKNESS OF PREDAWN ON *this bitterly cold January morning — two men. Shadowy figures dressed in the belted overcoats and fedoras that were the customary garb for those of their ilk, bursting into my bedroom shouting orders and brandishing pistols. Rude, boorish — Gestapo.*

And I thought: Well, here it is.

I had been expecting them, of course. Not in exactly these circumstances to be sure, but I had been warned. Still, I refused to allow them to intimidate me. There are times when having lived an entitled life prepares one for situations such as this — situations where others believe they are in control. At such times, the natural reaction of someone like me is to be momentarily stunned by their very daring, followed by getting immediately to the business of reminding them of their place.

Pushing myself to a half-sitting position, I leaned on pillows piled against the deeply carved headboard and switched on the bedside lamp. From elsewhere in the house I heard voices and movement and knew these two were not alone. Reaching for my cigarettes, I kept my eyes on their faces. "Gentlemen, are you lost?" I snapped the lighter closed, inhaled, and slowly blew out a thin line of smoke.

They blinked under the sudden flare of light and glared at me. Over time I had learned those who use threats, intimidation, and humiliation to get their way are far more comfortable in the shadows. Bullies always are.

I heard others moving through the downstairs rooms of the house — angry voices mingled with exclamations of surprise.

What followed was worthy of a Charlie Chaplin film, had the realities of the circumstances been less dire. One of the men straightened to his full height — which was unimpressive — and cleared his throat. "Monica Beresford Wichfeld," he intoned, "you are under arrest and ordered to come with us at once."

"In my nightgown then." I made a move to throw back the covers as they glanced uncomfortably at each other.

"You may dress, but be quick about it," the one in charge said.

"And do not think of escape," the other chimed in, pushing aside the draperies and raising the blackout shade.

From my position in bed, I could see the grounds surrounding the house, now illuminated by bright lights backlighting helmeted soldiers with machine guns pointed at the house. I made no other move to rise, further irritating my "guests." Sighing with exasperation at their failure to grasp even the simplest elements of common courtesy, I stubbed out my cigarette. "Some privacy, if you please?" My tone was harsher than I intended, but now that they were here, I was impatient to get on with it. There was much to be sorted out. My husband, Jorgen, knew nothing of why these men had come for me, and Viggo, the youngest of our three children — home from university — would be equally as perplexed.

Finally, one of the two I had privately labeled Tweedle Dee and Tweedle

Dum jerked his head toward the door. "We'll be just outside. Be quick."

"Five minutes," Tweedle Dee called out as the two of them positioned themselves in the hall without bothering to close the door.

I will confess that once they were out of sight, I gave in to the stew of panic and fear and uncertainty that churned in my stomach. I had certainly had ample warning to go into hiding. So, why had I elected to stay? I had always known that decision would come with a price — hours of questioning, possibly torture, even death. Feeling the sour taste of bile rising, I swallowed, forcing it back, its sting burning my throat and filling my chest. Throwing back the bedcovers, I crossed the room on bare feet, savoring the silky warmth of the Oriental rug that covered most of the floor, catching a whiff of my favorite perfume as I stepped past my dressing table. But once I opened the double doors of the wardrobe, I found myself frozen with indecision. What did one wear to an interrogation? Something practical and warm. Something heavy that might blunt the blows should they beat me. My favorite tweed walking suit with a caramel-colored matching cashmere sweater seemed appropriate. A pair of the heavy wool stockings Jorgen gave me last Christmas and my most comfortable thick-soled shoes. Dressing quickly, I turned my attention to the details that would be key to the impression I would make on these underlings and their superiors — hair, makeup.

From the hallway I could hear the two agents conferring in low voices. "One minute," one of them suddenly shouted in German, as if calling troops to attention. I leaned into my reflection in the full-length easel mirror to apply some lip rouge, then stepped away and stared at the woman looking back at me. I looked every bit the middle-aged matron I had become, with streaks of silver in my hair, thickening around my middle. I understood that the lines accenting my mouth and eyes could no longer be hidden with cosmetics. But despite my fear of what might lie ahead, I had no doubt I had done what I could to at least shorten this horrid war. My children and their futures were what I saw as important, and the work I had done had all been with that in mind. Whatever was in store for me, I had had nearly half a century of happiness along with adventures I could not have imagined or predicted. Frankly, I viewed these changes in my appearance as hard-earned marks of a life lived without regret – or apology.

I took a moment to straighten the covers on the bed before placing my cigarettes and gold Dunhill lighter in a jacket pocket. Then I strode past my captors, pausing a moment at the top of the stairway leading down to the sitting room I had turned into a library. Along with the private office I had set up in an outbuilding that held the servants' quarters, this room had become my refuge in this beautiful house where I had lived most of my adult life. Realizing there was every possibility I might be seeing it for the last time, I once again felt my throat close and my chest constrict. I squeezed my eyes shut and took a couple of deep breaths, knowing the key to getting through these next hours and days would be maintaining my composure.

One of the men gave me such a rough shove that I had to tighten my grip on the bannister to stop myself from tumbling down the spiral staircase. Just then Jorgen and Viggo were ushered into the room at gunpoint. Both were fully dressed. Jorgen even sported his signature monocle. The years fell away, and I was back in London, at the party where Jorgen and I met during the first war. Back then I had seen the monocle as an affectation. Now I found it endearing. But as my eyes filled with tears, I realized this was not about a monocle. This was about me collecting the images that would get me through the hours of interrogation I was certain to face and comfort me in my imprisonment. I met my husband's gaze, memorizing details – his pale golden hair streaked with silver, his blue eyes, bleary with confusion and, at the same time, icy with indignation. A decade older than my own forty-nine *years, he looked drawn, his fair complexion turned sallow and his hair thinning. In just over a quarter century of marriage, we had been more companions than lovers, and yet, despite the difference in our ages and our contrasting desires and interests, it had been a good union. From its beginning we each got what we needed from the marriage – Jorgen, the heirs necessary to keep his centuries-old familial estate going and the life of leisure he treasured, his time taken up with his beloved gardening, bridge, tennis, and socializing. In return he had never wavered from the promise he had made that I would have the freedom to live life on my sometimes-unconventional terms.*

Having followed me down the stairs, the Gestapo agents pushed past me to confront Jorgen, their belted overcoats protecting them from the chill of a room where the fire had not yet been lit. Dear Jorgen. As many times as I had tried to persuade him otherwise, he had refused to have central heating installed. "The fireplaces and stoves have worked perfectly well for over three centuries," he had insisted.

"You are this woman's husband?" Tweedle Dum barked as he took a step closer to Jorgen in an attempt to intimidate him.

"My family has nothing to do with this," I protested. Of course, it was only a half truth. Our daughter, Varinka, was even now hopefully being whisked to some haven of safety. "You can see for yourself," I continued. "My husband and son are completely perplexed by your presence in our home at this hour. It is me you have come for. Why muddy the waters?"

"We have our orders," Tweedle Dee retorted, swinging around to face me.

I knotted my fingers into fists. They were so tiresome, these pathetic beings who refused to even consider thinking for themselves. "And, naturally, you will follow those orders blindly as you and your like have done throughout this horrid war," I snapped. "Did you never once question the morality of those orders – the sheer madness of what your superiors demand of you, of others who are innocent?"

It was hardly surprising to observe the way the man's eyes widened in shock that anyone – much less a woman – would talk to him in this manner. Jorgen was equally stunned. Of course, it was foolhardy of me to speak to these men in such a way. They could have me shot – have all of us shot – and no one would say a word.

Jorgen stepped between us. "What precisely is this about? Why have you and your men invaded my home?" he demanded, just as our house-keeper arrived with an armload of kindling and knelt to light the fire.

While Jorgen assumed the role of outraged Danish aristocrat, I gave my attention to deciphering the sounds of heavy boot steps tramping about in the rooms above and beyond the library. Rooms were being searched – drawers and cupboards roughly opened and rifled through, glass shattering, soldiers shouting directions to one another, their voices high-pitched with the excitement of the hunt. I shuddered to think of the mess these hooligans were leaving in their wake – a mess others would need to put right once they took me away. I mentally ran through every cabinet and drawer and closet, hoping I had not failed to conceal the documents and other items that might provide the proof they needed for my arrest.

And in that instant, I finally abandoned any idea that I would ever return to Engestofte – this vast Danish estate I had come to think of as home. The home where we raised three incredible children; the home where we hosted parties and celebrated holidays; the home we had shared for over a quarter of a century. But these Nazis were not here because we had been one of a few wealthy aristocratic Danish families. They were not here because of Jorgen or our children.

They were here because of me.

They were here because Jacob Jensen had betrayed me and dozens of others. I had received that news shortly after his arrest. I had never fully trusted the man.

Of course, that was but the start of it, and who can say where the nightmare will end?

I write this from my new home – a cramped and dank prison cell that would easily fit inside my wardrobe. I am surrounded by unfamiliar sounds and smells. Scratching noises in the dark – rats, I think. Stale air and the overpowering odor of urine rising from the torn mattress on the cot. The slamming of a door down the way, jackboots pounding out their dance of power as orders are barked out in German.

The muffled sound of someone sobbing...

another someone screaming...

someone in pain or perhaps dying?

Later as I looked up at the small, barred window through which I could just see a sliver of the waning moon, I heard the key in the lock and the protest of rusty hinges as the door to my cell swung open and a guard motioned me forward.

I am ready, I tell myself as the guard took a grip on my upper arm.

I have lived my life at full throttle, and I believe I have made at least some difference.

And so, it begins....

PART ONE

Another Time
Another War
1915–1930

London – Spring 1915

MONICA GAVE THE WARPED, narrow-planked floor of the canteen a final swipe with the mop. If anyone had told her she would be mopping floors and cleaning toilets when her life should be one constant round of parties and weekends spent at country estates with friends, she would have laughed. But all Great Britain was at war, and for the last several hours she had served countless cups of tea to soldiers passing through on their way to the battlefields on the Continent. She had listened to their stories, admired photographs of their wives or sweethearts or stern-looking parents, heard the tremors in their boyish voices as they talked of adventure to come as if it were a rugby match, but trembled at the thought of leaving home for the first time. These lads – so noticeably young, barely able to grow a mustache although they tried – reminded her of her brothers. Both Tim and Jack were serving in France, along with their father, who was too old to fight but had volunteered as an ambulance driver.

Everyone was anxious to play some part to settle this war to end all wars, even women. Rather than sit out the war at St. Hubert's, the family estate in Northern Ireland, Monica and her mother, Alice, had come to London.

"We must do whatever we can," Alice had announced in that theatrical style that Monica so loved. Alice Massy-Beresford was a woman to be reckoned with. She was well educated, spoke fluent French and German, and had insisted her children learn other languages as well. She had little in common with the dictatorial, sports- and alcohol-loving man a decade older she had married. She found contentment in life in her love of the arts, her home, and her children. And with two sons serving in France, she was determined to do her part.

In addition to the hours Monica spent at the canteen, both women met trains bringing the wounded home from the front, offering the nurses and medic what help they could. Monica preferred the canteen. At least here she did not have to wonder if one day she might look down and see one of her brothers or her father being carried from the train on a stretcher.

While London was hardly the social scene she had imagined before the war, she still found life in the city far more exciting than staying at St. Hubert's could ever be. She and another volunteer, Alix, a lovely and lively Dutch girl, worked well together. Like Monica, Alix came from a well-to-do family with a strong sense of civic duty. The family had moved to London recently, and she and Monica had first met at a party, and then again at the canteen, delighted to renew the acquaintance. "Do you have plans for this evening?" Alix asked now as she polished the coffee urn after returning freshly washed mugs to the shelves.

Setting her mop and bucket aside, Monica perched on a table and lit a cigarette, a habit that had begun as fashion but was quickly becoming a necessity. "Not really." She grinned at her friend and cocked an eyebrow. "I assume you will be spending the evening with your Danish lord of the land?"

Alix talked constantly about the man she'd met at a dinner party hosted by her parents shortly after the family's arrival in London. She'd been seeing the man steadily ever since and was always eager to share the details of her romance with Monica.

"He's hosting a party at his flat in Mayfair. You should come and bring your mother. There are always so many interesting people at Jorgen's parties – from the embassy and such. There will be dancing, of course. Jorgen is a wonderful dancer. Say you'll come."

Alix had a way of speaking in sentences that ran together, especially when she spoke of Jorgen Wichfeld, the Danish aristocrat who currently served as an attaché to Denmark's ambassador to Great Britain. Monica had wondered, but never openly questioned why, Alix's beau was not at the front like seemingly every other eligible bachelor in the region.

"Of course, at his age – he's nearly thirty – he could have stayed at home," Alix explained without the need for Monica to state the question. "But he insisted on doing what he could. Of course, his connections with the ambassador have been useful, and even though his is mostly an honorary post, still…" She frowned as if trying to find the words necessary to justify Jorgen's part in the war. "He certainly does not need to work, and as Denmark is neutral, it's not as if he has a duty," she continued, her tone defensive.

"And what would going home mean?" Monica asked, deliberately changing the focus to what she hoped might be more pleasant. She was so weary of war talk.

Alix brightened at once. "Ten years ago, when his father died, he inherited the family's estate. It is in the southernmost part of the country – near the German border – on the island of Lolland, a hundred miles or so from Copenhagen. His family has owned it for centuries." Alix hurried across the room to where they had left their coats and purses. She rummaged through hers and returned to show Monica a faded black-and-white photograph of a large house on spacious grounds next to a lake.

"Three thousand acres," she reported breathlessly. "And just look at that enormous lake, not to mention this grand house, and of course, the farm buildings. Oh, and there's a chapel."

"Suitable for a wedding, I presume?" Monica teased as she studied the photograph. The house was indeed impressive, situated on a knoll of parklike grounds that rolled down to the lake. Although it looked to be considerably larger, it reminded Monica of her family's home in Ireland – St. Hubert's was also on a lake. Upon closer study of the photograph, she observed another parallel to her family's home: there appeared to be no other house or dwelling nearby, even in the distance. Monica and her brothers had grown up in near isolation, their closest neighbor miles away, and had depended mostly on one another for companionship. "Does he have siblings?"

"Jorgen's mother and sister live there now," Alix explained. "He has a younger brother who lives in America. In Jorgen's absence, they've hired an estate agent to manage the property. But Jorgen says that when he marries, his mother and sister will move to other quarters the family owns."

Monica noticed that apparently the man had spoken of *his* marriage – a union that might or might not include Alix.

"Say you will come out tonight," Alix pleaded, grabbing the

mop and dancing around the room with it.

A party. Dancing. Just two years earlier, Monica had been presented at court to the king and queen. That night she had danced with one handsome young man after another, and she had been so certain this was to be the pattern of her life until she married. Before the war, her calendar had been filled with fetes – picnics, balls, and outings to the theater.

Before the war...

She took a last draw on her cigarette and stubbed it out. It seemed every waking thought these days came down to what had been life before and life since war had come. Alix was offering a chance to return to *before* at least for a few hours.

"If you're sure Mother and I would not be intruding."

Alix laughed. "The more, the merrier, especially in these times."

Alice was delighted at the invitation. "Perhaps you will meet someone," she suggested as they rode together through the streets of London in a carriage sent for them by their host. It had become increasingly evident to Monica that her mother's reasons for coming to London had not been entirely altruistic.

Monica laughed. "Mother, any eligible man still in the city is either old enough to be my grandfather or young enough to be my little brother."

"Don't exaggerate, dear. Your friend Alix seems to have found someone suitable," her mother reminded her.

Monica ignored her mother's comment. She understood Alice Massy-Beresford wanted nothing so much as to see her only daughter – her impetuous, cheeky daughter – settled in a suitable marriage. And Monica was also aware that at age twenty, society dictated she should want that as well. The truth was, she didn't much care whether she ever married. Despite the war, the day they had arrived in London, she had delighted in the bustle that was life in a cosmopolitan city. And, because the war had left every agency shorthanded, women had stepped into roles of management and decision making unheard of in the social circle Monica had known as a child. The very idea that a woman could work, could have a say in how things were done, could state her opinions openly bolstered her ambitions to do one day something that might make a real difference in the world. After all, this new century was still in its infancy, with plenty of time for new ideas to take root.

The carriage came to a halt outside a residence alive with lights and laughter and music, and once they stepped inside the spacious and lavishly furnished town house, a butler in full livery took their wraps.

A party! A real party!

Unable to contain her excitement, Monica squeezed her mother's hand as the two were directed to the large drawing room. She saw that furniture and rugs had been removed to allow space for dancing, and her smile widened. Along the way, they passed men in uniform or formal attire along with ladies dressed in beautiful silks and satins chatting and laughing as waiters wove their way through the throngs of guests, bearing silver trays loaded with canapes and flutes of champagne. Monica ignored the champagne, preferring to drink in the luxurious surroundings. It occurred to her that perhaps Alix had downplayed the extent of Jorgen Wichfeld's wealth. The house and its furnishings were opulent beyond description, yet tasteful. Large colorful floral displays added to the decor. She was glad her mother was with her to see the place for herself.

Alix hurried forward to greet them.

"Come meet Jorgen," she said to Monica after introducing Alice to the ambassador and his wife, who immediately included her in their circle of conversation. Taking Monica's gloved hand, Alix pulled her through the room to where a trio of men stood near the fireplace. Monica smiled politely as Alix made the introductions.

"And this is Jorgen," she said, linking her hand through the crook of his elbow.

Jorgen Wichfeld was not much taller than Monica. He had a delicate, slender build, to which his evening wear had been expertly tailored. His blond hair and fair skin were presumed, given his Scandinavian heritage. The monocle fitted to his left eye was not at all expected. Nor was the way he looked at her, assessing her hair and makeup before glancing at her gown – not exactly haute couture but certainly not inappropriate. He gave her a tight smile and a slight bow. She felt dismissed. She was well aware that most of the guests were from families with far more money than her family had, but the Beresfords could certainly not be considered poor – or common. She decided she did not especially like the Danish aristocrat.

Alix clung to his arm as she offered more context for Monica's presence, and when the small orchestra played the opening bars of a waltz, she insisted Jorgen and Monica must join the other couples who had taken to the floor and were swirling around the room in time to the music. He smiled stiffly and gave Monica a courtly bow before he removed the monocle, allowing it to hang by its gold chain, and offered her his hand. And because it had been far too long since she had danced and because she so loved to dance, Monica accepted.

They fell seamlessly into the rhythm of the waltz, moving as one around the room, weaving their way expertly among the other dancers. She felt his hand at her waist, guiding her subtly to follow his lead. She met his gaze and smiled. He returned her smile and appeared to take a fresh look at her, perhaps surprised to find someone as accomplished on the dance floor as he was. And suddenly the evening promised to be everything she had hoped it might be. After all, she had come for precisely this reason: a respite from the war. And if that respite came in the form of a thirty-year-old diplomat who could dance circles around any other man she had ever known, so be it.

Throughout the evening, she danced with others – men closer in age to her father, boys not yet out of university. She sipped champagne and nibbled canapes. And she danced twice more with Jorgen.

For several days after, she did not give him another thought. She had enjoyed that evening immensely, but she had felt no envy for what her mother referred to as Alix's good fortune. At the canteen it seemed as if they hardly had time to catch their breaths, much less enjoy a cup of tea and a catch-up, so it was a bit of a surprise when Alix told her of the final break, dismissing it with a toss of her blond hair before going on to tell Monica of her new love. Even then Monica's focus was on her friend's latest romance rather than Jorgen Wichfeld. The truth was, she was slightly jealous. Alix had found not one, but two eligible suitors, while Monica seemed destined to rely on her mother's generation for any social activity.

But a few days later when Monica and Alice attended a dinner given by a distant cousin of her father's, Jorgen Wichfeld was also a guest. He looked up as soon as she entered the grand house and immediately excused himself from the group he was engaged with, crossing the room to greet her. His blue-gray eyes sparkled with pleasure, but his smile was shy and reserved.

"This is a surprise," she said.

"A pleasant one, I hope," he replied, and when their host's butler announced dinner was served, Jorgen offered her his arm. "Shall we?"

She was a little taken aback to see they had been seated next to each other and wondered if her mother had had anything to do with that. "I suppose since we are each here unaccompanied," she murmured.

After holding her chair for her and taking his seat, Jorgen nervously cleared his throat. "I cannot lie," he said in a low, accented voice. "When I learned you would be here, I switched the place cards. I apologize for my presumption, but I wanted the opportunity to know you better."

Monica could not have been more shocked. The act was so out of character for how she had viewed this stuffy Dane. "You switched the place cards?" It was a social faux pas that she would never have imagined Jorgen capable of pulling off, and the fact he had delighted her.

Above his starched collar, she saw the telltale sign of a flush of embarrassment. "That's not all. I also sought the invitation once I learned you would be in attendance," he admitted sheepishly.

Monica could not help being flattered. Certainly, Jorgen was an attractive man, well educated and with that charming accent. The war would not last forever, and why not take this opportunity to enjoy herself?

In the weeks that followed that evening, it seemed as if Jorgen showed up at any gathering Monica attended. They danced, making such a striking couple that other couples often stepped aside to give them free rein on the dance floor. But she discovered even more to like about this quiet man. He had a curious mind and was certainly a good listener. He seemed to take her opinions on news of the day seriously, unlike so many other men who could not seem to fathom a woman with a brain. She began to look forward to these evenings and felt a keen disappointment on those rare occasions when Jorgen was not among the guests. Still, he made no overture to invite her for dinner or even a walk in the park.

"It seems unlikely your being where I am on so many occasions is an accident," she said one evening as they stood on their host's balcony enjoying the night air. It was a mark of how comfortable they had become with each other that she was able to tease him when they were alone.

He ducked his head and cleared his throat. "The truth is, Monica, I am quite taken with you. Would you rather I cease trying to win your attention?"

She laughed. "Is that what this is? When we first met, I was quite sure you were not at all impressed."

"And then we danced," he reminded her.

"Hardly a solid foundation for a long-term relationship."

"But since then, we have talked and discovered much in common beyond dancing."

She shrugged, trying to interpret his expression in spite of the shadows of the night, the moon playing hide-and-seek with the clouds. She was certainly no innocent when it came to reading the signals of someone wanting to take the relationship to a deeper level. "Jorgen – "

"May I call on you tomorrow?" he interrupted. "I have something I wish to discuss with you."

She hesitated. He made the invitation sound almost like a

28

business meeting. Perhaps she had misconstrued the signals.

"Very well."

He called for her just after noon, and walking side by side, they followed a path on the grounds of Hyde Park. Jorgen set a brisk pace. He was, as always, impeccably dressed.

"Had I known we were out for a sprint, I might have chosen different footwear," Monica prodded, although she was having no trouble matching his stride.

Jorgen slowed, then indicated a nearby bench. "I apologize. Shall we sit?"

He loosened his silk scarf, removed his leather gloves, and placed one hand on hers. "Monica, the truth is I have come to a time in my life when I must seriously consider taking a wife. I recognize that there is a significant chasm in ages between us."

"Eleven years is not so great," she replied. *Not in these times,* she thought.

His mouth twisted in a sardonic smile. "A decade may as well be a century when it comes to some of the women I have courted."

"And are you courting me?"

"I would like to do precisely that, but I do need for you to understand what a life with me might entail."

She thought of the dreams she'd had for this time of her life – handsome young men, like her in their early twenties, sharing in the carefree activities of the young. The more mature man seated next to her did not fit that picture.

"Really, Jorgen, is it not enough for two people to care for one another, to appreciate the gift of having the opportunity to explore the possibility of simple friendship when so many are dying on the battlefields?"

He was silent for a moment, his expression one of conflict.

Finally, he sighed and said, "The fact is that I have a duty to marry – a duty to produce an heir."

"Like the king and queen?"

"I suppose it is a bit of the same. Allow me to explain."

For the next several minutes he regaled her with the history of his family – a family that had held the same land and estates in Denmark for over three centuries. A family whose fortune had come from the wool industry. He told her of his father's death and how the responsibility for sustaining the dynasty had been thrust upon him. "I was only just in my twenties – my life at its beginning in so many ways."

Like mine is now, she thought wistfully. But she understood what Jorgen was telling her. How many times had she lain awake, thinking of all she wanted to do in her life? At least she was not tied to some dynasty that set boundaries impossible to overcome. "It must have all seemed quite daunting," she offered. "Was there no one to share the duty?"

"My brother, Axel, had already left for America to make his life there. My mother suggested I hire a manager to handle the business end of things while she and my sister maintained the house. I was to come to London, work in the embassy and – as my mother put it – mature."

Monica could not resist a smile. "Mature as in ripen? You are not a crop in the fields, Jorgen."

"Precisely," he replied, tightening his hold on her hand. "And now the time has come when I must secure the future by producing an heir. In short, I need to wed," he said in a tone that dripped with misery.

"How romantic," Monica replied, desperately trying to insert a touch of lightheartedness into this somber conversation.

He grasped both her hands in his. "Oh, my dear Monica, I am stating this so badly. Please allow me to finish. Until now – until you – I had despaired of ever finding any woman who might share my need for complete autonomy over my time and activities. Alix wanted to share, and in some ways dictate, every moment we were together. I found that quite wearing. I could see that in the future, her need to be constantly entertained would become a problem for us both. You, on the other hand, have a maturity and an independent spirit that women twice your age seldom possess."

"Hardly the most affectionate way to put that," Monica said, not sure whether to feel insulted or simply amused. "You make me sound like a dowager." Her nerves were on edge. She was almost certain where all of this was leading. When Jorgen first showed interest, she had thought of his attentions as a welcome respite from the dreariness of wartime London. But now...

"Monica, you do not see what others – and I – see. You have a beauty that glows from within. You have a way of gaining the affection of complete strangers and making them friends. In short, the estate would be fortunate to have you as its mistress. I also understand that at this stage of your life it would be difficult to walk away from the chance for romance and adventure."

He had evidently thought this all through, and Monica had to admit the idea was intriguing, certainly worth serious consideration, given the lack of other options. "And yet, you wish me to consider a life with you in a country I have never even visited on an isolated estate where – "

"And yet," he interrupted, deliberately using her words, "I can offer you a great deal: financial security and, more to the point, the freedom to go about your life, pursue whatever interests you may have now or develop in the future without question or interference. Given our conversations these last few months, I suspect that is extremely important to you."

He was not wrong. While she had certainly entertained fantasies of being swept off her feet by some dashing young swain, Monica had also admired the approach to marriage taken by her parents. Theirs was more a union founded on mutual respect for their differences. Her mother was an educated woman with a love of art and theater and music. Her father was an avid sportsman and lover of the outdoors. They each pursued their separate interests and came together when decisions needed to be made for the future of their children or the good of the family business. Another similarity, Monica realized, was the age difference. Her father was thirteen years older than her mother.

Jorgen continued to press his case. "We would travel – shopping trips to Paris, weekends in the country, theater, and parties with our friends here in London. And the children, once they come..."

"But at the heart of our union would be my duty to give you an heir, Jorgen," Monica said softly. "Nothing more?"

He smoothed a tendril of hair from her temple. "Had I simply needed an heir, Monica, Alix would have sufficed. I need you – your grace and lively personality. At some point, I will be expected to return to my family's home and take up the duties and responsibilities associated with that heritage. You have to have realized by now how dreadful I am in most large social gatherings."

He had not once mentioned love, and yet by the time the war came to an end and young men of her age came home, would it be too late for her to find a match? She liked Jorgen, enjoyed his company, and had found much in common with him. Their childhoods had been similarly isolated, for one thing. Given his wealth, she would never want for anything. And he was promising the independence to pursue her own interests – much as her father had given her mother.

"You may find that 'lively personality' a burden as time goes on," she warned.

He chuckled. "Yes, your mother hinted that you have always been a bit of a rebel."

"You spoke to my mother?"

"In the absence of your father, yes. She has no objections."

No wonder her mother had been unusually critical of Monica's choice in clothing before Jorgen called for her earlier.

She slid her hand free of Jorgen's and stood. "I need time to think," she said.

He stood as well. "Of course. I understand." He clasped his hands behind his back. "Shall I see you home?"

"No. I'll walk a bit more." She touched his cheek. "Thank you, Jorgen," she said, her voice husky with emotion. "I am truly touched by your offer, and I promise to give you my answer soon."

Releasing his hands, he leaned into her caress and nodded. Then he placed his hands gently on her shoulders and pulled her closer as he kissed her cheek, before turning to walk away.

It was the first time he had shown her such affection. There had never once been a moment when she felt he was restraining himself from the desire to kiss her. She thought again of her parents' marriage – the absence of passion. Devotion, yes. Respect? Yes. But passion?

How many times had her mother dismissed that idea?

"You want romance? Passion?" she had scoffed. "Oh, my dear child, you are so incredibly young. Such things – like physical beauty – fade, and then, where are you? It is all well and good to enjoy such frivolities in your youth, but marriage? That is a union that requires a good deal more."

Perhaps her mother had a point. Perhaps marriage was more a partnership aimed at some practical end and founded on mutual esteem than the kind of lusty hunger written about in the romance novels her friends devoured. Monica had to wonder if the newly formed friendship she and Jorgen had forged would be enough on which to build a future – a life. On the other hand, he had demonstrated his respect for her opinions and her ideas, seeking them out when caught up in discussions of world affairs with his friends and colleagues. He had never once dismissed her thoughts on the news of the day or what might be done to bring the war to a quicker end. And although marriage had never been a priority, she did so love children and often thought of what it might be like to have little ones of her own. So perhaps in time...

Thinking on his proposal through a sleepless night, she further realized that Jorgen was offering her a chance to move on with her life – to leave her childhood home behind and seek new horizons despite the war that had interrupted the future she'd imagined. Jorgen was here, and although she did not love him, other than her brother Jack, she had never known anyone who understood her the way this quiet, uncomplicated man did.

"I will not be a traditional sort of wife," she warned him when they met a few days later. "Mother was right to caution you, for I will have my own way."

"Ours will not be a traditional sort of life," he replied as he gently stroked her cheek with the backs of his fingers. "But I assure you it will not be without excitement. We will travel, starting with Paris. I want to introduce you to people there who will take your natural beauty and bring it to the fore."

She stiffened, recalling suddenly the way he had assessed her through that monocle the night they first met. "I don't need a Pygmalion, Jorgen. I am perfectly content with the way I look and dress, and if you are not – "

"Are you averse to Parisian couture then? Some designer frocks to brighten your wardrobe?" Jorgen interrupted.

"Of course not. It's just – "

"Then allow me the privilege of giving you that gift – a wedding present?"

"Do not try and remake me, Jorgen," she said firmly.

He sighed. "I am an aficionado of beauty, Monica. You are a natural beauty. I wish only to bring that essence to full bloom. As for what lies in your mind and heart, only you can shape those parts of you and I assure you, I will not stand in your way." He took a step closer and looked directly into her eyes. "I want you to be happy, Monica. Only then do I believe together we can make a good life."

He was offering her the independence she craved with the security she needed. He was offering her a future that could begin the day they married. How could she refuse? And still, she hesitated.

"Come to St. Hubert's and meet my father and brothers, who will be home on leave next month," she said. "After that I will give you my answer."

Monica was inordinately nervous the weekend Jorgen came to visit at St. Hubert's. Her father, now returned to Ireland permanently, had made no secret of his concern that she was making a poor choice. He certainly agreed it was time Monica married – past time, according to her mother – but Jorgen did not fit the

Beresford model of man who focused his time and energies on competitive sport and political debate. Jorgen was, in her father's opinion, soft. "His interests are frankly effeminate," he told her. "Gardening and arranging flowers? Bridge and tennis?"

Her brother Tim focused his disapproval on the difference in their ages. "Eleven years may seem nothing now, but in another ten years when you are at the height of your vitality and his is waning?"

"No one 'wanes' at forty," she snapped.

Monica turned to Jack, the younger brother she had sought out for advice at every new crossroads of her life. Jack was the one person who had always seemed unmoved by her need to control every situation, often simply walking away from her demands for obedience to some childhood scheme or other. It was Jack's opinion she respected.

"The world is changing, Monica," he said as they walked together arm in arm through the woods where they had spent countless hours at play during their childhood. "This war..." His voice trailed off.

"Don't go back," Monica pleaded. "You've served your time and Father says the war is coming to an end and – "

Jack smiled down at her. "You know me better than that. I have a job to finish, and do not tell me you would not do the same were you in my position."

"You mean if I were a man and permitted to make a real contribution?"

"You are doing your part – and you are changing the subject at hand. This Dane – do you love him?"

Monica chose her words with care. "He is a good man."

Jack released a hoot of laughter. "Then your answer is no. So why marry him? Why marry at all if it doesn't suit you?"

"Spoken like a typical male," she snapped. "What other choices do I have? Stay here and play nursemaid to Mother and Father in their dotage? Live out my days as the spinster sister-in-law with you and your wife once you choose one?"

They walked in silence for some time, stopping on the banks of Lough Erne, where at age ten Monica had dared her brothers to "borrow" a rowboat and join her in crossing the broad lake for a visit with friends on the opposite shore. As always, Tim had surrendered to her demand while Jack had shoved his hands in his pockets and walked away, whistling.

"Does he know you, Monica? I mean, the real you?"

"I believe we understand each other."

Jack pressed his lips together. "And he will make you happy?"

"Happier," she amended.

He wrapped his arm around her shoulder as they turned back to the house. "Then that's your answer."

"But you still don't approve."

"Monica, you have never sought the approval of anyone."

"Except you," she protested.

"No, dear sister. You frequently use me as a sounding board, but only, I suspect, to make sure you are not overlooking some detail that might change the decision you'd already made."

She ducked her head and grinned. It was true.

"You have always looked at whatever the situation might be and made your choice, no matter the opinions of others," Jack continued. "I trust that you know what you are doing now."

She knew it was as close as she would ever come to sanction from Jack to move forward. She also knew if he genuinely believed she was making a mistake in marrying Jorgen, he would not give up so easily. She wrapped her arm around his waist and matched her stride to his. "Thank you," she said softly, and they never spoke of the matter again.

London – Summer 1918

Monica sat at her dressing table staring at her reflection in the oval mirror. She still marveled at the changes Jorgen's friends in Paris had wrought in her outward appearance in the two years since they had married. Now she wore her dark hair parted in the middle and pulled away from her face into an intricate chignon at the nape of her neck, secured by a pair of ivory combs. Her clothing was specifically designed to show off her angular frame. For the evening ahead, she wore a gown of sapphire silk designed by the famous French couturier House of Worth – a gown that showed off her long neck and creamy shoulders to perfection. Her posture was flawless, even regal, thanks to a governess from her childhood who had had her practice walking the length of the long hallways of St. Hubert's with a pitcher of water balanced on her head and a broomstick stretched across her back and secured under her arms.

"You have turned an ugly duckling tomboy into a swan," she had recently teased Jorgen.

Her husband had clearly been filled with pride and pleasure, and later that evening he presented her with a gift of yet another piece of jewelry for her collection.

"Jorgen!" she had protested.

He had smiled that shy, boyish smile she found endearing. "It was just sitting there in the shop window waiting for the perfect home, and I knew at once where it belonged."

After their marriage in June of 1916, followed by a honeymoon to Brighton, the couple had settled into a lavish apartment in one of London's most fashionable neighborhoods. Jorgen hired a cook, butler, and lady's maid – Rose, a member of the Beresford family's staff in Ireland. "She brings us a touch of Ireland," he said on the day he surprised Monica by bringing Rose from the train. "I want you to feel at home, darling, wherever we are."

Money seemed to be of no concern, and practically every night the young couple entertained or went out to parties or dinners or plays. Tonight, they were attending a concert at Albert Hall. She stood and examined her silhouette in the full-length, gilt-framed easel mirror. She ran her palms over her stomach and smiled to find it as flat as ever beneath the soft silk of her gown – a gown unencumbered by the petticoats, bustles, and other obstacles so common in her mother's day. A gown that would soon reveal the swell of her stomach.

She was finally pregnant. She planned to tell Jorgen following the concert – or maybe she would tell him now. This was the news they had both hoped for. Hearing footsteps approaching from outside her door, she leaned into her reflection as she touched up her lipstick. Her heart raced with the anticipation of seeing Jorgen's face when she gave him the announcement they had both waited two years to hear.

"*Entre!*" she called out gaily in answer to the light knock.

But it was Rose, not Jorgen, who opened the door and hesitated before fully entering the room, her expression one of concern. The housekeeper held a small silver tray that carried a telegram – the crisp pale yellow of the envelope unmistakable. Monica froze. Telegrams were harbingers of bad news – especially in times of war – even now that this war was winding down. She motioned Rose forward. On the dressing table, Monica's recently lit cigarette sent up a thin stream of smoke, the acrid scent of it mingling with her perfume as she slid a polished thumbnail under the envelope's flap.

The paper crackled as she pulled it free and read the message: *Regret to tell you Jack dead...very quick...love from Mother.*

Her heart convulsed and she felt as if she could not breathe. The room faded to a mist of disbelief. "Rosie," she managed. But as she crumpled the telegram into a tight ball, she could not seem to find her voice.

"I'll ask Mr. Wichfeld to come to you," Rose murmured and fled the room.

Slowly Monica turned back to the mirror. Acting purely on reflex, she extinguished the smoldering cigarette and scrubbed the freshly applied lipstick from her mouth. Behind her, Jorgen, dressed in the new tuxedo the tailor had delivered that afternoon, entered the room and crossed to her, picking up the telegram she hadn't realized she had dropped. He flattened it out before reading it. "Oh, my darling," he murmured as he placed his hands on her shoulders and gently pulled her into his embrace. "We'll leave for St. Hubert's first thing in the morning."

Monica gathered herself. Of course, although Jack had died in France, they would go home to Ireland so that arrangements could be made and she could find out exactly how this horror had happened.

"We'll leave tonight," she corrected her husband as she slid down the side zipper of her gown and mentally chose her traveling clothes.

The trip itself and the days that followed flowed together in a river of grief and disbelief. They were told that Jack had died courageously fighting one of a long campaign of battles in the north of France. They were told that he would be buried there due to the British government's decision to cease repatriation of war dead as of 1915. They were told that they would receive information about the exact location of his grave.

Monica filed each item away, unable to process anything more than the fact that Jack was gone. At a hastily arranged memorial service, she felt dizzy and swayed unsteadily against Jorgen.

"Are you unwell, dearest?" he whispered.

She realized that in her grief and the rush to get to St. Hubert's, she had never told Jorgen their news – news he had longed to hear since their honeymoon, news they would have celebrated together. But now, she wondered if bringing a child into such a world made any sense at all. Tears rolled down her cheeks, and Jorgen wrapped his arm around her, pulling her closer.

Once the service – which to Monica seemed interminable – ended and they were once again outside where she felt she could breathe, she took her husband's hand and led him away from the other mourners. She urged him to sit beside her on a stone bench in the church's graveyard. The stone was cold and still slightly damp from rain that had fallen the night before. The fact that Jorgen showed no concern for possible damage to his suit, but immediately sat next to her and took her hands in his, touched her deeply. He was the dearest man.

"What is it, Monica?"

She forced a weak smile. "Some good news," she said softly. "I am – we are – a baby, Jorgen. An heir."

She watched the expected emotions play out across his handsome face. Surprise, followed by a split second of delight, and then the somber understanding that this news was not the cause for celebration it might have been just a week earlier.

Jorgen stroked her cheek. "I know your loss is unimaginable, my dear, but in time, with this blessing..."

How often had she heard those words these last terrible days: *in time...with time...once time passes...?*

On her desk back in London was a letter she had never finished. She had begun it on the day she learned she was pregnant. Giddy with happiness, she had written Jack. Her plan had been to give Jorgen the news, show him the letter asking Jack to be the child's godfather, and, assuming her husband agreed, post the letter the following morning.

But now she realized that even as she wrote that message, Jack was already dead. "The others are leaving," she said, not yet ready to think of the years to come – years without her beloved brother there to share the joys, and yes, the sorrows to come. "We should go."

As summer turned to autumn, Monica's mother found solace in religion, attending Mass at least once a day and often receiving the priest for tea and a session of private prayer. Her father and Tim took their comfort in the familiar things they had shared with Jack – hunting, fishing, drinking. But Monica wandered the grounds and woods of her family's home, the places she and her younger but wiser brother had shared, hoping to find some comfort in those haunts of the past. Instead she felt as if half of her was missing.

September and October passed, and the rains came with such a vengeance that crops rotted in the fields. Jorgen was patient and extraordinarily empathetic, but Monica found it impossible to accept that the one person whose opinion and support she relied upon above all others was gone. And with the realization that Jack had been buried in a military cemetery in France and would not be coming home, she became determined to go there. Nothing – not even the fact that she was pregnant, nor that a deadly virus was raging across the continent – would stop her.

Once the armistice was finally announced that November, Monica impatiently ticked off each passing day on the calendar, seeking the exact moment it might be safe to travel to France and see Jack's final resting place for herself. The holidays came and went, barely noticed in the grieving household. And then in mid-January, Monica saw her opportunity. The Allies had announced a Peace Conference at Versailles to begin on January 18. Surely there could be no more definitive signal that the war was indeed over or that it was safe to travel.

She came to the dining room for breakfast for the first time in weeks and announced her intention to leave as soon as possible for France. "I will see for myself that he is truly gone," she said firmly.

Her parents exchanged a look. Jorgen stirred his coffee and stared out the windows that framed the snow-covered gardens. Having made her intentions clear, Monica turned on her heel, climbed the stairs to the second floor, and shut herself inside her room. Minutes later, Jorgen brought her a tray. On it were a crystal goblet filled with orange juice, two thick slices of potato bread accompanied by small silver containers of butter and jam, and a silver vase that held a single sprig of the *plur na greine* he'd nurtured in her parents' greenhouse. The flower's multiple pale-pink heads gave off a fragrance of vanilla. Monica knew the blossoms would turn throughout the day to follow the sun. It was so like her husband to try and reach her through the flowers he loved. Jorgen had used his love of gardening and horticulture to say what he had no words to offer. She knew he would do whatever she asked of him.

He placed the tray on a small table and hesitated. "If the fragrance is too much..."

"It's lovely. Thank you."

"I thought I might do some work in the greenhouse today," he said. "Will you join me?"

Jorgen had delighted Monica's mother with his gifts for cultivating unusual plants and for floral arranging. The rooms of St. Hubert's always came alive with lavish floral displays whenever Jorgen was in residence. In the past Monica had often sat in the wicker rocking chair near his planting table, reading or sharing the latest letter she had received from Jack.

"Not today," she said. She gently touched her protruding stomach. "I'm feeling a bit fatigued – perfectly normal at this stage, according to Mother and Rose." The smile she forced felt more like a grimace, and she knew Jorgen saw that she was lying, using their child as an excuse to remain alone in her room.

"I'll ask Rose to bring you some ginger tea," he said. "Perhaps by dinner..."

The hope in his voice was heartbreaking, but she was incapable of giving him more than a whispered, "Perhaps." Another lie, for she knew she would have no energy for what it would take to dress and make herself presentable for dinner.

Later that night, she sat alone, wrapped in the blanket that had covered Jack's boyhood bed, watching snow fall through the open French doors that led to the small balcony outside her room. From the library below, she heard someone open a window, followed by her father's booming voice. She opened the French doors wider and stepped onto the balcony to listen.

"She is your wife, Wichfeld. You need to take charge for once in your life and forbid her to go." Her father, John Massy-Beresford, had lost patience and was shouting at her husband.

Clearly the discussion had been going on for several minutes. Clearly her father was deep in his cups. Clearly Jorgen was, as usual, refusing to engage.

"Jorgen, dear, we must all face facts," she heard her mother plead. "Monica is not thinking straight these days. It has been months since we received news of Jack's passing, and her grief has only deepened. She refuses to speak of it or to allow any of us to speak of it in her presence. Her health, especially in her delicate state and with this flu still at large...What possible good will it do her or the baby to make such a trip?"

But Monica knew her husband. Jorgen might feel as powerless as her parents did to bring her out of her despair, but he would support whatever she felt she might need to do to find her way back from the devastation of Jack's death. She heard the clink of ice on crystal glass and knew her father was fortifying himself with another drink for another attack on Jorgen's role as a husband. To her relief, Jorgen calmly took control of the situation.

"As you have said, sir, Monica is my wife. She and I will work through this together. And now if you will both excuse me, I want to be sure she has at least tried to eat something. Goodnight."

She envisioned him leaning down to kiss her mother's cheek and giving her father a respectful nod as he left the room. Minutes later she heard him climb the stairs and come to her door. He knocked and, receiving no response, opened it slowly.

"Dearest?"

"I am going to France," she said, her voice raspy.

He crossed the room and sat next to her on the chaise. Taking her hand in his and following her gaze out the open French doors to the winter scene before them, he nodded. "We shall go together," he said. "I'll make some calls to colleagues in the embassy first thing tomorrow."

Had she any tears left in the deep well of her grief, she would have shed them then, so touched was she by his unending commitment to the bargain they had struck on their wedding day. She rested her head on his shoulder. "Thank you," she managed.

After a moment, Jorgen stood and closed the French doors. "You need your sleep, my dear," he advised. "The journey will be difficult."

She knew he was thinking of the emotional rather than the physical toll the trip would take on her. He held out his hand to escort her to her bed, already turned down.

"I'll sleep here on the chaise," she said. "I like looking out at the snow."

"Very well." He brought a pillow from her bed and then covered her with Jack's blanket.

And because he showed such understanding and did not judge how she chose to find her way through her mourning, she felt the fight to have her way fade and curled onto her side on the chaise. He leaned in and kissed her temple before once again crossing the room and switching off the light as he stepped into the hall and closed the door.

In contrast to the dreariness of Ireland, the north of France was awash in sunlight. But the fair weather only served to illuminate the devastation of war. On their drive to Calais, the town closest to Jack's burial place, they passed once rich farmland now scarred by deep trenches and craters created by a constant battering of artillery shells. The houses they passed had been nearly obliterated, walls collapsed into piles of rubble, with no sign of the former occupants whose personal belongings were visible in what rooms had been spared. Rooms missing an outer wall, like the dollhouse Monica had played with as a child. Only these rooms were real, as had been the people who lived there. This was what Jack had seen in his last hours. She closed her eyes against the scene, but her mind re-created the noise, the fear, the panic of those terrible days.

Jorgen had arranged for them to stay in a small hotel on the Boulevard Jacquard. His brother, Axel, and his wealthy American wife, Mabelle, had once stayed there. As the second son, Axel had left Denmark for the United States years earlier, taking a job as an investment banker until he met and married Mabelle Swift, the daughter of a multimillionaire American businessman. These days Axel no longer needed to work, and Mabelle was a generous spouse. In addition to their Manhattan residence, Mabelle's fortune paid for leased properties in England and Scotland, used for hunting and fishing vacations, as well as a suite at the Ritz in both Paris and London where the couple could stay whenever they decided to travel abroad. Mabelle wore the latest in French couture, and because she never wore a gown or outfit more than once, the more frugal Monica became her fashion beneficiary.

Of course, alterations were necessary as there was a significant difference in physique – Mabelle was short and plump, while Monica was tall and slender. But somehow the dressmaker made it all work, and more to the point, Monica and her sister-in-law developed a close friendship. The distinctions between them extended to their personalities as well. Mabelle was outgoing and carefree, while Monica was quieter and far more serious minded. Still, the friendship blossomed, despite their differences and the geographic distance between them. Mabelle had been the one to insist they choose this hotel for their stay, and as soon as the bellman opened the door to their room, Monica understood why Mabelle had been so taken with the place. A golden afternoon light streamed in through the windows of the small suite, easing the memory of what she had witnessed on the way to town. There were two small bedrooms to either side of a cozy sitting room. Since it was early February, a fire had already been lit.

While Jorgen directed the bellhop regarding where to place their luggage, Monica settled onto the damask-covered loveseat next to the fireplace and kicked off her shoes. She was six and a half months pregnant and exhausted after a long day of traveling. As was his custom, Jorgen had arranged for each room to be furnished with a bouquet of fresh flowers. The furnishings of the rooms were colorful if a bit on the shabby side, but then no doubt the hotel had suffered a great deal during the war.

Monica felt her depression deepen and reached for her cigarettes. Once the bellman had unpacked for them, Jorgen thanked him with a generous tip and closed the door.

"Shall we dine in tonight?" he asked.

Monica shrugged. Food held no interest for her, and increasingly, she was incapable of making such routine decisions as when or what to eat.

Jorgen removed an envelope from his inner suit-jacket pocket. "The concierge gave me the information we need to find our way at the cemetery tomorrow," he said. "Our driver will be here at nine o'clock if that suits."

"Not earlier?"

Jorgen released a sigh of weariness. "I will see if it can be arranged," he said and picked up the telephone.

Monica knew she was not being fair to him. He had worked miracles in securing the permissions and transportation necessary to get them here. How many telegrams had he sent seeking the help of former colleagues in the diplomatic world? And when one insisted the trip must be delayed, he moved on to someone else until finally he succeeded. He was trying his best to do whatever she wanted, no doubt in the hope that something might break the logjam of her grief. As he hung up the telephone after ordering an eight o'clock pickup, she stubbed out her cigarette and turned to face him.

"Let's go downstairs for dinner," she said. "It will do us both good to be around other people. And," she added, placing her hand on her stomach, "we never had a chance to celebrate."

The tightness in Jorgen's handsome features softened, and she knew that she had given him hope.

"I'll get changed," she said and headed for the larger of the two bedrooms. They had always maintained separate rooms, agreeing that they were old-fashioned, and besides, their nocturnal habits differed so that neither would get a good night's rest if they shared a room. Behind her she heard Jorgen dial the concierge and request reservations for dinner, adding a request for a bottle of the hotel's finest champagne to be put on ice and delivered to their table.

In the dining room as they were ushered to a table for two near the windows that overlooked the street, Monica was aware of the few other diners watching them with admiring glances. She and Jorgen made a handsome pair – his fair blondness contrasting with her dark hair and flawless complexion. She was thankful they did not see anyone they knew. These people were strangers who had no idea of her pain. They did not look at her with pity, but with approval.

"Shall I order for us?" Jorgen asked once they were seated.

"Yes, please." She doubted she would have much appetite, and Jorgen might as well have a meal he enjoyed. As each course arrived, Jorgen kept their conversation focused on memories of that first trip to Paris. He teased her about her sessions with several top designers – how she had questioned them on the reasons they chose a particular fabric or color or style for her. "You are always soaking in information, Monica," he said, adding with a chuckle, "Even information that might seem trivial to the rest of the world."

She did her best to play her part, reminding him of how he had denigrated her choice in clothing style in those first days after he began courting her. "You do know that I almost sent you packing," she said.

"But when we danced, you forgave me every flaw," he replied just as the waiter brought coffee for them both, and a dessert of fruit in a delicate puff pastry topped with a swirl of whipped cream for Jorgen.

Monica could not imagine ever wanting to dance again. She pretended her frown had to do with the coffee being too hot, her hand shaking as she replaced the porcelain cup on its saucer.

In the far corner of the room, a trio of musicians had accompanied the diners' meals with a selection of soft music. Monica had paid little attention. The music, like the conversation from other tables and the clinking of silver flatware on china, was all part of the overall ambiance of the setting. She was about to retrieve her coffee when the musicians struck up a song too poignant for her to ignore.

"Roses of Picardy" had been popular two years earlier when Jack returned to the front. She and Jorgen had danced to it at their wedding reception. Monica had also danced to it with Jack – her brother softly singing the words as he guided her across the dance floor.

> Roses are shining in Picardy, in the hush of the silver dew;
> Roses are flow'ring in Picardy, but there's never a rose like you.
> And the roses will die with the summertime;
> And our roads may be far apart;
> But there's one rose that dies not in Picardy;
> Tis the rose that I keep in my heart.

Jack had left a few days later to return to duty in France. Tomorrow Monica would visit his grave in Picardy.

London – Autumn 1921

Monica's visit to Jack's burial place early in 1919 did little to assuage her depression and grief, but the birth late in March of her son, Ivan, coupled with the young family's move to a sun-filled, four-story Victorian home in Kensington, rekindled her passion for life. She insisted on nursing the baby even as she and Jorgen steadily revived their social network, attending parties and concerts and entertaining lavishly. That first year after the war ended, they accepted numerous invitations for weekends in the country and, once the threat of the flu epidemic had waned, made several visits to a reinvigorated Paris. Monica reveled in her role as a new mother, delighting in every surprise and discovery life with Ivan brought. His first steps; his first words; the way he had of framing his mother's face with his chubby little hands – she relished it all. With each passing day, Monica felt certain she had found her true calling – motherhood – and she and Jorgen had found the perfect place to raise their family.

"Darling, I have news," Jorgen announced one September afternoon after returning from his post at the embassy. "Apparently my government has decided to have only career diplomats serving at the embassy. I'm afraid your husband is unemployed." He handed his coat, hat, and gloves to his valet and went to the table that held the crystal sherry decanter. He held it aloft with a glance toward Monica.

"Not for me," she said, still digesting what his news actually meant and trying to decipher his mood. Was he disappointed? Upset? Concerned? "Surely there's somewhere you can serve," she said, testing the waters of what Jorgen's reaction to this change might be. At the same time her mind raced with the possibilities of what this news might mean for them as a family. She was pregnant again, and Ivan was still a toddler.

Jorgen shrugged and took a sip of his sherry. "The ambassador expressed his regret, of course. Most kind and appreciative, but he has his orders." He smiled, his eyes twinkling. "The news is hardly calamitous, my dear. I'll have more time to spend here with you and Ivan – and the new baby."

They had been shocked and overcome with joy when they received news that Monica was once again pregnant. "A brother for Ivan," Jorgen had exclaimed.

"Or a sister," Monica had reminded him.

Now she felt the shadow of uncertainty they had known during the war years. What would this mean? "It's ridiculous," she declared. "You've served the embassy for years."

He took a seat beside her on the divan and leaned into the cushions, crossing his legs and studying the color of his sherry. "The truth is that I've been thinking it may be time we return home," he replied. "Mother is especially keen that our next child should be born at Engestofte."

While they had talked often of at least visiting the estate, something always seemed to take precedence – Mabelle and Axel were coming for an extended stay or Monica's father was having health problems and they needed to spend time at St. Hubert's. For Monica, Jorgen's family estate had remained an image in a photograph. But now, clearly, the time had come for her to see this place her husband thought of as home.

Monica pursed her lips. Shortly after Ivan's birth, Jorgen's mother had seen to it that the young couple hired a Danish nanny. Ivan as well as the child she carried would be expected to become fluent in the languages of each parent, and of course, one day Ivan would – as Jorgen had – inherit the family's vast land holdings. Monica, on the other hand, had tried to learn her husband's native tongue and failed miserably.

After the months of mourning Jack, she had finally found contentment in their London home, their friends, and the anticipation of a brother or sister for Ivan. She had always known this day might come, the day when Jorgen would not only be needed at home but would wish to return. She tried not to dwell on all they would be leaving behind – a life that revolved around the two of them and their children, not to mention proximity to her family. Of course, she was his wife and as such committed to certain duties. And the truth was his family's estate had been a mystical place she could only imagine. It was past time she should see it for herself.

"It's not forever," Jorgen assured her, as if reading her thoughts. "We'll still go on holidays, return here and to Paris for visits with friends, and of course, your family is always welcome at Engestofte."

It occurred to her that over these early years of their marriage, she and Jorgen had found their footing. They understood each other. More to the point, she realized now, they each held the other in high esteem and respect. She found his quiet and reclusive persona a comfort, while more than once she had heard him boast to friends and associates about her curious and quick mind. The two of them had formed a bond as parents, delighting in their son and often choosing to provide the fundamentals of caring for the child themselves rather than relying on the nanny. She pressed one palm to her swollen stomach where their next child was making its presence known with a restlessness that made Monica smile.

Let's get on with it, the baby seemed to urge with each shift, protesting the confinement of Monica's body.

Monica snuggled against her husband, resting her cheek on his shoulder. "Absolutely we should go. It's high time I actually visited this place I have only ever seen in photographs," she agreed.

Jorgen chuckled with relief and gratitude. "Not a visit, darling. Home. You'll make it your own," he assured her. He raised his sherry glass in a toast. "To the new mistress of Engestofte!"

The weeks that followed were a whirlwind of farewell parties and luncheons interspersed with shopping and packing for the move. The staff brought trunks from the attic, filling them with items from Monica's trousseau. In large wooden crates, they packed the many wedding gifts the couple had received. The Danish nursemaid oversaw the purchase of new clothes for Ivan and a warmer layette for the baby to come – apparel she assured Monica was necessary for living through the long Danish winters. "Snow can come as early as October," she announced in her thick accent.

"One can only imagine what January and February might be like. You'll need a suitable coat," Monica's sister-in-law, Mabelle, insisted later that afternoon as the two of them sat in a cafe, making lists of what was yet to be done. Jorgen's brother and his wife had been at the London Ritz for several weeks, and Mabelle had been a godsend in helping Monica with accomplishing everything she needed to do for the move.

"One can only imagine finding a coat great enough to cover

this," Monica said, pointing to her pregnancy. The two women laughed, and in the end, they chose a lynx-lined leather walking jacket that did not quite close over her expanding waistline. "Once the baby comes," Mabelle assured her, turning up the collar to frame Monica's face, "it will fit perfectly."

But there was nothing that brought Monica closer to understanding the change her life was taking than the day she and Jorgen went to the embassy, where she relinquished her British passport for the Danish one that confirmed her new citizenship. She hesitated for a moment, studying the well-worn cover and familiar lion and unicorn artwork as well as the pages stamped with the history of her many travels as a British citizen, before handing it to the clerk. In the car on the way back to their Kensington home, she turned the crisp new unstamped pages of her Danish passport and wondered what the future might hold.

The following day they left for Denmark.

The monochromatic photograph Monica had seen of Jorgen's family estate certainly did not do it justice. For one thing, the property was even more remote than she had imagined. After crossing the North Sea from Kingston-on-Hull to Copenhagen, the family boarded a ferry for the trip to Lolland, a large island near the German border. She could not help being surprised when they were met at the dock by an elderly driver, whom her husband introduced as one who had served the family from the time Jorgen was a boy. With a shy smile, the man led them to an old vehicle pockmarked with rust. The interior also showed wear – cracked leather seats and patched floors. Once the luggage was loaded, they passed through the town of Maribo with its quaint buildings and narrow streets of thick cobblestones, worn round and smooth by centuries of foot and wagon traffic. For the most part, their driver was silent, nodding whenever Jorgen made a comment or asked a question – always in Danish. Monica began to regret that, despite Jorgen's hiring a tutor for her in London, her lessons had not progressed beyond a few social essentials.

Hello – *Hej*; Thank you – *Tak skal du have*; Goodbye – *Farvel*; Pleased to meet you – *Det glaeder mig at mode dig.*

This last one had very nearly been her undoing, but she would not give up as she had back in London. She already had so many questions, and since she was now a citizen of Denmark, she would not be someone who clung to her past. As soon as they were settled, she would ask Jorgen to find another tutor for her, and this time she would conquer the language – extra three letters to its alphabet and all.

She turned her attention to the passing scenery. The land was flat, with deep stands of forest opening occasionally onto fertile fields. As their driver turned onto a side road, once again she was struck by the similarities of the estate to St. Hubert's. A tree-lined entrance curving on to the house and outbuildings. A lake. She had been happy in that home of her youth – mostly. She would find her way here.

The sporadic interplay of sunlight through the trees caused her to alternately squint and blink. It was the canopy of a double row of elms that threw everything into dusky shadow from time to time. Suddenly the vista opened before them, revealing the neoclassical house. Monica leaned forward, eager for a closer look. She was delighted to discover the house was a soft ocher color that blended perfectly into its surroundings. It stood backlit by the sun, spotlighting the deep blue of the lake that stretched out in all directions behind it. On their approach to the house,

Monica had caught glimpses of the lake dotted with small islands and coves and could not help recalling the adventures she and her brothers had shared on a similar, although far smaller, lake in Ireland. In years to come, Ivan and his siblings would have such fun exploring the property. She felt herself relax. This felt more like home than she could have imagined. They could make a life here.

As their chauffeur pulled to a stop on the gravel drive, a man Jorgen introduced as Christian Grieg, the agent who had managed the estate in his absence, stepped forward to meet them. As he led them inside, Monica was relieved to realize he spoke English.

"Your mother and sister have moved to Troldebjerg as planned," he said, addressing his remarks to Jorgen.

"Eighty kilometers from here," Jorgen murmured in explanation.

Monica suppressed a smile. Her mother-in-law was daunting, to say the least, an expression of displeasure seemingly permanently etched on her florid face. On the few occasions Monica had been with her, the older woman had dominated the room – and Jorgen. On at least two occasions, Monica had observed his mother questioning Jorgen with sidelong and disapproving glances at her. Sometimes translations were unnecessary.

"Your mother does not like me," she had complained to Jorgen one evening.

He had placed his hand on her cheek. "My mother does not especially like me, my darling."

Once Monica entered the home that had been so welcoming from the outside, her high spirits plummeted. The dour and cold reserve of her mother-in-law was everywhere in evidence. She entered an interior made almost claustrophobic with the onerous decor made popular in the last century. Hardly the lighter decor so fashionable in this new modern era she might have hoped to find. Heavy drapes hung in layers floor to ceiling, blocking the view and the sunlight, while massive pieces of furniture in dark walnut and mahogany seemed to fill every inch of space in the large rooms she could see through doors that opened off the reception hall.

She stepped into what appeared to be a sitting room with barely visible French doors that she suspected might provide a view of the lake and looked around, allowing her gaze to land on the portrait of a lovely young woman that hung above the fireplace. "Who is that?" Monica asked, certain it could not possibly be either Jorgen's mother or sister, even in their younger years.

"My grandmother, Varinka," Jorgen said, coming to stand next to her after discharging the agent to see to the luggage and arrangements for a light meal. "Come, have a look at the gardens." He led Monica to the windows and pulled back the drapes, exposing a view of the grounds, tiered to roll down to the lake beyond. "My grandmother created the terraces with an eye to extending this room outdoors. In her time these rooms were quite different, I assure you. I recall her saying that in countries such as Denmark and Russia where darkness comes early and stays beyond its welcome, one needed to find ways to bring the light indoors."

"She was Russian?" Monica turned back to study the portrait, feeling a closeness to this woman she already regretted she would never meet.

"She spent time there, but no. Her uncle was Niels Rosenkrantz, who served as prime minister of Denmark and later ambassador to St. Petersburg. She was his sole heir and used a part of her inher-

itance to redecorate the estate once she married my grandfather."
He paused, then quietly added, "My mother preferred this."

"But you do not?"

He shrugged, then smiled as they both looked up at the portrait.

"She's so lovely," Monica mused.

"She was much loved as well. As I am sure you will be, my
darling. Welcome home."

Their second child, a daughter, arrived in February, and Jorgen's
eyes misted over when Monica suggested they name the child
for his beloved grandmother. Ivan could not seem to master his
sister's name, so called her "Inkie," a nickname that was soon
adopted by everyone – except her paternal grandmother.

True to his promise Jorgen gave Monica carte blanche to redecorate, and once layers of dark wallpaper were removed in the
public rooms on the main floor, she was delighted to see the house
coming to life as the lighter touch of Varinka's style revealed itself.

Through the long winter Monica continued to explore the
rooms – forty by her count, along with attics and closets, uncov-
ering the treasures of the past. Although Jorgen's mother and
sister had taken most of the household staff with them, Jorgen
hired a new staff to supplement the nanny and Rose, the Irish
maid who had served Monica in London. Monica had to admit
that having Rose in the house made her feel more at ease in her
new surroundings.

"Jorgen, today Rose and I opened a closet and it was filled with
the loveliest assortment of hand-embroidered linens," Monica
reported one evening in late April as the couple walked along the
path that led down to the boat launch. They had donned heavy

coats and galoshes for the walk through the slush and mud. But Monica's spirits were undaunted. There were hints of spring in the snow-covered woods that bordered the property. Soon she and the children would be able to explore the property outside the house. "And Rose discovered a small watercolor by Varinka. It will be perfect for the alcove outside the nursery."

"I'm so impressed with all you've done already, darling. We should plan to entertain as soon as you think the public rooms are complete."

Despite her feeling that before long the house and its furnishings would truly feel like home, Monica was nervous about meeting Jorgen's friends. Her Danish was improving, but certainly not yet to the standard she wanted. "Perhaps in summer," she hedged.

Jorgen smiled, guessing the reason behind her hesitation. "And how are your Danish lessons coming?" he asked.

"I am making progress. Peter is a wonderful teacher and has been such a treasure, helping me communicate with the painters and other tradesmen working on the house." Her young tutor arrived early each morning and had made himself an integral part of the household. "He even tries to teach Rose, although I'm afraid she's far more hopeless at the language than I ever was."

"Speaking the language or not, you have already endeared yourself to everyone at the estate, Monica." Jorgen took her hand as they stood together on the dock, looking out at the lake. "The question is, are you content?" he asked.

"I am." The admission surprised her. They walked on, turning back when the trail became too icy. "Did I tell you Christian told Ivan there is a tree house in the woods?"

Jorgen laughed. "That was Axel's. Mother forbade him to use

it after he fell from the platform and broke his wrist. Ivan's far too young for it now, but I'll ask Christian to have one of the men examine it for needed repairs so it will be ready for him." He turned to face her, turning up the collar of her coat against the evening chill. "Still, I worry about you, darling. I mean, once you've brought the house to life, what will occupy your day?"

"We've only just begun the work. Fully renovating the house will take months, Jorgen. Besides, I have the children," Monica replied, but the truth was he had raised a question Monica had been asking herself. Other than the staff and tradespeople who made deliveries or served her on the rare occasions she went into the nearby village of Maribo, she had not met anyone who seemed likely to share her interests or whom she might eventually think of as a friend or confidante. From time to time she'd overheard one of the staff or a delivery person refer to her as "the young mistress," always with respect, even fondness. But that made her aware that Jorgen's friends were more likely to be his age or even older. She doubted they would approve of her outspoken ways. She thought of her mother-in-law and suppressed a shudder.

They turned back toward the house. "Perhaps until such time as everything is done to your satisfaction, we might at least call on our neighbors," Jorgen mused.

Monica looked out over the vast lake. There was not another dwelling in sight. There were days when she paused in one room or another – all of them with windows that faced the lake – and thought how peaceful it all was. There were also days when she felt overwhelmed with loneliness. Certainly, life at Engestofte was vastly different from the active social life they had enjoyed the years they'd spent in London, and yet she did not feel ready to entertain. Calling on others might be the perfect interim solution. She felt a flutter of excitement at the prospect. "Do you think my Danish will suffice?"

"Your Danish is certainly as good, if not better, than their English," Jorgen assured her.

Over the following weeks, they made their visits, and Monica was pleased to realize there were many who had traveled extensively and had definite and outspoken opinions about world affairs. And contrary to Jorgen's earlier remark, most spoke at least passable if not fluent English as well as the French and German Monica had learned in her youth. She began developing the connections she had been missing since leaving London, and was especially delighted to meet Suzanne Lassen, a writer and illustrator whose mother had attended boarding school with Monica's mother. Suzanne was also recently married and a countess to boot.

Jorgen also introduced her to cousins of the famous Danish writer, Karen Blixen, who was known worldwide by her pen name, Isak Dinesen. Although Karen was away in Kenya, Monica looked forward to meeting her one day, delighting in the stories her cousins related of her adventures. These were women who were doing exciting things – and they were doing them without the need for a man's guidance or blessing.

However, despite Jorgen's entreaties to change her mind, there was one neighboring family she refused to call on. The brothers, Heini and Kurt Haugwitz-Reventlow, were their nearest neighbors, but they were also German and the younger one, Kurt, had served in the German Army during the war.

"The Germans killed Jack," she reminded Jorgen.

"Kurt did not kill your brother," Jorgen argued. "And Heini is my dearest friend since childhood." He rarely lost patience with her, but she could see she was testing him when it came to this point.

"I am not asking you to cut those ties," she replied. "Just do not include me." She truly hated refusing Jorgen anything. He asked for so little and gave her such leeway. She understood that she was being unfair to the brothers, but her unresolved grief and anger over her brother's senseless death made her irrational and petty.

Over the days that followed, Jorgen tried other tactics. "Did you know Hans Christian Andersen wrote that story at Hardenberg Castle?" he asked one evening after stopping by the nursery and hearing Monica reading *The Ugly Duckling* to Ivan before tucking their son in for the night. "No doubt he found inspiration in the fairy tale structure of the castle."

Hardenberg Castle was the Reventlow home, far larger than Engestofte. According to Monica's new friend, Suzanne, the centuries-old structure included a moat, turrets, and expansive parklike grounds where deer grazed. "One expects to see fairies fluttering about and perhaps the occasional unicorn," she reported with a girlish laugh.

When Monica rolled her eyes, Suzanne persisted. "You have to know you and Jorgen are the talk of the island. We were all certain that Jorgen was a confirmed bachelor. Most speculation regarding the next wedding focused on Kurt – he's the younger of the Reventlow brothers, incredibly good looking, and a bit of a rogue, especially when it comes to the fairer sex. But once Jorgen showed up with you, everyone forgot about what Kurt might be up to. Frankly there hasn't been this much curiosity and speculation about anyone in years." She pursed her lips. "Of course, we don't get many newcomers."

"I imagine people are merely curious to see what I've been

doing to the interior of the house," Monica replied.

"Don't play coy, Monica. You must realize everyone is quite taken with you. Those who have met you admire you immensely. You are interesting as well as interested, and you have this unique ability to make others feel important. Even those who have not yet had the pleasure of meeting you are anxious to be part of your circle."

"Jorgen and I plan to entertain just as soon as the redecoration of the house is completed."

"Lovely, but all the more reason to make a connection with the Reventlows now," Suzanne advised. "The social circle here is small, Monica, and both Heini and Kurt are well liked. If you continue to snub them, you are forcing others to choose – and they will not choose a newcomer over men they have been friends with for decades."

Monica knew her friend was right and continued to struggle with how best to handle the situation. One day while she sat at her desk writing her mother, two men arrived in the courtyard on horseback. She watched from behind the lace curtains of a nearby window as they dismounted, handing off the reins to the boy who managed the stables before approaching the front door. Hearing the rise and fall of the knocker and the butler on his way to open the door, she hurried to stop him. Motioning him to follow her, she pointed to the men outside the window.

"Who are those men?" she asked in her schoolgirl Danish.

The butler smiled. "Herr Heinrich and Herr Kurt Reventlow, Fru Wichfeld."

"I am not at home," she said. "If they have come to call on my husband, he will return later this evening."

"*Ja, froken,*" the butler replied, and a moment later she heard him deliver that message to the brothers. She watched as they collected their mounts and rode off, taking particular note of the younger, Kurt, who was about her age and, indeed, undeniably handsome. Heini was older, closer in age to Jorgen. He seemed nice enough, although what could one tell watching from a window? Of course, Suzanne was right. If she continued to ostracize them, Jorgen and even the children would pay a price.

I do not have to be overly friendly – just polite.

As the weather warmed, the invitations began to pour in. The social set on the southern end of Lolland took full advantage of the short summer season, taking turns hosting a variety of events that included tennis and shooting matches, trips to the beach for bathing and picnics, and weekend parties at their estates. Because the work was ongoing at Engestofte, Jorgen and Monica were guests at the homes of their neighbors rather than hosts. And in a community made up of less than a dozen estates, Monica could not avoid crossing paths with the brothers. They attended every gathering, and Monica realized to her chagrin that she was far more aware of Kurt than would be deemed proper.

She did not want to like him, but his carefree, outgoing personality was hard to resist. The man was definitely charming, and while he did not specifically seek her out, there were times when someone of Jorgen's generation would make a remark that had Monica inwardly rolling her eyes and Kurt would glance her way and blatantly roll his, causing her to stifle a girlish giggle. She had begun to feel a connection – one she told herself was because the two of them were closer in age than she was to any of the other men – and most of the women – she encountered.

So, after a few such encounters, she stopped avoiding him, even going so far as to banter with him when he seemed a bit full of himself. On such occasions, he would duck his head and give her that devilish smile that had no doubt conquered female hearts since he was a lad.

She found herself thinking of him often – something he had said usually to someone else that had made her laugh, or the way he talked with his hands, making grand dramatic gestures that enhanced the story he was telling. At such times, he would catch her eye, and more than once she was sure his performance was meant to impress her. Twice he even winked at her. And with seemingly no effort at all, she had to admit he had won her over. German or not, Kurt Reventlow was fun to be around. Being with him made her feel lighter – younger.

Engestofte – Summer 1922

When Suzanne learned the bedrooms at Engestofte were being readied for renovation, she insisted Monica, Jorgen, and the children stay with her. Not that there weren't extra rooms at Engestofte they could easily move to, but Suzanne pointed out that the fumes from the paint and turpentine could not be pleasant or good for the children. Jorgen had been delighted to accept the invitation.

Monica could not deny she found Hovdinsgaard, the estate Suzanne's father-in-law had acquired at the turn of the century, a welcome respite from all the work and workers filling the rooms and corridors at Engestofte. Suzanne and her husband, Emil, were charming hosts eager to make sure their guests had whatever they desired to make their stay more pleasant.

One afternoon after the nanny and Rose had taken Ivan and Inkie, still in her pram, for an outing, and Jorgen was deep into a game of bridge with his hosts and other guests, Monica decided to take a walk. The trails on the Lassen estate wound their way along the lakeshore and on into deep woods that separated one property from the next.

Striding along with the energy that came with being outdoors and free of any social or parental obligation, Monica relished the solitude. Her tutor, Peter, had come up with the idea of improving her understanding of the Danish language through folk songs. It had worked well with Ivan, now a very verbal toddler, and Monica thought, since she was alone, she might give it a try. She hummed a bit of "Mester Jakob," a song her mother had sung in French to her, then sang the words in Danish.

> *Mester Jakob, Mester Jakob,*
> *Sover du?*
> *Sover du?*
> *Hører du ej klokken?*
> *Hører du ej klokken?*
> *Bim – bam – bum*
> *Bim – bam – bum*

She tried it again, louder this time, as she pushed through each syllable, skimming her fingers along the evergreen branches that lined the path, but when she finished the rhyme, she heard someone else singing, making a round of the melody. A strong male baritone coming closer, sounding the last line.

"*Hvem der?*" she called out, hoping she'd managed the correct Danish pronunciation for "Who's there?"

Kurt Reventlow stepped out from behind a cluster of trees. "*Tilgiv mig, Fru,*" he said with a sweeping bow, as if he had just encountered royalty.

Monica could not help but laugh. He looked so ridiculous as he tried without much success to maintain his footing on the path made slick by a morning rain. "English, if you please, kind sir," she replied, dropping into a half curtsey.

He stepped toward her. "I was not stalking you, Fru Wichfeld. I heard you coming and did not wish to interrupt your privacy. But then you began the song and..." He shrugged and grinned sheepishly. "Am I forgiven?" Another step, so near now that she could see his long lashes.

The closeness and the fact they were alone for the first time since meeting each other triggered something in her – a feeling she had not experienced before. A desire to touch his face. He clenched his hand at his side, opening and slowly closing it as smiles faded and their eyes met in a silent debate of should or shouldn't. The attraction arcing between them was both undeniable and shocking. Perhaps for the first time in her life, Monica felt the bashful reticence more usually experienced by a carefree girl than a married woman with two children, both still in nappies.

She moved half a step back and looked away, down the path behind him. "I should get back," she murmured.

"Or we could finish the walk together," he replied softly, then cleared his throat and spoke in a more normal – and appropriate – tone. "The truth is there's something I've been wanting to ask you." He held out his hand. Jorgen – or any other man, for that matter – would have offered his arm. Handholding seemed too intimate, and yet she linked her fingers with his as they walked on. After all he was a neighbor, a friend to her husband if not to her, and where was the harm?

They did not speak for several seconds, she matching her stride to his, both looking straight ahead toward the distant sun-dappled opening that would lead them back to the beautiful two-storied, whitewashed manor house with its glazed, black-tiled roof gleaming in the sunlight.

"You have a question?" she prompted.

"Yes. Will you dance with me tonight? When it comes to the waltz, I am not Jorgen, to be sure, but for weeks now I have tried to work up the courage to ask you."

Her head told her to refuse him, but her heart...

"It really is quite simple. One-two-three," she said, postponing the need to answer his question.

"Perhaps we could practice now," he suggested, as he stopped walking and faced her.

"Here?"

"We're quite alone, and there's no one to see me make a fool of myself."

His smile filled her with such pleasure that she blushed. All her life she'd had a reputation for rash actions. Her father had often despaired that his daughter would ever find a man capable of keeping her in line. But surely this was different. Or was it? If she agreed, she was giving this man who was clearly infatuated with her permission to persist. Local gossip had it that Kurt was exceptionally good at having his way and getting what he wanted. What if he wanted her?

He hummed the tune to the nursery rhyme and held out his arms, his arched eyebrow and dimpled smile a challenge for her to refuse. She placed one hand on his solid shoulder and the other in his outstretched palm. He tightened his hold on her waist but kept his distance. It was true he was not as gifted a dancer as Jorgen, but at the same time, dancing with him engendered feelings within that she had never experienced with Jorgen. She was nervous and far too aware of the scent of his cologne, the warmth of his palm on hers, the difference in the way he held her. For the first time, she felt what she had once heard described as the romance of the dance – an inner heat that spread through her like a fire and hinted at things that might come once the dance ended.

"Bim – bam – bum." He whispered the last line of the folk song as he finished the dance with a dip, then brought her upright so that their faces were barely separated.

He kissed her. This was not a kiss of affection between friends, but rather one of restrained desire. She knew she should protest, but the truth was she did not want to. In Jorgen's arms she had found comfort and security. In Kurt's she suddenly discovered the passion she had dreamed of during the war years. "I should go," she said, stepping away but not letting go.

"You do not strike me as a woman who pays attention to what she *should* do," Kurt replied, moving closer for another kiss.

Monica pressed two fingers to his lips to stop him. "Then allow me to rephrase. I want to go back now, Herr Reventlow. I need to...think."

To her relief, he did not press her, and this time as they fell into step, he offered her his arm. "Under the circumstances," he said, "do you think we might use our Christian names, Monica?"

She felt the twitch of a smile. He was indeed a rogue, flirting shamelessly even after being rebuffed. "Very well, but for now only when we are alone."

His smile was devastating. "That will hardly be an issue, Monica, as I plan to spend a good bit of time alone with you."

She laughed and slapped him lightly on his chest before walking ahead. "We shall see about that."

He stayed where he was, watching her go. "Say my name, Monica," he shouted, startling a flock of birds nesting in the trees.

"Shush," she scolded, with a glance toward the house.

"Shush, who?" he called out.

She was laughing now, feeling lighthearted and girlish. "Kurt," she replied. "Shush, Kurt."

And when she returned to the house, she hoped the flush she felt in her cheeks could be easily attributed to the exercise of a brisk walk rather than the memory of the kiss.

That evening they danced – at Jorgen's insistence. In fact, he encouraged her to dance not only with Kurt, but also with Heini, clearly delighted to see her opening her heart and mind to his close friends.

"You do understand that Kurt has fallen madly in love with you," Suzanne said a few weeks later as the two women sat in Suzanne's drawing room, sipping tea and feasting on a plate of small sandwiches and sweets.

Monica made no effort to pretend she was immune to the signs. She and Kurt had shared two waltzes the night after their encounter in the woods, when Suzanne hosted a dinner that was followed by dancing. He had kept a proper distance, but the things he had murmured to her as they spun around the floor – praising her beauty and what he called her "delectable mystery" – had made her pulse race. "He's infatuated. I am different from other women he has known."

"He told you that?"

Monica shrugged. She was not about to admit that she was captivated by Kurt's charm and good looks, that her thoughts went to him more often than they should whenever she was alone, that she could not help but compare his youthful exuberance and spirit of daring to Jorgen's predictability. She was not about to confide that since her woodland waltz with Kurt, the eleven-year age difference between Jorgen and her felt far greater. Or that she sometimes grieved for what she occasionally thought of as the sacrifice of her youth to the war and a marriage founded more on a business agreement than passion.

"He's in love," Suzanne repeated firmly. "The question is only one of whether or not you return those feelings – " Monica was about to protest when Suzanne raised her hand and continued. "And assuming you do, what does that mean for your marriage?"

"My marriage is only affected should matters move beyond the stage of flirtation."

Suzanne choked on her tea. "Flirtation? Monica! It is perfectly obvious, at least to me, that things have already advanced beyond such innocence, at least in Kurt's mind. Have you kissed?" She sighed in resignation. "Of course, you have – and more than once, judging by the sudden pink highlights in those delightful cheek- bones of yours. He's going to want more, you know. Kurt is not a man who takes things slowly, and the fact that he is never more than an arm's length from you tells me he is making advances and they are being, if not received, certainly considered."

Monica sat forward and placed her teacup on the tray. She glanced over her shoulder, checking to be sure no one was lis- tening. "We are not living in the times of our parents, Suzanne. Things have changed, and..." She paused, flailing about for the words necessary to have her friend understand. "Jorgen and I have a unique relationship," she began. "He understands me – my needs. I am as devoted to him as he is to me, but..."

"You do not love him."

"It's more complicated than simple labels," Monica explained. "Jorgen and I respect the right of the other to live the life that will bring the greatest happiness. For Jorgen that is the hours spent with the children or male friends. He's content to fill his time with bridge or tennis or in his gardens."

"And for you?" Suzanne arched a penciled eyebrow.

Monica hesitated, then admitted, "I need more."

Suzanne chewed her sandwich as she studied her friend. "And if there is gossip? A scandal?"

Monica could not hide her chagrin at that idea. "What business is it of anyone how I choose to live my life? I do not judge others, and as long as my choices do no harm, I simply do not understand why I should be judged."

Suzanne took a sip of her tea. "My guess is any criticism coming your way will be rooted in jealousy. Kurt is possibly the most beautiful male any of us has ever seen, besides which he is charming, kind, and witty, and he has clearly chosen you."

Monica could not hide a smile. "He has asked me – in the presence of Jorgen – to help him decorate the house on the farm he's taken over on their property. He says the castle is his brother's domain and he needs something of his own."

"And Jorgen approves?"

"Jorgen thinks it's a wonderful idea. Now that our house is nearly finished, he says it will give me a new project to fill my time. We have his full support."

"Still..." Suzanne frowned.

Monica reached over and touched her friend's hand. "Jorgen is no fool, Suzanne. He has seen what you and others see when it comes to Kurt's feelings for me. I suppose it does seem odd, but ours is an unusual union. If you must know, Jorgen has made it clear that in some ways Kurt's attentions are a relief to him. When it comes to intimacy, Jorgen is...how can I say this...reserved."

Suzanne blushed scarlet, and Monica realized – not for the first time – that her penchant for openness had gone too far. This might be the 1920s, but for women like Suzanne, there were some topics that were still taboo, even between close friends. "Thank you, for listening and for your caution, dear friend," Monica said.

Suzanne met her gaze. "People are going to talk, Monica. They already are."

Convinced that she was fully in control of what might or might not happen between Kurt and her, Monica began making plans for decorating Kurt's new home. A few days after her lunch with Suzanne, she loaded the Stutz convertible Jorgen had bought for her with swatches of fabric and wallpaper as well as rough sketches she had made. As she drove the winding roads that led from Engestofte to Kurt's farm, she considered what might lie ahead. It was already late afternoon by the time she got the children settled and alerted the staff that since Jorgen would be dining with friends, there was no need for them to prepare an evening meal. "I can fend for myself," she assured their cook.

Had she already been thinking of staying at Kurt's before she even got in the car? Surely not the night, but perhaps sharing a light supper with him before returning home in time to read the children a bedtime story?

When she pulled up to the farmhouse, he was waiting for her, pacing along the edge of the unpaved lane that led to the house. She slowed the car and leaned out the open window. "Am I late?" she asked with a laugh that stopped in her throat when she saw his expression.

"I thought perhaps you had changed your mind," he said, his eyes wide with what could only be described as relief. "I thought..."

"I'm here, Kurt," she said softly, a little taken aback at his agitation. "Shall we go inside?" She pulled the car to a stop and he opened her door, holding his hand out to assist her, and, once she took hold, not letting her go. "I brought things for you to consider," she said, motioning toward the back seat.

"We have time," he said as he led her to the house. Once inside he closed the door, and, as she removed her scarf and gloves, placing them on the side table with her pocketbook, she felt his hands on her shoulders gently urging her to face him.

Before she could think or find the will to protest, he was kissing her – a lover's kiss, one that demanded participation and promised more intimacy to come. She should have pulled away, she should have refused to engage, she should have...

You do not strike me as a woman who lives life based on what she should do, she recalled him telling her.

Was she so very transparent, or was it that Kurt already knew her so well because of the common opinions, likes, and dislikes they had discovered they shared even after knowing each other for such a short time? She felt a bond with this man and realized she was returning his kiss, clutching at his shoulders, urging him closer, giving permission with every passing second for whatever he might have in mind.

"I want you, Monica," he whispered, trailing kisses along her temple and ear as he removed the combs holding her hair in place, then spread the thick dark strands over her shoulders.

We cannot. I am married. The thoughts came instantly, but were as quickly followed by: *But where is the harm?*

Jorgen had taken note of Kurt's interest in her. He had even made it clear that he was well aware of Kurt's attraction. "He's a man with a reputation when it comes to the women he pursues, Monica. Have a care that he understands you are different."

"Yes," she had replied, laughing. "I am married."

Jorgen had arched one eyebrow. "That has hardly mattered to him in the past. No, darling, I am saying you should have this time to enjoy what the war – and marriage to an old man like me – robbed you of. Just make sure it is on your terms, not Kurt's."

"You are not an old man," she had protested.

Jorgen had smiled. "Mature then. The point is, you have made a number of sacrifices for me and if Kurt makes you happy, I see no harm."

"People are already gossiping," she replied.

"It is none of their business, darling. This matter lies between you, me, and Kurt. All I ask is that you not leave us – me and the children."

As if she ever could. She'd been both surprised and touched by Jorgen's pragmatic acceptance of the situation they faced. She might not love Jorgen in what others viewed as a conventional way, but she was devoted to him and to their children.

Now as Kurt drew her close once again, she placed a restraining palm against his chest. "Kurt, please. The servants..."

"I sent them off on errands. We have the house to ourselves at least for the next hour or so." He took her hand and led her into the large room that overlooked his property and served as his library and office. A fire crackled in the tile fireplace, and a sofa upholstered in a woven tweed wool proved irresistible when Kurt sat at one end and drew her down so that she was seated next to him. He opened the crystal decanter that sat with two glasses on a large silver tray on the ottoman next to the fire. Once he'd filled the glasses and handed her one, he leaned back and wrapped his arm around her. After taking a sip of the liquor, she removed her shoes, curling closer to him and resting her head on his shoulder. His fingers stroked her hair as they sat in comfortable silence watching the flames dance.

"I will do as you want, Monica," he said after a time. "But you must already know what it is that I want."

She sat up so she could face him. "And that is?"

"You, Monica. I want you. I have fallen quite madly in love with you. You must at least sense that."

"We barely know one another," she protested.

His answer was to set his glass and hers on the tray and take her in his arms. "I am going to kiss you and then we shall see if perhaps you wish to revise that statement."

This time his kiss was one intended to seduce. Monica felt herself throwing all caution aside. She did not stop him when he pulled her blouse free of the waistband of her skirt and ran his palm over her slip, cupping her breast. In return she tugged at his shirt until she could feel the warmth and smoothness of his muscled back beneath her fingers. She did not stop him when he positioned her so that she leaned against the arm of the sofa, nor when he began opening the buttons of her blouse. He kissed her collarbone, her exposed shoulder, and the heave of her breasts against the pressure of her slip and brassiere. She dug her nails into his back, an action he took as a signal to return his open mouth to hers.

Their gasps at each new discovery and the crackle of the fire were the only sounds. *So, this is true passion,* Monica thought as the fire nearby seemed suddenly to be raging inside her. Kurt pushed her open blouse off her shoulders and lowered the straps of her undergarments. She buried her fingers in his thick hair, thinking all the while she should stop him. But she did not want this incredible feeling to end. This was what she had dreamed of as a girl – a man who would make love to her with unbridled passion, as if he hungered for something only she could provide.

Making love with Jorgen was...

She banished that thought. *I will not compare them.*

Kurt gently set her a little away from him, his hair tousled and his eyes blurry with desire. "I want you, Monica," he said again, his voice husky. "I want to take you to my bed and lie naked with you, making love to you through the night."

Slowly she slipped the straps of her garments back in place. "I need time, Kurt."

He gently brushed her hair away from her face with his fingertips and smiled. "Then it is something you will consider?"

She had expected annoyance. His casual acceptance disarmed her, and she laughed as she stood and retrieved her blouse. "You are impossible, Herr Reventlow. Now what did you do with my combs, and where is the loo? I need to do some damage repair while you bring in my samples and sketches from the car."

"Yes, ma'am." He gave her a mock salute before reaching into the pocket of his trousers and producing the ivory combs. "The 'loo,' as you Brits call it, is just through there."

Following that visit to Kurt's farm, Monica forced herself to keep her distance. One day passed, then two. But by the third day she was so agitated and restless, she could not find peace. Jorgen had left with the children and their nursemaid for a visit with his mother and sister. They would be away overnight.

She picked up the telephone, then immediately replaced the receiver in its cradle. What was she thinking! She started down the hall and was stopped by the ringing of the telephone.

"*Hej*," she answered.

"Come to me," Kurt said, without bothering with the usual greeting.

"I –"

"Or I will come there," he continued, not as a threat but as if the possibility had just occurred to him.

"I'll come to you. We need to talk," Monica said, resolved to end this thing before it began.

Kurt groaned. "Talking was not exactly in the plan, darling." He lowered his voice to a sensual half whisper. "On the other hand, perhaps in the afterglow of our lovemaking, we could – "

Monica could not seem to stop the bubble of laughter that erupted. "You're impossible," she protested.

"And you are still there. Shall I call for you?"

"I'll come for lunch," she bargained.

"I've given the staff the day and evening off," he replied.

"Then you'd best explore the wilds of your kitchen and see what you can find." She rang off without saying goodbye. She touched her fingers to her cheek, feeling the heat of her excitement as she ran up the stairs to change.

Kurt was waiting when she arrived. Without a word, he led her inside and straight to his bedroom. There he'd set out a feast of cheese, bread, apple slices, and wine. Between kisses, they took turns feeding each other morsels from his makeshift picnic. But soon, they abandoned food for peeling away layers of garments until they were both naked on the soft linen sheets.

"Kurt, I – "

"Sh-h-h, my darling," he murmured as he ran his palm over the flat of her stomach and down to urge her legs apart.

She expected that he would mount her then, push in, and in moments it would be done. Surely the kind of lovemaking she imagined was only the stuff of fiction. But Kurt took his time, and he seemed to be as much concerned for her pleasure as his own – in fact, her pleasure seemed only to add to his. And when at last she felt she might explode from the way he had discovered erotic places on and in her body she had never dreamed existed, she clutched at his shoulders, urging him to take her.

"Please...," she pleaded.

Kurt balanced himself above her. "Please what, Monica?"

"I want..."

"Say it," he whispered.

"I want you," she said, the refrain to what he had said to her that day in the woods.

Kurt kissed her deeply. "Then you shall have me," he said.

Engestofte – Autumn 1922

Over the next several months Monica's affair with Kurt flourished. They spent hours together, mostly at his farmhouse, but he also was often part of life at Engestofte. Ivan and Inkie adored their "Uncle Kurt," and Jorgen always welcomed him warmly, insisting he stay for dinner or in some cases the weekend. The two men played chess or discussed matters of business or current events as old friends do. Kurt accompanied Monica and Jorgen to parties or concerts, and there was certainly no harm to Jorgen's lifelong friendship with Kurt's older brother. There was gossip, of course, but after a while their friends and neighbors realized Jorgen had fully embraced the triumvirate of his household.

One afternoon after both children had gone down for their naps, Monica decided it was time she tackled several boxes of books and papers that had recently arrived from storage in London. She had left the library doors to the terrace open and taken a seat nearby, hoping for a breeze in what had been an unusually hot summer that had lasted well into the autumn. She studied a letter she had found stuck between the pages of a thick volume and noticed small specks of some dark substance spotting the paper. As she brushed them away, they smeared like wet ink, staining the document. She looked outside and saw flecks of what looked like black snow swirling through the air. At the same time, she became aware of voices raised in panic. She stepped onto the terrace and tried to take in the various elements of the chaotic scene. At the foot of the terraced grounds that sloped down to the lakeshore, she saw several cows race by, with one of their tenant farmers in pursuit. She realized he was not chasing them but driving them away from... *What on earth?*

Turning toward the source of the distant shouting, she saw plumes of black smoke rising from the thatched roof of the barn and immediately understood the flecks coating her clothing and bare arms were ashes. For a moment it was as if she were incapable of action, her mind a jumble of emotions that ran the gamut from shock to denial to duty. This was their property – on fire – being destroyed. Jorgen was in Copenhagen, called there by his solicitors for a meeting regarding the family's finances and new laws that applied to estates like theirs. She was the one who needed to take action. She ran barefoot across the lawn toward the barn just as the wail of the fire brigade's siren announced their arrival from the road that served the farm buildings. She saw their estate manager, Christian, directing the firemen as they raced to unfurl the hoses.

"Christian," she called out, but he was still too far away to hear her above the noise of the firemen shouting to one another as they dragged the hoses to the lakeshore. And she realized there were other sounds – the sounds of terrorized livestock squealing and squawking. The air was caustic, not only with the stench of smoke, but with the distinct scent of cooked meat. Monica shook off her horror at the thought of how many animals might be dead or dying and focused on the brigade's captain. The man was mopping sweat from his face as he motioned toward the lake and then the barn, shaking his head as if there were nothing he could do. Immediately Monica understood the problem. The summer had not only been unusually hot, but also uncommonly dry. The level of the lake was well below normal, and she understood the hoses would never stretch from the lake to the barn.

Monica reversed direction and ran back to the house. Inside the library, she picked up the telephone.

Kurt answered on the first ring.

"Hello, darling," he said as soon as he heard her voice.

"The barn is on fire," she said, her voice raspy with inhaled ash and smoke.

"I'm on my way," he replied and hung up.

After alerting Rose to the disaster and sending her to be sure the children and their nanny stayed in the nursery, Monica put her shoes on and hurried back outside. Several interminable minutes passed before she heard the roar of Kurt's bright yellow Hudson convertible speeding up the long drive. She ran to meet him. He leapt from the car, gave her a quick kiss on the cheek, and took off toward the disaster, shouting instructions. In minutes he had joined the workers and firemen to form a bucket brigade, and after what seemed like hours, the fire was contained. While the others continued to stamp out smoldering embers, Monica crossed the barnyard and Kurt came to meet her. His shirt and face and hands were covered in soot and sweat, but she was so grateful, she ignored all that and embraced him.

"How bad?" she asked.

By now he understood her well enough to know better than to try and sugarcoat the facts. "Most of the livestock was rescued. However, the barn, and this year's harvest..."

"A total loss?" she asked, looking past him to where the skeletal ruins and acrid smoke from a fire that had spread from the barn to other outbuildings told their own story.

"I'm afraid so. You can rebuild, of course."

Behind them they heard a second car pull onto the drive. Jorgen was home. While the driver unloaded his luggage, he stood staring at the turmoil before him. Monica hurried to his side, and as she told him what had happened – the low water, the too-short hoses, Kurt arriving to save the day – she saw in his expression that he had returned with bad news of his own. "We're ruined, Monica. The new laws are draconian, and now this?" Ever mindful of propriety, he moved past her to thank Kurt and the fire captain, then shook hands with each member of the fire brigade and each of his workers, some of them still holding buckets.

Kurt waited with her. "I should go," he said.

She wanted so much to plead with him to stay, but clearly this was not the time. Whatever Jorgen had learned in Copenhagen, he would not yet wish to share that news with Kurt. "Yes. Call me tomorrow," she said, as she walked with him to his car. "Thank you, darling. I truly don't know what..." Tears welled, closing her throat, making further words impossible.

"You'll get through this, Monica," he said, squeezing her hand. "We'll find a way."

That evening over dinner, Jorgen explained the new laws to her. After decades of favoring landowners like Jorgen and Heini, a new political movement had managed to get laws passed that were far more favorable to the small tenant farmer. These new tax regulations had restored laws requiring estate owners to pay a land tax. More to the point, they were now required to pay a dual tax, one on land and the other on buildings and improvements – both substantial.

"Clearly with today's catastrophe, we shall need to find means other than those we have relied on in the past for meeting those requirements," Jorgen said. His despair was so great that she was at a loss to reassure him, and she was undeniably relieved when he decided to retire to his study shortly after dinner. For her part, she wandered through the large house, trying to process everything that had befallen them in just one day. She paused to study the portrait of Jorgen's grandmother and recalled there had been a large inheritance passed to her after the death of her Russian uncle – an inheritance she had left at least a portion of to Jorgen.

Would Varinka's estate be enough to offset the losses from the fire and help cover the taxes being imposed on the estate by the government? More to the point, was the money still available?

Alone in the silence of the grand house she had worked so hard to make a home, Monica returned to the library where the papers and books she had been sorting lay scattered about. She methodically put them away. Then she stepped outside, fastened a cigarette in a filigreed silver holder, lit it, and walked down to the lake, so low that a stretch of mud flats, slippery and sucking at her bare feet, prevented her from reaching the water's edge.

As was her habit when she had something she needed to think through, she twisted the bangles of gold and silver she wore daily. She had so many *things.* The furnishings Jorgen had insisted she buy while redecorating, the fur coats that filled the wardrobes in her dressing room, the jewelry Jorgen had given her for special occasions and for no reason other than that this or that bauble had caught his eye in a shop window. Surely all of that was worth something.

The following morning, she came to the dining room for breakfast carrying a leather valise filled with jewelry, cigarette holders of exotic woods, compacts of gold, and evening purses encrusted with precious jewels.

"Are you going somewhere?" Jorgen asked, folding the newspaper to a new page. He appeared perfectly calm, as if the events of the previous day were no more than a bad dream.

"I want you to sell these," she replied, opening the case to show him the contents. "I have more of everything here than I can ever possibly wear or enjoy, and we need the money."

Jorgen laid his paper aside as he reached over and caressed her cheek. "Dearest, it has hardly come to this. True, we will need to cut back on some things, but we also have an image to maintain. In the more than three hundred years my family has lived on this land, we have certainly seen hard times before and weathered them." He stood, his hand resting on the lid of the case. "Have Rose put these away." Before closing it, he chose one necklace – a double strand of gold and coral beads – and opened the clasp. "All but this piece. It's perfect with your sweater." He placed the necklace he had given her on her last birthday – her twenty-eighth – around her throat and fastened it. "Perfect," he said as he admired his handiwork. "It has always been one of my favorites."

Relieved by his calm demeanor and the absence of any sign that he was overly concerned, she would do as he asked and have Rose return the items in the valise to their proper places. Clearly his melancholy of the evening before had been healed by a good night's sleep and the dawn of a new day. She was further comforted when, after his daily meeting with Christian, she saw him leave later that morning for a tennis match with Heini. Reassured, she busied herself with the children, a visit with her friend Suzanne, and going over plans for a weekend with friends that she and Jorgen would host the following week.

But a few days later when the mail arrived, she realized any respite from worry would be short lived. A week before the fire, she had driven into the village to shop for some necessities. It had taken some time for her to grow accustomed to shopping in a store that carried everything from toothpaste to livestock feed and fertilizer, but she was pleased with the way she had been accepted by the locals. Thanks to her Danish lessons, she was even able to hold a casual conversation with the shopkeeper – inquiring as to the health of his family and such. As the shopkeeper wrapped her purchases, he asked if she would like them charged to the estate's account. She agreed and then as an afterthought asked to see the account. It had been a whim, perhaps born of her upbringing. Her mother was known to keep a sharp eye on the family's finances.

The man behind the counter had hesitated. "That might take some time to prepare," he said. "But, of course, I will see that it is done and delivered to you."

Monica assumed his hesitation was because she had asked and not Jorgen. Would the older generations ever find their way into the twentieth century? "*Tak skal du have,*" she replied with a smile, taking her package and giving the man a little wave as she left.

Now, a week later, she held a thick envelope addressed to her. Opening the seal and scanning the contents, she realized how badly she had misinterpreted the man's hesitation. Although the accounting was in Danish, the language of bookkeeping was universal, and there was no mistaking the facts. The charges were exorbitant, and no payment had been made for months. Clutching the pages in one fist, she strode across the grounds until she reached Christian's office. At her entry – without knocking – the estate agent stood, a worried frown furrowing his brow. "Fru Wichfeld," he said, a mixture of shock and concern evident in his greeting as he hurried to clear a chair for her.

Monica spread the papers on his desk. "I received this in today's post. Surely there is a significant error in the balance owed," she said in English, pulling the chair closer and seating herself as an indication she would not be leaving until she had an explanation.

Barely glancing at the columns of figures, Christian sat and burrowed his fingers in his hair. "There is no mistake, Fru Wichfeld. Your creditors have been most patient for some time now."

Monica pulled the papers closer. "But there are charges here that have remained unpaid for months."

"*Ja.*" He looked as sick as she felt. Sighing heavily, he began a tale that went back not just months but years, all the way to the time Jorgen had lived in London before they even met.

The money he had used for his – and later their – lavish lifestyle had been paid for by funds diverted from the running of the farm and estate to Jorgen's personal account. "Your husband is my employer," he reminded her. "I did try to warn him that the level of spending could not continue indefinitely." He stood and opened a file drawer, drawing out a thick folder. "These are copies of letters I sent him in London."

Monica rifled through the correspondence, pausing now and then to read one of the letters. Although they were written in Danish, she had become quite good at reading the language. One letter that caught her attention mentioned the loss following the Russian revolution of what had remained of Varinka's inheritance.

The bonds and stocks are quite worthless now, Christian had written.

She released the letter and leaned back in her chair. Christian poured a glass of water and handed it to her.

"And then you returned and took on the redecoration of the mansion." His voice held no condemnation.

"You should have objected," she managed.

"I did, but Herr Wichfeld would not hear of it. I was to find a way to cover whatever expense you felt necessary to make the house your own."

"You should have come to me," she murmured and saw by the expression on his face that such an idea was beyond his comprehension. She was a woman, not to mention a foreigner. To discuss family business with her was unthinkable.

"As I said, it is your husband who is my employer." He cleared his throat and replaced the correspondence in the file drawer. "Perhaps had we not suffered the fire and losses attached to that, and had the government not changed the laws..." His voice faded.

Monica stood and gathered the pages listing their debts to just one creditor. She did not wish to think what the full debt owed might be. "I will speak with my husband tonight. In the meantime, should you have any thoughts about how we might begin to address the situation, please share them with me."

He shot her a surprised glance and appeared about to protest that idea.

Monica smiled. "After all, it is my understanding that I am in charge of the management of the house." She held up the envelope that held the tallied bill from the Maribo store. "Looking at the matter from that point of view, a sizeable part of this debt is mine to manage."

Shortly after leaving Christian, she drove to Kurt's farm. In the months that had passed since their affair began, Kurt had become far more than her lover. He was her confidante – someone with whom she could discuss anything. As she navigated the narrow winding roads, her thoughts ran the gamut from fury at Jorgen to shame. After all, she had never once questioned their extravagance. She had relished the shopping trips and servants and travels as much as he had. She had not once declined his gifts. Surely she was as much at fault in this as he was.

"That's rubbish," Kurt protested when she confessed her feelings to him while cradling the snifter of brandy he'd insisted on pouring for her as soon as they were inside the house.

She sat perched on the edge of one of the sofas she'd helped him choose for the place, while Kurt sat on an ottoman facing her. A fire sparked and, although the day was pleasant, she savored the warmth. "It's not just a matter of the crop losses and the new state laws," she said. "What was left of Jorgen's Russian inheritance is worthless, and the estate agent has borrowed so much against the property that at this point, I doubt we can even pay the interest on the loans." She had always prided herself as one who could find solutions, but this was more than even she could master.

"The insurance from the fire should help," Kurt said. "You've filed the claim?"

She shrugged. "Jorgen said he would ask Christian to do that, but frankly..."

"I'll speak to Jorgen and offer to take that on. In the meantime, you need time to recover from the shock. Stay the night."

"I can't – the children. And Jorgen is putting on a good act, but I expect he is far more distressed than I am." She gave Kurt a weak smile. "He does not handle disappointment as well as I do."

"He is not nearly as strong as you are. The man is fortunate to have you in his life, but perhaps the time has come for you to think of yourself, Monica. Leave Jorgen to handle his money problems – they are of his own making."

"I had a hand in some of it," Monica said as she sipped her brandy. "I never once questioned all the money we were spending."

"And why would you?" Kurt stood and paced the room. "Leave him, Monica, and marry me. We have our whole lives in front of us – think of all we might do."

"Please don't add to my distress, Kurt."

"Then at least stay the night, darling," he begged.

She was tempted. "Perhaps I could get away for a few days in Copenhagen this weekend," she said.

He was standing at the hearth, his back to her, his broad shoulders hunched in frustration. "That's the best you can offer?"

"For now." She set her glass aside and stood, going to him and wrapping her arms around him from behind, resting her cheek against the warmth of him. "Day after tomorrow? Copenhagen? I think I can manage three days."

He turned to face her. "Three nights," he bargained as he pulled her close.

"Yes," she agreed and kissed him.

Two days later she drove down the tree-lined lane and away from Engestofte and all the worries and stresses it represented. By midmorning she would arrive at a hotel in Copenhagen. She had called ahead to reserve her favorite room – one with a small balcony that overlooked the hotel's courtyard. Kurt would arrive later in the afternoon, taking a separate room next door that connected to hers, and for three glorious days they would walk the city, dine in small cafes, and, best of all, lie in each other's arms through the night.

After returning from Kurt's she'd confronted Jorgen with the bills from Maribo and the details of the conversation she'd had earlier with Christian. He made a weak attempt at defending himself.

"I thought – "

"No," she interrupted. "The problem is, you did not think. You do not think when it comes to money." She felt her anger harden. "We have the children's future to consider, Jorgen. Have you even thought of what it will cost to properly educate Ivan?"

"Surely..." His voice trailed off.

Monica knew she was very close to saying something she would regret once she calmed down. "I'll be having my supper in my room," she said and climbed the stairs. "Kurt has generously offered to handle filing the papers necessary to collect on the insurance from the fire. I suggest we accept his kindness."

Later he had slipped a note under her door, pleading with her to forgive him and promising he would do better. So, the following morning when he saw her luggage stacked in the foyer, his entire body had seemed to cave in on itself.

"Monica, please, we can work this out. I cannot lose you. Please..."

"I am not leaving you, Jorgen. I simply need a few days to myself." She had no doubt he knew exactly where she was going – and with whom. And yet, neither by word nor gesture did he express the slightest disapproval. He never had.

He followed her to the car, once again offering his remorse for the problems he had brought on them, surprising her by adding, "I'm not as certain we will make it through this business as before, darling, but I will be eternally grateful to Kurt for his offer to deal with the insurance." He handed her a vellum envelope she recognized as his personal stationery. "Please see that he gets this, will you? It is a very inadequate attempt to express my thanks."

"Rose has the number for the hotel should you need me,"

she replied as she tucked the envelope in her purse and kissed Jorgen's temple.

"Drive safely, my dear, and enjoy yourself."

Thinking on their parting as she drove, Monica understood that she loved Jorgen – in her way. He had come into her life at a time when she longed for freedom and independence, and he had never once waivered from his promise to give her just that. For his part, he was the father of their children, who adored him, and together they had built a life. It might be unconventional but it suited them. Still, the escape to Copenhagen was going to be such a relief. For a few days she could pretend everything was all right.

Once he arrived later that afternoon, Kurt forbade any discussion of Jorgen or their economic worries. He arranged activities for their days that had nothing to do with shopping or spending money – long walks or biking trips through the old part of the city, where he regaled her with legends of earlier times. They ate simple food at cafes and giggled like school chums at the stories they invented about the passing parade of people. In the evenings, they attended an outdoor concert or rode the Ferris wheel in Tivoli Gardens before walking back to their hotel and preparing for bed as if they had been married for years. Not once did Kurt press his case for her to leave Jorgen and marry him, and for that she loved him most of all. He gave her three days and nights of the respite she needed to gird herself for what she knew would be the difficult days ahead. And when she arrived home a few days later, she felt rested and revived, ready to face whatever might come.

Engestofte – Winter 1924

In spite of his apologies and obvious regret, Monica knew it would take time before she could fully forgive Jorgen for being so cavalier about their finances. More to the point, he seemed incapable of coming up with a plan for paying off their creditors, some of whom had actually shown up at the door. Horrified by what such incidents might do to damage their social standing and reputation, Monica once again turned to Kurt.

"Is there anything you might sell?" he asked.

Monica thought of the jewelry Jorgen had insisted she keep. "Yes, but if word got round that I was doing that, Jorgen would be humiliated."

"We could sell it in Copenhagen," he suggested, then added with a wicked grin, "Another opportunity for a romantic diversion?"

Monica laughed, but the idea definitely had its appeal. She had not slept well since the day one creditor had accosted her on the terrace, having bypassed the front door. The man waved a sheaf of invoices in her face, demanding payment. Fortunately, Christian heard the commotion as he arrived for a meeting she had scheduled to go over the most pressing debts.

The estate agent took a firm grip on the bill collector's arm and escorted him away. When Christian returned, he assured her he had placated the man enough that he would not trouble her again. Still, Monica had been deeply rattled by the incident. The children had been sailing their toy boats at the lakeshore, and while the nanny attending them had looked up at the sound of the man's raised voice, to Monica's relief she had turned her attention back to the children rather than attempt to intercede.

Clearly something had to be done, and when Kurt made his suggestion of taking some of her jewelry and perhaps one or two smaller paintings to Copenhagen to sell, she readily agreed. Over the next several weeks, she would announce her intention to go into the city to meet friends or for a dental appointment and set off. On most occasions Jorgen seemed hardly to notice she'd gone. But one afternoon when she returned from an overnight stay, her husband met her on the circular drive, Ivan at his side and Inkie in his arms. Monica rushed from the car to hug her family, as happy to be home as she had been to get away. As they walked to the house, the children prattled on with all that had happened while she was gone. Rose and Christian had taken them out on the lake in the rowboat.

"And we caught a fish," Ivan announced proudly. "And Rose cooked it for our supper and..."

They were inside the house now, and Monica was aware that while he was trying not to show it, Jorgen's anxiety had returned. His smile was forced and his pale blue eyes had none of their usual sparkle at seeing her. Although she had to admit that lately he looked at her warily, still filled with remorse for his poor handling of their finances. She took Inkie from him and set her on the floor next to her brother. "Darlings, I want to hear and see everything, but – "

"You cannot see the fish, Mama," Inkie declared. "We ate it."

Monica laughed and tweaked her daughter's button nose. "Perhaps once I've had a chance to change clothes, we can catch another fish. Will you go ask Rose to gather the fishing rods and bait?"

Ivan grabbed his sister by the hand, pulling her along behind him. "We'll meet you at the pier," he shouted.

As soon as they were gone, Monica turned to Jorgen. Suddenly it was as if all the light had been sucked from the house. "What has happened?"

He gave her a weak smile. "The State has appointed public trustees to handle our affairs – or at least those of Engestofte. The first order of business is to close the house for the winter."

"Close the house? And we are to stay where?"

"Believe it or not, they have decided it will be far less expensive for us to travel abroad than to remain in residence." His expression was one of utter bewilderment.

"But where will we go?"

"It will take some time to arrange things. Perhaps you could take Inkie and go stay with your family in Ireland. You've been talking of a visit."

"And you and Ivan?"

"We'll stay here until everything is organized and then join you."

Within days she, Inkie, and Rose were on their way. Her father's health had been a concern her mother tried unsuccessfully to conceal in her letters, and as much as Monica had wanted to be at St. Hubert's to relieve her mother and care for her father, she had hesitated to plan anything because of the expense. As soon as she arrived, she knew she had done exactly the right thing in coming. Having a vivacious toddler in the house brightened everyone's spirits, and Inkie was more than happy not to have to share her grandparents' affection with Ivan.

That year the damp Irish winter lasted well into May, and even the summer winds of June occasionally struggled to find their way through the last dregs of an abnormally cold spring. With the weather finally improving, Monica began taking daily walks, delighting in the sight of late spring perennials and wildflowers poking through the ground and buds swelling on the trees. She realized she was showing signs of a different sort of birth. She was pregnant – and she had little doubt that the news would again set tongues wagging in their social circle. Some, she knew, would assume Kurt was the father, but to her mind, there was no question of the child's parentage.

Earlier that spring when the weather had begun to wear on everyone's nerves, Kurt had come to St. Hubert's for a visit. Jorgen was away for the evening, playing backgammon at a local pub. Her parents had retired early, and the children were also in bed. She and Kurt had the house to themselves and a long lovely evening to enjoy. But instead of the idyllic hours she had hoped for, they had argued. With the escalation of their affair and the larger role he had taken on helping her deal with the financial woes, he had stepped up his campaign for her to leave Jorgen and marry him. After he stormed off that night, she retired to her room certain that he would return, contrite and shame faced as always. But as the hours passed, she accepted the fact that he would stay away the entire night. His pettishness annoyed her and was becoming more habitual with the rising intensity of their affair. He wanted more, much more than she could give.

Restless, she pulled on her robe and wandered down to the great room, where she was surprised to find Jorgen sitting near the fire smoking his pipe and staring at the glow of the embers. Normally he would have simply gone off to bed after a night at the pub. The large floor-model radio was tuned to a station that featured popular music, and Louis Armstrong played "West End Blues."

"You're back," she had said, surprised but not alarmed. Kurt often stayed over even when Jorgen was in residence, the two men sitting up late discussing politics or playing chess. On such occasions, Kurt would be discreet, retiring to one of several guest rooms, but later coming to Monica's room.

That fateful night, Jorgen had set his pipe aside and held out a hand to her, inviting her to come sit with him on the sofa. He had covered her with the afghan her grandmother had knitted and hummed along with Bing Crosby as he sang "Makin' Whoopie," a song that carried memories of the days of their courtship. She closed her eyes, savoring images of parties and walks in the park and rainy evenings when the two of them had decided to stay in rather than dine out or see friends.

"We danced to this last summer at our anniversary party," she reminded him.

"*Ja.*"

The song ended and another began – Fanny Brice singing the mournful "My Man."

Jorgen kissed her hair. "It seems so long ago," he murmured.

"We could dance now," she suggested, and she laughed when Jorgen pulled back in surprise.

"Here?"

She shrugged and threw back the afghan. "There's music and a floor." She stood and held out her arms to him. "We've never needed more than that." Although the room was crowded with bookshelves and other furnishings, there was just enough open space in front of the fireplace. Jorgen took her in his arms, and together they swayed to the music. Sometimes he stepped back to allow her to pirouette, still holding her lightly. They moved as one, their bodies slipping effortlessly into the harmony that had first brought them together.

For the next hour they danced to the variety of music that crackled across the airwaves, laughing as they found ways to improvise in the cramped space. At one point Jorgen threw up his hands in frustration and moved a chair and two end tables to give them room for performing the Charleston. Then, exhausted, they had both collapsed on the sofa, their hands still linked. Once their breathing steadied, Jorgen sat up and kissed her fingertips.

"It's late," he said. "I promised the children an outing just after breakfast." He stood and banked the fire before turning to her. "Goodnight, darling."

He had made it almost all the way to the foot of the stairs when Monica called to him.

"Wait."

Not wanting to be alone and feeling such affection for this man who never questioned her or made demands, she crossed the room and, cupping his face between her palms, kissed him. "Stay with me tonight," she whispered, surprising him yet again.

So let others raise their eyebrows and study the child closely for a resemblance to Kurt, she thought as she paused to gather a bouquet of wildflowers for her bedside table. She was certain she knew precisely when conception had begun. Kurt had stayed away for three days and nights, and in return, Monica, annoyed by his childish need to punish her, had denied him access to her bed for weeks.

She breathed in the fragrance of the flowers, then whistled for her father's dogs that had accompanied her on her walk before turning back toward the house. Suddenly she was anxious to share the news with Jorgen. Kurt would not be pleased about this child that would only tighten her bond to her family and her determination to remain in the marriage, but Jorgen would be as delighted as she was.

To Monica's surprise, Kurt did not abandon her. Even after learning of her pregnancy, he returned to St. Hubert's, where he continued to take Ivan and Inkie on outings, charm her mother, and maintain his friendship with Jorgen. Once the baby, a boy christened Viggo, was born a few days before Christmas, Kurt announced he had found the family a perfect flat in London where they could spend the winter. Most of all, he did not press her to resume their affair. As she had so many times before, Monica found his kindness and concern irresistible and welcomed him back into her life – and her bed.

The Wichfelds moved to London and resumed their social life with friends there. Kurt came and went, and, despite the need to absent themselves from Engestofte for several months each year, Monica settled into her new routine. For the next few years, the main house continued to be closed every autumn, eliminating the costs of heating, staffing, and otherwise maintaining the place, and reopened when the family returned in summer. The children seemed unaffected by what Monica sometimes thought of as their vagabond lifestyle. They were delighted to spend the short summers at home and in autumn leave Denmark for an extended visit with Monica's family or at one of the lush properties Jorgen's brother, Axel, and his wife, Mabelle, owned. Despite her fears that the children might be upset by all the moving, the truth was they seemed to thrive on the adventure of it.

And then one year over Christmas dinner, Jorgen proposed they move to a hunting lodge in Scotland that Axel and Mabelle had leased for the year but would not be using over the winter. Over the years, Monica had left the arrangements for where they might spend the winter while Engestofte was closed to Jorgen. She was all too aware that he and her father had little in common and that once the holidays were over, Jorgen would be ready to leave St. Hubert's. But although she was as ready to leave St. Hubert's as he was, Monica had so often thought of the highlands as isolated and lonely. She hated to sound ungrateful, but the idea of long days in Scotland was not the most appealing option. And what of the children? Ivan was now nine, Varinka six, and little Viggo a precocious four. They were used to having their days filled with activity, people coming and going. Still, they were less likely to be tempted to spend money they did not have shopping than if they went to London or Paris.

"Scotland?" Her father's voice resonated with the question uppermost in her mind. "Bloody desolate there, son, especially in winter."

"Winter is winter, in Scotland or here. Am I not right?" Jorgen directed his response to Monica. "There is some better news. The insurance claim for the fire has finally been paid in full, thanks to Kurt. You should ask if he'd like to come to Scotland with us. The children enjoy him and I could use a chess partner."

It had taken years for the payment to come through, but Kurt had not allowed legal and regulatory obstructions to deter them.

"I'm trying to find ways we can perhaps recover some of the losses we've suffered, darling," Jorgen added. "If we stay at the lodge, our expenses will be minimal, and it is my understanding that the nearest village is some distance from the lodge. Surely by this time next year, or the year after that, things are bound to be much improved."

Given the depths of their liabilities, Monica was not so sure, but what choice did they have?

Scotland – Winter 1929

The hunting lodge was perhaps a quarter the size of their home, built of thick gray stones and set on a knoll against a background of rolling hills. The road leading to the house crossed a stone bridge above a rushing rivulet that ran down to the river they had followed on their way to the property. Inside, Monica was a bit taken aback by the number and sizes of wildlife specimens mounted on the high walls of the great room. The massive fireplace, made of the same stone as the bridge outside, soared up two stories to the wooden rafters. The second-floor bedrooms, nine of them, opened onto a walkway that overlooked the great room below.

A caretaker and his wife – a stoic, humorless couple who did a lot of nodding and very little smiling as they unloaded the car's boot – got them settled. The woman served them meals of sturdy stew or wild game that Monica felt would have been vastly improved if served with a nice wine sauce. But when she suggested the idea, the woman simply nodded, and the meat served later that evening was covered in a thick, tasteless gravy. Still, to Monica's surprise, the weeks passed quickly as the family made the best of their new life in Scotland. Kurt came for short visits, complaining about the isolation and lack of any decent place to get a proper meal before leaving for London or Paris, always pleading with Monica to come with him. She refused. She was beginning to understand the isolation of Scotland was exactly the respite Jorgen needed, reviving his energy and enthusiasm for rebuilding their future. Recently he had announced plans for starting an antiques business.

Admittedly Monica felt a flutter of dismay at the idea. "A shop?"

"No, darling." Jorgen chuckled. "I really cannot imagine me behind a counter, can you?"

"Then what?"

"Remember when Axel and Mabelle were looking for the perfect Louis XIV table for their foyer?" His voice practically trembled with excitement.

"Yes, of course." How could she forget the hours Jorgen had spent scouring shops in Copenhagen and telephoning friends who knew someone who might know of such a piece? He had found it to Mabelle's delight and then, with Monica's full agreement, insisted on making the expensive piece his gift to her for the generosity she had shown them through the years. "But, Jorgen, that was family."

"This is different." He waved an impatient and dismissive hand, clearly miffed at her failure to grasp the possibilities of his idea. "We have friends, Monica, and they have friends, and the people in our social set are always in the market for adding to their collections or decor."

Monica swallowed and forced a smile. Jorgen needed this and perhaps it could work. His impeccable taste and knowledge of fine things was admired and respected. "Well, clearly you have given this a great deal of thought, darling, so tell me your plan and how I might help."

He hurried to the desk set up in a corner of the great room of the hunting lodge, returning a moment later with a handful of papers. "I've made lists," he told her, tucking his monocle in place. "Potential buyers, potential resources for finding the goods, initial expenses – business cards and such...." As he spoke, he handed her one page after another. "And last week when I was in the village, I sent out some wires to potential clients. I have a luncheon with Tallulah next week in London, and..."

The actress Tallulah Bankhead was an acquaintance, hardly a close friend, but Monica had to respect Jorgen's thinking. If she became a client, others in her circle would follow. "Perhaps I could also make some calls or simply mention your new venture in correspondence to friends," she offered.

"Splendid!"

It had been some time since she had seen Jorgen so excited about anything. How she wanted him to succeed at this, and yet she felt a niggling doubt. She knew her husband's penchant for spontaneity when it came to shopping, and the venture he was proposing was firmly rooted in shopping. Had he learned his lesson? It occurred to her she should warn Christian to alert her to any unusual requests for funds Jorgen might require, lest they find themselves even deeper in debt. But then she remind-ed herself the estate and its finances were now being managed by men who had no ties to Jorgen. Surely they would keep his spending in check.

She relaxed and gave the papers her full attention. "Perhaps you could put together a portfolio of ideas to show Tallulah," she suggested.

Jorgen beamed. "Excellent idea."

"Mummy!" Inkie's high-pitched shout was followed by a clatter on the stairs.

"What on earth?" Monica and Jorgen looked up to see their daughter, wearing a pair of Monica's high-heeled shoes, standing halfway down the stairs that connected the great room to the open loft above. She carried the stuffed Steiff bear she was never without by one leg. "Ivan will not play," she announced petulantly.

"I am reading," Ivan calmly replied, poking his head above the back of a large sofa in the loft.

Monica met Inkie on the stairs and gently relieved her of the bear. Then she sat on a step with the bear perched on her knees. "Yes, dear Billy Bear, they are arguing – again." She paused as if listening. "Oh yes, very distressing, but I'm afraid I see no solution, and look how sad their spats make their father."

She turned the bear toward Jorgen, who played his role to perfection with downturned mouth and a heavy sigh. Inkie edged closer, sitting next to her, and she heard Ivan start slowly down the stairs. She kept her attention on the stuffed toy. "What's that?" she asked and held the bear to her ear as if hearing a whisper. "That's brilliant," she said with a delighted smile.

Inkie tugged at her sleeve as Ivan sat on the step behind them.

"What does Billy say?" she asked in a whisper.

"Billy has an idea," Monica replied, once again perching the bear on her knees. "He would like to hear a story and suggests perhaps Ivan might read aloud to him and the Princess Varinka."

"But I want to play tea party," Inkie protested, reminding Monica a good deal of her younger self when Tim and Jack failed to march to her tune.

She turned the bear quickly to face Inkie. "Billy asks you please to allow him to finish," she said sternly.

Inkie folded her arms across her chest and pouted. Every feature on her face said she was not going to like whatever the bear might have in mind.

"What is the rest of it?" Ivan asked.

"Well, if I have this straight, Billy suggests that once Ivan has read a story, then he would like the five of us – Inkie, Ivan, Viggo, Papa, and me, to join him in the dining room for tea."

"Tea with cakes?" Ivan bargained, his eyes on the bear.

Monica jiggled the bear as if he danced with excitement. "Billy says, 'What a lovely idea!'"

"And cream and jam," Inkie crowed – a statement rather than a question.

Jorgen climbed the stairs to where they all sat and offered Billy Bear a solemn handshake. "Once again, Sir Billy," he intoned, "you have saved the day. We are in your debt."

Ivan stood and shook the bear's paw, then held out his hand to his sister. "Come along," he said. "Let's go find Nanny and Viggo."

Kicking off the shoes, Inkie grabbed the bear and followed her brother back up the stairs. "Does the story have fairies?" she asked.

"Perhaps," Ivan replied.

"Does it or not?" Inkie demanded. "Billy wants fairies and elves and – "

"Wait and see," Ivan said, his tone mildly victorious.

Jorgen and Monica stood watching them go, then smiled at each other as Jorgen took her hand and kissed it. "Shall I send word there will be five for tea?" he asked.

"Six," she corrected. "Billy?" she added when Jorgen raised a quizzical eyebrow.

He laughed. "Yes, of course. The guest of honor."

As hints of spring along with definitive downpours came to the highlands, the family decided they'd had enough of Scotland for the time being. Jorgen took Ivan and returned to Denmark. He would meet with Christian and the trustees, and they would stay with Heini. Monica and the other two children left to stay with Monica's family at St. Hubert's. Her father's health continued to fail, and he died later that summer.

The day after the funeral, Monica's mother surprised everyone with her announcement that she planned to move to Rapallo, a small village on the Italian Riviera where the family had often spent holidays. Monica's brother, Tim, expressed his concern that she was acting in haste, but Monica understood.

"This is her time, Tim," she told her brother. "She has done for all of us for years. She deserves to do something for herself."

After helping Alice pack for the move, Monica returned to Engestofte, where she found Jorgen suffering from bronchial pneumonia and their finances little better off than they'd been the previous autumn. The antiques business had to be put on hold, although in truth it had yet to come close to fulfilling Jorgen's lofty plans.

Kurt and Heini arranged for Jorgen to be admitted to a Swiss hospital, while Monica decided to take the children and stay with friends in London. She saw no reason to open the house for only a few weeks.

"London? Why not stay here with me?" Kurt's tone was etched with self-pity. "Why do you always insist on leaving me?"

"I am not leaving you, Kurt. I am simply taking the children to London." Between grieving her father and her worry regarding Jorgen's health and the ongoing financial problems, Monica had less and less patience with Kurt's refusal to think of what she might be dealing with instead of focusing on his own disappointment. "Don't be so dramatic," she retorted.

This triggered one of Kurt's increasingly frequent and volatile outbursts. "I am asking you to be my wife," he shouted. "Why you choose to play the martyr is beyond me."

Monica forced herself to remain calm. "I have to think of my children, darling. They adore their father, and at the moment, having just lost their grandfather, they are frightened by Jorgen's poor health. London will be a distraction, and by the time we return, hopefully Jorgen will be much improved."

This time, to her surprise, her logic calmed him. "I'll come with you," he announced, his face brightening.

I don't want you to come. The truth of that surprised her. She forced a smile. "Let me get settled and make sure this is the right thing for the children." She closed her suitcase and snapped the locks in place. "Suzanne is waiting to take us to the station. I'll call you once we arrive," she promised, kissing his cheek.

"Kurt did not seem pleased," Suzanne ventured as they headed to the rail station in Maribo, Monica with her and the luggage in the lead car, followed by the children and Rose in another.

"Kurt is being a child. He knew the terms once we started down this road," Monica replied.

"And yet...?"

Monica ignored her friend's query. "I am so tired of his peevishness. Have I not endured the whispers and raised eyebrows our affair has elicited? Just because our friends and neighbors are perhaps too embarrassed or well-bred to express their disapproval openly does not mean it is any less obvious."

"You and Jorgen have silenced any such criticism," Suzanne protested. "His devotion to you and your loyalty to him have turned gossip to shrugs of indifference. Besides, it's been years and times have changed. People have affairs. And you and Kurt have always been discreet. Your children adore you, and with good cause. You are a wonderful mother, Monica. And in your own, shall we say unconventional way, a wonderful wife."

Monica grasped her friend's hand in gratitude for her reassurance. Once they arrived at the station, Suzanne suggested they enjoy a cup of tea while waiting for the train to arrive. At an adjoining table, Rose tended the children and kept a watchful eye on the luggage.

"Things between us have changed," Monica said as if there had been no break in the conversation the two women had shared in the car. She lit a cigarette. "The truth is, I have little doubt that eventually Kurt will leave me for good."

Suzanne did not argue the point. "And when he does, will you have regrets?"

Monica shrugged. "Perhaps. But I know that I could never live with myself if I abandoned Jorgen."

"You could end it, you know. Leave Kurt before he leaves you. You have that kind of strength."

"It may come to that," Monica admitted.

On the train to London, Monica thought about her conversation with Suzanne, and recalled a similar discussion she'd had with her mother. Early on, Monica's parents had accepted the story of Kurt's relationship to their daughter's family as a friend of Jorgen's, and Monica's father had welcomed this broad-shouldered young man who could hold his own in whatever sport the men of the family suggested.

But on the day Monica had helped her mother pack for the move to Rapallo, Alice surprised her by admitting she had often envied her. "You have Jorgen and the children, and despite financial challenges, you have had the opportunity to travel." A pause, and then, "And, of course, there's Kurt."

"Kurt is – "

"Your lover," Alice Massy-Beresford said bluntly. "Do not take me for a fool, child. I see how the two of you look at each other, the subtle touches when you think no one is looking. I assume Jorgen has given the affair his blessing?"

Monica was rarely speechless, but her mother's frank discussion of her situation stunned her. "I...we...he..."

Her mother waved off her attempt at a response. "I simply want you to be mindful that what you have with Jorgen is not dissimilar to what I shared all those years with your father – stability, devotion, a shared joy in your children, and, perhaps most important, the certainty that when you wake each day he will still be there."

"I am aware of all that," Monica replied, somewhat annoyed by her mother's lecture. "Kurt is – "

"Kurt gives you the passion that has never been a part of your relationship with Jorgen. I understand that. Heaven knows I certainly do not blame you for wanting that or for taking advantage of it once it came your way. But, Monica, passion is of the moment, and you need to keep that in mind for the good of the children if nothing else."

"I will always put my children first," Monica protested. "They are my life."

"I believe you, and one day Kurt will finally realize that, and he will move on. And on that day your heart will no doubt break and you will question if you have made the right decision. I just want to assure you now that as long as you choose Jorgen and the children, the answer will be 'yes.'" She took Monica's hands in hers and smiled. "But until that day comes?" She winked. "I see no reason why you and Kurt should not enjoy yourselves."

Rapallo, Italy – Autumn 1929

Once Alice was settled in a rented villa in the scenic seaside village, she invited Jorgen, Monica, and the children to come stay with her.

"This place is far too large for one old lady," Alice said. "And besides, it will be a comfort having you and the children with me."

Monica did not protest her mother's generous offer. There were more than enough bedrooms for everyone, and the children were delighted at the idea of living near the seashore. Once again, they had closed the house at Engestofte and the farmlands and livestock had been leased to tenants, providing the modest source of funds necessary for paying down debts with enough left to cover the expenses they would incur while living with Alice in Italy. Jorgen's health was so improved that he had been able to return to managing his antiques venture. And despite Monica's concern for both his health and his financial acuity, he traveled often to London and Paris to court potential clients. Monica spent her days with the children and her evenings with Kurt, who had been unable to resist the sunny warmth of a villa on the Riviera.

Along with her mother, she developed friendships with other expatriates. Most had come to the seaside to escape the harsh winters in the north, but some had chosen to leave behind communities where they felt uncomfortable with what they perceived to be subtle shifts in the political climate. Often after discussions with these friends, Monica struggled with a sense of foreboding she could not label – a sense that, as her sister-in-law Mabelle sometimes said, another shoe was about to fall.

"Turn on the radio," Kurt shouted one October afternoon as he rushed into the villa brandishing a copy of the daily newspaper. "The American stock market has collapsed – banks are closing and everyone is in a panic." He spread the paper open on the table. "People are ruined – people like us."

Monica picked up the newspaper and scanned the story. "I need to call Jorgen. He'll want to wire Axel and Mabelle immediately to be sure they have not been victimized in this disaster."

Certainly she and Jorgen would be all right. They had lived with the pain and stress of financial loss for several years now. For them, money continued to be an issue even though the cost of living in Rapallo was vastly more reasonable than staying in Denmark could ever be. Besides, according to the news, the crisis had not yet spread to Europe.

Still, she knew she could no longer afford to keep silent when it came to Jorgen's antiques business. His plan for soliciting friends and colleagues included presenting himself as someone who was in this for the fun of the hunt, not because he needed money. To that end he often treated prospective clients to lavish dinners or expensive gifts. Recently, a carefully worded letter from Christian had alerted Monica that her husband had fallen back into his old habits and was once again spending a good deal of money on credit, with no results. His so-called clients were happy to have him entertain them, but they did not reciprocate by using the services he offered. The trustees warned the estate could not handle any further depletion of its already limited income.

So for the Wichfelds, the fall of the American stock market was that other shoe Monica had been waiting for, and when it dropped, it did so with a force that touched all their lives. A wire from Axel to Jorgen came with the startling news that Mabelle's fortune was gone. There would be no more shopping trips to Paris or weekends spent in rented country houses in the highlands of Scotland or ritzy hotel suites in Paris. They were scrambling to cancel all their leases on such properties.

With each passing day, Monica considered how they might have Mabelle and Axel come for the holidays and an extended stay on the Riviera. But just a few weeks later, she received a letter from her sister-in-law. She removed the single sheet of Mabelle's signature rose-colored monogrammed stationery and unfolded it.

Axel has abandoned me as have my friends. I am quite alone now. I beg you not to forsake me, dear Monica. I need your strength.
                            With love,
                            Mabelle

Monica showed the letter to Jorgen. "This is unconscionable," she raged. "Your brother is a cad, and his behavior at such a time is positively villainous." She stormed around the room, waving the letter. "And the children? What of them?"

"They are not Axel's offspring," Jorgen reminded her.

It was true. Before marrying Axel, Mabelle had been married to a man who had died on the Titanic, with whom she had had four children. "I understand that, but they are Mabelle's and as such a part of his responsibility. Mabelle has treated him like royalty for all their married life, and this is how he repays her generosity and kindness? Her love and devotion?"

"My dearest Monica," Jorgen said as he took hold of her shoulders, "I am as distressed by my brother's actions as you are, but we have our own problems to conquer. This business in America is bound to spread across Europe. We need to protect *our* children's futures – not worry about what will happen to Mabelle."

"Still..." Monica stumbled for words to persuade him of her need to do something for Mabelle, but for once Jorgen remained firm.

"I am not asking you to abandon your friendship with Mabelle, Monica. You would not do that even if I did. But Mabelle has resources. Surely she has real estate and personal property she can sell. She will be all right. Give her your advice and counsel as she finds her way through this, but beyond that..." He shrugged.

She knew he was right. She also hated that he was right. What could she do beyond giving her sister-in-law and friend comfort and sympathy? She read the letter again. It appeared not only Axel, but Mabelle's host of erstwhile friends had deserted her. Monica thought of how worried Jorgen had been that their social set in Maribo would pity them for the need to leave Engestofte for much of the year. To set his mind at ease, Monica – dressed in one of Mabelle's designer castoffs – had convinced them she and Jorgen were not struggling at all. In fact they were blessed to be able to afford to escape the Danish winters and spend time with friends in London and relaxing in the sun in Rapallo.

She thought of those gowns now. Perhaps she could sell them and send the money to Mabelle. It would not be much, but surely anything might help. Of course, she had to be realistic. If banks were failing and stocks had become worthless in America, how long before the same would happen across Europe? And what would that mean for their already tenuous financial situation?

The holidays were celebrated under this cloud of still more financial insecurity. Alice helped the children set up a nativity scene in the villa and insisted the entire family attend midnight mass on Christmas Eve. Although Monica had abandoned any semblance of religious faith after her brother Jack's death, she found herself hoping for better days to come as she sat in the back of the church. And if silently repeating a mantra of *Please* constituted prayer, then she would not deny that she had prayed as the eve turned into Christmas Day.

Just after the New Year, Monica and Jorgen received word from the trustees, informing them that, given the added debts Jorgen had acquired while trying to get his business venture started, closing the house for the winter and leasing out the farmlands to tenants would no longer be enough. The house itself needed to be offered for year-round lease. Jorgen assumed Kurt would take them in over the summer as he had in the past, but Monica was reluctant to do that.

"I'd rather we found some other place," she told him, and while he gave her a look of surprise, he did not question her.

"I suppose we could stay with my mother and sister until we could work out other arrangements."

"The children would hate that," Monica said before she could censor herself.

Jorgen chuckled. "As would I."

They walked on without speaking, Monica thinking this was no casual walk along the shore. This felt more like a forced march to the future – a future over which it seemed they had so little control. She supposed they could each find work, but Jorgen would be as bad at working in some shop as he was at trying to manage his own business. He was a proud man who had been served by others his entire life. The truth was he had no idea how to live any other way. It would be up to her to find some way they might earn enough for the children's schooling and their own daily expenses.

"You know Mother will be delighted to have us continue living with her," she reminded him. She did not add the balance of what she was thinking: *We can stay here while I come up with some way to make a living.*

"Yes, but for the summer, surely we can accept Kurt's invitation while we work out what comes after," Jorgen replied. "That seems the best plan. The children will have a summer at home – or as close to home as possible – before Ivan goes off to boarding school. I cannot think why we would refuse such a kind and generous offer."

Of course, Jorgen was right, but she understood the greater cost of staying with Kurt.

As expected, from the day they arrived, Kurt used any time he had alone with Monica to intensify his efforts to persuade her to leave Jorgen and marry him. He took every opportunity to remind her that it was Jorgen's fault she and the children were in such dire straits. His tactics ran the gamut from wheedling, to showering her with gifts intended to remind her she would have no need to worry about money if she chose him, to the one time he became so incensed that he raised his hand to her. He had not followed through on that threatening gesture, but Monica realized it had taken a great deal for him to lower his hand and apologize. Thankfully she was able to get away from time to time for lunch or a walk with Suzanne.

"Do you still love him?" Suzanne asked one morning as the two friends walked through the house at Engestofte, making sure everything was ready for the tenants the trustees had found.

"Kurt?" Monica shrugged. "It all began as such fun. It's been almost a decade since we first met at your party. We were so young then, and he was so charming and handsome. That he chose me was irresistible, especially when I thought no man would ever look at me the way he did. I was so certain that any chance I might have had for that kind of attraction had passed."

"And now?"

"It's become so complicated. In the beginning we both agreed this was a fling, however long it lasted. And I cannot deny that even after all these years during which we've gone past the thrill of discovery, just seeing him enter a room still makes my heart race. If I were single, or if Jorgen and I had not had children, or..." She shook her head and faced her friend. "I will always have feelings for him, but I have to think first of the children and their futures – not my own. And I must wonder if I am being fair to Kurt. Should he not have the opportunity to marry and have a family of his own? You've seen him with the children – he's wonderful and they adore him."

"He wants to marry you," Suzanne reminded her. "He has been intent on that for years now. The man is obsessed."

"Yes, he makes that clear several times a week. But the time we might have had once for such fantasies has passed." Monica was struck by the truth of that statement. In years past she'd had no concerns about where and how they might live; how they would build solid futures for their children; how they would sustain themselves in their old age. But recent events had opened her eyes to the realities that everything could change without warning. Surely Mabelle had learned that lesson. Her letters since Axel left had been rare, and those she sent were full of sadness and disbelief at her circumstances.

Monica understood it would be up to her to make sure her children had the future they deserved. She also understood that while she did not love Jorgen with the same hunger she and Kurt had known, she did love him. He was a devoted husband and father, and she would not abandon him.

"Perhaps it's time Kurt and I came to a different understanding," she mused, more to herself than to her friend.

She took Suzanne's failure to reply as agreement.

Days later Monica sat at the desk in Kurt's library typing out lists of expenses and potential income resources that might sustain the family for the foreseeable future. Suddenly the door to the garden banged open and Kurt strode into the room, bringing the chilly May air with him – a cold warmed by his smile and obvious good mood.

"I have decided," he announced. "The answer to all your problems is to stay here with me, permanently. It has been here before us all along. I will speak to Jorgen – it can hardly come as a surprise. He and I will settle on a mutually suitable calendar for visits with the children, and of course, I will take on all expenses for you and them, leaving Jorgen the full amount of the monthly stipend you receive from the trustees. It's the perfect plan for all involved."

As he made his declaration, Monica's fingers, poised over the keys of the typewriter, stilled, and the black ink on the page wavered before her. She squeezed her eyes shut to clear her vision and then went on typing. Always before, when she lost patience with Kurt, what she felt was exasperation. What she felt now was different. Staying the summer was not going to work. No matter how many times she refused him, Kurt would not stop his campaign to have her leave Jorgen, and his assumption that he would wear her down – that he would win – enraged her. Clearly the time had come. She pulled the paper from the typewriter, adding it to a stack on the desk before rolling in a fresh sheet. All the while, Kurt continued laying out the details of his master plan for her life.

She typed the first three items on her list before speaking, the typewriter's bell pinging each time she shifted the carriage to a new line. "You have decided?" She felt her jaw clench as she repeated his words. "Unfortunately, you do not decide what is best for me, Kurt. What I have decided is that Jorgen and I will leave as soon as possible for Rapallo," she replied calmly, although inside she felt anger flow through her like the thick hot lava of a volcano.

How dare he assume he could simply rearrange her life without so much as a discussion? How dare he expect her to simply acquiesce to his plans when he knew very well her opinions on the subject? How dare he...

She paused for a moment but did not look up at him or remove her fingers from the keys. "It is time to face facts, Kurt. We are both well aware that we cannot go on as we have. I have never deceived you when it comes to my loyalty to Jorgen, and you have always known I will not abandon him. If that means you and I are finished, so be it. I will always hold deep feelings for you and what we have shared, and I hope we can remain friends."

She continued typing, aware that Kurt was the one now frozen in place. In truth, she knew if she looked at him, she might falter in her resolve. Certainly she had done it before. How many times had they argued and one of them had stormed out? She knew if she stopped typing she would not be able to control the shaking in her hands. He would see that as a sign that she didn't mean what she'd said.

She heard him release a breath as he walked to the French doors that led to the garden. "The frost is heavier than usual for this time of year," he said, ignoring her pronouncement.

Had those words come from someone other than Kurt, Monica might have suspected a double entendre. But this was Kurt – a simple man used to having his way and clearly determined not to give credence to her decree. As usual he had simply changed the subject, assuming she would come round in time. She continued typing, and a moment later, she realized the click she had just heard was not the typewriter keys, but the soft closing of the door as Kurt left the room.

Her shoulders slumped. What had she done? A life with Kurt could indeed solve everything. While others had suffered in the financial downfall, Kurt continued to thrive, his farm secure and prosperous. With Kurt, she and the children could live a life of ease. No need to worry about next term's tuition for Ivan or where they would live. No need to play the game with their friends that everything was all right when it wasn't.

She closed her eyes and thought of the questions she'd told Suzanne she always asked herself at moments like this. If she stayed with Kurt, would her actions cause others harm? The children were everything to Jorgen, and whatever she felt for her husband, he clearly revered her. She had always understood that while Jorgen accepted her affair with Kurt, he trusted she would never desert him. If she chose Kurt, Jorgen – and the children – would certainly suffer. If she remained firm in her decision to end the relationship, Kurt would be the one damaged. One way or another, one of the two men she had loved most would be hurt. And what of the aftermath? The real question was only which one of the two men in her life might more easily recover.

Kurt, she thought as she stacked her papers and stood. He had the emotional and financial resources to move on. Perhaps in time they could be friends again. Perhaps one day, once the children were grown and well settled into lives of their own, she and Kurt might...

She shook off that thought. Satisfied she had taken the first step toward focusing all her energy on her family's future, Monica crossed the room, pausing only a moment to look back. She took in the sofa placed in front of the fireplace, where she and Kurt had shared so many trysts. How she would miss all this – the refuge that Kurt had provided. If she went in search of him, apologized, he would take her back in an instant.

She swallowed around the lump that had formed in her throat and hurried from the room, calling for Jorgen. She would tell him Alice needed them. She would remind him with Ivan leaving for school in the fall, it was important the family, including her mother, be together for this last summer. Once again it was time to pack up and move on.

The following day as the family waited to board the ferry that would take them to the train station for the journey to Rapallo, Monica handed Kurt a letter. She had stayed up most of the night composing it, the tears flowing as she sought the words to thank him for the love they had shared without giving him the false hope that she would change her mind.

After placing the envelope in his coat pocket without reading it, he turned to shake hands with Jorgen, then leaned in to give her chaste kisses on both cheeks. "We are not done, you and I, *liebchen*," he whispered.

PART TWO

Hard Times
1930–1939

Rapallo – Autumn, 1930

"WHAT ARE YOU GOING TO DO?" Monica's mother asked one morning as mother and daughter walked through the village together. Monica sighed. How she wished the fairy-tale life they enjoyed in Rapallo could turn into reality. How lovely to enjoy walks to the seashore, where local women sat in the sun tatting intricate lace patterns to make into curtains and tablecloths they would sell, while the men mended their fishing nets. They bought fresh fish at the local markets and dined alfresco on the patio outside Alice's villa. The children traipsed to and from the seashore with Rose, while Jorgen spent most of his days playing cards or visiting with other expatriates at the local casino on the beach.

"Monica?" her mother prodded. "You must find a way to better your circumstances, or at the very least, maintain the status quo."

"What can I do?" Monica replied. "The trustees say we need to continue to economize – never more than now. Jorgen's business venture was a setback. I've looked for work here, but there is nothing for me."

Alice snorted. "You mean there's nothing Jorgen doesn't consider beneath you."

"That's not the whole of it," Monica said. "How can I take a position that might make a real difference for a local family? We are the intruders here, Mums, and I will not be guilty of putting my own needs and those of my family ahead of someone in far more difficult circumstances. As for Jorgen – "

Linking arms with her daughter, Alice grunted. "Darling, I have always liked Jorgen. He is a wonderful father, and he is clearly devoted to you. Still, I'm afraid unless you take charge, you and the children may find yourselves in even more dire straits. I wish I could help more, but my own finances have also begun to take on water, so to speak."

Monica released a sardonic laugh. "Things for us are well past the 'dire' level, I'm afraid."

She knew her mother was right, that it was up to her to salvage what she could of the life she wanted for her children – a good education in schools that were not free and the future for Ivan that was his birthright.

"I might need to go elsewhere to find something," she said.

"If that's the only choice, we will make that work, Monica." Alice looked up at her. "I am here to do whatever is necessary for you and the children – and Jorgen."

Over the next days and weeks Monica considered and rejected a number of possibilities, until one day she noticed an article in a magazine about the growing rage for "costume" jewelry. Despite Jorgen's objections, she had quietly sold off several pieces from her collection as well as precious accessories, adding the money she received to her savings for school expenses for her boys. On a trip to Venice before they'd been called back to Denmark, she had been intrigued by a costume collection featuring colorful glass beads in place of the usual precious stones. She'd made contact with the designer and bartered with him to replace the real stones in a choker necklace with his glass beads, letting him keep one of the precious gems as payment. As usual she had been a trendsetter, wearing this unique piece that reflected light in a rainbow of colors and garnering the admiration of friends and strangers alike.

According to the article, the fashion trend continued to flourish, with famous designers offering their unique collections. What if she could find a way to work with her contact in Venice to produce pieces of her own design? On the other hand, in their current state, how could she risk investing what little money they could spare in something that might turn out to be as disastrous as Jorgen's antiques business?

She glanced at a framed photograph of Mabelle, Axel, Jorgen, and herself in happier days. News of Mabelle's failing health had reached them by way of a brief message from her eldest child just after they arrived in Rapallo. The woman who had been her sister-in-law and dear friend had indeed been totally abandoned by her husband and friends, the properties Jorgen had assured Monica would fill the gap sold to pay off creditors. At least she and Jorgen still had each other and the friends they had made in Italy. And they still owned Jorgen's familial estate – barely. If they lost that, she did not know what might happen to Jorgen. Furthermore, Engestofte was Ivan's birthright. More than that, it was "home" for Varinka and Viggo. As much as they loved the life they lived in Rapallo, they were proudly Danish – especially Varinka.

One night while dressing for dinner, Monica paused as she dabbed her wrists and throat with her favorite perfume – one introduced by Coco Chanel a few years earlier. Chanel No. 5 had been developed by Coco's master perfumer, Ernest Beaux, a man Coco had introduced Monica to one day when she was in Paris. They had talked of his work, and Monica had offered her ideas for fragrances. Coco had been impressed with her grasp of the intricacies of the business. "Perhaps one day, *cherie,* you and I might go into business together?"

Monica set the signature bottle of fragrance on her dresser and stared at it. Could that be the answer? They were not close friends, but still...

"I'm going to Paris," she announced at dinner. Jorgen and her mother exchanged a look. "And I am going alone," she added and held up her forefinger to forestall their objections. "This is a business trip. I have an idea that just might be profitable."

"The children – " Jorgen protested.

"Can stay right here. Mother?"

"Of course," Alice replied.

Jorgen offered no further objections. Instead he reached over and covered Monica's hand with his. "I'll make a few calls and arrange for you to stay..."

"No. I do not wish to announce this trip. It is business, not social. I need to be discreet until I know for certain I can make this work."

Jorgen frowned. Alice cleared her throat.

Monica lifted her glass. "Cheer up, darlings. It is not as if this is a permanent move. I will be back, and when I return, with any luck at all, I expect our world to look a great deal brighter."

As Monica stepped off the train in Paris, she drew in a long breath. The platform was crowded with passengers waiting to board, railway employees rushing about unloading and loading luggage, families and lovers sharing farewells, and a loudspeaker crackling with announcements of arrivals and departures. It was exactly the kind of chaotic energy on which Monica thrived. She turned to the porter who had gathered the mountain of belongings she found essential for travel and motioned for him to follow her to the taxi stand. The day was overcast with a threat of rain, but nothing could dampen her spirits. She was on a quest to save her family and she would not fail. While she already missed Jorgen and especially the children, she could not deny that it was exhilarating to be on her own, solely in control of her time and decisions.

Once the luggage was loaded into the boot of the taxi, she gave the driver the address and sat back to enjoy the passing view – places she and Jorgen had frequented, the cafe where she and Kurt had argued, and then a few blocks on, the hotel where they had later made love. She'd heard nothing from him since the day she and Jorgen had left Kurt's farm for Rapallo. She couldn't help wondering if she would come to regret making a final break with him. For that matter she couldn't help wondering if she had the strength to stand firm in her decision. For nine years Kurt had been her refuge – the one person she could share anything with, the one person who could take a day when she felt overwhelmed and turn it into a night of laughter and romance. But over time there had been fewer nights like that, fewer holidays for just the two of them that did not include repeated arguments with Kurt storming out, then returning hours later with flowers or some bauble and an apology.

No, she had done the right thing. Kurt was never going to stop pushing her to leave Jorgen, and she was not going to abandon a man who was the father of her children – one who might not have given her passion, but had certainly given her respect and devotion.

Respect. That was the difference. In the final analysis, Kurt's rants had shown no understanding – no respect – for her choosing to stand with Jorgen, especially during these times when he needed her most. Kurt saw no reason she should not simply abandon Jorgen, leaving him to deal with problems that she was certainly complicit in creating. How many times had she explained that to him? Perhaps if Kurt had suffered the financial setbacks she and Jorgen had endured, he might be more understanding. And if he could so cavalierly expect her to forsake her husband, might there not come a day when he would be tempted by another woman and leave her?

She had made her choice, and she would not regret it.

Leaving the more fashionable neighborhood behind, the driver made several turns until he stopped in front of a four-story building that barely clung to a hint of having known better times.

It suits me, Monica thought with a wry smile. *We're both a bit worn around the edges.*

Inside, she met her landlady, who was obviously surprised to see the amount of luggage the taxi driver stacked inside the front hall. "You are staying how long?" she asked in French.

Monica shrugged. "Indefinitely," she replied, her own French so flawless that the landlady appeared to relax. She paid the woman in cash for a week's stay and accepted the key.

"Second floor, end of the corridor on the left," the landlady instructed as she pocketed the money and stepped aside. Monica picked up her phonograph and cosmetic cases and mounted the stairs, the taxi driver following, dragging her trunk behind.

The hall leading to her room was narrow and poorly lit, and it smelled of cigarettes and the accumulation of years of tenants coming and going. Monica unlocked the door to reveal a small room with a window that overlooked an alley. The driver deposited the trunk and hurried back downstairs for a second load. When he returned, Monica rewarded him with a generous tip in addition to his usual fare. "*Merci,*" she said. She noticed he looked at her in her beautifully tailored suit with equally fashionable hat, shoes, and gloves and then at her surroundings and seemed to hesitate.

She smiled and ushered him toward the hall. "*Merci beaucoup,*" she said as she gently pushed him into the hall and closed the door. She removed her hat and set it with her gloves and purse on the bed – little more than a narrow cot, really, that had seen plenty of use. Then she kicked off her shoes and unbuttoned her suit jacket, hanging it on one of a series of pegs that were apparently to be her closet. Pushing back the sleeves of her silk blouse, she studied the furnishings. In addition to the bed, there was a small armchair upholstered in frayed and faded chintz, a floor lamp that leaned like the Tower of Pisa, a battered writing table, and a straight-back wooden chair. In one corner was a tiny sink and towel bar. Her landlady had told her she would share a bath with other tenants, and there was to be absolutely no cooking in her room.

Monica opened the window and leaned out, allowing the sounds of the city to envelop her – the honk of car horns, the click of heels on the pavement below, the distant sound of children at play. She lit a cigarette and sat on the window ledge, blowing the smoke out slowly – a respite before setting to work making this tiny space a home she could endure for however long might be necessary. This was Paris and with any luck at all, here she would find what she needed to save her family.

By late afternoon she had transformed the room, moving furniture to better suit her needs and unpacking the items she considered necessities: the phonograph and box of records, her typewriter, framed photographs of the children, a vase for the flowers she would buy when she went out later to purchase bread, cheese, and wine for her supper, the pillow and blanket from her bed at home. She positioned the steamer trunk in a corner, open to give her access to its drawers and hanging space. On a small shelf above the chipped and rust-stained sink she placed the cosmetics she considered essential – lipstick, perfume, nail polish. Finally she set a crystal wine glass on a small corner shelf she had lined with a lace doily made by one of the women in Rapallo, then stood back and surveyed the room.

"It will do," she murmured aloud. She changed into a simple dress and flat shoes and hurried down the stairs. "I need to make a telephone call," she told her landlady, who was lingering just inside the small parlor, her small dark eyes squinting with suspicion.

"Calls are an extra charge," the woman replied.

"Of course," Monica said agreeably, standing her ground as she waited for the woman to leave.

Finally her landlady gave a snort of derision and headed down a narrow, dark hall and through the swinging door to what Monica presumed was the kitchen.

Monica perched on the edge of the chair next to the telephone and pressed the receiver several times to rouse the operator. She gave the woman the number to Coco's business office, and smiled as she waited. An appointment with Coco was step one. The two of them had exchanged telegrams, and Coco had urged her to call as soon as she was settled. Once she had secured the meeting, she would head off to the market for some flowers and her supper items and the one luxury she had no intention of giving up – a decent bottle of wine.

Monica's meeting with Coco opened her eyes to new possibilities. The designer might be petite, even fragile, in looks, but she had a will to succeed on her own terms that resonated with Monica. Their consultation at the Chanel salon included Ernest Beaux, the master perfumer.

"The formula for number five was a happy accident," Coco reported.

"How so?" Monica could not imagine this incredibly successful woman allowing anything to happen by accident.

Beaux gave the designer a sheepish smile. "Sometimes – like the great chefs – I do not measure precisely. A little of this or more of that," he explained. "In this case I was a bit heavy handed when it came to adding aldehyde."

Monica was well aware that aldehyde was the synthetic compound most perfumers used. It was sometimes said to add a hint of effervescence to the scent.

"But you did insist," he added, glancing at Coco.

She shrugged. "Perfume should smell like a woman, not a vase of roses."

"I agree. There are perfumes that announce themselves almost before the woman is even in the room."

Coco laughed as she fitted a cigarette into a gold holder and leaned into Ernest's offer of a light. She inhaled and blew out a long stream of smoke, all the while studying Monica with a shrewd eye.

"Did you know that I make only pennies on each sale?"

Monica was taken aback. Chanel No. 5 was the most popular fragrance in Europe. She'd assumed sales had paid for a large part of the opulent surroundings they were sitting in.

Coco smiled. "You see, *cherie,* in business one makes choices, often difficult choices. I needed an investor, someone to provide funds for other aspects of my business – the clothes and accessories do not assemble themselves. But I gave up far too much. I was naive. Do not make the same mistake."

"But you are so successful well beyond the perfume," Monica protested.

Coco leaned forward. "Fashion is not something that exists in dresses only, Monica. Fashion is in the sky, in the street – it has to do with ideas, the way we live, what is happening. You wish to start a business. You clearly have a strong sense of design. What will you create?"

Monica started to answer, but Coco held up a finger, stopping her.

"My question is rhetorical. You are not here for my design advice. You are here because once we discussed the idea of perhaps you working with Ernest to develop a new fragrance. My guess is that this is not the business you plan to pursue. Rather, you seek an investor."

She took another long inhale of tobacco. Monica prepared herself to be dismissed. It had been a far-fetched idea, thinking a casual conversation at a party could be taken seriously.

Coco tapped ash into a heavy crystal ashtray. "So here are my terms," she continued. "I offer you an advance of a thousand francs for you to meet with Ernest and give him your ideas. Should those ideas result in an actual product we can market, it will carry your name. However, you will receive the same revenues I currently receive for Chanel No. 5 – ten percent of the net once the initial advance is recovered."

Monica did not need to think for even a second. "I accept," she said before the designer changed her mind.

Coco smiled. "Ah, Monica, I see that you understand what every woman in business must. Success is often achieved by those who don't know that failure is inevitable." She offered Monica her hand. "I'll leave you and Ernest to work out the details of your collaboration, while I call my solicitor to draw up a more formal agreement."

"Thank you," Monica said, her voice cracking with the attempt to restrain her joy at having taken what she hoped was her first step toward achieving her purpose in coming to Paris.

That night Monica set to work. She had no formal training, but through the years she had developed a unique sense of style others seemed to admire. She thought of when she had completely redesigned Engestofte and Kurt's farmhouse. But beyond that, with the help of Jorgen's friends in the fashion world, she had developed a personal style that set her apart from other women without intimidating them. She had always been able to sketch, and she set to work developing a few basic – and she hoped classic – designs for standard pieces of jewelry like necklaces, bracelets, earrings, and brooches.

Unable to sleep, she took out the pieces from her own jewelry collection she'd had the designer in Venice redesign using glass beads in place of precious stone and polished them, using a soft cloth. These would become her samples, and hopefully the small advance Coco had offered for rights to the fragrance would be enough to keep things afloat until she had garnered some actual orders.

The following morning she posted her sketches to her contact in Venice, asking him to get back to her with estimates of costs and time to produce. Then, after a brief meeting with Coco to sign their agreement and a working meeting with Ernest Beaux, she decided she was ready to let others know she was in town.

As she had hoped, the invitations poured in. She wore her samples to lunches and dinners, and once she had heard from her friend in Venice, decided she was ready to seek orders. After only a month, she had sold enough from the original collection to sketch out more dramatic pieces – bracelets and hair accessories in polished tortoiseshell, as well as watches and compacts inset with intricate and colorful enamel. After that she was able to secure orders based solely on her sketches, and her stash of profits grew.

"I am succeeding," she murmured to herself one night as she sat at her writing desk making entries of that week's sales in the ledger she kept before writing her nightly letter to Jorgen, her mother, and the children. After years of living with uncertainty, she had found a way to bring in an income that would enable Ivan to attend boarding school in Switzerland in the fall.

"What if I could replicate this entire venture in London," she said aloud, her excitement rising as she tallied the columns on her ledger sheet. It would be taking a risk, but she knew exactly the person she needed to open doors there for her – if he was willing.

She ran down the stairs and slid the pocket doors of the parlor shut as she picked up the telephone and asked the operator to connect her to Kurt's flat in London. After months of no contact between them, he'd called her one night a few weeks earlier to say he was in Paris and had heard from mutual friends that she was there as well. He asked to take her to dinner. Monica had made it clear that she would be delighted to see him on a strictly platonic basis, and to her surprise, he had accepted her conditions. They had taken a couple of long walks in the Tuileries Gardens, visited the Louvre, and shared a second dinner before he left for London.

He had been the perfect gentleman, and she had realized how much she had missed him – his friendship most of all.

He answered on the third ring.

"Kurt, I have wonderful news," Monica said. "I'm coming to London."

His response was hesitant and wary. "Why?"

She considered how to present her reasons and decided, as usual, to state them outright. "The truth is I need your advice. I am considering an expansion of my jewelry business. It is going very well here in Paris, and it occurs to me that in London – "

"I see. My advice – not me?"

"I won't pretend this is not about enlarging my business, darling, but I have missed you," she continued. "We got on so well when you were here in Paris last month, I thought perhaps we had decided to be friends?"

"Let me be sure I understand you, Monica. When I make decisions about our relationship, I am overstepping. But when you do something quite similar – "

"I read the society columns, Kurt. You have not been living the life of a monk since we parted ways."

He released a long breath, and she could almost see the cigarette smoke she imagined him exhaling. "When can you be here?"

"Is the day after tomorrow too soon?"

"I'll be waiting...with at least one if not two porters for all your things."

Monica laughed and hung up.

If she'd had any doubt about her decision to keep her relationship with Kurt purely platonic, those doubts were soon erased. After making some calls to colleagues he knew might be helpful, Kurt seemed to regard her business as more a hobby than a necessity. He sulked when she put a meeting with a potential vendor or a lunch with prospective clients ahead of the outing he had planned for the day. Her attempts to explain the urgency of her plan to expand her business fell on deaf ears. But fashion was a fickle business, and she knew the current popularity of her jewelry line would not last. She had to make her London venture a success while pursuing yet another venture she'd recently discovered – one she hoped might prove even more successful than the jewelry line.

Practically every woman she knew never appeared in public without full makeup, and that included manicured nails painted a glossy pink, red, or coral. The price for such vanity came in the form of dry, cracked nails, flaws that over time showed through the polish. Recently a friend in Paris had introduced Monica to a product created by a local chemist that repaired damage caused by the constant application of nail polish. The product had worked beautifully, and when Monica learned the chemist planned to retire and give up production, she had risked a portion of her savings to purchase the patent and formula from him, thinking, if nothing else, she might have someone make up a batch for her when her personal supply ran out.

"But what if I marketed the product to women everywhere?"

she asked Kurt one night as they shared a late supper of fish and chips at a local pub.

"What does this concoction do again?" Kurt asked.

"It keeps a woman's fingernails from cracking – I could call it 'No Cracks,'" she joked.

"I don't know, Monica. How do you know after prolonged use it might not have adverse effects? Or even initially, someone might experience a bad reaction. You could lose everything."

He had a point. If Monica had learned one thing with all she had been through, it was to always proceed with caution. "I have the formula," she told Kurt. "I can take it to a laboratory for analysis."

Kurt studied her for a long moment, his eyebrows lifted in surprise. "You are quite good at this," he said.

And there it was at last – a measure of respect. Unfortunately it came too late to salvage more than the friendship Monica hoped they might maintain.

"I may know someone you can trust to give you an honest and thorough analysis," he said. "I'll make a call in the morning before I leave for Zurich."

"You're going away?" Monica gave her full attention to finishing her fish and chips and keeping her voice calm.

He shrugged. "Skiing with friends. You're welcome to come, of course."

For all his charm – or maybe because of it – Kurt was incredibly transparent. The entire time they had spent together in Paris and now all during her stay with him in London, he had made it a point to let her know he was not sitting around pining away for her. He spoke of parties where he had accompanied some young woman half his age for the evening. He hinted at dalliances with former lovers. He insisted he would need to consult his calendar before agreeing to come to Rapallo for the holidays. In short, he was letting her know that with or without her he had a life, in the obvious hope that his actions would spark her jealousy and she would come to her senses.

"What he fails to see is that I have outgrown the thrill of an affair," Monica told Suzanne later that evening. Suzanne had come to London to visit friends and insisted Monica share her suite at the Ritz. "I simply do not have time for such frivolity. I have a business to manage, and between that and my family – "

"You've changed," Suzanne observed.

"I've matured," Monica corrected her, and recognized that statement for the truth it was.

Rapallo – Spring 1936

Over the next several years Monica settled into a routine of splitting her time between London and Paris, business trips to Venice to buy supplies and meet with the artist who made up her stock pieces collection, and visits back to Rapallo. When she could not be with the family, she called weekly or wrote long letters in answer to their far briefer ones. She tried to be at the villa every school holiday. The children were growing up so fast – Ivan nearly a man now at sixteen and Varinka always off with her cluster of friends on some adventure. Monica worried most about Viggo. He was the quiet one of the three.

Occasionally Jorgen would join her in the city for a few days, and they would see a play or dine with friends. Occasionally she thought of Kurt or saw some item on the society pages about him. Since their parting in London, he had not called or written. She had decided not to reach out to him. Such gestures on her part only seemed to give him false hope. Besides, she had little time to keep up with the news of the day, much less Kurt's life.

And the years had passed.

In order to make it back to Rapallo in time for Easter, Monica had barely slept, but although it had been late when her train arrived the night before, all three children and Jorgen, along with Alice, had been at the station to welcome her. That was more than enough to revive her.

The following morning the telephone rang as Monica descended the stairs from her room feeling rested and eager to enjoy this respite from work and worry.

"*Pronto,*" she greeted the caller gaily.

The line crackled, and then she heard Kurt's familiar voice. "Monica?" Her breath caught. The years – five years with no call or note – since the day he left for Zurich fell away in a heartbeat.

"Hello," she managed. "This is a surprise."

He chuckled and she envisioned him seated in some luxurious hotel suite, perhaps sipping a sherry. "I am thinking of marrying," he said quietly.

"Really?" Was he seeking her approval?

"She's American, Barbara Hutton. You may have heard of her?"

Monica was aware of the gossip. One could hardly miss the photographs on the society pages of Europe's newspapers showing the pretty young heiress and Kurt skiing in Zurich or dining in Rome. *She's a mere girl,* Monica thought. Kurt was nearly forty.

"She seems a bit young for you," she couldn't stop herself saying.

"The age difference is no different than yours and Jorgen's," he reminded her, his tone edgy. There was a pause and then, "But before I decide," Kurt continued, "will you hear me out?"

"Of course." The villa's telephone was in the hallway that connected the public rooms of the house. She was aware of her mother's housekeeper, Olga, and other servants moving about and of the children starting to gather, Inkie's voice especially high pitched with excitement over a tennis victory. Jorgen and her mother were already seated on the palazzo. All were within earshot of her conversation.

"I'm listening," she said, removing an earring and pressing the receiver more tightly against her ear.

Kurt took a deep breath. "As you well know, I have loved you since the day we met, Monica. More to the point, regardless of claims I may have made to the contrary, I have been faithful to you through almost all that time. You know that, and you also know for a man like me, that was not easy. I would walk through fire if you asked – if that meant you would finally agree to be my wife. It is you I wish to spend my life with."

"I –"

"Let me finish, please. This is not a threat, darling. But the time has come when I realize I want what you have always had – commitment. I am tired of the social scene, of pretending that's a life. Your children are coming of age, Monica, and – "

Monica lowered her voice to a whisper. "Do not bring my children into this, please."

"Yes, that was unfair." He drew in a long, audible breath before continuing. "We could have such a good life, darling. I have the financial means for us to do whatever we want, live wherever we want, and that is obviously a great bonus. Still, the core of this is that it would be enough if we could just be together." His voice broke as he added, "So I will ask one last time – will it be yes or no?"

Monica thought about all the years of struggle she had endured to assure that the future for her children was secure – the lonely Paris apartment; the constant need to dress and play the part of the aristocratic woman whose business was simply a pastime, not a necessity; the long weeks and months away from her family. Kurt could change all of that, and she had loved him – once.

"Monica?"

"I think you know my answer," she said.

There was a long silence.

"Then your answer is still no," he confirmed.

"I made my choice years ago, Kurt. I will not rethink that decision. I wish you and Miss Hutton much happiness. Know that I will be your friend and you are always welcome here." She felt the tears coming and added a whispered, "Goodbye, darling," before slowly lowering the receiver to its cradle.

Behind her, she was aware that her mother and husband were no longer engaged in conversation. Had they heard? Had they understood? She didn't really care. Without a word, she climbed the stairs, entered her room, and closed the door. She stood frozen in front of the collection of framed family photographs she carried everywhere with her. And slowly she reached out and took the silver frame that held Kurt's image, and without looking at it, opened the drawer of her nightstand and placed it facedown inside.

For the rest of the day she remained cloistered in her room. Through the open windows she heard Alice explain to Ivan, Varinka, and Viggo that their mother was exhausted and needed time to rest, assuring them that by morning she would be just fine.

Later that evening she listened as everyone gathered for supper. The conversation was subdued, but occasionally she heard Ivan's deep laughter. His voice had changed – another step toward manhood. And Varinka's self-assured pronouncements regarding the news of the day reminded Monica of herself at that age. And dear Viggo, silent for the most part, but later the scrape of a chair and his voice. "I'm going to look in on Mother."

Moments later Monica heard a light knock at her door.

"Mummy?" he called. "I brought you cake."

And his kindness and concern finally unleashed the tears she'd held at bay throughout the day. Tears that were more relief than sorrow. She had made the right decision.

"Thank you, dearest," she managed. "Could you leave it there?

I'll see you in the morning, all right? We'll go fishing."

"Just the two of us?"

"Just the two of us," she promised as she pressed her hand to the closed door as if caressing her youngest child's face.

Once she heard his retreating steps and the click of his bedroom door closing, she retrieved the cake and sat cross-legged on the floor eating it while making her plan for going forward. There was no reason she could not manage her business interests from right here in Rapallo. It was time to come home to her family.

In the weeks that followed, it was hard not to think of Kurt. His photograph was often in the papers as plans for what in America constituted a royal wedding to the heiress went forward. But Monica had made her choice, and she did not regret it. With her usual determination, she threw herself into work and shared activities with the children. Unless the weather prevented them, each morning she would pack a picnic and they would set off for a day at the beach. At night the family would dine together, sometimes with friends, but always as a family. Once the children had retired or gone off with friends for the night, she and Jorgen would sit together with Alice, discussing the news or playing a board game or simply enjoying a glass of wine. While they were certainly not rich, their finances had recovered enough that Monica felt she could afford to indulge in this blissful family time. For the first time in years, she reprised her favorite role as wife and mother. Her business ventures could, for the time being, be managed through mail orders and the occasional telephone call.

As was his custom, one summer morning Jorgen was enjoying breakfast al fresco overlooking the blue waters of the Mediterranean. The children had left the day before to visit Jorgen's mother and sister. Alice was in Vienna seeing friends. Monica and Jorgen had the day to themselves. "Good morning, darling." Monica kissed Jorgen's thinning hair.

As usual her husband was immersed in his newspaper. Monica had developed the habit of avoiding the news. It was all so disheartening. Recently the Germans had enacted a series of laws that were thinly disguised measures to restrict what Jews could and could not do in that country. Hitler seemed intent on driving out the entire population. Meanwhile there was Franco in Spain, and in Italy, Mussolini seemed to be taking his cues from Hitler when it came to amassing power. Still, one could not stand on the sideline as matters worsened. She had always prided herself on being informed.

"What's happening in the world?" she asked as she filled a glass with juice squeezed fresh from the oranges on their tree.

"A good deal of news about the coming Olympics," Jorgen replied, folding the paper to a more manageable size for reading.

Monica's hand tightened on the glass. The 1936 Olympics were to be held in Berlin, and Adolph Hitler had clearly decided to use the spectacle as a showcase to promote his political agenda. The economic depression coupled with the harsh penalties imposed on Germany following the war that had taken Jack's life had given rise to this man whose strident talk represented a wave of such nationalistic ideals. He was a man Monica had dismissed early on, thinking intelligent people would never line up behind someone so unsophisticated and unschooled in the way government worked. But they had – by the thousands, tens of thousands – shouting his praises at mass rallies throughout Germany.

She and Jorgen had become friends with one Jewish couple who had left Germany for Rapallo quite suddenly. They never spoke in detail about what had caused them to leave, but Monica had noticed whenever Hitler's name or that of his Nazi party were mentioned, the Rosenbergs remained silent, and their eyes reflected something Monica could only define as fear. And earlier that spring, before returning to Rapallo for Easter, as she traveled to Berlin for her business enterprises, Monica had been shocked to observe firsthand the closed shops marked with vile language. On another occasion, she had witnessed an elderly Jewish man accosted in broad daylight, berated and humiliated by his attackers with no interference from the police or passersby. And when Monica had prepared to protest such abuse, a total stranger had gently taken her by the arm to stop her.

"Stay out of it," he warned before leaving her and walking quickly away.

On another of her trips, a prospective distributor for her jewelry had insisted she attend one of Hitler's mass rallies. She had stood with thousands of others as they all thrust their arms out in the Nazi salute and roared "Heil, Hitler," in unison. She had kept her arms tightly folded across her chest, watching their faces, reviled by the zeal of their devotion to this man she had come to fear might be capable of leading the world straight into another war. But on her most recent visit to Austria, it was seeing the hundreds of boys and girls – blond, blue-eyed, and fervent in their belief that Hitler was akin to the Second Coming – that had caused her the greatest concern. Youth with the same features as her own children. Youth already in uniform, the same age as Ivan, eager to serve.

She shuddered as she sipped her orange juice, the day now dampened by memories of what she had witnessed.

Jorgen closed the paper and set it aside as he gave his full attention to his meal. "I was thinking we might try and attend at least some of the contests," he said as he buttered a slice of bread.

"Never!" The word was out before she could temper her response.

Jorgen's butter knife wavered slightly, his gaze on her. "Darling, the Olympics are a global event, and I think seeing some of the world's elite athletes compete would be – "

"Why this sudden interest in sport?"

Jorgen gave her a sheepish smile. "I admit it is more the spectacle that intrigues me."

"Perhaps another year, when the games are held somewhere other than Germany."

"Monica, my darling, I know well your feelings when it comes to the Germans, but Jack – "

"This is not about Jack's death fighting in the war. This is about our children, Jorgen. What if..." She could not find the words to express her fears, irrational as they might be.

Retrieving the paper and searching for a specific page, Jorgen murmured, "It seems Kurt will be going." He pointed to a photograph.

"These days it seems Kurt goes anywhere there is likely to be a photographer," she said, ignoring the offer of the paper.

Although Kurt's marriage to Barbara Hutton was old news by now, it seemed as if photographs of the popular couple were still featured almost weekly on the society pages of every newspaper in Europe. His young wife was indeed a beauty – her blond features complementing Kurt's dark hair, deep-set eyes, and tanned face perfectly. They were always smiling as if life were one grand party, but Monica was aware that often Kurt's handsome smile did not reach his eyes – or perhaps that was just wishful thinking. Monica did not begrudge him the joy of true happiness. But she did have her doubts that he could find it with this child bride.

She sipped her espresso. "As I have told you, Jorgen, Kurt's whereabouts are no longer a concern," she said softly.

Jorgen folded his paper and leaned closer. "Do you understand that I am both glad of that and at the same time sad?"

"Why sad?"

He shrugged. "I miss him. He was a decent bridge partner and always a lively addition to any gathering. The children miss their 'Uncle Kurt' as well." He paused, studying her features. "But most of all, his absence makes me sad because it makes you sad, and there is little I can do to alleviate that."

Monica's eyes filled with tears. "Darling Jorgen," she murmured, linking her fingers with his. "You have your own place in my life, and no one – not even Kurt – can ever change that."

They did not go to Berlin. Kurt and his American bride continued to make headlines on the society pages. But what held Monica's attention more than anything else was a sense of impending disaster – not so much for her family, but for the world her children would inherit. Surely by this time next year or the year after that, Hitler would be exposed for the madman he was.

Rapallo – Spring 1938

Despite her desire to spend as much time as possible in Rapallo, Monica could not avoid the need for regular trips to Venice, Paris, and London if she wanted to maintain the success of her business venture. She longed for the day when they might be assured by the trustees that their financial situation had rebounded, and she could focus all her attention once again on her family. With that in mind, she found any opportunity she could manage to return to the seaside village that in many ways she'd come to think of as home.

The train slowed as it moved around the curve that would bring it into Rapallo, and she pressed her nose to the window, looking through the smoke from the engine for her children. They would be there – tall and suntanned, waiting to greet her, as eager to have her home as she was to be there.

The station was flanked by neat beds of blue salvia interrupted by lemon and orange trees that stood like soldiers marking the way to the platform.

Soldiers.

She shut her eyes. It had been twenty years since Jack was killed, but she still could not think of men in military uniform without thinking of him.

"Mummy!" She turned back to the window and saw her children waving madly at her, their voices a chant orchestrated by Inkie that she heard above the noise of the train's brakes and exhale of steam. She waved and blew kisses at the three of them. At nineteen, Ivan favored his father in looks, but he was every bit as gregarious and social as Monica. And her beautiful daughter, Inkie, dressed in tennis whites, clearly having been pulled away from a match to meet the train, her blond curls catching the sun. At sixteen, she had a quick and curious mind and was already fluent in three languages. And standing just slightly apart from his outgoing siblings was Viggo. She studied him for signs that his spirits had lifted since arriving home from his Scottish boarding school – a place where he had struggled to fit in. In the days to come, Viggo would need her most.

As the porter arrived to help with the usual assortment of items Monica refused to check with her larger pieces, she stood, pressed wrinkles from the skirt of her gabardine suit, checked her hair and hat, and followed the porter down the corridor to the exit. At the sight of her, all three children pushed forward.

"M'lady," Ivan said, offering her his hand and a courtly bow.

"Thank you, kind sir," she replied, stepping down and holding out her arms to them. Hugging them tight, she drew in a deep breath. At least here in Rapallo, thoughts of war could be kept at bay. Although Mussolini made no secret of his desire to create an empire to rival that of Hitler's, his ambitions had not yet affected their idyllic seaside village. At least here, she could put aside the things she had heard and seen. At least here, with Jorgen and the children, she would reclaim the title she treasured most – that of mother.

"Come along, darlings," she called out as she led the way through the station. "Let's not waste a moment of this glorious day."

A second homecoming awaited her once they reached the villa. Jorgen and Alice stood at the entrance, waving as they arrived. Monica was first from the car, embracing her mother and her husband. She felt her heart bubble over with the simple pleasure of being with them. The coming days and weeks could be filled with reading and adventures with the children and reconnecting with the growing community of expatriates that had blossomed in the years since Alice had first taken up residence.

"Olga has prepared lunch," her mother announced. "Go and change out of those traveling clothes." Olga was a local woman Alice had hired to manage the household. She waited with Rose just inside the courtyard. "*Benvenuto a casa, signora,*" Olga said with a shy smile.

"It's so good to be here," Monica replied, giving her and then Rose a hug. She noticed that Rose had aged, but then realized she had as well.

"May I put those in water?" Rose asked, with a slight nod toward the flowers Monica had held since receiving them from Viggo at the station.

"Yes, thank you." Relieved of the bouquet, Monica wrapped her arms around Viggo on one side and Varinka on the other. "Let me change and then I want to hear everything that's been going on," she said as they entered the house.

Her daughter would not be deterred from launching immediately into a litany of gossip as she followed her mother up the stairs. "And most recently, several people from Spain have moved into town – fleeing the civil war there according to Father. Oh, and there are two more lovely families recently arrived from Germany – one of the men had a fine jewelry business in Berlin, so you should have much in common with him, Mummy."

She flopped onto Monica's bed to make room as Ivan and Viggo delivered Monica's luggage, then continued talking as she pushed herself off the bed and began unpacking the cartons, placing the items around the room in the spaces they occupied whenever Monica was in residence. She shooed her brothers away. "Mummy needs to change," she reminded them.

As she stepped out of her traveling suit, Monica savored her surroundings. The soft dusty-rose and white color scheme she had chosen was such a welcome respite from the blandness of her hotel room in Paris. While the furnishings there were make-do, here she had filled the space with pieces in the lighter French provincial style that added to the room's illusion of openness and size. One corner of the room featured a glazed terra-cotta fireplace. The windows were large and covered with voile curtains that moved with the breeze. On the walls she had hung framed antique maps of the three places she thought of as "home", Ireland, Denmark, and Italy, while on nearly every surface a vase filled with Jorgen's expertly arranged floral creations – small nosegays to large bouquets – filled the room with their delicious perfume.

She was home.

"I'm famished," she announced as she opened the door to the hallway and waited for Inkie to precede her down the stairs.

The patio was dressed in a veil of fragrant jasmine and climbing roses – roses Jorgen had planted and lovingly tended over the time they had lived with Alice in the villa. He had made a life here, as he had in Paris and London in those years when they first met.

The years before...

Monica often thought of those times, of how naive she had been, of how sure she had been that she knew what the future held. She thought of the bargain she and Jorgen had struck – a bargain that had over time become a marriage. For in spite of her affair with Kurt, it was Jorgen who had never once questioned her choices. It was Jorgen who had leaned on her when their financial situation became dire; Jorgen who had gratefully accepted her determination to secure a future for their children; Jorgen who was always there.

She supposed in her way she loved him, and she understood that to the degree he could love any woman, he cherished her. He was a wonderful father. How often had Inkie turned to him with her triumphs on the tennis court or her achievements in the classroom? Times when Monica had been preoccupied with weightier matters. How often had she observed Jorgen quietly talking with Ivan as the two of them walked along the beach? And in a world where men wanted their sons to present themselves as strong and confident, not once had she ever seen Jorgen chastise Viggo for his lack of the self-confidence that came so easily to his siblings.

Spontaneously she reached across the table and covered her husband's hand. "It's so good to be home, darling," she said, and Jorgen smiled as he laced his fingers with hers.

"You look tired, Monica," her mother commented. "You've been working far too hard." Her eyes flitted briefly to Jorgen, expecting his agreement.

Monica laughed, releasing Jorgen's hand as she lifted the glass of lemonade her mother had poured for her. "I'm not as young as I was," she teased, pointing to the silver streaks that contrasted with the rest of her dark hair.

"None of us are, darling," Jorgen agreed with a rueful gesture toward his own silver threads among the blond.

"Monica is just past forty," Alice huffed. "That hardly places her in her dotage."

"Forty-three, Mother," Monica corrected, winking at Jorgen, who she knew understood that Alice Beresford did not like being reminded that her daughter was middle-aged. "And you are..." She gave her mother a sly smile, pretending to count the years on her fingers.

"Never mind," Alice murmured as she stood and busied herself refilling their glasses. "The sun is too hot. I'm going inside to read."

"More likely to nap," Monica whispered to Jorgen as soon as Alice left. Her smile faded as a new thought struck her. "She isn't unwell, is she?"

"Darling, I fully expect your mother will outlive us all," he assured her.

Monica leaned back and lifted her face to the sun. "Heavenly," she said. "It's always like coming back to a completely new world."

"Is it so terrible in Paris?" Jorgen asked.

Monica frowned. "There is so much talk of Herr Hitler and his band of Nazis," she said. "According to reports on the BBC broadcasts, Lord Chamberlain seems unconcerned, but I – "

"You worry far too much about things you can do nothing about, Monica."

She opened her eyes and gazed at him. "And if war comes?"

Jorgen shrugged. "Denmark will remain neutral, of course, and if that is the case, while there will be shortages and other difficulties to be sure, with the crops and livestock already in place, we could surely sustain ourselves were we to return home to Engestofte."

And in that moment, Monica recognized the single trait of Jorgen's she had never understood or accepted – his sense of entitlement that prevented his understanding that there were far more universal matters to consider than whether his family's estate would survive.

The summer flew by, with days spent at the shore or bicycling through the countryside for a picnic, and evenings spent with neighbors and locals in a cafe or at the villa. Once the boys left that autumn – Ivan to Denmark to apprentice with a neighboring estate manager in preparation for the day he would take over Engestofte, and Viggo, reluctantly, to the Scottish boarding school he abhorred – Monica and Jorgen filled their days pursuing their separate interests. For Monica that meant time spent with her daughter, and increasingly, included taking a more serious interest in the news. Not only was she concerned about the ongoing rise of Adolph Hitler and Benito Mussolini, but the local papers had begun touting the need to silence outspoken liberals, especially those expatriates who had left their own countries to settle in Italy. Nightly, Monica sat close to the villa's floor-model radio, straining to hear through the static the news from London.

"Mummy would rather die than miss the evening news on the BBC," she heard Inkie dramatically report to Rose one day.

"She's just worried," Rose replied. "After all, she knows a good deal more about what's happening in the world than we do. She's actually been in London and Paris, and even Berlin, where these things are happening."

"But we're fine," Inkie argued. "I feel sorry for people like those who have had to leave their home in Berlin because of what Hitler is doing to the Jews, but that hardly – "

"Varinka!" Monica had heard enough. She stood at the window of her room that overlooked the garden bench where her daughter sat shelling peas with Rose. Both Inkie and Rose looked up at her. Rose shaded her eyes and had the good sense to look abashed to have been caught gossiping, while Inkie met her mother's gaze directly and without apology. She was, Monica thought, truly her daughter – so sure of herself, of the rightness of her position.

"It's nearly time for the news," she called in a softer tone. "I'll see you downstairs?" At first she had been glad that her daughter had little interest in what was happening in the rest of the world. But recently, she had decided Inkie needed to be aware that life in Rapallo was a fantasy compared to what others were suffering. That's when she had insisted her daughter join her for the BBC report each evening.

Rose gathered the bowl of peas and walked quickly to the kitchen, while Varinka's shoulders slumped as she turned away.

"Afterward, I thought we might go for a coffee in the village," Monica added. "Just us girls."

Her spirits restored, Inkie ran up the stone steps and into the house.

Monica smiled as she closed the casement window and headed downstairs. She knew all too well that Inkie would be full of opinions after listening to the news. The outing would be the opportunity she intended to massage her daughter's sense of compassion for those deeply affected by the current political and social climate. Meanwhile her outspoken daughter could bask in the self-confidence that, given the chance, she could certainly tell those world leaders a thing or two.

The mail had arrived. Monica shuffled through the stack until she spotted the familiar scrawl of her brother, Tim. She slid her lacquered nail under the sealed flap and pulled out the single sheet of onionskin paper.

30.9.1938

Monica,

Matters are escalating and, even if you insist on staying, you need at least to get Mother out of Italy as soon as possible. No doubt your

Danish passports will buy you and Jorgen some time, but rest assured if matters continue on their current path, even Rapallo will be no place for someone with British citizenship. I'll make arrangements on this end.
    Tim

Monica read the note a second time while her mind sorted through what would need to be done. The boys would be all right, and Inkie could travel with Jorgen back to Denmark. Monica would return to her business in Paris, so the first order of business was to get Alice safely back to England.

"Rose?" she called as she headed for the kitchen.

It took only two days to pack Alice's things and make travel arrangements. Locals and friends came to help, for in her time living in Rapallo, Alice had endeared herself to the entire community. Olga was perpetually sniffing back tears, and other locals adopted stoic expressions that clearly stated they would do what they could to help, but they did not like it that their dear friend was essentially being forced out.

And then, the day came. The cab arrived and was loaded with Alice's belongings. It seemed to Monica that most of the townspeople had gathered to see her mother off. The impending gloom of war hung over the scene in spite of a brilliant blue sky, and Monica felt an undercurrent of dread that the world was about to embark on something far more horrid than the war of her youth. She had just given her mother one final hug when behind her she heard her husband calling for the cab to wait.

"There's news!" Jorgen shouted as he hurried up the path from town, waving a rolled newspaper. "Chamberlain has agreed to appeasement." He flattened the English newspaper on the hood of the taxi and pointed to the headline.

Chamberlain Declares Peace in Our Time.

"I don't have to leave?" Alice asked, pressing closer to her daughter and son-in-law as she ran a finger down a column of type.

Monica quickly scanned the article, then looked to Jorgen for confirmation. Their eyes met and Jorgen nodded. Turning to Alice, he announced, "It appears you have been granted a reprieve, *Mor.*" It was a mark of how close the bond between Alice and Jorgen was that he called her "Mother."

Alice stared wide eyed at the stacks of luggage, and then she laughed. "Shall we put everything back in its rightful place?" she asked, and she spent the rest of the morning directing the unpacking before hosting a dinner for everyone as a gesture of her gratitude and relief.

Paris – Autumn 1939

For over a year, life at the villa in Rapallo returned to normal. It seemed that perhaps disaster had been avoided. Monica resumed her routine of spending holidays and summers in Rapallo and returning to Paris every fall to attend to her business ventures. At first glance the city appeared to be unchanged from the scene she had left the previous spring. The streets and cafes were crowded as always, and there were the usual assortment of markets – flowers, paintings, books, produce. It occurred to her that in Paris, one could probably live quite happily from what was available on the street without ever entering a shop. There were even weekly flea markets, where more than once, she had refreshed her wardrobe with a cast-off designer blouse or beautifully tailored coat for far less then such a garment would have cost her new.

In concert with the success of her business ventures, she had moved out of the garret where she had gotten her start and into a spacious room in a decent hotel. Here she could have tea with prospective clients in the hotel's cafe while showing them her latest designs, or better yet, sketching out a design for a one-of-a-kind piece for which she could charge a good deal more. Having un-packed after her trip back from Rapallo, she stepped outside and lifted her face to the sunny October sky with its hint of autumn.

The doorman started to raise his hand to call a taxi, but Monica waved him off. She wanted to walk, to savor the moment. After all the uncertainty they had endured in Italy that summer, Paris seemed like a refuge. It was still the most beautiful city in the world to her way of thinking. She passed through a flower market where the vendors were beginning to close for the night. A young man about Ivan's age presented her with a single lavender rose. It had been years since she'd felt so young – so carefree. She was quite certain that women in their forties did not twirl around in public like schoolgirls, but she found the urge irresistible and was rewarded by the smiles of the flower vendors, if not all their more high-society customers.

And as suddenly as her giddy mood had arrived, it disappeared. For as she continued on her walk, she found herself facing a wall plastered with posters warning all citizens of Paris to prepare for "military mobilization." A crowd had gathered around a newsboy standing next to a pile of evening editions of the paper, which he was passing out to those gathered as quickly as they could hand him their coins. Monica moved closer, wanting yet not wanting to see the headline.

"What does it say?" an American asked, pressing closer to her as he strained to see the newspaper.

"It says: 'Since this morning at eleven o'clock, a state of war exists between France and Great Britain against the Reich,' – Germany," she added just in case. The man's face turned an alarming pasty white, and Monica placed her hand on his arm. "Perhaps you should sit," she suggested with a nod toward a nearby park bench.

A well-dressed woman that Monica assumed to be his wife came alongside him. "Herbert, what's happened?"

The man recovered enough to tip his hat to Monica before steering his wife down the street, muttering something about the need to pack and leave immediately.

Her high spirits totally deflated, Monica paid for a copy of the paper and hurried back to her hotel, stopping at the front desk to request her room key and any messages that might have arrived. While the desk clerk collected her mail and key, she overheard someone say, "The German invasion of Poland was the trigger. They had no provocation – none at all."

Her fingers trembled as she opened a telegram from Jorgen, urging her to leave Paris at once for England, and then read the handwritten note on stationery from a neighboring hotel:

Have dinner with me. I need a friend. K

So, Kurt was in Paris, and he had managed to find her. The most recent news she'd had about him had been about his divorce from the American heiress – the story had made headlines throughout Europe. There was a child involved – a son – and knowing how Kurt had longed for a family of his own and knowing the likelihood that the mother would be given custody, Monica's heart went out to her old friend.

She returned to the desk clerk, and scribbled her reply:

Yes. Eight o'clock at Cafe de Flore.

It was the best choice. Likely to be crowded, and yet, they could find a quiet corner to talk – Kurt about his acrimonious divorce and Monica about the looming specter of yet another world war. She folded her message and gave it to the clerk with a tip for the bellboy he would send to deliver it.

Kurt was waiting outside the cafe when she arrived. He had aged, but then so had she. What had not changed was the smile that once could set her heart to beating in double time and still made her feel a youthful flush. Opting for a lighter meal, they dined on onion soup and quiche, shunning the entrees. But neither could resist sharing the most sinful chestnut-pear *tartin* Monica could ever remember tasting. They talked late into the night, exchanging wine with dinner for espresso as the tables around them emptied. To her surprise, Kurt dismissed more than a cursory review of his divorce in favor of asking Monica about her children, her mother, and even Jorgen.

"And you, darling?" he asked. "How are you?"

She shrugged. "The business is doing well. Despite your doubts at the time, the nail-restoring serum has been a huge success. And I did name it NoCrax – with an 'x' to give it some panache, yet still make its use more obvious."

Kurt smiled. "That was not the question. I am asking about you."

"You've seen the headlines," she replied. "My homeland is at war, Kurt."

"Denmark is your home now, Monica, and Denmark will not engage. Leave Paris and Italy and take your family home. Clearly you've done what was necessary to save the estate."

"Perhaps. Mother is in London visiting friends, with plans to make a stop here in Paris on her way back to Rapallo." She felt a sudden chill as she recalled the news of the day. "Of course, given that both countries are now at war with Germany, who knows when or even if she'll be able to return to Rapallo."

"And you, Monica?" Kurt brushed an errant tendril of hair from her cheek.

Monica felt the weight of uncertain times fill her chest. "I don't know what to do," she admitted. "Stay here in Paris? Be with Mother? And what of the children and Jorgen?"

"I have business in London next week," Kurt said. "Come with me. The Drurys are hosting a weekend in the country. Alice could come as well, and a weekend with old friends might lift her spirits – and yours."

She was tempted, recalling the many weekends she and Jorgen and the children had enjoyed in the days when their friends had hosted such gatherings.

"The Churchills are likely to be there," Kurt added with a sly grin. He knew only too well how Monica had championed the politician's sometimes radical ideas during his early career.

"I do have clients in London that I could call on," Monica mused, as she fingered the handle of her espresso cup. "And one can always use a respite...."

Kurt's smile changed to a frown. "What's your hesitation?"

Monica drew in a long breath. "If I agree, Kurt, we need to be perfectly clear that there is nothing more than friendship between us now – I do not want to leave you with false hopes that – "

He burst into laughter. "Monica, let me assure you that at the moment, after everything that went on with Barbara, I haven't the slightest interest in a romantic entanglement. I need a friend – and so do you."

The one thing she knew best about Kurt was that he wore his true feelings on his sleeve, so she believed him. "Then, if the Drurys agree, I would love to come to their country house for a long weekend."

"They'll be delighted," he assured her. "In these dark times, you'll be like a breath of spring air."

The last waiter hovered, repeatedly wiping the tables around them, even going so far as to upend chairs so the floor was clear for mopping.

"We should go," Monica said.

After leaving an amount on the table that was double what the bill had been, Kurt draped his suit jacket over Monica's shoulders and held the door open for her. Sometime while they were deep into their conversation, it had rained, and the street glistened with moisture while the air smelled of a potpourri of decaying leaves, flower-filled window boxes lining the shops along the street, and a hint of colder weather to come.

Monica could not help but think the seasonal change was an apt environment for the ominous shifts taking place in their world. In September, Hitler had, without provocation, simply marched his troops into Poland and proclaimed victory, provoking England's response. Chamberlain's 'peace in our time' had turned into a cruel joke, and now both England and France were at war with Germany. "I'm going to have Inkie join us as well," she said.

To her surprise Kurt readily agreed. "Yes, send for her. The Drurys will be doubly delighted."

Dear Kurt, Monica thought as she took his hand. If nothing else had come of this evening, this horrible day, at least Kurt was there. They were older now, and the flame of their passion had ebbed into companionship. Tonight, she felt they had moved to yet another level – the kind of deep bond that exists between two people who know they can count on the other to always be there when needed.

At her hotel, he saw her to the elevator, gave her a hug, and then headed for the bar. As the accordion-folding cage door of the tiny elevator slid shut, Monica caught a glimpse of Kurt walking away. He was still a stunningly handsome man. She had little doubt that despite his recent troubles, whatever the months and years to come might bring, Kurt would be fine.

On the surface, the weekend at the country home of the Drurys was like any other such gathering Monica had enjoyed through the years. The days were filled with activities such as riding and croquet matches and, on the one day it rained, a marathon bridge tournament. Plenty of Inkie's friends had been invited for the weekend, and once they had all gathered, Monica barely saw her daughter.

By evening the skies had cleared, and as Monica dressed for dinner, she saw the sliver of a new moon – always an omen of adventures to come, at least to her. How many times had she and her brother Jack walked along the cliffs in Ireland under a starry and moonlit sky sharing their dreams for the future? How often had they stood side by side seeing the moon's light reflected in the water of Lough Erne? "There it is," Jack had said once, "the pathway to the stars."

And here she was again – on the precipice of this new war. Well, this time she would not sit idly by. She would find some way to take action. Even if they continued living in Italy, there had to be something she could do to help stem this madness that was once again engulfing the world.

Hearing other guests exiting their rooms and heading down the corridor to the grand staircase, she quickly checked her reflection, added one additional piece of jewelry from her collection, and hurried to collect Alice and join them. Already three of the women staying in the house had admired her wares. One had even slipped a note under her door, placing an order for a brooch Monica had worn. Dinner would include not only the houseguests but neighbors as well – new clients for her to woo.

But as the evening progressed, Monica found she was the one being wooed – not by Kurt, but rather by her old friend Max Aitken, the owner of one of Britain's largest newspapers and a close friend of Churchill's. Having made the mistake of printing Chamberlain's prediction that Britain would not join the conflict, he was determined to erase that misstep from his legacy and make his mark now that war was at hand. During dinner, he had listened intently as Monica freely offered her opinions about Hitler and his gang of thugs, as she called them, and her certainty that Mussolini was every bit as bad. She had met Max years earlier at a similar country weekend, and they had remained friends since, staying in touch by occasional letters or meeting for coffee whenever Monica was in London. Max was as famous for his amorous adventures as Kurt was, but Monica was well aware he preferred younger women. She assumed his interest in her political commentary was more likely because he understood how her outspoken political views shocked other guests.

Certainly, Max was familiar with her political rants, so she was not especially surprised when he sought her out as she sat alone on the terrace enjoying a cigarette and the cool night air. Her mother had retired to her room just after dinner, leaving Monica free to enjoy the night air on her own.

"Ah, my lord," Monica intoned with mock deference for his title. "May I join you?"

Through the open French doors behind them, Monica heard Kurt entertaining the other guests with tales of his recent marriage and the foibles of the nouveau riches in America. "Of course," she replied and motioned to the filigreed iron chair next to her. She pushed her gold-enameled cigarette case closer to him, and he took out a cigarette and lit it before sitting.

"I see Reventlow is nursing his wounded ego by embellishing his time with the Hutton woman," Max said. "I would think you might find that amusing?"

"I've heard the story before," Monica replied.

Max chuckled. "I suspect you've heard that story and several others. Word has it Kurt has not been exactly monastic since you broke things off with him, my dear. Will you take him back now that he's once again unencumbered?"

"We're friends."

"You were lovers," Max replied bluntly.

"And we outgrew that – or at least I did." She gave him a side-long look. "One day perhaps you'll mature as well, Maxie. Find someone you can be serious about?"

He laughed. "Hard to imagine when I am having so much pleasure."

"We aren't getting any younger, my friend, and there's something to be said for stability and a loyal partner."

"I have both," he protested and rubbed his thumb and forefinger together in the universal gesture that signaled wealth. "Mine simply comes in the form of being quite rich – money does indeed buy a great deal, love."

"Fortunes can disappear," Monica reminded him. "Even those that are centuries old."

He reached over and patted her forearm. "I apologize, Monica. That was crass of me. I understand you've managed to add a bit of business to your stay here?"

She shrugged.

"Come now. You know you are your best advertisement for your collection." He fingered a bracelet she wore. "I know a young lady who would do unspeakably delightful things to me if I but put this bauble on her arm."

Monica laughed. "You are impossible."

"But charming?"

"Impossibly so." She stretched her arms above her head and sighed. "Such a lovely night. Hard to believe we are at war."

They sat in silence looking up at the starlit sky and smoking, until Max cleared his throat and turned to her. "Earlier, I was frankly a little surprised at how informed you are on matters of the day. After all, with managing your business interests and a family, one could understand how such issues as politics and war might not be at the forefront of your concerns."

"Anyone not paying attention is a fool," she said bluntly.

"And yet there are those who refuse to see what is clearly before us all."

"Chamberlain? Or you?" she teased.

He grimaced. "Both – among others." Drumming his fingers on the arm of the chair as they enjoyed their cigarettes and the clear quiet of the night, she was aware that he repeatedly glanced at her, as if trying to come to a decision.

"What is it, Max?" she asked finally.

"It occurs to me that someone as dedicated to your family heritage as you have always been, Monica, could be useful now that Britain has joined the fray."

Her heart fluttered with cautious excitement. "In the first war, I'm afraid my usefulness extended only as far as serving tea and mopping the canteen floor," she said lightly. "If I were to find a way to help, it would have to be more significant – a good deal more significant."

Aware that Max was well connected, she waited anxiously to see what he might suggest.

"Clearly time and your natural bent toward absorbing information have enhanced your options for doing your part."

Ever impatient to have people get to the point, Monica stubbed out her cigarette in the crystal ashtray on the small table between them, and sat forward so that in the light spilling out from the drawing room, she could read his expression. If he was teasing her... "Exactly what is it that you think I might do to help, Max?"

He took his time, drawing on his cigarette, inhaling deeply, blowing the smoke out slowly. She punched his arm. "Tell me," she demanded.

"It occurs to me that the occasional letter that included your insights on the situation in Italy might be helpful. I mean now that we are at war, the flow of information regarding our adversaries will be challenging. The BBC will be reaching out to those caught in enemy surroundings, of course." He put out his cigarette and stood. "Think it over, Monica. It may seem like an innocuous task, but you must have a care, for you will be fulfilling that role from the very core of enemy territory. There is a danger to be considered – not just to you but for your family as well."

Monica waved away his warning. "I'll do it," she said, almost giddy with excitement to be asked to take part in anything that might have a real effect on the length and outcome of this war. "I'll write you every week and – "

Max held up a restraining hand. "Nothing can raise alarms. As a former Brit in Italy, you will be watched and anything that appears to be a change in your normal routine will be seen as suspect. You'll write to me monthly via an address in Portugal, and in between, you'll write Tim."

As a brigadier general, Monica's brother, Tim, had at least as many contacts in the government as Max did. No doubt Tim would object to her getting involved, but Tim was not Jack. She had always been able to persuade Tim to her way of thinking.

After a sleepless night, she wired Jorgen to say she was returning to Rapallo, and that she thought perhaps the time had come for them to take up residence in Florence, hinting that living in the larger city would benefit Viggo and Inkie. Viggo could pursue his interest in architecture and art history, while Inkie could spend more time with friends she had made while pursuing her studies there. Monica knew it was unnecessary to add that Florence was more pro-Ally than the rest of Italy, and she saw no need to tell him of her true reason for the move. Gathering information in a larger city like Florence would be far more expedient than waiting for news to filter down to Rapallo. Living in Florence made perfect sense, not only for the children but also for her business interests, and Jorgen would assume that was her reason. During the remainder of her stay at the Drury estate, she took long walks with Tim as he instructed her on ways to deliver information in code by speaking of the weather or family members.

"Mention 'Mother' and I will know you are speaking of Britain," he told her.

"But what if I have a question or news that relates to our actual mother?"

"Mummy or Alice," he replied.

"Of course," she said, her excitement barely contained. "And I see how the weather can be useful as well – clear, cloudy, rain – "

Tim sighed. "Do not get carried away, Monica. We need to be very sure about what you are telling us. Information you provide could find its way into a report on the BBC that reaches pro-Ally groups in Italy or elsewhere. Accuracy is key. Just follow the script Max and I are giving you. Don't go making up things on your own."

"Aye, aye, my captain," she replied with a mock salute.

Tim frowned. "This is not a game, Monica, or one of your childhood plots. Lives will be at stake – *your* life."

"All right," she replied. "I was only – "

"And that's brigadier general – not captain," Tim interrupted with a smile. He tucked her hand in the crook of his elbow as they turned back toward the grand house. And as they walked, it occurred to Monica that it might be some time before she would enjoy such a carefree weekend again.

Florence – Late 1939–Early 1940

After returning to Rapallo, where they packed up items Alice had requested be sent to her and convinced Rose to return to Ireland, Monica and Jorgen bid farewell to their friends there and boarded the train for Florence. When they arrived, Viggo and Varinka met them at the station, both eager to show them the living quarters Viggo had secured for them.

"You should have seen him," Varinka bragged as the taxi navigated the busy streets. "Signora Imperiali was reluctant to let the space when she learned it would be for only a short time, but my baby brother here answered all her objections," she added.

"She likes me," Viggo said with a shy smile. "And I am nearly eighteen – hardly a baby," he added.

Inkie pinched his cheek. "Signora said he was the nicest boy she'd ever met," Varinka corrected. "And wait until you see all he's managed since yesterday."

The space was at the back of a large villa near the center of town. While Jorgen and Viggo unloaded the luggage and paid the driver, Varinka linked arms with her mother and led her through colonnades dripping with wisteria and on across the courtyard to the entrance. "Ta da," she announced with a dramatic sweep of her arm as she ushered Monica inside.

Wandering through rooms where a table was set for supper, beds were made up, and fires and bouquets of fresh flowers warmed and every room, Monica could not contain her surprise and delight. And when she came to the room that was to be hers and saw that her children had filled a vase with her favorite pink carnations, she could barely speak.

"Viggo bought those for you," Varinka said, pointing to the carnations. "He also hired the cook, ordered the food, and chopped wood for the fireplaces. My little brother is quite something."

"Indeed he is," Monica agreed. Despite the uncertainty, perhaps things were not as dire as she had first feared. The city of Florence was known to be pro-Ally, and certainly in a more cosmopolitan locale such as this, she would have access to far more information that might be helpful to Max. Of course, all communication with England had been disrupted, but she could still send her letters through other means – friends in Portugal, Sweden, or even America who could forward them. Her mind was already racing with the logistics of how she might best do her part.

A new adventure! She was anxious to get started.

Within days they had fully settled into their new surroundings, reconnecting with friends, including Muriel Mavrocordato, an English woman and former neighbor from Rapallo, who called on them a few days later.

"You're going to thrive here," Muriel exclaimed. "There are so many interesting people. Do you know Bernard Berenson?"

"I know of him," Monica replied. Berenson was considered the world's foremost authority on Italian Renaissance art. He would most certainly be someone Monica would enjoy getting to know, especially because Viggo had taken an interest in art history and particularly admired the Old Masters.

"Oh, the two of you must meet," Muriel insisted. "I'll set something up. Bernard will be delighted to have someone with your insights to talk art and politics with. I'm afraid he's been abandoned by others – politics and all that." She dismissed the current state of the world with a wave of her hand. Monica recalled reading somewhere that Berenson was American – and Jewish. "You will not believe what he and his wife, Mary, have managed to do with their estate. It was little more than a farmhouse until they took it on." She lowered her voice as if sharing a secret. "Of course, Mary has not been well. Her nerves, you see – all this nonsense about the Jews."

"Then perhaps another time," Monica suggested.

"Heavens, no. I've told Bernard all about you, and he's so looking forward to your visit."

On the day Monica and Jorgen arrived with Muriel and her husband for tea, Monica saw that *Villa I Tatti* was a great deal more than a simple Tuscan farmhouse. The dwelling had been transformed into a grand villa, and the grounds surrounding it, which had once been a vineyard, had morphed into a formal Italian garden worthy of some royal estate. The ride from Florence had been short, and yet she felt as if they had traveled some distance into a peaceful valley surrounded by hills covered by forests of cypress trees. The esteemed collector and art critic was waiting for them. Bernard Berenson was a small man with a neatly trimmed goatee and a ready smile. He wore a three-piece wool suit with a silk rose pinned to the lapel. As he took her hand and kissed both her cheeks, Monica knew instantly that, despite the difference in their ages, the two of them were destined to become friends.

The hours of their visit flew by. Jorgen was as entranced by the formal gardens as Monica was with Berenson. While Mary Berenson said little during tea, she seemed pleased when Jorgen asked if he might have a tour of the gardens and readily agreed.

"Monica and I will join you in a bit," Bernard said. "I want to be sure she has time to see my library."

"Truthfully," Muriel teased sotto voce to Monica, "Bernard sees this home as the library with rooms for living attached."

"That's right," Mary added. "It is where he spends nearly all his time now that..." Her voice faded and she looked away, her eyes glistening with the threat of tears. A moment that had seemed lighthearted had suddenly come under the shadow of the war. On the drive out to the villa, Muriel had explained that because they were Jewish, Bernard and Mary were virtually under house arrest. They could not travel or engage in the normal activities that had been so much a part of their lives.

"This, too, shall pass, my dear," Bernard said softly as he tenderly stroked his wife's shoulders.

Recovering, Mary turned a bright but clearly forced smile on her guests. "Shall we?" As she led the way out to the terrace that overlooked the grandeur of the gardens, she glanced back at her husband. He stood at the open doors leading to the terrace watching her, his expression one of deep sadness.

After that first visit, Monica went often to the villa, spending hours with Bernard in his beloved library as they sipped tea from china cups and enjoyed the luscious Italian pastries his cook provided. They discussed art and the effect the war was having on culture overall. One day she arrived to find Bernard leaning close to the radio, intently listening to a voice she recognized. The renowned American poet Ezra Pound had recently decided to make his home in Italy. His devotion to Mussolini was so ingrained, he had written an ode to the dictator and presented it to him. Now he had been given the opportunity to deliver radio broadcasts, spouting his certainty that the economic woes of the world could be laid squarely at the feet of the Jews. The world's problems could be blamed on Jewish bankers, according to him, infiltrating governments and outlets for distributing information such as radio broadcasts, newspapers, and even films in their efforts to sway public opinion while lining their own pockets.

"Have you heard this dribble?" Bernard asked, rising to greet her and signaling his valet to bring their tea.

"I have had the dubious pleasure of being at several social events he attended," Monica said as she took her usual chair next to Bernard's. "My impression is that he has always had a love affair with words – those spilling from his mouth."

Bernard chuckled and switched off the radio. The tea arrived, and as had become their habit, Monica poured while Bernard filled two china plates with a variety of pastries. Once the tasks of serving were complete, he leaned back in his chair, crossing one thin leg over the other, and took a sip of his tea. "Nectar of the gods," he murmured. "Now, what news have you gathered about matters in Denmark?"

Monica shrugged. "Danes are by nature nonconfrontational. In times such as these, most will simply take a wait-and-see position. So far, according to our son, Ivan, at least newspapers are still being distributed and the radio broadcasts continue as well."

"And yet for you it is not enough?" Bernard conjectured.

Monica stirred her tea. "Britain is at war and my heart is with them. Jorgen constantly reminds me the situation in Denmark is different. Sometimes it's almost as if he thinks Denmark would do well to work with the Germans."

"He is not mistaken, you know. Your fellow countrymen stand to gain a good deal economically if they play along with the Germans – at least those who are landowners. If the country can grow grain and provide other food supplies for the war effort, they are bound to prosper."

"But it's wrong," Monica insisted.

Bernard plucked a small cake from his plate and popped it into his mouth. "Shall we talk of more pleasant matters? How are Viggo's studies coming along?"

Monica smiled as she always did when any conversation turned to her children. "I'm afraid you have a convert. He's developed quite a fascination with the Florentine art of the Renaissance, thanks to you."

"He is welcome here any time, if my library might be of interest. In fact" – he rose, selected a copy of his own *Florentine Painters of the Renaissance*, and set it on the table next to Monica's chair – "give him this with my compliments."

"That is so generous of you," Monica said. "Viggo will be thrilled."

Bernard was still standing, scanning the shelves across from where she sat. "And what are you reading, my dear? The winters here can be quite daunting if one has nothing to engage the mind." He ran his finger along a row of books, paused at one, and pulled it out. "Ah, this one is by a fellow Dane." He handed her a copy of Isak Dinesen's *Seven Gothic Tales*. "There's enough humor in there to sustain you through some gray days."

"I've met her," Monica said, leafing through the pages. "An interesting woman and a wonderful writer."

And so it went over that cold winter they spent in Florence. Monica existed on visits with Bernard and others, reading, and maintaining correspondence with friends as well as Max and Tim. Despite a growing number of newspaper editorials and broadcasts that called for patriotic Florentines to cease association with foreigners who might hold anti-fascist ideals, she continued to make her opinions known whenever she and Jorgen attended social events or visited with friends. As a result they found themselves being left off guest lists they had once taken for granted.

"No matter," Jorgen assured her. "The truth is with the disruption of the post and the irregularity of receipt of our monthly stipend from home, we'll save money by dining here at the villa rather than going out. But, my dear, you must learn to control your opinions. We are in enemy territory after all."

Recalling that conversation, Monica pushed aside the letter she was writing to Tim and walked out to the terrace, savoring the soft April breeze. She was a middle-aged woman who had raised three children and set them on paths of their own while managing successful business ventures that had made a real difference in her family's future. Now, by all rights, she should be looking forward to years of leisure as her friends were. Soon Jorgen would celebrate his sixtieth birthday, and she knew he longed to return to Engestofte to live out what years he had left tending his beloved gardens and spending his time with friends. But such sedentary pursuits did not appeal to Monica – never had. Even as a child she had tested the boundaries of what was expected and what she saw as necessary. For that matter, she hated the reality that she was getting older and there might come a day when she would need the care and support of her children, rather than the other way round. She had always lived her life at top speed, and the thought the day might come when that was no longer possible and she would need to rely on others was the single thing she dreaded most.

While Jorgen and his friends had hinted that war could be

good for the economy of small, neutral countries such as Denmark as well as their personal finances, Monica firmly believed war was never the answer. From the moment she had seen those headlines in Paris, her every waking thought had focused on finding ways she might be part of the fight to shorten the reign of terror sweeping across Europe – however insignificant in the greater scheme her contributions might be. She would do what she could to ensure the future she'd fought so hard to secure for her children. She would do it to honor her beloved brother who had returned to the front in that other war, knowing the price he might pay – and paying it.

"Monica!" Jorgen's voice, raised in alarm, brought her back to the moment at hand – Florence and the letter she'd been writing.

"What's happened?" she asked, seeing the telegram he held clutched in one hand.

"They've taken Denmark," he said, his voice faltering as he held the telegram out to her. The message was brief.

Denmark has fallen. All is safe. Ivan.

The paradox of the two short sentences was not lost on Monica. No one was safe if the Nazis had taken charge. She understood Ivan was letting them know that he and Engestofte were secure, but secure was not safe. She mentally accounted for the whereabouts – and safety – of her other two children. Viggo continued to live with them in Florence, while Varinka was staying with friends in Vienna. Only Ivan was in Denmark. She wondered if the Danish government might mount a counterattack, might recruit Ivan and his friends to serve. Her heart thrummed with anxiety and fear.

Hurrying past her husband, Monica switched on the radio. Amid the static, they were able to make out the announcement of the invasion of Norway and – worse – the complete capitulation of Denmark.

What was happening?

Following the invasion of Poland and declaration of war by France and Great Britain, they had been advised to remain in Italy for the time being. But for months now, everyone they knew had lived with uncertainty. Having learned that only one ocean liner would be leaving for the United States in the foreseeable future, their American friends had booked passage, and Monica and Jorgen had driven to Genoa to see them off. Now she recalled the scene she had witnessed there when the ship's leaving had been delayed. By then the rumors of wholesale roundups of Jews and others considered enemies of the Reich were widely accepted as truth. From the day the dictator first came to power, many German Jews or Jewish expatriates living in Europe had taken refuge in Italy, perhaps hopeful that they might someday return to their homes. But very quickly they realized that Italy was following Germany's lead, and even the more liberal city of Florence was no longer considered safe. That afternoon, as their friends waited for the *Conte di Salvoia* to depart, Monica had seen hundreds of families – most of them Jewish – flood the dock area, fighting for any available space on the ship.

Despite the deterioration of the political scene in Italy, Jorgen and Monica decided to remain in Florence. For the time being, neither Ivan nor the estate appeared to be in imminent danger, as the Danish government had fully acquiesced to its designation as a "protectorate" of Germany, and at least the Nazis had allowed the king and his family to remain, along with the prime minister and Parliament, who held the actual power to govern.

Then one morning in early June, Monica witnessed men installing loudspeakers around the town square as she walked back to their villa. Outside the hotel, members of the usually subdued staff spoke rapidly in Italian to each other, gesturing dramatically as their voices vied for space to state their obvious jubilation. Monica caught the gist of the conversation. *Il Duce* – Benito Mussolini – would be speaking to the country that afternoon. That explained the loudspeakers as well as the unusually large number of peasants from the hills already filling the town. As she turned onto the narrow lane leading to their dwelling, Monica saw their landlady standing just outside their gate, nervously wringing her hands. Monica quickened her step.

"You have visitors, signora" she said. "The *carabinieri*." She nodded toward the entrance to the house, where Monica saw two local police officers conferring with Jorgen. She hurried to join them.

"Ah, Monica, these gentlemen have come to give us some distressing news," Jorgen said. "It seems that we are no longer welcome here in Florence."

"Why not?"

One of the officers turned to her. "You are British, no?" His tone was deferential, even a bit apologetic. "Unfortunately, given our two countries are at war..."

"We are Danish," Jorgen replied.

The officer shrugged. "Still, not Italian – and we have received a number of reports that your sympathies clearly lie with the opposing side. I am most sorry, but we have our orders."

"Perhaps once things are more clear," his partner added, offering the hope they might return.

"We understand," Jorgen said as he escorted the officers to the street. As soon as they had gone, he returned to the house. "I'll make some calls."

"There must be someone you can speak with who can arrange for us to stay," Monica said, thinking of the information she continued to send Max and Tim. How would she continue to do her part if they were forced to leave?

"Monica, it is time to go home," Jorgen said softly, taking Monica in his arms, and she knew he was right. For outside their door, against a background of the crackle of the loudspeakers and the chatter and eventual cheers of those filling the streets, Mussolini announced Italy had joined forces with Germany.

They spent the remainder of that afternoon rearranging their lives – again.

A few days later, when the taxi arrived to take Monica and Jorgen to the train depot where Viggo and Inkie would meet them after bidding farewell to their friends, Monica was touched to see several locals gathered to see them off. Some, she knew, were fiercely loyal to Mussolini, and yet, here they were, their faces showing their distress at the parting. Muriel handed Monica a handwritten note of farewell from Bernard Berenson, and their landlady pressed a basket filled with bread and cheese and a bottle of wine on Jorgen.

"For the journey," she insisted.

Oh, how I hate war, Monica thought once they had boarded the train and found their compartment. It was not the larger political differences between governments she hated so much as what war did to the lives of ordinary people. She thought of their Jewish friends, now hopefully safe in America, but at what cost? Displaced from their homes and businesses in Germany and now displaced yet again. *Refugees.* Was that who she and Jorgen were to become? She had a vision of men and women, bent under the burden of carrying whatever they might salvage as they trudged from one place to another – innocents caught up in the petty infighting of men who protected their power by destroying the lives of those they never knew. On the train, she rested her head on Jorgen's shoulder and slept. She was so very tired, and there was still so much they would need to face.

In spite of having traveled extensively, Monica was still unprepared for the differences they encountered crossing the continent in wartime. Just after they left Florence, their train was placed on a side rail for hours to allow trains carrying troops and supplies to pass. Once they reached Genoa, she realized the city had recently been bombed. It was the first time Monica and her children had witnessed the actual destruction of war, not just on buildings and land but on people. Everywhere they looked men and women seemed to be on the move, their faces masks of bewilderment. The trains were already crowded – the depot platforms even more so. As they made stops in Milan and Verona, they heard shouted commands as troops marched past, their boots stamping out a drumbeat of warning that sent anyone in their path scurrying for shelter. Once they crossed the border into Austria, German officials boarded, patrolling the aisles of each car and demanding to see travel documents as the train moved slowly forward.

Weary of being cautious and determined to deliver whatever message of resistance she might to these buffoons, Monica pulled out a copy of Winston Churchill's latest work and set it on her lap, its red cover a vivid backdrop for Churchill's name in large yellow letters. The door connecting their car to the next opened and closed. A German officer walked slowly down the aisle, his eyes shifting from side to side until they settled on Monica. He took the empty seat across from her. The officer nodded, but Monica ignored him, turning her attention to the Churchill book. When she spoke to Jorgen or the children, it was in English. The officer remained with them through the night with not a word exchanged. Her family slept, as did the German, but Monica continued to read, her mind racing with ideas for how she might make some genuinely significant contribution toward ending this horrible war once they reached Engestofte.

She'd heard that Churchill had labeled Denmark "Hitler's tame canary." The very idea of her adopted country being seen as some caged bird infuriated her. Churchill did not know the Danes as she did.

The following morning they arrived in Berlin. The city was dressed in enormous banners that seemed to hang from the upper floors and rooftops of every building, the black Nazi cross emblazoned across large swaths of red silk that rippled like wheat fields on a summer's day. Jorgen went in search of someone to help convey their luggage to the hotel, where they would leave it until it was time to leave for the ferry later that night. Monica turned her attention to the aftermath of the RAF bombing raids she'd heard about on the BBC. The extent of the destruction was not what she had hoped. There was damage to be sure, but all around her shops were open and people were going about their routines as if they were confident they would be the victors in this conflict.

"Monica!"

She turned to see Jorgen walking toward them with an elderly man who pulled a rickety cart. Once he'd loaded their belongings, they followed him to the hotel, where Jorgen had often stayed and where they were warmly greeted by the manager. Anxious to get back outside and see more of the city so she could send a report to Max, Monica left Jorgen to enjoy a glass of schnapps with the hotel's manager and headed toward the Brandenburg Gate with Varinka and Viggo.

"I'm starving," Inkie moaned.

"We've no ration cards that will work here," Viggo reminded her.

Inkie shrugged, grabbed his arm, and headed for a nearby cafe. Monica took a seat on a nearby park bench to wait for them. She watched as her children spoke to the owner of the cafe and smiled when Inkie touched the man's arm, gave him that wide-eyed gaze that had captivated more than one male, and then followed him inside. Viggo glanced back at his mother before hurrying after his sister. Moments later they emerged.

"*Danke,*" Inkie shouted back toward the cafe's open door as she and Viggo crossed the street and presented Monica with a cup of steaming hot – if bitter – ersatz coffee. "It's not exactly Olga's espresso," Inkie apologized, and, while Viggo held her coffee as well as his own, she divided a chunk of bread into thirds.

"It's hot and at the moment that's all that matters. You two are quite the negotiators."

As they strolled up the broad avenue, Monica saw some evidence that all was not perfect for the Germans. They passed subway stations that were closed, and the zoo – an always-popular destination – was also shut down. On side streets shop windows were boarded up, making her wonder if those shops had belonged to Jews. But what interested her most was the sight of a sort of camouflage netting placed over the trees near a main intersection with fake trees added, creating the appearance at least of a new street grid. Overhead she heard a plane, and it dawned on her the deception was not for people on the street, but rather meant to confuse the Allied bombers.

"Viggo," she said, tightening her grip on his arm, "I want you to memorize the changes I'll point out to you and once we return to the hotel, draw a map of what we are seeing. Can you do that?"

"Of course." Viggo straightened to his full height as his eyes darted from side to side, taking in details of their surroundings.

"But Mummy, what good is a map?" Varinka protested. "We know our way, and besides, we aren't to stay here, are we?"

"I want to share the changes we're seeing with your father." It was half a lie. Of course, she should show the map to Jorgen, but although her contributions to the war effort were minimal, it seemed best to keep him out of it. On the other hand, if she could get the information to Max or Tim, maybe it would help. Once they returned to the hotel, Viggo recorded what they had seen, following Monica's instructions to make it appear to be a guide for tourists. Once he'd finished, she dashed off a cryptic note, shoved the map and note in an envelope, addressed it to Max in care of his friend in Sweden, and asked the friendly hotel owner to post it at his earliest convenience.

After more delays while traveling later that afternoon from Berlin to the town of Warnemunde, where the ferry terminal was located, it was well after midnight when they finally arrived during a blackout. With no shelter nearby, they stood or perched on their luggage for what seemed like hours.

"We need to find somewhere for the night – or what's left of it," Monica said, knowing there would be no ferry until dawn, if then. "The children are exhausted."

Jorgen gave her a weary smile. "The children? Not you?"

"Never," she replied, but she returned his smile.

"I'll see if I can find someone," Jorgen said as he walked away.

In the blackout, he was soon swallowed up by the dark and the others from the train milling around on the platform. But moments later, she heard his voice. "Pardon. This way, *bitte*."

He emerged from the shadows followed by a trio of sailors pulling a hand cart. In minutes he had directed the loading of the luggage. "These gentlemen know of a possible room in town, above a pub. We can get something to eat and rest until morning."

"Hooray," Inkie murmured as she uncurled from her position lying on one of the trunks and smiled at the sailors. It did not escape Monica's notice that the young men seemed suddenly more inclined to play the hero. "This way," one of them directed as he fell into step with Inkie and parted the crowd to make way for the cart – pulled by his two friends – to follow.

Monica found their hosts at the pub to be a pleasant couple, even if they were German. They made space for the mountain of luggage in a back storage area, then directed the family up a narrow stairway to a loft furnished with half a dozen cots. Viggo claimed the one closest to the back wall, collapsed onto it, and was breathing deeply before the rest of them had time to settle in. The owner of the pub arrived with a tray that held a pot of tea and some sliced apples and cheese.

"*Danke*," Monica murmured as she relieved him of the tray while Jorgen handed him several folded bills. She realized he'd managed to exchange their Italian money for German during his time at the hotel in Berlin.

Monica poured the tea into cracked cups while Inkie woke Viggo and sat next to him on the cot, the two of them silent as they savored the meal. Monica had to admit as she took her first sip that nothing had ever tasted so good. Jorgen sat on the cot across from her. He offered her a piece of cheese. "Tomorrow, we shall have whatever we want to eat," he said. "Tomorrow we shall finally be home."

In the weak light that filtered up from the pub below, she saw a single tear slip free and slowly wind its way down his lined face. She leaned forward and caught it with her thumb. He was so very tired, and perhaps she had underestimated how much returning to Engestofte after all this time meant to him. "Yes, my darling. Home at last." She took his empty cup. "Let's get what sleep we can," she said as she gathered their cups and placed them back on the tray, then covered her children, who were already half asleep, with the rough blankets folded at the end of each cot. She kissed their foreheads, smoothing back their hair as she had when they were babies, then kissed Jorgen's forehead as well before lying down.

It seemed she had just shut her eyes when the air-raid sirens shrieked. Below them they heard shouts, then the pub owner was shouting for them to follow him. They stumbled down the stairs and out into the street, where they joined a crowd of people hurrying toward the neighborhood shelter. Bombs were falling several blocks from them, a fireworks display that was nothing to celebrate, for this was not a sky lit by festivity, she realized. This was a sky lit by death and destruction.

Jorgen pulled her into the shelter and they sat huddled together, their arms around Varinka and Viggo, while the explosions continued to rock the small town. And then as suddenly as it began it ended. The shelter that had reverberated with shrieks and nervous chatter was suddenly quiet. The silence was eerie, as if no one dared even to breathe much less speak. Finally the sirens sounded the all clear. Wearily the throng that had crowded into the shelter shuffled back into the street and dispersed, everyone trudging back to home or business to assess the damage.

They arrived at the pub to find the owner and another man dragging their luggage from the storeroom to the street. Jorgen hurried forward to stop them, but soon was in the thick of it, grabbing what he could carry and adding it to the pile in the street. "Stay back," he shouted when Monica started toward him. "There's an unexploded bomb inside."

Ignoring her husband, she organized Viggo and Varinka into a sort of bucket brigade line so they could hand bags and drag trunks further from the danger. The all-clear sirens were replaced by the whine of police vehicles arriving to disarm the bomb.

The family waited along with the tavern owner and his wife and several neighbors, their breaths shallow with dread. Then, as dawn broke, the two officers tasked with disarming the bomb emerged with their arms raised in victory. The pub owner shouted with relief and hugged his wife. Monica watched them and understood that this was the real cost of war – the disruption it caused for innocent people like these. They had no stake in what was happening now that Hitler had marched into Russia. They had no idea that in cities miles from where they stood, Jews and members of the intelligentsia and others were being herded onto trains and taken to unknown destinations. All they knew was that once again their businesses, families, and friends had survived an attack and for now they were safe.

But she also understood that, if asked, they would place blame for their plight squarely on the shoulders of the RAF. They had no understanding of or interest in the geopolitical reasons behind the attack they had just endured. They knew only the immediate fact: they had been targeted by British planes.

As dawn arrived and everyone went about their business, Viggo retrieved the cart the sailors had used the night before and left outside the tavern. The four of them loaded it and then made their way down the cobbled street to the terminal to wait for the next ferry. They were beyond exhaustion and in desperate need of a shower or bath, their clothes coated with the dust that blew around in the aftermath of the attack. So when they arrived at the terminal and saw the Danish flag hoisted above the bow of the ferry, they cheered.

The captain recognized Jorgen from previous crossings and hurried down the gangplank to greet the family and orchestrate the loading of their luggage. They were led to a bathroom, where they took turns washing and making themselves as presentable as possible, before joining the captain in the ferry's salon, where a lovely lunch served at a table with real china and white linens awaited them. There were silver servers piled high with fresh bread, dishes of butter and jam, fresh fish, an assortment of fresh fruits and cheeses, and real coffee.

As the large ferry moved across the Baltic, Monica found a place near the bow, her gaze on the horizon waiting for the moment she would see the familiar coast of her adopted country. And as they docked, there was Ivan, waving his arms above his head in greeting, and she felt as if for the first time in days she could breathe free again. But as the family hurried down the gangplank to be reunited with Ivan, she could not ignore the presence of German soldiers carefully observing their Danish counterparts examining the papers of the new arrivals.

"Are they always around?" Monica asked her son, with a side-long glance at the Germans.

He shrugged. "We are not completely free, Mummy, but at least there is no war in Denmark."

Yes, there is, Monica thought, and in that moment she knew she would need to do more than writing letters to send to Max and Tim if she were to truly do her part in making sure freedom was restored – at least for her children.

PART THREE

Occupied
1940–1944

Engestofte – 1940–1941

AS MUCH AS SHE HAD ENJOYED THE MEAL they'd been served on the ferry crossing, once they were settled and began accepting the occasional invitation from friends and neighbors who had remained in Denmark, she found the excess of food served at such gatherings annoying. Through letters from her mother she heard daily of the strict rationing and lack of some of the more basic foodstuffs people in Great Britain were suffering. In Poland, people were close to starving, according to the BBC reports. She found some hope in America's passage of the Lend-Lease program and the fact that, while they still waited on the sidelines of the war, their government had established a process for selective service.

But with Germany on the brink of invading the Soviet Union, across Europe innocent citizens had to endure the nightly bombings launched from both sides. Denmark was an anomaly in that the country's declared neutrality and forced collaboration with their German occupiers meant their larders and stomachs were full. They could go about their business and sleep soundly knowing they were unlikely to be bombed. Of course, she was happy her family did not have to suffer as others across Europe were, but at the same time, she found the smugness of some of their friends and neighbors so unbearable that at one dinner, she could no longer hold her tongue.

"Perhaps you will discover your patriotism only when your stomach suddenly feels empty," she snapped at one guest, a comment for which Jorgen chided her later that evening.

"Darling, you cannot blame others for appreciating what we have," he argued.

"I can and I will," she replied. "This new foreign minister has as good as surrendered to that Nazi madman. Where are those who will stand against him? In Norway, the Resistance is already well organized. Where are they here?"

"That's hardly fair," Jorgen said, his voice tinged with irritation that she was questioning the patriotism of his countrymen. "As soon as our ships at sea learned of the occupation, they made for Allied ports, rather than return and serve the Reich."

He had a point. But the truth was that since the occupation, even small acts of protest had been sporadic at best. "We can and must do more," she insisted.

Still, she was happy to be back after over a decade of living in Italy. She had left Denmark as a young wife and mother in her thirties facing unforeseen hardships in terms of their financial well-being. Now she had returned as a middle-aged matron whose children were fully educated and prepared to move forward with lives of their own. Then, she had still been naive about how the future she had imagined for her family and herself might suddenly shift. Now, she was wiser – and far more confident in her ability to deal with whatever new challenge life might send her way. That first new challenge presented itself the moment she set foot in their beloved house – a place she had not entered for nearly a decade.

Over the last six years their beautiful home had been occupied by a large, rowdy family. Every room was badly in need of painting, with stained carpets and damaged furniture requiring replacement or repair. And, because the home had no central heating and they had to rely on the wood or coal-burning fireplaces throughout the mansion, the dust and smoke added to the damage done by the lessee's five rambunctious children and two large dogs.

Fortunately, as her business ventures had flourished, Monica had been able to either purchase or barter several rolls of French upholstery fabric and linen. These she had sent back to Christian at Engestofte to be stored in the attics along with the Victorian furnishings she had removed when she'd first redecorated the house – pieces, she realized, that could now be sold to pay for repairs. On top of that, she was pleased to learn the trustees had held back funds they could not trust getting safely to the family in Italy, and with all of this she set to work restoring at least the public rooms and bedrooms to their former level of welcoming comfort. Meanwhile Jorgen was impatient to get to work taming the overgrowth on the grounds and reestablishing the orchard and gardens. With the shortages in gas, bicycles and horse-drawn carriages were the main means of transportation for visits or shopping excursions into the village. Those restrictions, along with the inclement weather, meant they were more isolated than ever, but they hardly noticed. There was so much to be done.

By spring, with the house finally set to rights, Monica looked for other projects she might take on to fill her time. During their stay in Rapallo, Christian had written to suggest refurbishing a small half-timbered cottage on the island across from the main house and offering it for rent. The years of struggle had made Monica keen to take advantage of any opportunity to supplement their income. One never knew when financial disaster might strike again, so she urged Jorgen to give Christian his permission. A month later their estate agent wrote to say the cottage had been rented to a couple from the northern part of Denmark – one of whom was a writer. Now that she had returned, she decided it was time to introduce herself.

She and Inkie rowed across the lake, then walked through the thick woods to the cottage. As they approached they could smell meat frying, and Monica was pleased to see the cottage seemed to have weathered the harsh winter with little damage. The name Christian had given her was Hilmar Wulff, who leased the cottage with his wife and their friend, Halfdan Rasmussen.

"The poet?" Monica had exclaimed. Rasmussen was well known and quite respected in Danish literary circles. She'd read his work and recommended it to Inkie and her friends. How delightful to have such a person in residence!

As she and Inkie passed the kitchen window on their way to the front door, Monica glimpsed a woman moving about the kitchen. She heard the low murmur of conversation. "They're home," she said as she knocked on the door she'd painted a bright azure blue. They waited. Monica knocked again, keenly aware of the silence that had suddenly descended on the other side of that door.

Finally the door opened and a man who was not quite as tall as Monica peered up at her over the rims of his glasses.

"Good day, sir. I am Monica Wichfeld and this is my daughter, Varinka."

His caution turned to a smile as he swung the door wide to invite them inside. "Ah, the ladies of the manor have come calling, my dear. Welcome. I am Hilmar Wulff and this is my wife, Grete. Sit. Sit." He removed a stack of papers and books from one chair and set them teetering on top of a similar stack on the table, then pulled out a second chair for Inkie.

If the outside of the cottage had seemed none the worse for wear, the interior was a mess. Everywhere she looked Monica saw rows of books stacked on the floor. Every table surface was covered with papers, ink bottles, and empty beer bottles. It occurred to her that Wulff fit his surroundings, his thick hair in need of a cut or at least a comb. He was dressed in a flannel shirt with a frayed collar, over which he wore a shapeless corduroy jacket. His trousers were stained and baggy and his shoes scuffed. But he had a ready smile and a self-deprecating manner that made Monica like him immediately.

"We won't stay long," Monica said with a glance toward Mrs. Wulff. "We really just stopped by to see if you had settled in and might need anything?"

Hilmar laughed. "As you can see, we have indeed made ourselves at home." He swept his hand around, taking in the scope of clutter surrounding them. Monica noticed neither he nor his wife made any excuse nor effort to set anything to rights. She had no idea why or of what, but she felt that was perhaps a good sign. She also took note of a small mimeograph machine half-hidden behind one pile of books.

She and Inkie stayed for about an hour, enjoying tea and a slice of the coffeecake Mrs. Wulff had baked earlier. They learned Rasmussen was away for the moment, but were assured he would be delighted to meet them. Plans were made for getting together at the main house once he returned. Monica also learned that they had established friendships with some of the same townspeople and shopkeepers in Maribo that she knew. By the time they left, Monica's heart was racing. After seeing the mimeograph, something told her this man might be her entree into the Resistance. She had caught glimpses of some of the titles of his reading material and a phrase or two from writings scattered on the table tops. She was fairly certain the man was a communist, and that with his close ties to Rasmussen, this meant in taking sides in this war, he would not choose the Germans.

A few days later she returned alone for a second visit, and was pleased to learn that Hilmar's wife was away, shopping in the village. She took the opportunity to come straight to the point. "Do you read *Frit Danmark* by chance?" she asked. *Free Denmark* was one of several underground newspapers she'd become familiar with since her return.

In answer, Hilmar went to a corner of the cottage, and after rummaging through one of the stacks, returned to the table, handing her the last few issues. "Would you like to borrow them for reading?"

"What I would like is to help with the distribution," she replied.

Hilmar hesitated. "You do understand the politics of this?" he asked. "People of my leaning are not especially well received in any circle these days."

"You mean communists."

Hilmar smiled. "You have a way of coming directly to the heart of a matter, Fru Wichfeld. Still, we are not exactly on the same page when it comes to what we think might be best for this world postwar."

Monica placed her hand on the stack of forbidden newspapers. "It's Monica, please, and what I care about at the moment is fighting the Nazis. Anyone who is in that fight, I consider a colleague. The rest we can sort out once Hitler and his thugs are defeated. Now, what can I do?"

Hilmar leaned forward, his normally jolly expression suddenly intent and serious. "Distribution is but one of our problems, dear lady. We need funds, and as you can well imagine, raising them can be difficult."

Monica shrugged. "No one needs to know the true purpose for what they give. All they need to know is that they are doing their part for a good cause."

By week's end she returned to hand over an envelope stuffed with several hundred kroner. This time Halfdan Rasmussen was in residence. The young poet had a long, thin face and a delicacy about him that stirred Monica's maternal instincts. "There will be more next week," she told both men almost apologetically. "There's a large party planned for the weekend at a neighboring estate. I expect I will have every opportunity to double or perhaps triple this amount."

"This will help so much, Monica," Rasmussen said. "You've no idea...." Seeming at a loss for words, he added, "Thank you."

Later that autumn, Monica took comfort in the news that a group of schoolboys, calling themselves the Churchill Club, were actively imitating the Resistance fighters in Norway by performing various acts of vandalism in Jutland. She delighted in their efforts to sabotage military vehicles and airplanes. These were children – their reported leader a mere fifteen – refusing to simply stand by while their country was occupied. She felt like celebrating and suggested that once the holidays passed, she and Jorgen host a party to mark their silver wedding anniversary.

"We were married in June," Jorgen reminded her.

"But we have our family together now. So much can change in a matter of days, much less months," she argued as she began making one of the lists her children well knew meant the plan was already in motion.

The day of the party, guests arrived in a parade of conveyances from pony traps to carriages that had served their ancestors in the last century. They wore their finest furs and sat under the wrap of heavy wool and fur blankets. Monica and Jorgen greeted them while Varinka and Viggo escorted them to the rooms assigned to them for their stay, if overnight, or for changing clothes for the afternoon's festivities. Ivan and Christian took care of the luggage. The house was soon alive with chatter and activity. Late in the afternoon everyone gathered in the dining room where Monica, dressed in a satin gown Mabelle had given her years earlier, served Russian tea from Jorgen's grandmother's silver samovar. The long table featured a selection of crustless sandwiches and petite cakes. Once guests had filled their plates, they adjourned to the drawing room to play card or board games while the younger friends of Ivan, Varinka, and Viggo cranked up the gramophone and rolled back the carpets in the grand entry for dancing.

"Shall we show them how it's done?" Jorgen asked later as he and Monica stood watching the young people fox-trot to the music of Benny Goodman and Glenn Miller.

Seeing his parents ready to take to the dance floor, Ivan lifted the needle and restarted the record as Jorgen and Monica swung into a lively quickstep. That was followed by a Charleston, and although they were both a bit breathless, they agreed to one more dance when they saw all their guests had gathered around the perimeter of the room. Ivan placed a new recording on the turntable – a tango.

"Ah, the dance of love," Jorgen murmured as he took her in his arms. "And after twenty-five years, my darling Monica, I still adore you."

How far they had come, she thought as she effortlessly followed his lead through the intricate steps of the dance. Theirs had been an unusual union, to say the least, but in spite of everything that might have pulled them apart, that union had survived. He was her husband and dearest friend, and she knew she had made the right choice in rejecting the temptation to follow passion over practicality. As for Kurt, he no longer held any place in her life – not as a lover and not as a friend. He had chosen to go to America and sit out the war in California among a new cast of friends who saw no need to take any part in the conflict. Learning of his choice, Monica had at last understood that Kurt – a bit like Jorgen's brother, Axel – would not stand up for something, but would rather simply stand by, waiting to see which side came out the victor. Only then would such people choose.

Later that night, after their guests had left or retired to their rooms, Jorgen came to her bedroom. He carried an extra blanket. "You'll need this," he said, throwing back the double layer of blankets and comforter already piled on her bed and lining the sheet with the soft flannel blanket. "The temperatures are predicted to drop well below freezing, and the fire can only do so much."

"I can't recall a time when the lake was completely frozen over this early in the season," she replied as she sat at her dressing table removing her makeup. "Christian says the ice is so thick one cannot easily drill through it for a decent round of ice fishing."

Jorgen stood gazing out the window, lost in thought. After a long moment, he pulled the draperies closed. "What would you think of spending the worst of the winter in Copenhagen?"

She understood his hesitation in making the suggestion. Certainly she had made her abhorrence of the Nazi banners that swathed the city well known. Still, the idea of spending at least the next few months in the city had merit, and at least for the time being, the presence of German soldiers was minimal as Germany made a show of permitting the Danish government to be in charge. "The children would like that, I'm sure," Monica replied. There Viggo could continue following his passion for his studies in architecture, and Varinka had several good friends who now lived and worked in the city. More to the point, it occurred to her that being in the city would open the door to finding her greater role in resisting this horrid war.

"The children would indeed like to go. And you?" Jorgen asked, stepping behind her so they were both reflected in her mirror.

"Can we afford it?"

Since their return to Engestofte, Jorgen had been quite firm in his decision that Monica was no longer to feel it was her responsibility to keep their finances in order. Her line of costume jewelry continued to yield orders from time to time, but with the war, business was waning. Jorgen had earned her trust and she was ready to move on to other pursuits – such as raising funds for the Resistance.

"I have learned my lesson," Jorgen had assured her, and from that day forward he had worked closely with Christian and the trustees to continue to enhance the profits provided by the farm. Now he placed his hands gently on her shoulders. "Yes," he replied. "We can."

She smiled. "Will there be proper heat?"

"I promise," he said as he leaned down and kissed her cheek. "I'll make the arrangements first thing tomorrow." He crossed the room, stoked the fire, and then opened the door. "Sleep well, my dearest."

He was just about to close the door before moving on to his bedroom down the hall when she called out to him.

"Jorgen? I love you," she said softly in Danish, surprised at the tears that sprang to her eyes.

"Happy anniversary," he whispered and blew her a kiss before closing the door.

As predicted, Varinka and Viggo were delighted by the move. Ivan would continue his work managing the neighbor's farm, promising to come to the city whenever time allowed. As for Monica, she could not quite recall why she had been so against the idea of being in Copenhagen. As she wrote her mother:

Truly, it is a bit of paradise. I wish you could be here as well. We have rooms on the top floor of the hotel, and I've but to press a button and someone appears to fulfill my slightest wish. There are no vermin or fowl taking refuge in the walls or ceilings and no need to keep one ear open at night for the possibility of beggars trying to break in as there is in the country these days.

She described the small luxuries that came with living in a fine hotel, the comfort of the beds and the fresh flowers – not up to Jorgen's standards, she assured Alice, but still a nice touch.

And warmth! I have never seen so much snow in Denmark. Still, despite waking to the sound of shovels scraping paths through the snow that fell overnight; and in spite of traversing a tunnel created by piles on the rare occasions I venture out; and although even as I write this I am looking out the window through a valence of icicles and the delicate lacework of frost that coats the window panes, I am supremely comfortable.

The canals and river were frozen over, and Viggo and his friends often went skating, enjoying a hot beverage in the warming house afterward. Varinka preferred meeting her friends at cafes, although she and her father developed a habit of collecting leftover bread from the hotel kitchen and walking down to the shore to feed the water fowl.

The shops continue to do a brisk business. I am particularly fond of the bookstore on Stroget. It stocks a wonderful selection of works in English and I have been reading for hours every day.

She hesitated to write what worried her most – the news she had heard that the Nazis had built a walled ghetto in Warsaw and forced hundreds, if not thousands, of people to abandon their homes and move there for no reason other than that they were Jewish. She could hardly comment on such topics as the censors were bound to black out those sections. She leaned away from the writing table and stared out the window. The letter to Alice she had meant to reassure her mother of the family's safety and well-being had taken a darker turn. The Copenhagen she had described seemed like something straight out of a Hans Christian Andersen fairy tale, but beneath all that appeared normal lurked a darker scene.

She supposed she should take some comfort in the open displays of nationalism. The Danish flag and small pennants showing the national colors fluttered from every shop and apartment window. Businessmen wore enamel pins in their buttonholes that featured the royal insignia. Students flaunted their red-and-white knit caps and scarves. King Christian V, still in residence, took to the streets every morning for his daily horseback ride through the city, and on several occasions bicyclists formed a line behind, trailing him like the tail of a kite. Pedestrians would stop to wave at their king, and while he was not as popular as monarchs of the past, his people had come to admire his show of independence.

And yet, Monica thought, *what did it all matter?*

Putting the letter aside, she rummaged through a stack of reading material on the table by her bed and unearthed an underground newspaper she'd found inside one of the books she'd bought. It contained an article about airmen from England parachuting into the northern part of Denmark. It occurred to her that perhaps Churchill was preparing to build an underground movement in Denmark, and if so, she wanted to be part of that.

But how? Would these men ever consider using a woman in her mid-forties to further their cause? And where would she begin? Who would she approach?

She sealed the letter to her mother and went down to the lobby to post it. While there she treated herself to a cup of tea in the hotel's dining room, sipping it as she sat at a small table for two and stared out the large leaded glass windows. Again, she was struck by the way everything in Copenhagen seemed unaffected by the war. A trio of German soldiers strolled by. They were laughing and then waved to a Danish policeman directing traffic as if they were old friends, while in Poland soldiers in these same German uniforms were raiding homes and herding innocent families into ghettos.

Engestofte – 1941–1943

All that spring and into the summer, Monica redoubled her efforts to raise funds for the distribution of the Resistance newspapers. Of course the donors had no idea the money was being used in that way. She did not lie exactly. If she told them their money was going to help the people of Denmark, was that a lie?

Because of Denmark's flat terrain, radio communication from the BBC and Sweden was easier to access than in any other occupied country. Those bulletins, plus the burgeoning circulation of over four dozen secret newspapers, boosted Monica's morale even as the news about her own family worsened.

In early December, word came of the attack on Pearl Harbor by the Japanese. Monica's thoughts immediately went to her brother, Tim, who had been transferred to Singapore. And a month later her mother wrote that indeed Tim had been taken prisoner. Alice was inconsolable at the thought of losing yet another son. And as determined as Monica was to protect her own children, she knew they all had minds of their own, especially when it came to the war. But at the same time, with America now fully engaged in the war, she took hope.

Monica continued to raise funds for a growing number of underground newspapers. In addition she persuaded Wulff to allow her to become part of the network of men and women distributing the papers themselves. She took care to keep her activities from her family. Placing herself in danger was a small price to pay if it meant her children would one day have the freedom to do as they pleased. And then early one morning in 1942, Viggo called her from Copenhagen with startling news.

"Mummy, I'm leaving tomorrow for home," he said after a stilted exchange of pleasantries that was atypical of their usual free-wheeling conversations. His voice shook, and she realized he was quite nervous. At least he had stuck to the code the family had adopted for mentioning any place that might raise suspicions. "Home" was Great Britain, more specifically Ireland.

"To visit your grandmother?" she asked. Alice Beresford was back living at St. Hubert's and would not be able to return to her beloved villa in Rapallo until the war ended – if then. A visit with her grandson would certainly lift her spirits.

"If time permits," he said. "I have an appointment, and after that I may be away for some time."

Immediately she understood what Viggo was telling her. Her youngest son was going to England to join up. Monica's heart threatened to break through the wall of her chest, and she clutched the receiver so hard her knuckles turned white. "Surely this can wait. You have to sit for your final examinations after all," she said, buying time while she tried to think how best to stop him.

"The appointment is far more important than school, Mums." He cleared his throat. "I need to pack. Give everyone my love and tell them I'll write."

He rang off then, and Monica stared at the receiver before replacing it in its cradle. Then she grabbed her purse and the car keys, scribbled a note to Jorgen, and broke every rule of the road getting to the depot in Maribo in time for the train to Copenhagen. On the trip she sat forward in her seat, as if by doing so she could will the train to move faster. She arrived in the city by noon and, through calls to her son's friends and others, figured out that Viggo had taken a job as a deckhand on a Swedish schooner that sailed from Copenhagen to Stockholm before returning. It was a common way for young Danish men to get to England to volunteer – first make it to Sweden, then on from there. After learning the ship with its crew had sailed, and unwilling to trust the Danish police who she understood could be reluctant to go against their German counterparts, she called a close friend in Stockholm who might be able to help. Blessedly the ship made several stops between Copenhagen and Stockholm, buying them time. Meanwhile she waited for any news.

Late that afternoon she received word that Viggo had been taken into custody by the Swedish authorities, who had developed a habit of watching for young Danish men intent on getting to England to join the fight. Allowing such traffic through Swedish ports endangered the country's status of neutrality. When an abashed Viggo returned to Copenhagen later that evening, Monica met him at the pier.

"We've been invited for a visit with the countess," she told her son, invoking the name of the friend she had contacted to help bring Viggo back to Copenhagen. She knew her son admired Countess Nina Moltke, an American heiress and the wife of the former Danish minister of foreign affairs. He also admired her son, Bobby, a friend of Inkie's, a great deal. As Monica had assumed, the news had the desired effect of brightening Viggo's sullen mood.

"I was certain you would take me home and perhaps throw away the key."

"The thought occurred," Monica replied. "But a weekend in the country for me and perhaps longer for you seems a good idea for both of us."

To Viggo's delight, Bobby was also staying at the estate. Monica had met Nina's son once or twice but knew him more by his reputation as a bit of a playboy who edited a humor magazine in Copenhagen. He was a good ten years older than her daughter, but both Viggo and Inkie spoke highly of him, so Monica was curious to know him better. By the time she asked him to walk with her to the station at the end of her stay on Sunday evening, Monica was convinced by comments he'd made that Bobby Moltke was far more than a wealthy, carefree bachelor. She decided to come straight to the point.

As they approached the depot, she stopped suddenly and faced him. "You have ties within the Resistance, Bobby, and – "

He raised one hand in denial and laughed. "My dear lady, whatever gave you such an idea?"

"There is no time for game-playing, Bobby," she said, keeping her voice low as she took his arm and continued walking. "I overheard your side of a telephone conversation you had this morning. All very secretive. I want to help."

"I really do not think – "

"I am doing what I have been able to offer so far," Monica continued, "but it is hardly enough. I am aware of rumors of parachutists entering the country, and if such reports are true, there must be more than one such person with a need for safe haven. Where are they being sheltered, especially once they have completed their task, or more importantly, if they need somewhere to stay until they can leave the country?"

"I – "

"What I am asking is that you get word to those who can act on the information that Engestofte has the facilities to shelter those men – and do a great deal more in terms of receiving and distributing goods and even perhaps recruiting and training locals to…"

They had almost reached the station, and Monica's words came in a rush, as if she needed to make sure she got everything said before leaving. "I am determined to keep my children safe. The only way I can accomplish that is to do whatever I can to bring a quick end to this war," she said, her eyes brimming with tears. "Will you help me?"

Bobby no longer feigned innocence. He faced her and took hold of her shoulders. "Fru Wichfeld, the danger to you – your family…"

"I know all of that," she replied impatiently and felt tears of frustration fill her eyes. "But I'd rather they be here where I can watch over them than off on some battlefield." She had thought of little else over the last couple of days and was convinced this was the best course. There was more to be done – there was more *being* done. She had proven herself by raising funds and offering the estate as a center for Wulff and his work making sure the underground newspapers continued to be printed and distributed, but…

Bobby leaned closer as if kissing her cheek in farewell. "I'll see what I can do," he whispered. "But you must be patient. Please do not do anything rash."

Patience was hardly her strong suit, but she nodded in agreement. She would give Bobby a month, no more.

Through letters and the occasional phone conversation, Monica made sure she and Bobby stayed in touch. He tried placating her by pointing out the work she was already doing when it came to the distribution of the illicit newspapers around the country.

She now managed several underlings whose job it was to make deliveries to various outlying communities. Still, in her view, Bobby continued to limit her ability to make what she felt was any significant contribution. He had repeatedly dismissed her suggestion she could do more, as she urged him to present the idea of Engestofte as a perfect reception point for arms and supplies to his superiors.

"Far too dangerous for you to get involved at that level," he protested one afternoon in early January when they met in Copenhagen. "When will you understand there are limits to what you might do?"

"I don't accept that. I will never accept that," she snapped. "I believe I have proven myself capable, and the estate is perfect as both a safe haven for parachutists and others as well as a perfect storage and distribution center for arms and supplies." She decided to try another tactic. "Bobby, this is our time. Now that Hitler has tasted defeat in Stalingrad and North Africa – "

"The Germans are nervous and as a result have become less passive and more observant here in our homeland, my dear," Bobby interrupted. "In case you haven't noticed, the presence of German soldiers on the streets of our fair city has increased – not a great deal, but it's a clear sign that our occupiers are paranoid and questioning just how much they can trust the locals."

"I am well aware that on the surface our countrymen – and women – have limited their rebellious acts to such trifling actions as displaying the flag and singing patriotic anthems, but underneath? When I look into their faces, I see people ready to stand up to the Germans, Bobby. I feel that so deeply, and frankly my true abilities are wasted if you insist on limiting my contribution."

Bobby's lips thinned, and she could see he was annoyed with

her. "You have been given a good deal of responsibility already," he grumbled.

"I can do more," she repeated tersely.

They had been strolling arm and arm through Tivoli Gardens, their heads bent close together and their voices low. They might have been any mother and son, enjoying an unusually mild winter afternoon together. As they reached the gates, ready to join the throngs on the more crowded street, she searched for anything else she might say to persuade him.

He stopped just outside the gate and lit a cigarette. "You're not going to stop until you get yourself arrested or killed, are you?"

"I don't take unnecessary risks, Bobby," she replied, assuming he was preparing to leave her since he did not offer her a cigarette as well.

Bobby inhaled and slowly blew out a stream of smoke as he studied her. "Very well. If I can't talk you out of endangering yourself and God knows who else, perhaps there's someone who can. Come with me," he ordered, setting off at a brisk pace.

He threaded his way through the narrow side streets, not waiting to see if she had followed or was keeping up with him. She saw him approach a woman wearing the uniform of a hotel maid. Under the guise of assisting the woman with her packages, the two exchanged a brief conversation and Bobby slipped something into his coat pocket before the woman walked away.

Curious, Monica hurried to catch up with Bobby. She'd had enough clandestine conversations while delivering the under-ground papers to know what she'd just witnessed. "Who was that?"

"A friend," he replied and took off again, cutting down a narrow lane before emerging on the plaza and crossing to the Hotel Terminus. Once inside he bypassed the front desk where the clerk was busy with an arriving guest and, ignoring the elevator, started up the stairs.

Monica followed. "Where are – "

"Shush," Bobby ordered, and for the rest of the climb to the third floor, the only sounds were their footfalls on the worn marble.

When they reached the third floor, Bobby headed directly for the last room on the hall – a room positioned across from a rear stairway. *Escape route.* Her pulse quickened with excitement as she realized whatever Bobby was up to involved something far more dangerous than he'd trusted her with before now.

He knocked twice and then again before removing a key from his coat pocket and unlocking the door with a sign that read: *Rengoring.* He waited for Monica to enter a small room – a closet really, with brooms and mops hung on hooks and buckets stacked along the perimeter. Bobby pushed aside a stack of cardboard cartons to reveal a second door. Again he knocked before opening it to reveal a larger space lit only by a shadeless floor lamp near the single small, blacked out window. She made out a large desk cluttered with files and papers and maps, another side table that held a telephone and mimeograph machine, a cot rumpled with sheets and a flat pillow, and a coat rack on which hung a gray fedora and black overcoat.

A man stood near the blacked out window. He switched on the small lamp on the corner of his desk and stepped forward to greet them.

Behind her she heard the click of the door closing. Suppressing a surge of fear and suddenly concerned she might have misread the situation, she turned to Bobby. "What's going on?"

"Precaution," Bobby said as he stepped between her and the man. "Mrs. Monica Wichfeld, may I present Mr. Flynn Moller."

Monica's heart raced. Bobby had faltered over the man's name. She knew at once that the man before her was not named Moller. Wulff had told her of rumors of someone being sent from headquarters in London to step up Resistance activities in Denmark. Her pulse quickened as she realized this must be that man. She knew those most in danger of being arrested took pseudonyms and fake identities – sometimes disguises – to confuse the authorities.

"You are Danish?" she asked, accepting his handshake. She needed him to speak so she could gather more information about his background.

"I am, although I have been away for some time – London, Africa...." He shrugged and indicated she should sit. "I have heard a great deal about you, Mrs. Wichfeld." His English was impeccable. "Our mutual friend here has spoken of the services you are providing for our work, especially the monies you have managed to raise. We are in your debt, madam."

"I can do more," Monica replied, thinking she would keep repeating that until someone finally heard.

Moller studied her for a moment, inclining his head to one side as a painter might if trying to decide how best to portray her. "You are impatient," he said quietly, more to himself than to her. "That can be dangerous for others."

Now she understood why Bobby had brought her here. This was the man in charge. If he said she could not do more, then...

"I learned that lesson long ago, Mr. Moller. When my family was living in Florence, I was quite outspoken. It resulted in a neighbor I barely knew being arrested and questioned for hours before finally being released. The interrogation focused on me, and while there was no harm done, I vowed never to place anyone in such a position again."

Moller paced the narrow confines of the room, occasionally glancing from her to Bobby and then back to her.

Monica waited.

Finally this man with the power to offer or deny what she so desperately wanted stopped pacing and began rearranging papers on his desk. "Since my arrival a week or so ago, I'm afraid I have found it necessary to focus much of my attention on the northern provinces, but it was always my intent to give equal importance to Lolland and Falster. Bobby tells me you are quite familiar with that part of the country – and its people?"

"I am." Monica was still unsure of where this conversation might lead. Bobby had been so adamantly against her involvement, and yet, here she sat before the man she had to assume was the very person she'd heard about – someone the Brits had sent to oversee acts of resistance and sabotage throughout Denmark.

"The truth is, Monica – may I call you Monica?"

She nodded.

He smiled and continued. "We do indeed see a need for stepping up operations in the southern parts of our country. I will admit that I had not had much faith in the idea of a woman....However, now that I have met you in person, I am wondering if you might not be precisely who we need to help us in that regard."

Behind her, she heard Bobby suck in a breath. Moller peered at her through his black-framed glasses, his finger still poised over the part of Denmark she called home. After a moment she realized he was waiting for her to say something.

"Exactly what are you suggesting?"

He turned his attention to Bobby. "The more I think of it, the more it seems that placing a woman in the role would be less suspect – throw our enemy off track, at least long enough for us to establish the unit."

"She has a family," Bobby protested.

"Yes, so you said. Still, a woman...the wife of an aristocrat? And a mother as well?"

Bobby released a sigh of resignation. "There will need to be a period of...shall we say, orientation?"

Monica could hardly believe what she was hearing. They were discussing her as if she'd left the room, and yet, Bobby was coming round to the idea of placing her in charge of something they clearly both considered important.

She turned to Bobby. "I can do this. You know I can."

Her friend studied his shoes and did not return her gaze.

Moller chuckled. "Actually Bobby had been singing your praises until I brought up this idea. I'm afraid he is not quite as enthusiastic as I am. His friendship with your children – and admiration for you – have influenced that. However, as resistant to the idea as he was originally, by bringing you here today, it appears he has decided to allow me to make the final decision."

"I thought you would be the one to see the folly of this idea," Bobby retorted.

Moller moved the desk lamp closer and tapped a spot on a hand-drawn map marked *Engestofte*. "Tell me your thoughts, Monica."

She stood and removed her gloves, setting them and her pocketbook aside as she leaned over the map. "These fields," she said, pointing to several acres in the most isolated part of the property, "will not be planted this season. They are some distance from roads or houses, making them a perfect location for airdrops." She ran her finger down to the lake that took up a large section of the map. "The lake is also available, of course, but perhaps more suitable as a landing place for men than supplies. We would need to gather any parachutes, of course, but once laundered, the fabric makes a lovely christening gown."

Moller smiled.

"There are locals eager to help," Monica added. "Often whenever I go to the village, I am approached with a cautious inquiry. Just the other day the butcher offered his home should I need extra bedrooms for my guests. Everyone is well aware Engestofte has dozens of rooms – many of them bedrooms. I have little doubt the butcher was offering more than simple guest space."

"If we organized a team of high-level support," Moller reasoned, more to himself than to Bobby, who still seemed inclined to raise objections.

Monica straightened to her full height. "I am somewhat familiar with the work being done in the north, Mr. Moller," she said. "If you are asking me to head up a similar operation in Lolland, my answer is an emphatic yes."

She was aware of the two men exchanging a look. Bobby shrugged, and Moller rolled up the map.

"Thank you, Monica. I will take the matter under consideration. In the meantime, we are in immediate need of a safe house. One of our own has recently found his way here from Norway. He is fine for now, but the Germans are determined to capture him, and until we can secure his escape to Sweden, Copenhagen is far too dangerous a place for him. Do you think you might accommodate him for a short time?"

It was a test and she knew it. "Of course." If it meant she would finally be trusted to take on the greater work of fighting the Germans, she would defend the man with her very life.

Engestofte – Spring 1943

As it turned out, that was unnecessary. The young man arrived when Jorgen was away on business and none of the children were in residence. For the benefit of others who might be curious, Monica made up some story about a distant relative passing through and put the hunted saboteur in the guest room where visiting members of the family always stayed. Not for the first time, she was glad that Rose had gone back to Ireland and she and Jorgen maintained only a skeletal household staff. None of them lived on site. For the first time since the war started, she was also glad for the rationing of petrol, which meant casual visits between neighbors were minimal. The young man stayed a few days and then was gone. When Moller sent word of his need for additional safe houses, she knew she had passed her first test.

Over the spring she continued to shelter those in need. In June she received word that a man calling himself Jacob Jensen would need a place to stay indefinitely. Moller's heavily coded letter let Monica know this young man would also need a job that would allow him to move freely through the region. On more than one occasion she had managed to disguise someone's identity by introducing them as a new employee on the household staff.

Until she saw him, Monica's plan was to have him stay in the house in the guise of serving as her tutor. Everyone agreed her Danish could use some refreshing after the years she had spent in Italy and traveling throughout Europe, and that would explain a longer tenure. But when she met him at the train station, she knew there was no possibility the man before her could live in the house without raising questions. The man Moller had called "Jacob" had the physique of a longshoreman and a certain rough-around-the-edges speech and manner that told Monica no one would ever believe he was either a scholar or her latest Danish tutor. She immediately thought of Hilmar, and decided to make arrangements for Jacob to take up residence in the cottage. Rasmussen was no longer staying there, so she was certain they could manage.

On the drive back to the estate from the station, she was somewhat taken aback by Jacob's apparent need to impress her with his past exploits. She soon realized that he wanted her to understand that he would not be taking orders or direction from a woman. "We will collaborate," he announced.

Monica gave him a smile that held no warmth and spent the rest of the trip reminding herself that this man had been chosen by Mr. Moller, so he must be the best. But she could not help being glad he would not be staying in the house.

Meanwhile, with Bobby's guidance, she began assembling a network of support – a small circle of like-minded people who could help make things happen. The first candidate for such a role came via a request from Jorgen.

"Darling, I fear I have overbooked my calendar," Jorgen announced one morning as he refilled her coffee. "A young man is coming today to recommend some insurance for the estate. He's the cousin of one of our farm tenants and I thought to give him a hearing, but I need to meet with the trustees. I asked him to come for lunch and a tour of the grounds and house. Could you possibly meet with him in my stead?"

She had nothing else on her calendar, and it would be a distraction. "Of course," she agreed.

Erik Kiersgaard might have been sent from central casting to take on the role of a Viking for a play or film, Monica thought as the young insurance agent introduced himself. He was tall and blond, with the ruddy complexion of one who preferred to be outdoors. During lunch Monica carefully steered the conversation to topics intended to reveal his political leanings. Over the years and through her travels, she had learned it was difficult for anyone with strong feelings toward one side or the other to conceal them. Eventually some turn of phrase or unintended facial expression would give them away. Her suspicions that he had more than insurance on his mind as they toured the house, outbuildings, and grounds of the estate were confirmed when his questions turned to distinctly non–insurance related questions.

"That island," he said as they stood on the pier looking out across the lake, "is it occupied?"

"We rent out a small cottage." She studied him as he shaded his eyes with the flat of his hand and continued to consider the wooded island. "There's a hunting blind," she offered. "My sons have used that, as, I suspect, have the generations of men who lived here before we did. Would you like to see it?" She nodded toward the rowboat tied up next to them.

He caught himself just shy of an excited smile and agreed. "If it wouldn't be too much trouble," he said.

"No trouble at all." She indicated he should board and, while he steadied the boat, took his hand and sat on one of the two bench seats facing him. "It will give us the opportunity to discuss your true reason for wanting to tour our property."

Erik could not hide the sudden flush that rose to his cheeks as he took charge of the oars. "I don't know what you mean."

"Oh, please. You don't know the first thing about insurance. You are here to survey this property for other purposes. Who sent you?"

On the trip over to the island, Erik confessed he'd had a message from "Mr. Moller" in Copenhagen, who had suggested he contact Monica. "I thought if I met with your husband, I could ascertain the viability of the property before making contact with you."

"I see."

"We need a place to train recruits," he said. "The issue is not just one of a hiding place but of finding who we can trust not to give us away."

"You can trust me," Monica said.

Erik ducked his head. "So I am given to understand. However, forgive me, but a woman, and one of your…" He hesitated and swallowed.

"Advanced years?"

"I was going to say 'social position,'" he insisted.

Monica's laughter rang out across the calm water as she reached for her cigarettes. "Liar," she said as she lit one and blew out a stream of smoke. "It may prove helpful to know that I have explored most of the island on foot or bicycle. I know precisely where your people can gain access with no one the wiser. I know where they can conceal themselves. In fact, I know a great deal of what it would take you weeks to figure out. Do you want my help or do you want to waste time? Either way you have my permission to make use of the property."

Erik squinted up toward the sun. "Still, this estate belongs to your husband and – "

Monica placed her fingers lightly on his knee. When she had

his full attention, she said, "Neither my husband nor my children are to be any part of this. Understood? While I have given every possible consideration to the consequences of actions such as those we are discussing, they have not. Should the day come when they are questioned because of suspicions related to me, they will not need to lie because they will not know."

He considered her for a long moment, allowing the boat to drift toward the island. "You are not Danish, so why would you…"

She leaned back and took a draw on her cigarette. "This war is more far-reaching than any one nation or people, Erik. If you haven't yet understood that, perhaps you are not as ready as I thought."

His expression reminded her so much of Ivan's face whenever she'd reprimanded him for some failure to think clearly, she almost laughed. Erik was young – not as young as her children, but she could not help but feel a bit maternal toward him. "Ah, here we are," she said as she rolled the legs of her trousers to her knees, climbed out of the boat in calf-deep water, and guided it to shore. "Come along," she called, striding up the bank and on into the woods. "There's someone you'll need to meet," she added as she saw Hilmar waiting for them.

Meanwhile there were subtle signs the tide of the war was turning. Over the summer the Allies had prevailed in the Mediterranean, and Mussolini had been arrested. With him no longer in power, that fall the Italians reversed course and declared war on Germany.

Monica continued to build her inner circle. At Bobby's suggestion, she reached out to Thor Gerner Nielsen, director of the asylum in the small neighboring town of Sakskobing. Monica knew Thor and his wife were eager to do their part, and the asylum was perfect for holding weapons and supplies until they could be transported. It also was a place closer to the train station that could provide haven for those on the run. Erik introduced her to a young veterinarian who offered his van as a means of transporting goods. As each piece of the plan fell into place, Monica mentally ticked off the checklist Moller had developed for her.

Only one piece left, she thought. They needed a place where Jacob could train the young men they had recruited to make up the unit. These were the men who would hide near the fields and wait for planes to drop cigar-shaped metal containers filled with guns and ammunition so they could store them on the island before distributing them. They would also need to destroy the containers by "drowning" them in the lake.

The vicarage, Monica realized as she and Jorgen left services one Sunday and waited their turn to greet their friend, Pastor Marcussen. The vicar was a small man with a trim pointed beard and eyes that flared with the passion of his beliefs. Dressed in his black cassock, his face framed by the starched white Jacobean ruff, he occupied the intricately carved pulpit with authority. His Danish was what Jorgen called *hoj dansk* – that spoken from the stage of the Royal Theatre – and he used it to deliver impassioned sermons. When her turn came to greet the vicar after the service, she invited him and his wife to tea at Engestofte that afternoon. Pastor Marcussen's eyes widened in surprise. "We would be delighted." Monica understood his surprise. In all the time she had lived in Denmark, other than including him and his wife in large parties, this was the first time he or his wife had been invited for tea.

"I have something I wish to discuss with you," she added. "A personal matter."

"Of course."

Later that afternoon, after the four of them had enjoyed tea and cakes, Monica suggested Jorgen give the vicar's wife a tour of the gardens while she and the vicar adjourned to the library. "There's a volume of illuminated manuscripts I believe you would enjoy seeing, Pastor," she said.

In the library she retrieved the book and handed it to him, and while he carefully turned the illustrated pages, she told him about the plans to establish a resistance unit in Lolland.

"What can we do to be of assistance?" he asked.

"The gardens at the vicarage are expansive, and more to the point, enclosed by high stone walls. Could we make use of them for training volunteers?"

"Of course. What else?"

His readiness took Monica by surprise. "There's always a danger – "

"My dear Monica, we live in dangerous times, but freedom carries a price, does it not? If we are unwilling to do whatever might be required to meet that price, then..." He shrugged, but his eyes met hers with the fierce intensity required of anyone dedicated to do whatever was necessary to defeat Hitler.

"Our people will train at night," she assured him, "well after you and your wife have retired and the blackout curtains are in place."

"I'll leave the rear gate unlocked," he replied, bobbing his head with excitement. "Bless you, dear lady, for all you are doing for your adopted country."

Monica blushed, embarrassed that a man like this – a man of such fire and intellect – might admire the work she was doing. "My children are Danish," she reminded him.

"And you would walk over burning coals to make sure they

have the opportunity to live free again, would you not?"

"I would." She did not add the thought that sprang to mind – that she would die a happy woman if she could but achieve that for Ivan, Varinka, and Viggo.

Engestofte – Autumn 1943

"You seem to be a bit more content lately, darling," Jorgen noted one evening as they walked along the lakeshore.

Monica had suggested the walk. A heavy fog was predicted, and she needed to signal Hilmar there would be a drop that evening despite the weather. They received word through coded messages embedded in radio programming, usually the day of the drop. The codename for their unit was Frans, meaning free. Monica found it apropos to their mission. The radio broadcast might report something like, "The Olsen family is celebrating the homecoming of their son Frans this evening," as part of a long list of local news items to do with birthdays, anniversaries, and the like. Hilmar did not have access to the broadcast, so they had worked out the signaling process.

"I do feel there is cause for hope," she told Jorgen, stopping along the shore to light a cigarette. She assumed Hilmar Wulff or Jacob would be watching her through binoculars from the hunting blind on the island. By lighting the cigarette, she was signaling that she had received the message. In spite of the predicted fog rolling in, there would be a drop.

She flicked her lighter shut, took a deep draw on her cigarette, and turned back to Jorgen. "I fancy a hot toddy," she said, taking his arm. "Will you join me?"

Hours later, after Jorgen had retired to his room and Inkie and Viggo, who were both staying at the house, had also gone to their rooms for the night, Monica waited until the house was completely silent. Then she changed into the dark clothing she wore on such occasions and slipped out of the house, the consciousness of finally doing something substantial giving her the vitality of someone years younger.

Thankfully the fog had not lingered. The skies were clearing, and a full moon provided the light the pilot would need to pinpoint the site. Monica ran from the house to the dock without incident and within minutes had untied and settled into the dinghy. From the water she could hear the quiet sweep of muffled oars breaking the still waters as Hilmar and Jacob rowed from the island toward the shore closer to the fields. There Jacob and his crew of men waited in hiding to collect the heavy, cigar-shaped metal containers and unpack the contents of weapons and ammunition before bringing the empty receptacles to the shore, where Monica and others would let them fill up with water and sink in the lake. The system had been working almost nightly all summer.

Some nights the drop included men who parachuted in, landing in the fields or water. After shedding their parachutes, these men would be picked up by others and taken to the island. On these occasions Monica used the sodden weight of the fabric to refill the containers, making them sink more easily. The work continued in silence, any necessary communication conducted through hand signals. While she and Hilmar managed sinking the containers and parachutes, she knew others were shuttling the goods to hiding places in the woods that surrounded the fields, and Jacob was overseeing it all. She could not deny that he was quite good at his role, and the locals he had trained followed his orders without question.

Tonight there were more containers than usual, requiring her to make extra haste to get everything unloaded and secured and return to the house before first light. At one point, thankfully after the plane had come and gone, she caught a glimmer of light coming from the island, and her heart skipped a beat. What if the Germans had discovered their operation? What if they were even now arresting Hilmar's wife and searching the cottage? What if...

"Monica!" She heard Hilmar's sharp hiss. When she looked over at him, he pointed to the container she'd been sinking – the one she had released without thinking upon seeing the light. The one that instead of sinking had just floated close to Hilmar's boat and was now clunking against it.

She pointed toward the island and then grabbed her oars, bringing her boat closer to Hilmar's. "A light," she whispered. "There."

Hilmar retrieved the errant container, held it until it filled with water, and then watched it sink. "One of the men had not arrived before we had to leave. That's Mary letting Jacob know he's there now."

She felt both relief and annoyance. Relief that whatever had detained the man, it was not the Germans, but annoyance that apparently Jacob had worked out this signaling without telling her.

"We must hurry," Hilmar reminded her, casting an eye to the East, where the black night sky was already turning a more charcoal gray.

Monica nodded and got back to work. By the time she had sunk the last container, she realized that their cook and some of the tenant farmers would soon arrive to start their morning chores. There was a small window of opportunity between the hour of deepest night and the one when people began to stir. By the time she docked and tied up the dinghy and ran back across the lawn uphill to the house, she was covered in sweat and breathing audibly.

Reaching her room, she slipped inside, shutting the door with a quiet click and letting out a breath of relief – until she turned and saw Inkie sitting cross-legged on her bed. At just over twenty, Inkie was a beauty, with her mother's large eyes and flawless complexion. Monica's friends had often said how much they thought her daughter had turned out to be a younger version of her – not just in looks, but in personality as well.

"I want to help," Inkie announced now, clearly seeing no need to explain what it was she wanted to help with.

"It's too dangerous," Monica replied as she began stripping off her clothes.

"Then it is too dangerous for you as well," Inkie replied calmly. "I'm not a fool, Mummy. The last time one of your 'cousins' stayed with us, I took his luggage to his room and thought to do him the courtesy of unpacking for him. Do you know what I found inside his valise?"

Monica paused. "You should not have – "

"I found a pair of socks rolled up around a pistol as well as two boxes of ammunition," Inkie interrupted. "Do you have any idea what might have happened had we still employed maids who would have done the unpacking?"

Monica could not conceal the chill that ran through her. Since their meeting with Moller in Copenhagen, Bobby had sent several men in need of a place to hide for a few days to her. She had managed always to create some story to explain their sudden arrival – and even more sudden departure. "Still...," she said, fumbling for the words to deliver her counterargument.

But Inkie was not finished. "Of course, I was not as shocked as I might have been had I not already begun to suspect that our frequent houseguests and the tenants renting the cottage were not all they purported to be."

"Hilmar?"

Inkie nodded. "I stopped by a week ago to see if they might need anything from the village. Mrs. Wulff asked me to bring back a bottle of peroxide, and when I protested that her natural hair color was so lovely, she stammered something about how a friend needed it to change his appearance so he could more easily make his way to Sweden. Seems he had gotten himself in some trouble with the authorities here. Mrs. Wulff apparently assumed I knew whatever has been going on around here all summer."

Monica wrapped herself in her robe and sat on the bed with her daughter. "Your father and brothers know nothing," she began. "That is for the best, because should they ever be taken in for questioning, they cannot reveal what they don't know. Thankfully Ivan is consumed with his farm work and has little interest in the war, and Viggo is so young." She thought of how she had managed to stop him from running away to England to join the fight and shuddered. Tightening her grip on Inkie's hands, she pleaded her case. "Hilmar's wife should never have asked you for the peroxide or given you further information about its purpose, and as for the others – "

"I am Danish, Mummy. Denmark is my home, and I will do my part to defend it with or without your approval."

The defiance Monica saw in her daughter's eyes was like looking in a mirror. She could stand her ground as a parent, knowing full well Varinka would do as she pleased. Or she could perhaps keep her safe by overseeing just how deeply she became involved in the Resistance. "Very well," Monica said and watched as defiance shifted to surprise.

"Tell me everything," Inkie whispered. "Where were you tonight? Who are these men who come and go? Why..."

Monica could not help but smile even as her heart thumped with fear that she was making an enormous mistake. It was one thing to place her own life in danger. She had recognized and accepted the possible consequences of her actions from the start. "We will do things my way," she insisted.

Her daughter nodded, eyes wide with eagerness to hear more.

"I need your word on that, Varinka. Any mistake – even a minor one – places your father and brothers in grave danger."

She saw by the tightening of her daughter's lips that she understood. Monica rarely addressed her by her formal name unless the matter was critical. "Varinka?" she repeated firmly.

"I promise," Inkie replied, her voice barely a whisper. "You can trust me. I just want to do my part. Surely you can understand that."

"Yes. What I question is whether or not you fully understand what that might entail in the long run."

"I might be arrested. I might be beaten. I might be imprisoned. I might suffer torture. I might die." Inkie ticked each penalty off on her fingers as if repeating a shopping list.

Monica shut her eyes for a moment. She knew Inkie did not believe any of that would happen – not to her. It was the way of the young to believe they were invincible. In that moment she knew that she would have to find some role for her daughter where Inkie would feel needed and yet would be as far from real danger as Monica could manage.

Monica continued to make trips to Copenhagen under the guise of keeping medical appointments or visiting Viggo, who had moved there to be closer to friends. On every trip she had a meeting with Moller to bring him up to date on all that was happening in the southern region. On the rare occasions when she was unable to get away, she sent Inkie in her stead. On one such occasion, she met her daughter at the train station and felt a wave of relief when Inkie excitedly reported Mr. Moller had asked her to serve as his secretary.

In her own meetings with the man, Monica had made no secret of her concern for her daughter's safety. "She needs a position where she can be protected should things become...difficult," she'd told him. And now her beloved daughter would be in Copenhagen, close to escape routes to Sweden, should that become necessary. "And what precisely will your duties be?"

"I'm to translate the leaflets sent from England to begin with, but once I prove myself there, Flemming has – "

"Flemming?" Monica arched an eyebrow. By now she had learned that Flynn Moller was really Flemming Muus. Jacob Jensen had let that slip.

"Mr. Moller," Inkie hastened to correct herself. She leaned closer. "I've been given a code name as well. Kirsten." Her smile spoke volumes. Monica realized her daughter was not only rejoicing in her new position, but also in this opportunity to spend more time with Muus. She knew that sparkle in her daughter's eyes because once – years earlier – she had seen that same sparkle in her own reflection after meeting Kurt.

Inkie was falling in love.

With her children away from the estate, Monica could focus all her attention on the underground activities she'd been given responsibility for orchestrating and carrying out. According to reports in several of the underground newspapers, across Denmark each night there were now as many as fifty acts of sabotage and vandalism. Established units throughout the country – including members of Frans – destroyed sections of railroad tracks and bridges, interrupting the transfer of goods for the war effort headed to the eastern front. Factory workers did their part as well, disabling critical machinery or finding other means for slowing or stopping production.

At Engestofte, parachutists in need of a haven for a night or longer continued to show up, and the frequency of their coming and going made Monica decide to set up an office over the garage across the hall from the unused servants' quarters. The space was perfect, with an outside stairway that would allow those in need of shelter to come and go in the night, unseen, and without the need to create some reason for their presence.

"I simply do not understand your thinking, Monica," Jorgen protested the morning she had two of their farm hands move an old desk and chair, as well as her sewing machine, to the new space. "There are whole rooms right here that are unused."

"Indulge me, darling," she replied. "I want a space away from everything to do with the management of the house – a place where I can close the door and know no one will come knocking. With Ivan's wedding coming, there are so many details to attend to – not the least of which is sewing gowns for the various events for Inkie and myself. I need solitude to get it all done."

It was but half a lie. Ivan was indeed betrothed to the lovely Hanne, and both families were overjoyed at the prospect of planning a celebration during war. "Besides," she added with a wink, "all the mess I make whenever I am in the throes of creating something will be contained there and you won't have to see."

Jorgen could not deny his tendency toward neatness had sometimes butted up against Monica's habit of leaving the evidence of whatever project she was working on scattered about, sometimes for days. "That is something to consider," he replied with a smile. "Very well. Just remember you do have a home – and a husband in need of your attention."

The office and unused servants' quarters were not Monica's only resources for shifting those in need of shelter in and out of the property. The space above her bedroom in the main house contained a series of attic storage rooms, and Monica had the only key. As the need increased for transporting more parachutists and others out of the country, she furnished the attic space with cots, blankets, towels, and sets of spare clothing. Having men stay there would be a last resort, but she wanted to be ready in case. There was a small mirror over a wash basin, and she kept a large pitcher filled with water at hand as well as supplies of food. In addition, at least once a week she would slip away from the house and down to the pier, where she launched the heavy old rowboat and started her journey – two miles round-trip. Her mission was to pick up a large bag of weapons or explosives dropped in the fields during the night and deliver it to the vet when he arrived later that morning. He would pull his van close to the barn where she had hidden the contraband under piles of hay in an empty stall and make a show of examining one or more of the estate's livestock before leaving.

Some nights were cold with rain and gusty winds that made the rowing more difficult, and she was no longer a young woman. But there were some nights when the moon cast its light across the still water and the sheer beauty of her surroundings gave her renewed energy and passion for the work. On such nights she thought of Jack, and all he might have done had his life not come to such a senseless and premature end. Was that – at least in part – why she did this? Risked her life in his name? And if that were true, what would her brother say?

She closed her eyes and saw him as he'd been that day they walked through the woods, talking of her engagement to Jorgen. What was it he'd said when she'd pleaded with him not to return to the front?

"I have a job to do, and do not tell me you would not do the same."

He had known her so well.

By September, any hint of collaboration between Denmark and its German occupiers came to a halt. The Germans took total control, with no further pretense of allowing the Danish Parliament to hold any power. To add to the deterioration of matters between the two countries, word spread that Hitler had decided the time had come to rid the ungrateful country of its small Jewish population. No official announcement or warning was forthcoming from Berlin, but the underground was alive with reports of a plan to stage a major roundup and arrest of Jews on one of their holiest days – Rosh Hashanah. Apparently the plan was to strike when the Nazis knew most Jews would be at home celebrating the holiday or attending services.

Monica was outraged, and to Monica's frustration, Erik informed her the Lolland Resistance unit would take no part in the rescue plan being developed by others.

"Why on earth not?" She had always respected the way the citizens of Denmark, for the most part, put aside religious or political differences when the entire country was threatened. In Denmark, Jews were of no less importance than Lutherans or

Catholics. They were all Danes. Country came before religion. "We could certainly provide shelter here at Engestofte for those living in this region," she argued.

"We cannot risk the work we are already doing, Monica. So far we have been fortunate, but there is no reason to add to the risks we are already taking. There are others ready to help the Jews. You need to stay out of it."

He was right, of course. How many times had she had to deflect a question about the presence or sudden absence of a downed pilot posing as a laborer or some distant relative? But wasn't her experience in helping the pilots and saboteurs proof of her ability to help the Jews?

As if reading her mind, Erik took her hand. "Monica, I wish we could all do more, but each group has its purpose, and this particular one is not ours."

Monica had occasion to recall this conversation a few weeks later when Mrs. Kann, the real estate agent who had found tenants for Engestofte during the years the family spent in Rapallo, came calling. "This is a pleasant surprise," Monica said as she ushered the realtor inside and took her coat.

Mrs. Kann gave her a nervous smile as she glanced toward the doors leading to the main rooms of the house. "Are we alone?" she asked in a whisper.

"Quite," Monica replied. "Come sit by the fire. Your hands are shaking. I had not thought it was so cold out."

Once seated, Mrs. Kann leaned forward, her dark eyes pools of worry and something more. *Fear,* Monica realized. "My dear woman, what has happened?" she asked, her own voice hushed.

"I have friends – a mother and her three children – who are

in need of a place to stay – a safe place – until they can travel to Sweden." Mrs. Kann paused, allowing the true nature of what she was about to ask to register.

"Go on."

"I have been able to secure housing for the two youngest with the Gerner Nielsens. However…"

Monica understood the facilities at the asylum were stretched beyond capacity already. "The mother and her daughter need a place," she finished as her mind ticked through possible solutions for the pair. "For how long?"

"A few days – a week at most," Mrs. Kann replied.

Hiding hardened soldiers and airmen was one thing, but a mother and daughter? Even she had to admit that most females would be unused to living so rough. "Jorgen and I have been thinking of hiring additional household staff," Monica said slowly. She studied Mrs. Kann's reaction and saw by her expression that the friends in question were probably not used to performing such menial tasks. "Of course, if that does not suit…"

Mrs. Kann stood. "It will suit them just fine," she said as she took Monica's hand between both of hers. "Thank you." She squeezed Monica's hand before releasing it.

"Very well. Have them report to the kitchen entrance first thing tomorrow. Our cook will see that they have uniforms and show them to my office."

"I will make sure they are here. The Kauffman family…"

Monica held up one hand. "I do not wish to know their names, Mrs. Kann. They should present themselves as Olga Werner, and her daughter, Rose." She deliberately chose the names of the two women who had served the family in Rapallo. "And their dress should be that of people seeking such work, understood?"

"Of course. Yes. I will see to everything. Thank you."

Monica saw the realtor to the door and watched her walk down the drive, her demeanor a good deal more chipper than it had been on her arrival. For her part, Monica understood she had just agreed to something she knew neither Erik nor Flemming Muus would approve. But she had no doubt these people were desperate to leave the country before the Nazis could execute their roundup. Surely she could manage to shelter them for a few days. It was not as if she had opened the whole of Engestofte to displaced Jews.

But the following morning as she stood at the window of her office, observing the woman and her daughter as they crossed the yard, she had immediate second thoughts. The mother was dressed in a suit that had to have come from one of the finer shops in Copenhagen, while the daughter wore tailored trousers and a belted jacket that also looked expensive, if at least three seasons out of fashion. Each of them clutched the stack of uniforms the cook had pulled from the storeroom near the kitchen, and glanced around uneasily as if expecting at any moment to be accosted. It occurred to Monica that they could be one of her aristocratic neighbors – any one of whom would be equally as out of her element in these circumstances.

Monica sighed and opened the door to her office, stepping out onto the landing of the outer stairs. "Up here," she called out, at the same time giving a wave to the cook who had served the family for years. Monica knew she could trust the woman and her family. Her husband and son were among those who collected and transported the supplies from the airdrops. Still, even limited interaction with others on the estate could be dangerous. She would follow the plan she used when harboring a pilot or saboteur. She decided her Jewish guests would spend their days in the attics, ostensibly taking an inventory of everything stored there. That should keep them out of contact with anyone else.

Upon reaching the top of the outer stairway, Mrs. Kauffman gave Monica a beaming smile and began to thank her effusively.

"Please stop talking," Monica said as she led them inside and shut the door. She took her place behind her desk, and left them standing. The mother glanced around as if looking for a place to sit, while the daughter's eyes went immediately to the telephone on Monica's desk.

"Rule number one," Monica announced, pointing to the phone, "there is to be no communication with anyone other than me – no calls, no messages of any kind coming or going, nothing. You will not engage with other workers on the property. When you are not performing your work or accompanying me on some errand, you will stay in your room. Are we clear?"

The girl nodded. The mother's lips thinned and her eyes hardened. "Are we permitted to eat?" There was an edge of entitled sarcasm to her tone. Under similar circumstances, Monica was sure her tone might be just as mocking. Still, it was vital they understood the need for such restrictions.

"Your meals will be provided." Monica motioned for them to follow her through the connecting door that led to the servants' quarters. "At the moment we have no other employees living here on the property." She opened the door to the room closest to her office. "This will be your room."

"And my daughter?"

Monica swallowed a smile, again realizing how foreign this must be for them – how foreign it would have been for her in earlier times. "There are two beds, as you can see." She continued the tour from the open door of the room. "There is a bath with sink and toilet at the end of the hall, towels in the linen closet across from it."

The mother straightened to her full height and confronted Monica. "Mrs. Wichfeld, while my daughter and I are certainly in your debt, I hardly think it necessary to speak to us as if we were servants."

"Ah, but you are servants, *Olga*."

She deliberately placed an emphasis on the code name the woman had been assigned. "That is rule number two. You must both put aside the personas that dwell inside and, even with me, accustom yourselves to these new identities you have been given – or I am afraid I cannot help you."

She left them to get changed, then walked back to the house with them and on up the back stairway until they reached the attic, crammed with trunks and cartons and cast-off furnishings. She smiled at their shock when she opened a second door that appeared to be a stack of boxes, revealing not a musty, cramped space, but a well-organized room where sun streamed in through dormer windows. This was the space reserved for those who might need to stay a bit longer. The servants' quarters were for those who would come and go within a day.

She opened a trunk that sat between a pair of comfortable chairs to reveal its contents: some art supplies, puzzles, games, and books. "I don't expect you to actually perform household duties," she said, reading the surprise in their expressions. "I do need your word you will remain here from morning to evening before returning to your room."

"What if someone comes?" This from the daughter.

"That is unlikely, but should it occur, you should have warning enough to move to the first room. Make sure this door is closed before moving on to sorting through those boxes and trunks closest to the stairs. I suggest you unpack a few so they will be ready."

Monica was surprised to see tears brim at the edges of Mrs. Kauffman's eyes. Her earlier irritation with the woman evaporated. Mrs. Kauffman and her family were in grave danger, their lives turned inside out by Hitler's decision to remove the Jewish population from Denmark. They had left their home with nothing more than the clothes they wore. She understood the woman's previous bravado had been an attempt to cope.

"Thank you," the woman whispered and dabbed at her tears with a lace handkerchief she pulled from the sleeve of her uniform.

Monica's heart went out to her. She put her arm around the woman's shoulders. "We must all do what we can until this horrid war comes to its end," Monica replied. "Now, do you have any questions?"

"Do we sleep here?" the girl asked, pointing to a row of cots that ran along one wall of the room.

"You can certainly nap if that suits, but at five o'clock, you will return to your room above the garage, using the outside stairway. Your evening meal will be waiting. And remember, the less contact you have with anyone, the better."

"We understand," the mother assured her.

But apparently they didn't, because just two days later, Erik presented Monica with a letter. "Fortunately, this was given to Christian for delivery and he was on his way to give it to you when I arrived."

Mystified, Monica removed the page from the unsealed envelope that was marked for an address in a fashionable part of

Copenhagen. She scanned the unfamiliar writing and realized Mrs. Kauffmann was contacting *her* maid to ask for her husband's tallit and *kippah* to be packed and delivered to her at Engestofte as soon as possible. She had included several kroner to cover any expense. "You read this?"

Erik nodded. "She's asking the maid to send her husband's skullcap, or yarmulke, and prayer shawl here. Monica, we discussed this...."

Monica rarely allowed her temper to get the better of her, but in this case, she could not hold back. "I risked my life," she seethed. "I risked *all* our lives. I know these items are precious to her religion, but how dare she?" Clutching the letter, she strode across the yard and on to the attics.

When she stepped into the shadowy confines of the main room, lit only by a couple of bare bulbs hung from the ceiling, Mrs. Kauffman and her daughter were bent over an open crate, removing and examining the contents. Monica stepped between them, facing Mrs. Kauffman. "What is the meaning of this?" she demanded, handing the woman the letter. "Do you understand what might have happened had this not been intercepted? Are you so oblivious to the fate that could await you and your children were this to fall into the wrong hands or if your maid, who I must assume is not of your faith, were to turn it over to the Gestapo?"

"She would never – "

"You have no idea what others are capable of doing when their own safety is endangered. You have put not only yourself at risk, but my family as well, and that will not be tolerated."

Even as she raged, she understood why the woman had done it. These items were marks of her family's identity at a time when they would have next to nothing with them to recall the life they'd once known. Still, Monica was glad Erik had assured her he would immediately put plans in motion to get the Kauffmans to Sweden as soon as possible. To her relief, the transfer was accomplished a few days later with the help of Thor Gerner Nielsen. Once the deed was completed, neither of them reprimanded her for the risk she had taken. They didn't need to. Monica was fully aware of how foolish she had been.

Determined to make up for this near disaster, she focused her full attention on her responsibilities as a leader of the Lolland division. In every town and village across Denmark, streets were now patrolled by German soldiers, while in Copenhagen, the Danish government had resigned en masse and the royal family had been placed under house arrest. Hitler and the Nazis were now the law of the land, and they viewed the Danes as their enemy. This was exactly what Moller had hoped to achieve – in the presence of the Germans as more than occupiers, the fire of the Danish people to stand and fight had finally been ignited.

Engestofte – Autumn 1943–Winter 1944

In all the time she'd lived in Denmark, Monica could not recall a more beautiful fall. The universe around her seemed alive with color – the clear blue sky; the reds and oranges and golds of the trees, their leaves cascading like feathers around her as she and Jorgen took their daily walks; the mirrorlike surface of the lake reflecting the ring of color cast by the trees. And the air! When had it been so fresh, so invigorating at this time of year? Most days they took their meals on the terrace, rejoicing in the fine stretch of weather that more commonly would have been blustery and rainy, filled with signs of approaching winter. The war seemed as far away as the distant thunder of Allied planes dropping their payloads on strategic targets in Germany to the south.

Jorgen used the unexpected weather to make visits to friends around the region, often staying for several days and nights to enjoy tennis or bridge marathons. Monica begged off, citing her preference to be at home with Viggo, who was back living at Engestofte while he prepared for his final architectural examinations. Of course, that was only part of her reason. Lately, she'd begun to think more seriously of what might lie ahead. She – and others – had surely been skating on the thin ice of discovery and danger for months now. It was time she made sure her affairs were in order and her family well protected should the day come when she answered a knock at the door only to face the enemy.

One afternoon while sorting through boxes of personal papers that had traveled with her from London to Denmark to Rapallo and back again, she came across the letters Jack had written her from the front in that other war. Three of the envelopes were still sealed – letters that had arrived after Jack's death, that she had never been able to bring herself to open. That evening as she and Viggo sat next to the fire after dinner, she took out the letters and read them aloud. As usual Jack's description of his circumstances carried a wry humor and the intent to calm any fears she might have for his safety.

Must close for now. The chef has prepared a delightful repast of a lovely tin of beans served in the inspired setting of a trench where one dines standing. It could become all the rage by next season. Dining while seated is so passe.

Monica smiled wistfully.

"Why now, Mummy?" Viggo asked.

She shrugged. "It's time. I suppose part of me dreaded reading his words, hearing his voice in those words, while there was any possibility you or Ivan might suffer a similar fate. But you are both here and safe, and I have missed Jack so terribly." She ran her finger over the ink on the page. "This brings him back for me."

And for the first time since his death, she realized she was able to freely speak of Jack, regale Viggo with stories of his uncle, laugh at some childhood misadventure, and find comfort in his words without once feeling her chest tighten or tears threaten. Instead she felt happier and more content than she had in months.

Despite her high spirits, Monica could not avoid some reservations when it came to the members of her unit. Of everyone in her inner circle, the one she struggled most to trust was Jacob Jensen.

His work was flawless and productive. His ability to recruit and train locals for their unit's work impressed her, and yet she could not dispel the niggling doubts about his motivation that came to her in the night. For one thing, while others accepted the funds she distributed to support their families and their work as just one more piece of the process, Jacob seemed almost too eager to get his share. But more to the point, his conversation made it abundantly clear that he was not in this for some idealistic or patriotic reason. Jacob thrived on adventure – even danger.

On a visit to Copenhagen, Monica decided to speak to Moller about her concerns. Despite his growing romance with her daughter, Monica insisted on addressing him always by his code name, especially at times like this when they were discussing business. "There is no question the man is brave," she told him, "but I have to wonder how he might endure questioning under torture."

Moller removed his glasses and pinched the bridge of his nose. He looked exhausted, and Monica regretted adding to his worries. "The truth is, Monica, not every agent in our line of work shares your altruism."

"I fail to see why."

"Some are more pragmatic. The duty carries a real opportunity to achieve higher pay and an officer's commission – reasons enough to step up. Others like the cachet of being trusted with secrets that could change the course of history." He locked eyes with her. "Not everyone is you, Monica."

"Heaven forbid."

"As it happens, I am transferring Jacob to the Jutland unit for a few weeks. His experience will be invaluable working with our radio operator in the region." He smiled at her. "So, he is no longer your problem – at least for the foreseeable future."

But that proved not to be the case when in mid-November Erik reported Jacob's arrest along with the radio operator's.

"They were taken from a safe house in Aarhus," he told her.

"How? Why?" Monica realized the dull sense of foreboding that had been lodged in her chest for some time now had finally broken free.

"According to our sources, Jacob made several phone calls that were intercepted, exposing their location. They were taken for questioning."

"But he will follow protocol – the manual dictates he should take the cyanide pill before they can force him to give up names or..."

She thought of the training they'd all gone through in case they were arrested. Escape via a cyanide pill was certainly to be a last resort.

"He has already revealed names, Monica," Erik replied. "Yours among them. We're shutting down this unit for now, and we'll get you to Sweden as soon as arrangements can be made."

"Absolutely not," she snapped.

"Monica, be reasonable."

"You be reasonable. I leave for Sweden and what happens to Jorgen and the children? What reprisals will there be for them – for this estate that is Jorgen's legacy? I will stay and continue our work until the day they come for me. Just promise me that the moment that happens, my daughter will be moved to safety at once."

Later, as she walked along the lake digesting this latest news, Monica suddenly recalled a time she had visited a fortune teller during the years when her affair with Kurt had been at its most intense. She had never been religious, but her Irish heritage had included folklore and superstition. So when the fortune teller had given her enough detail of her life up to that moment to make her a believer, Monica had accepted the woman's dire prediction that she would die just before she reached the age of fifty.

She was forty-nine.

With Jacob's arrest and betrayal, Monica was not surprised to receive word that, for the time being, all Resistance activities in her region were to be put on hold. Hilmar and his wife left for the safety of Sweden, and Erik also went into hiding. There were no longer signals Monica needed to deliver to the island. Not only was there no one to receive them, but the airdrops themselves had stopped. She needed a distraction, or she was going to drive herself mad wondering just how much Jacob had revealed since his arrest a few weeks earlier.

To that end she focused all her efforts on staging a family celebration for the Christmas holidays. Ivan and his bride, Hanne, would return to the manor for the first time since their wedding the previous summer. He had taken on the role of estate manager for another property, and she looked forward to hearing all about that. A few days before Christmas, Viggo and Inkie arrived together from Copenhagen, talking over one another as they vied for their mother's attention.

"I have so much to tell you," Inkie whispered as she hugged Monica at the station. The way her eyes sparkled told Monica that her daughter's news had little to do with their work in the Resistance, and a great deal to do with her growing feelings for Flemming Muus. It was also clear Varinka knew nothing of Jacob's arrest or confessions. Muus had clearly honored Monica's pleas to shield her daughter as much as possible.

With Jorgen's expert direction, the young people gathered fresh evergreens and decorated the main rooms of the grand house. Giving the staff a holiday, Monica, Inkie, and Hanne prepared meals the family consumed while gathered around the dining room table. Once, they made the meal an impromptu picnic on the floor of the library next to a warm fire after returning from cross country skiing on the grounds. Heini Reventlow and other neighbors were often part of these festivities. And through it all Monica could not help wondering if this would likely be her last holiday with her family – at least until the war finally ended.

"You're very quiet, darling," Jorgen said as he joined her at the windows leading to the terrace. Outside their grown children engaged in the antics of their youth, pelting one another with snowballs, their laughter echoing like bells in the cold clear air.

"I was just thinking how quickly time has gone. Yesterday they were babies, and today?"

Jorgen chuckled. "In many ways still so incredibly young. We've done well by them, Monica – you especially. All those years you had to be away from them for long stretches..." His voice trailed off. Jorgen had never quite forgiven himself for the financial chaos his unchecked spending had caused.

She kissed his cheek. "They've turned out just fine, darling, and once this war is over..." She could not find the words to continue, and she realized she was close to breaking down. Would she be around to see what became of them? She hugged herself to stifle the tears she would not allow her husband to see. He was an innocent in all she had done – in many ways, had been an innocent for their entire marriage. He had been born to and of the manor and that aristocratic life. And yet together they had created this wonderful family – this happy family – and that alone would sustain her through whatever she might yet need to face.

On Christmas Eve, she and Inkie were finally alone, snuggled under comforters as they sat near the fire and admired the giant fir tree the entire family had decorated earlier that afternoon.

"Flemming has asked me to marry him, Mummy," Inkie said. "He loves me," she added in a tone filled with wonder.

Monica smiled. This was hardly news. Flemming was very skilled at his work, but when it came to hiding his feelings for her daughter, the man was like a lost puppy. "He has asked before," Monica reminded her. He'd been pressing his case for some time, even trying to enlist Monica in his pursuit.

"I think I may surrender this time," Inkie replied, her voice tinged with shyness.

Monica waited for more, and when it didn't come, she turned to her daughter so she could see Inkie's face lit by the fire. "Why now?"

"I thought we needed to wait – allow the war to play out. I thought it best we make sure our feelings were not simply part of the excitement of the work we were doing. But a few weeks ago, when he was returning from London and his plane was nearly shot down and, well, he could have died or been captured or – "

"That is no reason to make a lifetime commitment, Varinka."

"No, Mummy. It was what I felt when the news finally came that he was safe. I realized I had no idea how I might go on if he were not in my life. Surely that is love."

Monica could not help but consider the similarities between Inkie's situation and her own when Jorgen had proposed. There was the difference in ages. There was the war. And she could not help but wonder if Inkie – so like her in so many ways – felt the kind of passion for Flemming that Monica had known only with Kurt. Still, she could not deny the years she had shared with Jorgen had been filled with laughter and the promised freedom to live life on her terms. Would that be enough for Inkie should things turn out that way? "It's your decision," she said, stroking her daughter's smooth cheek, "but know that whatever you decide, you have my support and blessing."

Later, after everyone had retired for the night and the house was quiet, Monica walked through the downstairs rooms, pausing before the portrait of Jorgen's grandmother that still hung above the fireplace in the main sitting room. She recalled the day she and Jorgen had come to this house, and she smiled at the memory of how horrified she had been at the change from the sunlit exterior to the dark and musty interior. What fun she and Rose had had exploring the many nooks and crannies of the grand house, discovering treasures that had been packed away for decades, and bringing them back to their rightful places. In those days she had been so afraid she might do something that would upset Jorgen – or his mother. But these days she came and went without a thought, for this was her house – this was home.

Ivan, Hanne, and Inkie left just after the New Year dawned, and suddenly the gray skies filled with snow seemed more ominous than celebratory. The war was now in its fourth year, and Monica had begun to wonder if it would ever end. Jorgen and Viggo set out with friends for a day of snowshoeing, while Monica prepared to host Pastor Marcussen for tea. She was anxious to see him. He always had news. But on this occasion she was horrified at the update he brought.

"You have heard of my colleague, Kai Munk?"

"Of course." Munk was a renowned playwright as well as a vicar in Jutland.

"I'm afraid the good man has paid the ultimate price for speaking his mind in his New Year's Day sermon." Pastor Marcussen's hand trembled as he set the china teacup in its saucer without taking even a sip.

Monica felt her chest tighten. "Tell me," she said.

"He was taken from his home without warning, and later his badly beaten body was discovered in a roadside ditch." He hesitated as if trying to find the words he needed. "My dear lady, you must leave Denmark immediately, while there is still time."

"There have been no signs I'm being watched or followed," she assured him. "We've been cautious."

Marcussen leaned closer. "Word has it that the men taken in Aarhus have revealed more than names. Everyone associated with the movement is in grave danger."

Monica picked up the silver snuffer and put out the flame that warmed the teapot. "You should leave at once, of course. And anyone else who has not already...the Gerner Nielsens should go as well."

"And you," the pastor persisted.

"I am staying. I joined this fight with the full knowledge of where that might lead, and I have always been aware of the cost that might bring." Seeing the vicar's distress, she leaned forward and placed her hand over his. "If I go into hiding, I fear what may happen to my family in retribution. I have had a full and satisfying life, Pastor, overflowing with far more love and adventure than most. My children have all turned out well and are on their way to what I hope will be equally full lives of their own. I cannot protect them if I am in hiding."

She stood, signaling the visit was over.

"There is nothing I can say to persuade you?"

Monica smiled. "Not a word." She walked him to the door, helped him with his overcoat, then kissed him on each cheek before seeing him on his way.

Once he left, she closed her eyes as she gripped the newel post of the stairway and sank to her knees. The only sound was the ticking of the mantel clock in the room they had just left. What if she was being foolish? What if in her determination to make sure Jorgen and the children were safe, she was actually placing them in danger?

But no. She felt she was right in her choice to stay where she was. If they came, they would soon realize she was the only guilty one. Still, she could not deny the vicar's news had struck the flame of terror for what she might need to face in the days to come.

PART FOUR

Arrest, Trial, Prison
1944–1945

Engestofte to Copenhagen – Winter 1944

SHE DID NOT HAVE LONG TO WAIT. She had imagined many scenarios for her arrest, but being awakened in the deepest part of night to the sound of soldiers ransacking the house and the sight of two Gestapo agents standing in her bedroom had not been among them.

The men had allowed her to dress and then escorted her downstairs to the library. A moment later Jorgen and Viggo had been brought to the room by soldiers carrying rifles. The house was freezing, as the fires in the main rooms had not yet been lit. Monica had thought she was prepared for all this, but the truth was she welcomed the cold. At least if the invaders noted her trembling hands, she could assure them it had to do with the lack of warmth rather than her fear of them.

She clenched her fingers into fists and fought to maintain calm for the sake of her husband and Viggo. After all, she had been warned weeks earlier, and in a way, having to finally face the enemy was a relief. Further relief had come when Jorgen had been undeniably livid at this invasion of his home – so genuine in his outrage that one of the Gestapo agents had muttered an apology.

"Viggo, please light the fire," she instructed.

"No time," the lead agent, whom she'd labeled Tweedle Dee, announced. He waved some papers in her face. "These articles are all the proof needed...you are obviously sympathetic to the Allies," he sneered.

"Is that a question?" Monica moved a step closer and blew out a stream of smoke. "My brother is a prisoner of war in the Pacific, while another brother gave his life fighting your countrymen in the first war. Do you honestly expect me to be pro-German?"

The agent ignored her taunt, instructing his partner to assemble a detail to round up the two servants. Monica saw a soldier descend the stairs. He was holding the dark clothes she wore whenever she went out to help with the airdrops. When he showed them to Tweedle Dee, he looked at her and smiled.

"Let's go," he ordered, herding Monica, Jorgen, Viggo, and the two servants out the front door to where two trucks waited. Surrounded by soldiers with guns pointed directly at them, they were hustled forward to board the tarpaulin-covered trucks. Monica and her family were directed toward the first and their cook and her husband, the second. The soldiers closed in on them. Instinctively, based on the hunting adventures she'd shared with her father and brothers, Monica grasped the barrel of the rifle closest to her face and pushed it down. She ignored the sudden chorus of other weapons being cocked as she faced the young soldier directly – still holding the barrel of his gun.

"Young man," she said in her perfect German, "has no one

trained you in the proper handling of your weapon? You never point it at anyone unless you intend to use it." She met his eyes and added, "Is that your intent?"

"Nein," he whispered, and all around her, Monica was aware rifles had been lowered.

Tweedle Dum stepped between the soldier and her. "You are no longer giving orders, Frau Wichfeld," he informed her, as he took the rifle from the young soldier and pointed it at her. "I am, and I can assure you, if you give me the slightest cause, I do indeed intend to shoot you. Are we clear?"

Monica stood her ground. "Given the fate I understand Pastor Kai Munk recently suffered, may I assume there are two vehicles so that you can take my husband, son, and me to some isolated spot where you will indeed put a bullet in our backs and dump our bodies in the nearest ditch?"

The agent straightened to his full height. "That is not the plan, however..." Handing the rifle back to the soldier, he took hold of her arm and prepared to hoist her into the back of the second truck. She snatched her arm free of his grip and climbed aboard unassisted.

The agent stepped aside, motioning to Jorgen and Viggo to board. Two soldiers slammed and secured the tailgate, then banged on the side to alert the driver to leave. Monica sat on a hard wooden bench across from her husband and son. Unable to face them, she pulled aside the flap of the black tarpaulin and saw the Gestapo agents give final orders. Once they had gotten into their large black car, the procession began. Two trucks and a sleek black car rolled slowly down the long drive lined with snow-covered elm trees.

Monica leaned forward, straining to gather what she had to

admit might be her last glimpse of the home she had loved. Every window glowed with a soft golden light. Dawn was just breaking, with the promise of the kind of clear, cold day she had always found uniquely Nordic. She could imagine the pristine white of the snow sparkling like diamonds under that incredible aquamarine sky. She let the flap drop back in place and reached forward to take Jorgen's hand. He kept one arm firmly around Viggo's shoulder, and it was difficult to say whether he was giving or receiving comfort. They shared the space with four armed soldiers, who, now that their prisoners were in hand, seemed bored by the whole situation.

Monica began speaking to her husband and son in English, certain none of the soldiers would understand.

"No talking," the soldier closest to her shouted in German above the noisy rattle of the truck. He reached forward and jerked her hand free of Jorgen's, roughly shoving her back against the metal pipes that formed the frame supporting the canvas top. With the canvas enclosing them they rode in near darkness, and it was impossible to read the expressions playing out on her husband's and son's faces. Hopefully she had done what was best toward protecting them. They knew nothing, so how could they be held?

After awhile, she felt the truck slow and then stop. As the soldiers scrambled past them to stand outside the truck, their rifles once more at the ready, she heard music – faint but unmistakable. The truck flaps opened and, with a jolt of panic, she realized they had arrived at the Marcussen house. She watched in horror as the soldiers broke through the front door with the Gestapo agents following. The music continued – Schubert, Monica realized, and knew Pastor Marcussen's wife must be playing the spinet piano in their parlor. Occasionally the music would stop and then resume. Finally, the Germans left the house, but instead of reboarding their respective vehicles, they began a search of nearby streets and gardens. Monica caught a glimpse of the butcher from the village walking along the side of the road. She leaned out to catch his attention. Without fully acknowledging her, he jerked his head in the direction of the frozen fields behind the vicarage. Monica let out a rush of relieved breath when she realized Marcussen had been warned and made his escape. At the same time her chest tightened with the certainty that their next stop would be the asylum. She could only hope Thor Gerner Nielsen and his wife had also been warned.

But moments later, Thor was pushed onto the truck, followed by a German officer who took his place next to Monica – between her and the back of the truck – separating her from Thor and any chance they might have to exchange information. It seemed luck had run out – perhaps for all of them. How far could the elderly pastor get before he was apprehended? And Erik? Had his hiding place been discovered?

The second truck and car made two more stops, and when their truck reached the village, the driver pulled to the side to wait for the rest of the convoy to catch up. Jorgen seized on this opportunity to address the officer in German. Monica could hardly believe what her husband was requesting. He was pleading with the man to allow him to purchase cigarettes for his wife. The officer leaned forward and accepted the handful of kroner Jorgen had taken from his money clip. He pocketed all but one bill. This he gave to a soldier with orders to go buy cigarettes.

Monica watched as the soldier dashed across the town square and entered the store – the one where so many years earlier, Monica had first learned of their financial woes. Tears filled her eyes as she watched the soldier head back to the truck holding two cartons of cigarettes, followed by the shopkeeper, who insisted the officer take one of the cartons for himself. The headlights of the second truck flashed and the officer gave their driver orders to move on. To Monica's surprise, he allowed Jorgen to keep one carton of cigarettes. On the other hand, he made no gesture to share his own ill-gotten booty with his men.

Their odyssey finally came to an end at a barracks near the docks of Nakskov – docks men trained by Jacob Jensen had damaged with explosives collected from the fields of Engestofte just a few weeks earlier. The irony of the place she would be interrogated was not lost on Monica as she was separated from the others and taken to a large, sparsely furnished room. Her interrogators were Gestapo but clearly of a higher rank and maturity. They were not the fools who had invaded her home earlier that morning.

God, it was still morning!

They were officious but respectful, a ploy she suspected was intended to have her let down her guard. They allowed her to smoke, even providing the cigarettes since they had confiscated the supply Jorgen had gotten for her, along with her pocketbook. They knew a good deal. Jacob had apparently revealed many details of their operation. They dropped little nuggets of information into the midst of their questions, often switching from one topic to another, one event to another.

"What do you know of a family by the name of Kaufmann – Jews from Copenhagen?"

"You'll need to be more specific in your questions," she replied archly, fighting to maintain the aura of her position as a member of the aristocracy. She had seen how Jorgen's inbred entitlement had served him well while the house was being searched.

The agent ignored her, leaning close so that his eyes were level with hers, and said softly, "And who is Mr. Moller?"

Monica feigned confusion. "Is he a friend of the Kauffmans?"

The man made a sound of disgust and moved away.

The room was icy cold. The agents wore heavy coats and gloves. A guard had taken each prisoner's coat and personal belongings before they were separated and taken for questioning. Their belongings had been carefully recorded, and they had each signed a paper approving the inventory.

The other agent suddenly came at her from behind, reaching over to pluck her cigarette from her fingers. As he had intended, she startled and stiffened. He came around to face her, dropped the half-smoked cigarette on the floor, and took some time to crush out its light with the toe of his boot. Then he looked at her for a long moment, allowing the silence to brew, before leaning close and screaming, "You helped Mrs. Kaufman escape. We know this. We could have you shot on that charge alone."

"Then do it," she retorted, and immediately regretted giving in to his provocation.

"Trust me, dear lady, once we have gotten the information we need – from you or one of the others, we will happily oblige."

They continued to circle her. They lit cigarettes for themselves, but not for her. They blew streams of smoke into her face and laughed. She fought to maintain her composure by focusing on the others, especially Jorgen and Viggo. Where were they? What was happening to them?

She soon realized her examiners had a limited and repetitive repertoire. She also noticed that the centerpiece of their interrogation was the identity of Moller. They had a name they knew to be a code name. They needed the identity. Jacob Jensen had apparently told them Monica might know that identity. They interspersed their questions about her association with Jacob and Moller with questions about the Kaufmanns. After awhile they changed tactics and began grilling her about Pastor Marcussen and the others. Finally, after what seemed like days but was only hours, there was a knock at the door. The two men stepped into the hall and held a short but animated discussion with someone.

When they returned, they redoubled their efforts to get her to admit she knew the identity of Moller. But to her surprise, they used only shouting and repetition and intimidation. Not once did they touch her.

Sometime in late afternoon, when the shadows in the room deepened with the promise of twilight and she was so weary she could barely hold herself erect, she suddenly realized she had failed to slip her cyanide pill in her pocket while dressing. It had been right there on her dressing table in her little gold pillbox. For one moment she gave Jacob the benefit of the doubt. Perhaps he, too, had failed to carry the instrument of escape they had all agreed to use should their situation become unbearable. She remembered the night Inkie had confronted her after her return from recovering the night's delivery of supplies. How Inkie had ticked off what might be the penalties for such actions should she ever be caught. That night she had thought her daughter impossibly naive, and yet, was she any different? What an arrogant fool she had been! She could have left – gone into hiding. Her being there had made no difference when it came to Jorgen and Viggo being arrested. Exhausted and terrified of what might lie ahead for them, she swallowed back tears and continued to dodge the questions hurled at her with such hatred.

Another knock had both agents pausing and glancing at one another. When neither moved and there was a second, more urgent, knock, Monica sighed wearily.

"Shall I get that, gentlemen?"

One of them scowled at her while the other went to the door. When the second man followed his partner into the hall, and once again, they closed the door, Monica took advantage of their absence to stand. She had been sitting in the same chair, unable to move much, for hours. Her knees clicked in protest when she stood, and it took a moment for her to gain her balance. She'd had nothing to eat or drink all day and suspected she was on the verge of dehydration. She made her way to the window and looked out to the shipyard beyond – a shipyard that had been severely damaged recently by saboteurs trained by Jacob and using explosives collected and secured by Monica in the fields of Engestofte.

Was it enough? Was it worth risking her life – and now perhaps the lives of her son and husband?

Behind her the door slammed open, and she turned to see, not her interrogators, but two low-ranking soldiers.

"*Kommen Sie*," one said.

They escorted her back to a larger room, where her family and the others arrested that morning were being served a sparse meal of potato soup, crusty bread, and weak tea. Jorgen managed to arrange for her to sit between Viggo and him, and she felt the warmth of their shoulders and thighs pressed to hers as they ate.

"What happened?" she asked. It was, to be sure, a loaded question.

"One of the men Father worked with when he was in London

at the embassy heard we had been arrested. He insisted on seeing us, and now he's speaking with the Germans in charge," Viggo explained in an excited whisper. "Father was magnificent."

Jorgen shrugged and gave Monica a weary smile. "You see, my darling, sometimes being part of a certain social circle has its rewards."

She had never loved him more. His connections had perhaps saved them. His wry humor had certainly renewed her strength to face what might yet come.

But her euphoria was short-lived.

They had just finished eating when two German officers entered the room and ordered everyone to stand. With a gesture they indicated those whom the soldiers should take into custody – Monica among them.

Jorgen stepped forward. "My wife is – "

"Your wife is under arrest for crimes against the State, sir, and you have interfered enough. She and the others will be taken to Copenhagen immediately to await trial. I will give you a moment to say your farewells." He stepped away, orchestrating the removal of Monica's fellow saboteurs.

Monica turned first to their elderly cook, embracing her and assuring her all would be well. Then she shook hands with the blubbering husband, thinking of the service these dear people had given the family through the years.

"We'll never forget you," the man assured her, grasping her hand between his large, calloused palms. Monica understood that for him this was indeed a final farewell. He was certain she would never return to Engestofte – at least in this life.

Behind her, she was aware that Jorgen had taken the officer aside and was engaged in what appeared to be a serious conversation with the man. "Very well," the officer said, and to her surprise,

Jorgen grabbed the man's hand and shook it firmly.

The officer gave her a half smile as he crossed to the table. "Your husband has been most persuasive in requesting a staff car for your conveyance to Copenhagen," he explained. "Given the circumstance of your position as the only female under arrest, and your advanced years, I am in agreement. We are not without compassion."

He stepped aside, indicating the time had come. Monica reached for her youngest child, taking the moment to inhale the scent of him, the feel of his cheek against hers, the fullness of his strong body.

"Who shall I call?" he asked.

"Pray with me," she said as she squeezed his hand, hoping he would understand he needed to follow her lead.

To her relief, although her family was well aware Monica was not in the least religious, Viggo bowed his head. At the same time the officer took a step back, showing respect for this private moment. Monica spoke in English in the rhythm of a prayer, in the hopes neither the officer nor his underlings spoke the language.

"Take your father to your Uncle Heini's. He needs warmth and a solid meal, as do you. You should stay the night there, but once your father is settled, you need to return to our house and go to the attics above my bedroom. There's a revolver and ammunition hidden in the extra insulation stored there. Then go through the house and pack up any valuables – silver, my jewelry – and take them to the bank for safekeeping. There are sure to be looters once word gets out. Finally – and this is most important – you need to get word of what has happened to Ivan and Varinka."

As she gave each instruction, she felt her son's head bob against her cheek. She thought of the time they had lived in Florence and how it had been Viggo who had taken charge and made all the arrangements to settle them there. "Amen," she murmured and, after kissing his cheek, gently pushed him toward the door. When he made a move to turn back, the guard interceded and ushered him into the hall.

Monica watched until the door closed between them and then turned to face Jorgen. He looked so bewildered, and there was no way she could explain things to him. She walked into his embrace and, as he burrowed his face into the curve of her neck, she felt his shoulders shake. "Some day," she whispered, "I know you will understand – and forgive. For now, know that I have no regrets – least of all about the choice I made to marry you, my darling husband."

The officer cleared his throat.

The guard opened the door, then he and his partner took positions to either side of Monica. They did not touch her, but she saw by his expression that the officer's patience had run out. She cupped her hands around her husband's face and kissed him full on the mouth. She felt her heart catch, realizing this could be the last time she might see this dear man.

She took the coat a guard handed her. "Gentlemen, lead the way."

As they traversed the long hallway to the exit of the barracks, she realized all the rooms behind closed doors were dark and silent. She wondered what might have happened to the others. Outside, the German officer opened the rear door of a long black car. She turned back to where her family stood helplessly in the open doorway of the barracks. Once seated in the car that smelled of tobacco and too little fresh air, she pressed her palm to the window, her eyes on her husband and son until the car pulled away and turned a corner.

West Prison, Copenhagen – Winter 1944

The streets of Copenhagen were deserted as the car pulled to a stop in front of the somber Victorian building. Monica realized she had slept, lulled by the warmth of the car and the rhythm of the ride. She stirred and looked around. Somewhere along their journey they had apparently joined a caravan of vehicles, for now she saw her friends being led from the backs of two trucks like the ones used to take her into custody earlier.

The rear door of the car was jerked open, and she saw the highly polished boots of a German officer. "Get out," he snarled.

After the warmth of the car, the cold hit her like a slap. The others were climbing down from the trucks.

"Line up," the man in charge shouted, his men herding them toward the outer wall of the prison.

So, we are to be shot without delay, Monica thought, fighting back the acidity of fear that rose suddenly in her throat.

"Face the wall, hands in the air," came the next command.

She considered resisting. If they were going to shoot her, should they not at least look at her? But next to her, Thor Gerner Nielsen murmured, "Do as they say, Monica." He was right, of course. Defying them would only add to their sense of entitlement. If Monica and the others were shot, it would be over in an instant, but the German officers decided to release the snarling dogs that waited, barely constrained, with a line of soldiers a few feet away...

She faced the wall and raised her hands, flattening her palms against the rough, cold stone, glad she'd had the presence of mind to grab her gloves when they'd taken her away that morning.

No, yesterday morning, she thought. She straightened when she realized she had survived the first day of her captivity. Each day she repeated that was a day closer to freedom and a return to her beloved family.

They were left standing there for over an hour, by Monica's calculations. Behind them, she could hear the officer and his cronies talking and laughing, the scent of their cigarettes wafting through the air. Whenever any of the prisoners tried to shift positions for more comfort, there was a ruckus behind them of rifles being raised in unison, as always, a cue for the dogs to bay and howl.

Finally, they were told to line up single file in front of the entrance to the prison. As the only woman, Monica wondered how they would deal with that. Soldiers positioned themselves to either side of them and marched them forward until they stood inside a closed space facing yet another gate, this one manned by Danish prison guards. The heavy iron doors grated against the concrete, and they walked across a courtyard and through yet another gate, while behind them, the iron doors slammed shut. Monica understood there was a message in all this opening and closing of gates, rattling of chained locks, scraping of keys – there would be no escape. She could not help but note the power of the message repeated again and again as they made their way to the depths of the prison.

Suddenly they were led through a final gate and into a large space. A cathedral ceiling soared high above several floors lined with iron balconies. Through the skylights she could see the gray, turbulent sky. A guard took hold of her arm and pulled her from the line of prisoners. "This way," he said, half dragging her forward to a stairway. Her legs threatened to give way, she was so exhausted. She stumbled along through more metal doors with locks until she stood before a cell at the end of a corridor. The guard opened the solid metal door and stepped aside, waiting for her to enter. As soon as she was past the door, he slammed it shut, turned the key, and walked away, the leather soles of his boots echoing on the concrete walkway.

Welcome home, Monica.

She leaned against the door and took in her surroundings – a barred sliver of a window placed too high for her to see more than a bit of sky, a cot bolted to the wall and covered with a thin mattress, a chamber pot in one corner, and a single sputtering lightbulb threatening to go out, for which there was no chain or switch. Monica closed her eyes, forcing herself to breathe away the panic that threatened. The reality of her situation was finally hitting her full force. This was not some nightmare from which she would wake. For now, this was her life.

She opened her eyes and considered her options. They had taken her purse and the carton of cigarettes, but, anticipating that, she had managed to conceal three of the precious smokes up her sleeve. She had no way to light them, of course, but just holding one between her lips brought a measure of comfort.

By her estimation, the cell was not even half the size of the small room she had rented in Paris when she began her jewelry business. She turned the mattress, hoping to find the other side less stained. If anything it was worse. And the damp and cold had seeped into the fabric. But she was so drained that she stretched out anyway, wrapping her coat around her and pillowing her head on her folded arms. She gazed up at the patch of dawn she could see through the window, closed her eyes, and imagined she had all the personal items she had always taken wherever she traveled. Mentally she rearranged and furnished the space as she drifted off. But when she opened her eyes, it was unchanged – the same bleak and desolate cell.

Hearing footsteps in the hallway, she stood. She was determined to present herself as a woman to be reckoned with no matter who came to her door. The footsteps stopped, and she heard the rattle of metal on metal, then a small door near the base of the larger door was opened and a tray holding a tin cup and a bowl was pushed through.

"Hello?" she called out first in Danish and then in German, hoping to gather some information from whoever was on the other side of the door.

No response. The footsteps retreated, accompanied by the rattle of a cart as her server left.

Flemming Muus had once told her what she might expect should things ever come to this. "Their weapons of intimidation, Monica, are built on the absence of control – *your* control. In addition to its barren damp coldness, your cell will probably always be brightly lit, depriving you of any chance for proper rest. No one will speak to you, much less answer any questions. The food will be inedible, and yet you must force yourself. Likewise you must keep up your strength through exercise – mental and physical. You will wait for long periods of time for something – anything – to happen. Much of this will take place early in your detainment."

Above her the light flickered sporadically. She supposed she should take heart in the probability it would soon burn out. She considered the cup of water, flecks of unidentifiable debris floating on its surface, then the lumpy congealed concoction in the bowl. There were no utensils and certainly no napkin. At the same time she realized there was no way for her to wash herself – no sink or towel. Her hair was coming free of its chignon, and one of the combs she'd used to hold it in place was missing. Ignoring the food, she pulled the other comb free, as well as the few hairpins that remained, and laid them on the mattress. She removed her coat and suit jacket and shook them out, then tugged her sweater sleeves down, straightened her skirt, and smoothed her woolen stockings. During the short stay at the Naskov barracks, she had seen evidence that as long as she remained in Denmark, she would be treated with a certain amount of civility. Jorgen's connections with high-ranking Danish officials had played a role in gaining freedom for her husband and son, as well as their servants. The fact that she had not been ordered to undress and don a prison uniform was also a good sign. Understanding the importance of making sure her appearance and demeanor constantly reminded her captors of her standing in society, she combed through her tangled hair and pinned it up as well as she could, before putting her jacket back on. As she'd left the house, she'd had the presence of mind to grab a soft cashmere shawl from the bench near the door, but after they'd arrived at the barracks and been taken for questioning, she had not seen that again. The cell was damp and cold, but she decided to save wearing her coat until night.

Once she had groomed herself, she sat on the edge of the cot and consumed the meal. She cupped the bowl in her hands, closed her eyes, and slurped down the first bite of the cold contents, tasting a piece of undercooked potato and a strand of onion skin among the gelatinous base of flour and water. She chewed slowly, fighting back the reflux that threatened to bring whatever she managed to swallow up again. After finishing, she took a swallow of the water, rinsed her mouth, and spit into the chamber pot before drinking the rest of the water. Just as she finished, once again she heard footsteps, then a key thrust into the lock, the scrape of metal on metal, as the door swung open.

Two uniformed guards stepped inside her cell – Danish by their uniforms. She greeted them with a welcoming smile, hoping to inspire some empathy for a fellow Dane.

Neither guard looked directly at her. "Come with us," one said, speaking in Danish and stepping back into the corridor.

She dug deep for a reservoir of charm or humor or anything that might make these men see her as a person, rather than another prisoner, but after the sleepless night and the stress of yesterday, she had nothing. Without looking at them or speaking, she headed for the door. Alarmed at her sudden movement, the man standing outside her cell blocked the exit.

"Do you want me to come with you or not?" she snapped.

The guards exchanged a look, steeping aside to allow her to step into the hall. Once there, they surrounded her, each taking hold of one of her arms.

She jerked free. "I am perhaps to you an old woman, but I assure you I can walk on my own."

The guard to her right scowled at her. "We shall see if you feel the same when you return," he muttered.

Her jailers led her through a door at the end of the row of empty cells, then up a flight of stairs, through a second door, then along one of the balconies she had seen when she arrived.

"This way," the sullen guard snarled as he made a sudden turn down yet another seemingly endless hallway. Finally he rapped on the frosted glass panel of a door and then turned the knob.

"Frau Wichfeld," he announced, giving her a none-too-gentle shove that propelled her into the room.

Fighting to maintain her balance, Monica also made a quick survey of her surroundings. Bright sunlight poured in through a barred window at least four times the size of the window in her cell. After the dimness of her cell and the corridors, she squinted and resisted the instinct to block the sudden brightness with her uplifted hand. The room was sparsely furnished – a rectangular table, two chairs on one side, and another on the opposite, facing the sun. The two chairs were occupied by men in suits, their heads bent close together as they studied some document – perhaps the warrant for her arrest. They made no move to acknowledge her. Behind her the door to the room clicked shut, and she heard the retreating steps of the guards. A radiator clanked and hissed. She remained where she was, waiting, but the men acted as if they were unaware of her presence even though she'd been announced.

She cleared her throat.

Nothing.

I am far too exhausted to play these little games, she thought as she strode to the window and pulled the shade, before taking a seat in the only available chair – the one facing the window. "Gentlemen," she said with a quizzical smile. "You wished to see me?"

This got their attention. It also appeared to startle them, and Monica could not help but take a bit of comfort from that. Still, these were not the Danish prison employees who had accompanied her here. These men were clearly seasoned professionals – German, she suspected – and she would need to be on her guard at every turn.

One of the two bundled the papers and, with a nod to the other, left the room, passing her as if she were no more than a coat rack. The remaining man pulled a cigarette case from his pocket and pushed it, a lighter, and an ashtray across the table to her. She recognized it as her first test. Clearly they knew of her habit and intended to use that to either punish or reward her. On the other hand, it had been over twenty-four hours since she'd last smoked. A cigarette would calm her – help her focus. She did not miss the way the man smiled when she gave into her reasoning.

"Thank you," she said as she took the first deep draw, then pushed the case and lighter back toward him and pulled the ashtray closer to her side of the table. She turned in the chair so that she could cross her legs, determined to create at least the illusion of a woman at ease. "May I know your name?"

He waved a dismissive hand. "That hardly matters. In the days to come you are likely to meet so many of our agents, and keeping us all straight seems a useless exercise."

"Then how shall I address you?"

He seemed to consider this for a moment while he lit a cigarette of his own and took his time blowing out the first round of smoke. "*Mein Herr? Ja*, that seems appropriate. I quite like that."

I don't, she thought as she set about memorizing every detail of this man's appearance, already determined that once the war ended she would be able to identify him as one of *them.*

She tapped ash into the ashtray as she took the time to study him, looking for any distinguishing marks that could not later be hidden by peroxide or make-up. He had a definite cowlick and a scar on his left earlobe. His nose had been broken at some point. But it was his eyes she knew she would never forget. Enlarged by the thick lenses of his eyeglasses, they were a pale gray blue, the color of the Baltic in winter, and there was not one iota of warmth in them although at the moment he was smiling at her.

In a sudden move that startled her, he reached across the table, snatched her cigarette and stubbed it out. "Now then, Frau Wichfeld, let us begin."

He delivered his questions in a rapid-fire fashion, seeming not to care much what answer she might or might not offer before he moved on to another query.

"You are British. What contacts have you maintained with your countrymen?"

"I am Danish – "

"You have established a relationship with the minister, Marcussen, and one Thor Gerner Nielsen, have you not?"

"Pastor Marcussen is my – "

Her interrogator smirked. "Come now, Monica. It is well known you are an atheist." He leaned across the table, nose to nose with her, his eyes boring into hers. "You are more in sympathy with the communist, Hilmar Wulff, are you not?"

The inquisition continued in that vein for some time. Monica felt she was managing to maintain her focus and calm, until the moment the man – who had been pacing the perimeter of the room – suddenly came up behind her and placed his hands on her shoulders. He slowly massaged them, even as his fingers moved closer to her throat. She could not hide her revulsion and tensed at his touch. He leaned in and whispered, "I could snap your neck in an instant, Monica."

Her body went stiff with fear.

The man moved away, pausing to raise the window shade as he stared out the window. "Jacob Jensen," he said.

She waited, biting her lip to keep herself from making any comment.

"You know him, of course." He turned to face her and smiled.

"Certainly he knows you."

She gazed at a spot on the wall where once a framed painting or certificate had hung, refusing to look at him.

Suddenly he took hold of her chin, forcing her to face him, his fingers digging into her flesh. "How did the two of you meet, Monica? You have to admit you are an unlikely pair."

She met his icy scrutiny. "We were hardly friends," she replied.

The man released her and laughed. "No. In fact, he did not like you, and the feeling was mutual, isn't that right?"

"We hardly traveled in the same social circles. I was aware of him, but – "

"And what about Herr Moller? Did the two of you travel in the same circles?" He placed both hands flat on the table and once again leaned close. "I believe he is fucking your daughter."

Monica's heart threatened to stop. She found it difficult to draw a breath. They knew about Inkie.

Pull yourself together, Monica. You knew there would be something – here it is. Now deal with it.

She forced a hardness into her stare as she leaned forward herself. "How dare you speak of my daughter with such disrespect and vulgarity?" The fact that droplets of her spittle landed on the lenses of his glasses gave her renewed courage. She waited for him to strike her.

Instead, he removed the glasses, took a pristine handkerchief from the breast pocket of his suit, and slowly wiped them clean. "And so, we are making progress," he murmured.

Eight grueling hours later, she was led back to her cell. The young soldier had been right; she was so spent and exhausted she could barely stand. She had been given two small glasses of water and nothing to eat throughout the ordeal. But she had told "Mein Herr" nothing. Indeed she had gathered a great deal of information about what the Germans knew about their operation and what they were still looking to learn. In her case, it was clear the one thing they sought above anything else was the true identity of "Mr. Moller." It was equally clear they had no idea who or where he was, giving Monica hope that he and Inkie had been spirited out of the country and were safe.

The guard escorting her back to her cell was closer in age to Jorgen. Hoping to appeal to his sense of compassion, Monica accepted his hold on her arm as he navigated the twists and turns of the maze of corridors.

"Is there some way I can get word to my family, sir?" she asked. "A letter perhaps?"

"*Ingen*," he replied in Danish, his voice tinged with regret. "No letters and no visitors."

"But perhaps you might let them know I am well? If I give you the address or telephone number or..." Once the questioning had become so repetitive that she could almost answer by rote, Monica had turned her thoughts to her family and how worried they must be.

"I'm sorry," the guard murmured as he opened her cell and stood aside to let her enter. She paused in front of him, her eyes looking deep into his, where she saw a hint of kindness. "Perhaps some paper and a pencil then. After all, there's every chance I will not be leaving here alive. I would like to let my family know how much I have loved them."

His eyes widened in surprise. "They will not kill a woman," he said.

"Won't they?" She stepped inside and turned to face him. "Thank you for your consideration, sir. May you and your family sleep well." She stood facing the door while he closed and locked it.

She saw a tray that had been left on the cot probably hours earlier. It seemed to feature the same menu as her breakfast had offered, with the addition of a thick slice of bread. Next to it was a thin blanket. So, small rewards were to be doled out, delivering the message her jailers were not the monsters she might consider them to be. In the meantime, the overhead light seemed to have found new life, although it continued to flicker, the food was inedible, and the chamber pot she had used that morning smelled. She sat on the edge of the cot and dunked the bread in the potato onion concoction, tearing at the tough crust with her teeth and chewing thoroughly to make the little taste there was last.

She had made it through day two, or had she? She had heard of prisoners being awakened in the night and taken for questioning again. She needed a strategy to keep her wits about her. During the hours she'd spent with "Mein Herr," he had revealed perhaps more than he knew about what information they had gleaned from interrogations of others. If she could just keep her wits about her...

She scraped the last of the gravy from the tin dish with the heel of the bread and forced it down. She needed to remain as strong as possible, and that meant eating when she could and getting some regular exercise, since for now, it appeared they had no intention of giving her exercise time in the courtyard or elsewhere. Setting the tray aside, she paced the confines of her cell – up, down, across, repeat. Then she pulled back the soiled mattress and stepped onto the iron grid of the cot and back down to the floor, repeating the drill again half a dozen times. Finally she placed her palms flat to the damp wall under the window and, with her feet planted well behind her, improvised a kind of push-up. It was not her normal routine of walks through the woods, but it would do. She spread the blanket over the mattress and lay down, her forearm across her eyes to block out the incessant light.

The next time she opened her eyes, she saw the sky was a dull gray and realized it had started to rain in the night. She also realized she'd slept so deeply that her breakfast had been delivered through the slot in the door without her hearing a thing. Aware that the guards might come at any time to take her for more questioning and that they would not knock before entering the cell, she squatted over the chamber pot, used a bit of her breakfast water and her finger to clean her teeth, and repaired the damage a night of sleep had done to her hair and clothes. Satisfied that she was ready whenever they came, she set the tray of food on the cot.

And when she picked up the tin dish, she saw a sheet of blank paper that had been ripped from a notebook and a small pencil. Ignoring her food for the moment, she scribbled a message to Jorgen.

My darling, I am well. Please do not worry. Once they have realized I have nothing to tell them, I'll be home. Until then, take care of yourself until I can be there to be sure you do. Give my love to the children, and know that you and they are my life.

She folded the paper and then tried to decide how best to conceal it until she could hopefully pass it to the guard from the night before – the man she was sure had gotten her the paper and pencil. She thought of placing it in her jacket pocket or her shoe, but what if today they decided to have her undress, took her clothes, put her into a prison uniform? She glanced around the barren cell and remembered how the grid of the cot had included some places where screws had come loose. Throwing back the mattress and blanket, she slipped the folded paper between a space where the crossbars joined the frame. She barely had time to turn back the mattress and fold the blanket before she heard steps and the door swung open.

"*Kommen Sie,*" the less callous of the two guards from the morning before ordered.

She smiled. "Lead on, MacDuff," she said, forcing a jovial tone. When the young man seemed confused, she added, "It's Shakespeare. Actually the line is really 'lay on,' but close enough. Have you read any of his plays?" He refused to look at her, and his mouth hardened into a thin, determined line. "He's quite brilliant, you know. Everyone needs to read Shakespeare, regardless of their station in life. So much to be learned." She kept up this line of chatter all the way to the interrogation room, taking some comfort in the fact that, at least for the moment, she was the one in control, even though her escort was the one in uniform.

As the guard led the way, Monica realized that the route they were following was not the same as before. Her pulse quickened and she found it difficult to breathe. Perhaps she had done too good a job of feigning ignorance in the earlier round of interrogation. Perhaps her inquisitor had decided she was useless, or worse, decided to make an example of her by having her shot. Her mind raced with dire possibilities until, as she and her guard reached the catwalk that ran around the central court of the prison, she looked down and saw Viggo smiling up at her. Breaking free, she ran down the last flight of metal stairs, ignoring the guard's orders for her to halt. Her son caught her in his arms, his mouth next to her ear as he whispered the news that Inkie had gone into hiding and he had done as she instructed regarding the revolver.

By then the guard had caught up to them and pulled them apart.

"I brought provisions," Viggo announced, pointing to a suitcase, along with a basket filled with food and a carton of cigarettes.

"You cannot..." the guard began, but Viggo gave the man his most winning smile as he pressed a wad of cash into the man's hand.

"You have five minutes," the guard said. He took the suitcase and food and set them aside. "These will need to be searched."

"Yes, of course," Monica replied before turning once again to Viggo. "They told me no visitors and – "

Viggo grinned as he pulled out a letter with several official-looking stamps on it. "I pulled a few strings."

Monica almost laughed as she studied the letter. It had been written on their attorney's stationery but typed in German – a request for Monica to receive visits as well as necessary personal items from her son. One corner showed a large red stamp that read "Approved." She recognized the stamp as one Jorgen kept on his desk at Engestofte. It was anything but official, but somehow it had worked. She had never been more impressed with Viggo.

"That is five minutes," the guard announced.

Monica and Viggo embraced, and she felt him burrow his face into the curve of her neck. When the guard gently separated them, she felt the dampness of her son's tears on her jaw.

"Father is working to secure your release," he stated openly as the guard picked up the suitcase, took hold of her elbow, and led her away.

As she climbed the stairs, she called out messages for Viggo to deliver on her behalf. "Remind your father to take his medication.

And write to your sister and brother to let them know I am well. The trial should come any day now and – "

They passed through a door that the guard closed behind them, shutting off any further attempts at communication.

Following Viggo's visit, her days became numbingly the same – hours of interrogation without a break, then back to her cell for a meal that she forced herself to devour despite the bland sameness of the menu. As daylight faded, she huddled on her cot, the only place that provided even a modicum of protection against the pervasive cold carried on the winds of winter that raged outside and seemed to penetrate the very walls of the prison. She was so grateful for the extra clothing and personal items Viggo had brought. She'd been surprised when the suitcase was delivered. Of course, they had confiscated the food and obviously rummaged through the contents of the luggage, but they had apparently decided they had no use for her clothing or the other small luxuries, such as a favorite blanket, her hairbrush, and even a bottle of her favorite bright-red nail polish. As for the cigarettes, they had left her a single pack – as well as the lighter Viggo had packed. That was a surprise. Perhaps they had missed it.

Each night she lay on her cot, wrapped in the softness of her own cover. She never knew when they would come for her, when the next round of questioning might begin. Dawn? Middle of the night? Midmorning or afternoon? An hour after they'd walked her back to her cell or three days later? By now she understood that Jacob had painted a picture of her as someone who was at the very core of the underground movement.

Heinrich Nagel, the man who had replaced "Mein Herr," was now in charge of interrogating her. Immediately she had realized he was someone to be reckoned with. Clever and intelligent, he was clearly one of the Gestapo's best. He wove an intricate web of truth and lies as he questioned her, facts designed to demonstrate the uselessness of her trying to protect anyone and lies intended to make her question what they did and did not already know. In the early sessions with him she was allowed to smoke, and she did. Nagel even gave her cigarettes to take back to her cell with her. Through the long nights, using the lighter she now understood had been deliberately overlooked, she would light one after the other, feeding a habit that had sustained her in difficult times throughout her adult life.

Convinced that Nagel held a grudging respect for her, she decided to try engaging him in a dialogue rather than simply waiting for his next question. "Do you mind if I ask you a question, sir?"

He arched one eyebrow, a gesture she took to be his agreement.

"Rumor has it that others incarcerated within these walls are not treated as...shall we say, hospitably, as I am."

He shrugged. "You are a woman, Frau Wichfeld, and contrary to rumor, we Germans are not the monsters many have made us out to be." He leaned closer to light the cigarette she had removed from the ebony case he always sat opened on the table between them.

She drew in the rich and welcome taste of tobacco. "Still, you have allowed me a great deal of leeway for someone who is under arrest for crimes against the State." She pointed to her clothing. "Not only am I not required to dress in the usual prison garb, you have allowed my family to send me extra clothing and personal items. Not that I am ungrateful," she hastened to add. "On the contrary, I – "

"The truth is that you are a woman held in some esteem here

in your adopted country. Your reputation – and arrest – have made you something of a folk heroine to the locals. The last thing we need is for your supporters to decide to attempt some rescue effort. Your sons and husband have been most cooperative in our effort to subdue any such plan, assuring all who will listen that you are well taken care of." He closed the cigarette case with a gentle but clearly intentional snap and pocketed it. "Now then, there is the matter of your daughter..."

Monica froze. This was the first time Nagel had mentioned Inkie. She understood it would not be the last.

"My daughter has nothing to do with any of this."

"And yet it would appear that she has rather conveniently disappeared. In fact, her friends and associates in Copenhagen – her last-known address – tell us she has not been heard from since just after we showed up to arrest you." He stood at the window, gazing out. "I would think, as her mother, you might be more concerned. In fact the only reason I can think of that you might not show concern is that you know where she is – and more to the point who she is with."

He returned to the table and opened a file folder before pushing it toward her. There was a photograph of Inkie with Flemming Muus – grainy and blurred because it had been taken from some distance, but unmistakably them.

Monica forced herself to maintain a calm she did not feel. After accepting the position as Moller's assistant, Inkie had dyed her hair blond, changed her style of dress, and taken a room in a part of Copenhagen where she was unlikely to meet up with any of her university friends. She'd been given a code name and, other than the visit at Christmas, had not returned to Engestofte. She and Monica had exchanged correspondence through letters hand delivered by a member of Monica's unit.

Stay as close to the truth as possible.

"My daughter is visiting friends in Stockholm," she said. "I have advised her it might be a good time to look for employment there. I do not know the man with her. Perhaps he is someone she has met there?" Her mouth had gone dry, but she would not reach for the glass of water on the table, lest her shaking hands give her away.

"Ah, I see." Nagel closed the folder and said nothing more about Inkie during that session, but she was sure he would continue to probe the soft underbelly of her love for her daughter in his attempt to learn more about the mysterious Mr. Moller.

Determined this man would not break her, she sat across from him day after day, her hands folded to stem the shaking brought on by his sudden shift in demeanor, her eyes locked on his. With "Mein Herr," she had developed the habit of answering with a single word whenever possible, realizing that as she grew more exhausted, the less she said, the less likely she was to make a mistake. With Nagel, she considered inventing names and details in the hope he and his like would waste precious time tracking the false information. But she feared choosing a name that might lead to an actual person – an innocent with no ties to the Resistance. In any event, access to smoking was completely cut off, even as the interrogations intensified.

Thanks to the intervention of the Danish Red Cross, meals became heartier – more potatoes and onions, an occasional bit of beef, bread that was almost fresh. Her Danish jailers no longer simply shoved a tray through the slot in the door, but opened the cell. She realized they were curious – they wanted to see her.

She hoped she might use that to her advantage, and made sure to thank them and even attempt some bit of normal conversation.

"It looks like we're in for more snow tonight," or, "Please thank the cook for adding more seasoning to the stew."

Such comments went unanswered verbally, but one night she returned to her cell to find a heavier blanket had been left for her, and several times after she returned from an especially grueling interrogation, the door slot would slide open and an extra portion of bread or tea would be placed inside by an unseen Samaritan. Her most precious gifts came from the older guard she'd met early in her confinement. She knew him only as Heinz and thought of him as the angel who continued to provide her with supplies for writing to her family while taking the additional risk of smuggling the missives out for her. All visits since Viggo had managed to see her had been denied, and, while she was not allowed to receive letters, the news this man was able to bring her about the well-being of Jorgen and their children – at considerable risk to his job and very life – was a gift she knew she would never be able to repay.

After more than a week of denying her cigarettes, Nagel smiled as he sat across from her one morning. Removing a full pack from his breast pocket, he placed it on the table between them. "These are yours," he said. "Of course, in these times, everything has a price." He moved the pack of smokes an inch closer to her. "Your colleague – Mr. Moller? His real name? Where he might be found?"

Monica leaned in as if to take them, but instead flicked them with her long fingernail, sending them sailing off the table and under the radiator that hissed nearby.

Nagel shoved his chair back and stood, looming over her, one hand raised as if to deliver the slap she'd expected for days now. She had finally gone too far. She looked up at him, almost daring him to strike her. Instead, he lowered his hand, turned away, and walked to the door. "Take the prisoner back to her cell," he ordered the guard.

As she left the room, she saw Nagel go down on one knee to retrieve the cigarettes she suspected were far more important to him than they were to her. After all, in these times, there were shortages for everyone. It felt like a victory, and yet, once she returned to her cell, she had to face the fact that she had humiliated Nagel, and he was not likely to take kindly to that. She recalled how he had forced himself to lower his hand without hitting her. For some reason, he had been told he could not use such tactics. Surely that was a good sign?

A few days after Viggo's visit, Monica had been given the additional privilege of exercise time outdoors. Prisoners who were not being interrogated were allowed a single half hour each day to walk back and forth along a narrow three-sided space. Once a week they were taken from their cells carrying their chamber pots to empty them. Since Monica was the lone prisoner on her block, the time in the yard was her only opportunity to see the men who'd also been arrested on that bitterly cold January night. Whenever she saw any one of them, she smiled and winked. She was determined to send the message that all was well with her, even as she realized some of them had not fared as well. Pastor Marcussen had lost weight and aged considerably. Thor Gerner Nielsen was clearly in pain as he made his way along the path. But she took some solace in the fact that they were all there – all still under arrest, but not yet sentenced – and there were no new faces among them.

That lasted only until the day she saw her son, Viggo, coming down the corridor in a line with the other male prisoners. She was stunned, and her step faltered, causing a guard to grip her arm and push her forward. *Viggo? Arrested? On what charge?* When she caught his eye, she saw how frightened he was. She felt helpless – as if somehow she had failed in her role as a parent. After everything she'd done to keep her family out of this, how was it that her youngest child was being marched to a cell?

When she faced Nagel a few minutes later, she could barely control her fury. "You have arrested my son," she stated flatly.

"We could not find your daughter," he replied with a nonchalance that made her want to murder him.

"He's done nothing."

"He struck an official who refused to allow him to visit you here. That is assault – a crime in any civilized country."

Oh, Viggo.

In spite of his normally placid nature, Viggo had always had a temper – one that flared white hot when he did not get his way. She could only imagine the scene he must have caused to get himself locked up, and he was so young. But she felt some relief in knowing his so-called crime had no connection to her actions. Of course, he knew her, and that would be enough for Nagel and others to take an interest. Viggo might inadvertently give them some detail they could use in their interrogation of her. Worse, they might use the threat of torturing Viggo to break her. She racked her brain trying to come up with a way to contact Viggo and reassure him.

Fortunately, Heinz was the guard who led her back to her cell after her session with Nagel. He confirmed what Nagel had told her, but assured her that there were witnesses who had reported Viggo was deliberately provoked.

"He won't be here long," Heinz said as he opened her cell door and stood aside to allow her to pass.

A glimmer of metal caught her eye. "Heinz, could you wait just a moment, please?"

The guard glanced back down the corridor. They were alone – no other prisoners or guards. He nodded.

Through all the interrogations and searches of her cell during them, Monica had managed to hold onto one personal possession she treasured – her gold Dunhill lighter. In addition to its sleek outward design, the lighter had a small interior compartment meant to hold an extra flint. Viggo had been the one to show her that detail, and she hoped he would remember it now. She scribbled a note for her son on a single sheet of the toilet paper the guard had given her for writing letters, folded it into a sliver, and slid it inside the tiny compartment.

Stay calm, my darling. I am here. Mummy

She slipped Heinz the lighter, and was relieved when he seemed to understand without words its destination.

Late that night, the slot used to deliver her food opened and a tray with a cup of tea and her lighter was pushed through. She opened the flint compartment and pulled out Viggo's reply: *Do not worry.*

Having made contact, she breathed a bit easier.

As the weeks passed, conditions for all those awaiting trial improved bit by bit, thanks mostly to the ongoing intervention of the Danish Red Cross. The prison employed Danish guards, who gradually became more relaxed about exchanges of conversation during the daily half hour of exercise or when prisoners were taken from their cells, slop buckets in hand, to a communal washroom. And although visitors were still prohibited, Monica and the others were able to receive packages. Of course, all were opened by the guards, who saw no problem with taking anything that caught their fancy before delivering what remained. Monica understood times were hard for many, and she did not blame them for the petty theft. The interrogations had dwindled to no more than a couple of times a week, and Nagel seemed almost bored as he went through his usual round of questions. Viggo was still being held, although through her contact with the guards, she had learned he'd been moved from West Prison.

One day as she sat in her cell unraveling an old sweater that Ivan had long since outgrown – one used to cushion baked goods made by their cook – Monica heard footsteps coming her way. Hoping that at last she might receive the knitting needles she had requested so she could turn the yarn from the sweater into warm socks for Viggo, she waited for the slot to open. But as the footsteps came closer, she realized this was not a single guard but at least three, and they were marching. That meant either they were coming for her – perhaps to take her for another session of questioning – or something worse.

She shook off that thought and stood. When she heard the scrape of the door to the cell next to hers, her pulse quickened. *A neighbor at last.* The irony of her rejoicing did not escape her, but anyone new to the prison meant someone with information about what had been going on outside these thick stone walls. She heard the guards give instructions to their new ward, then slam shut the door and retreat.

Monica remained by the door, listening for the sounds of the multiple doors she knew had to open and close before the guards were truly gone. Flemming Muus had insisted every operative in his organization learn Morse code. "It may well be your only means of communication," he told them. So once she was sure she and the prisoner in the next cell were alone, she rushed to the wall connecting her cell to her new neighbor's, and using the heel of her shoe, tapped out a greeting.

Hello. My name is Monica.

Remembering her own first day in this place of defeat and uncertainty, she realized her new neighbor had probably collapsed on her cot, and perhaps thought the tapping was just one of the quirks of the building. Monica repeated the message, and waited.

Silence.

Deciding to give her neighbor some time, she returned to unraveling and winding the yarn. An hour passed, and she decided to try sending her message again.

There was a faint tapping in reply. Monica pressed her ear to the wall to catch the message. But the taps stopped abruptly when the guards returned. As they took the new prisoner away, Monica heard a shout.

"My name is Claire Schlichting."

Claire Schlichting? The actress?

Monica knew that name. She and Jorgen had attended a cabaret performance where the woman had performed. How they had delighted in her talent as a songstress and comedienne. Monica also knew from Flemming Muus that Claire's day job was that of managing the canteen at Dagmar House, Copenhagen's headquarters for the Gestapo. Flemming offered no further information, but seemed to trust her, although in these times, who knew?

Paranoia born of weeks of endless interrogation and, in the words of her sister-in-law, Mabelle,, "waiting for the other shoe to fall," made Monica suspicious of any changes in the daily routine, any new encounters. Why, after all this time, move someone next door to her? She needed to be careful. So far, Nagel had been unable to break her, and perhaps this was his newest attempt. Perhaps the actress had been offered a deal – in exchange for her freedom, she was to get the information Nagel had failed to glean.

The precious – and illegal – knitting needles were delivered along with Monica's supper, and still Claire Schlichting had not returned. Hours passed with no sounds from the hall or cell next door. At midnight, Monica assumed her nightly position of blocking the flickering ceiling light with her forearm and fell asleep. Sometime in the hours of deepest darkness just before dawn, she woke.

All was silent. But something had brought her awake.

And then...

Tap. Tap. Taptaptap.

I have news.

While Monica slept, Claire had returned to her cell. Monica lay very still, listening for more.

Yard today.

Monica pushed herself off the cot and hesitated only a second before tapping her one-word reply: *Yes.*

Just the day before, Heinz had brought news that her son had been transferred to an internment camp usually reserved for those about to be sent to Germany, ending any opportunity for mother and son to stay in touch. The news had terrified her. It was one thing to be jailed in Copenhagen, and quite something more unsettling to know her son might be headed for a German prison. Rumors had been rampant of labor and concentration camps in Germany and Poland, where anyone taken there was unlikely to come out again. She had heard of beatings and mass executions. There was even talk of gas chambers being constructed and put to use. Whatever this woman's game might be, there was always the possibility she might know something about Viggo.

But to her disappointment, shortly after dawn, the guards once again came for Claire, and she was not back by the time they returned to escort Monica to the courtyard for her daily half hour of exercise. Any opportunity for a connection was further thwarted when Monica was taken for questioning later that night, and Claire had still not returned.

To Monica's surprise, when she entered the interrogation room, Nagel was nowhere to be seen. Instead she sat across from three SS officers who took turns over the next several hours grilling her. Sometimes they made her stand for over an hour without posing a single question. As the day turned to evening, she understood what questions they did ask really had no purpose. Their game was to wear her down. But when she realized they were the ones who did not have the stamina to endure hour after hour of the process, she lost patience. Seeing the head of one officer bobbing as he fought against falling asleep, she'd had enough.

"Gentlemen, it would seem you have exhausted any ability to question me properly. Therefore, I request that you return me to my cell. This is a waste of your time – and mine."

One of the three jumped to his feet and advanced on her, his hand on the butt of his pistol. The officer who had been dozing looked up, bleary eyed with exhaustion. "Leave her," he ordered wearily. "We're done. Guard!"

The young man posted just outside the room opened the door and snapped to attention. As he escorted her down the endless corridors, across catwalks and on to her cell, Monica was aware he kept glancing at her, and she thought she saw him smile.

"Do I amuse you?" she asked.

The guard blushed. "*Nein*, Frau Wichfeld." Then, as they turned a corner, he added, "They could have had you shot for speaking to them that way."

So he had been listening outside the door. She shrugged. "One day I expect they will, but until then, I will not suffer fools like those three."

They had reached her cell and he fumbled with the lock. "Do you know what the guards – the Danes – call you?"

Monica chuckled. "I can only imagine."

"Queen of West Prison," he said. "No one has ever known anyone quite like you." He opened the door and stepped aside to allow her to enter.

"Thank you," she whispered, touched in spite of herself. She studied him for a moment. He was perhaps a year or two older than Ivan. He was a Danish man who was doing a job to provide for himself and possibly a wife and family. He had no blame in all this. She reached out and smoothed the collar of his uniform. "Get some rest."

This time the cell door closed with a soft click rather than the usual chilling slam meant to drive home the point that she no longer had control over her life.

Well, she thought as she lay down for what was left of the night, *at least I am apparently the queen.* It was the kind of ironic humor she wished she could share with Inkie. It was also the first time in weeks that she could recall laughing out loud.

Early the following morning, Monica received another visit from Dr. Helmer Rostling, the director of the Danish Red Cross. Over the past several weeks he had visited Monica and the others awaiting trial, and while he had made it clear that his sympathies were pro-German, Monica looked forward to their political jousts. It was obvious that he respected her. During this latest visit, she decided to gather what information she could about her new neighbor.

"You do know she was arrested because of you," he said as he leaned across the table to light her cigarette. They were meeting in a room designated for such visits. It was smaller than the interrogation room, but no less dreary.

"I don't see how that's possible. I had no contact with her prior to meeting her here," Monica protested. "I did see her perform once, but I have not once been inside Dagmar House, where I understand she managed the canteen."

Rostling shrugged. "The canteen was apparently a cover she used to gather information she could pass along to your sort and perhaps use to help the cause of those awaiting trial – like you. Unfortunately, she became involved in a plot to break you out of this place – one that nearly worked."

Monica had overheard the guards whispering and seen them giving her sidelong looks a few weeks earlier, and for several days, they had been especially strict in their monitoring of her movements. Now she understood. Flemming Muus must have tried to free her.

"Were others arrested?" Monica's mind went immediately to Inkie, who would have insisted on being part of any such plan.

"No one who had anything to do with the plot. Your husband and son – the older one – were unfortunately in the wrong place attending a wedding here in Copenhagen and were taken into custody. They are being held in the same camp where your younger son is."

Monica's hand shook as she took a deep draw on her cigarette.

"I doubt they will be held for long, Monica. It's quite apparent they knew nothing of the plot. They'll be detained for awhile and then released."

Monica was not so certain. Nagel could use this latest detainment of her family as a bargaining point to try and force her to reveal information, especially information about Flemming Muus. But betraying Flemming ultimately meant betraying Varinka, and there was no possibility she would ever put her daughter in danger.

"And Claire Schlichting?"

"Claire has other problems. She's half Jewish. That alone would be cause for bringing her in for questioning." He tapped the ash from his cigarette. "I fear she has not received the same...consideration you have been shown."

"Because she's part Jewish? The Nazis are beyond barbaric."

Rostling shrugged, and not for the first time, she wondered how it was possible for someone so obviously well-bred and educated to blindly follow the rantings of a madman.

"She will be all right in the long run," he said. "Like you she is a survivor, and she also has the advantage that she is a popular celebrity. The newspapers will follow her case closely and keep her name in the public eye."

Monica recalled the first time they'd finally met in the courtyard. Claire had fallen into step beside her as the prisoners paced the perimeter of the yard in pairs. Doubling up had become necessary because every day it seemed new prisoners arrived, filling even the cells on her corridor. If they had walked single file, they would have filled the space and been unable to move at all. The overcrowding had one other advantage in that it gave prisoners more opportunity to exchange a few words, or even written notes.

Over the next week, Monica and Claire met every day in the exercise yard. Monica had remembered Claire as a striking younger woman in her thirties, a woman who moved with dignity and confidence. But after the ordeal she had been subjected to since being incarcerated, she seemed increasingly fragile. There were dark purple bruises on her bare legs, and her facial features showed the effects of almost no sleep for days now. Although she wore her own clothing, the outfit never changed. Monica's heart went out to her, even as she realized how fortunate she had been. So far, in all the days and hours of interrogation, she had come close to being slapped and threatened by cigarettes held far too close to her face, but never tormented in the brutal way Claire obviously was on a regular basis.

Still, she had been concerned when Claire appeared to stumble and, as Monica steadied her, she felt a thin roll of paper pressed into her palm. Under the cover of making sure her companion had regained her balance, Monica pocketed the message and spent the rest of the exercise time impatiently waiting to be returned to her cell so she could read the contents.

Claire's handwriting was tiny, filling every inch of the thin sheet of paper. The fact that, despite her beatings, her sense of humor remained intact was a surprise.

Getting accustomed to our luxurious accommodations – the cuisine, the view, and how kind of them to provide a companion – a mouse I've named Oscar. He comes and goes through a small hole in the wall between us. So tiny and yet...

Monica had seen the mouse on several occasions, had even left crumbs and watched with interest as it warily approached the treasure, nabbed it, and scurried back through the crack in the wall. Now she made a thorough examination of the opening. Using the handle of her spoon, she pushed it as far into the slit as possible. The bowl of the spoon prevented it from going more than a few inches, and the wall was at least six inches deep. Still, if Claire worked from her side, they might be able to widen the tiny hole enough to pass notes.

Each night they scraped away at the opening. Monica had no concern about the small pile of plaster and dirt accumulating on the floor. It was not as if the prison sent a housekeeper to dust and sweep. Still, she made sure she spread the dirt with her shoe before turning in for the night. And then one Sunday afternoon when boredom threatened to be her undoing, Monica sat cross-legged on the floor of her cell, eye level with the hole. Using her knitting needle, she poked at the chalky barrier, and when the needle penetrated what seemed to be the last barrier, she placed her mouth close to the opening and called out, "Claire!"

A moment later she saw Claire's eye peering back at her and heard her laughing. "We did it," Claire crowed.

After that the two of them spent whatever time they could sharing stories of their families and life before coming to West Prison. There were times when Monica had to fight back tears. She had been so alone for weeks now, her family unable to visit, her only communication with the outside world being through her visits with Dr. Rostling and the increasingly rare letters the guard, Heinz, managed to deliver for and to her. She missed her family and friends more than she had ever imagined could be possible.

Claire filled that void, and she was a fountain of more official information as well. If Monica had earned the respect of her jailers, Claire was a popular celebrity they all seemed anxious to impress. Through her inside contacts, she was the one to tell Monica that Ivan and Jorgen had been released without charges, and Viggo was being returned to West Prison. But Claire's sources had failed to let her know what was about to happen late one night in May. Hearing the now-familiar stamp of jackboots coming her way, Monica set aside her knitting and waited for them to take her for yet another round of questions. Given the lateness of the hour, she assumed Nagel was making a point. The man was so transparent.

Her cell door banged open, slamming against the wall. A large, muscular guard filled the opening as he announced, "Frau Monica Beresford Wichfeld, you will be dressed and ready to leave at dawn for your trial at Dagmar House." Having delivered his message, he pivoted, then slammed the door shut.

So, here it was at last – the trial she had spent weeks anticipating. *At long last the other shoe had fallen.*

Dagmar House, Gestapo Headquarters, Copenhagen – Spring 1944

Outside West Prison, Monica waited with the others scheduled for trial. She had dressed carefully, in the tweed suit over the cashmere sweater she'd worn the night she was arrested, her hair pulled back in its signature chignon, her sturdy shoes polished as best she could using spit and a rag. The weather was cool but fair, the air sparkling in its clarity. She thought of Engestofte and days spent lounging on the terrace, watching the children swimming in the lake or Jorgen pruning his beloved rose bushes, and wondered if she might ever know such simple pleasures again.

She greeted her compatriots, pleased to see Thor Gerner Nielsen and the veterinarian, Hans Hovmand, as well as William Grandt, the editor of the Maribo newspaper, already seated in the back of one of the canvas-topped trucks. There was a woman she had not met, but felt drawn to at once – Pia Baastrup-Thomsen. From another prison door she saw Viggo and five others being marched to the second lorry. In their last session together, Nagel had informed her she'd left him no choice but to assume Viggo had been part of her operation all along.

Monica had to clench her fists to stop herself from running to him. Instead, she made eye contact and smiled. Once they had all boarded their respective vehicles, the procession, led by a sleek black Gestapo staff car, drove away from the prison and down the streets of Copenhagen. Having taken a seat close to the opening at the very rear, Monica drank in the sights she had missed for so very long. The verdant green of the grass and budding trees, the pops of color where crocus and other spring blossoms had taken root in the park despite small hills of snow that had not yet melted. She observed pedestrians, still bundled in coats and scarves, out for leisurely walks, clearly unaware of the drama contained in the car and two trucks rattling past. She saw a couple – young lovers – and thought of Kurt. How many times had they strolled through a park, their arms linked, their heads close? Not only here in Copenhagen but also in London and Paris and along the seashore of Rapallo.

It was all so very normal.

Her chest tightened against the flood of emotion that threatened to drown her as she watched the young couple walk away, their innocent laughter floating on the May breeze. This was why she had risked everything. It was not for her or her generation, but that her children and their children and the children of the passing strangers might know peace and a better life. Everything she'd been able to learn of the progress of the war gave her hope the Allies would prevail, and if she had played some small part in that, she would ask for nothing more.

Moments later the trucks lumbered down a ramp into a walled courtyard where the sunlight disappeared, and the reality of her world came rushing back. Armed German soldiers stood at attention as the trucks halted to discharge their passengers. Single file between a cordon of stern-faced uniformed men, they were escorted inside and up a flight of stairs. Emerging into a long hallway, they passed several closed doors, behind which Monica detected the sounds of typewriters in use and muffled conversation. The Gestapo agents were at the head of their procession. At the end of the hall, two uniformed guards – also German, their faces impassive – opened a pair of highly polished doors to reveal a large room where bare white walls reflected the sun streaming through a panel of windows. More soldiers, each balancing an automatic weapon, stood like columns around the perimeter of the room – a room already crowded with officials, attorneys, and spectators. At the end of the room that faced the windows, Monica saw two rows of chairs, the second row elevated above the first by a riser.

One by one the prisoners took their seats: Georg Quistgaard, at age 29, a charter member of the Resistance; Arne Lutzen Hansen, a man who, if passed on the street, might have been mistaken for a businessman, but who Monica knew had been a superb radio operator; Carl Jorgen Larsen, a bank cashier who had managed the secret accounts that funded the operation. Monica was led to the fourth chair in the first row. Behind them Pia, Hans, Thor, and Viggo stepped onto the riser and took their seats. Viggo was right behind her, a detail that gave her some comfort. She reached back and tapped his calf. She hoped he would take courage from her touch.

At a table to their left sat the prosecutor – young, confident, clearly pleased with himself. He wore the uniform of the SS, the silver skull insignia gleaming in the light. Next to him sat their accusers – Jacob Jensen and another man Monica did not know. She focused her gaze on Jacob, but he kept his eyes averted. At a far smaller and less impressive table sat a nervous older man who Monica realized had the unenviable job of offering their defense. She had never met him, nor did she suspect any of her fellow defendants had. The poor soul looked as if he would rather be anywhere – even the Russian front – than here. Near the window sat the secretary for the proceedings – a high-ranking officer given his uniform – and next to him the two Gestapo agents. The rest of the room was crowded with spectators – members of the press and others merely looking for an afternoon's entertainment. Monica had no doubt this so-called trial would be nothing more than a charade.

On orders from the secretary, all chatter ceased and everyone stood as three judges entered the room and took their places under a portrait of Adolf Hitler. The indictment was read – a long, involved recitation that boiled down to a charge of "giving aid to the enemy."

Monica was called on first, instructed to stand where she was and answer the charges. The young prosecutor was practically licking his lips in his excitement to show his superiors what he could do. Repeatedly he challenged her about the airdrops, the underground newspapers, the funds she had tricked her neighbors into providing, the people she had associated with – the communist Hilmar Wulff and the radical Jew Bernard Berenson, not to mention a weekend she'd spent in the English countryside with none other than Winston Churchill. And when repeatedly she denied that any of this was relevant to the charges, he turned to the judges and announced, "Denied, and yet proved by the testimony of this man, Jacob Jensen." And with each pronouncement, it seemed to Monica that Jacob sank a bit lower in his chair. The grilling, which was more harangue than interrogation, went on for nearly two hours with no interruption. It occurred to Monica that perhaps she should pen a note of thanks to Nagel. He had prepared her well to withstand the hours of such inane madness.

Taking each of the accused in turn, the prosecutor smeared their reputations, rambling on and on as one by one they were called to stand and remain standing even when the questions were directed at another. Monica could hear the town-hall clock chiming – quarter hour, half, three-quarter, hour, repeat. She kept her expression deliberately bland and gently shifted her weight to avoid cramping as she focused on a line of pigeons patrolling the ledge outside the windows.

Finally, in the early afternoon, the triumvirate of judges called a recess. The courtroom emptied except for the prisoners and soldiers. They were given food and water and allowed to smoke and talk freely. Monica noticed the napkins were imprinted with *Glædelig jul!*

Happy Christmas.

"They are only six months late," Viggo said bitterly.

"Ah, better to see it as an example of German efficiency, using up any surplus. We can learn from our enemies, my son."

Viggo rolled his eyes, and Monica was carried back to numerous times when she or Jorgen had attempted to teach their children some lesson and received a similar response. She gave his cheek a motherly caress.

The questioning resumed and lasted until after dark, when the prisoners were once again loaded onto the trucks and returned to their cells at West Prison. Monica was exhausted, her entire body ached, and she found sleep nearly impossible. She passed a good part of the night stretching her stiff limbs and filling Claire in on what had transpired. The following morning the entire process was repeated, only this time there was no testimony. Rather, the first hour or so was occupied by the prosecutor's summary of the charges, a diatribe on the despicability of these traitors, and a suggested punishment of ten years in prison for Monica, a lesser sentence for the three men seated with her in the front row, two years for Thor Gerner Nielsen, and a warning for the rest.

As the prosecutor rested his case, the defense attorney stood. Twice, one of the judges had to chastise him to speak up. His face was shiny with perspiration, and he frequently ran his forefinger beneath the collar of his shirt as if seeking room for more air. Repeatedly he would clear his throat and start down a path of logic designed to refute the prosecutor's case. Then, after fumbling for words, he would stop and look almost pleadingly around the room for help before hurrying back to his table to review his notes. Finally he looked imploringly at the panel of judges and requested that Monica's sentence be reduced due to her gender and age, although he hastened to add that his request came in spite of the obvious fact that she was guilty as charged.

Once again court was recessed – this time for the judges to deliberate. The prisoners were taken to an anteroom. Once there, Monica hurried to reassure Viggo, who seemed close to breaking down.

"Ten years, Mummy," he lamented. "Perhaps they would allow me to serve in your place."

"Ten years is nothing," she told him. "Especially because this war will not last that long. Besides, that is but the prosecutor's suggestion. The judges may see things differently. Either way, I can wait it out for however long it takes to put the world right again. You must go home and see to your father. You must – "

The door to the anteroom banged open, and several soldiers surrounded them and herded them back to the courtroom. This time they were told to remain standing as the secretary read off the particulars of their lives – name, age, birthplace, occupation, and so forth – followed by a detailed description of their crimes. Finally, they were ordered to face the panel of judges. Monica was aware of the silence that had suddenly blanketed the room, as if every person in attendance had stopped breathing. Outside the window a pigeon cooed, and then in a voice clearly intended to strike terror, the presiding judge pronounced their sentences.

"Georg Brockhoff Quistgaard, condemned to death."

An audible gasp from the spectators and reporters at the unexpected harshness of the ruling.

"Arne Lutzen Hansen, condemned to death."

A growing murmur of alarm, but the judge's banging of his gavel cast the room back into silence.

"Carl Jorgen Larsen, condemned to death."

A deliberate pause, and then the judge turned his icy glare to Monica.

Did he smile?

Her pulse thundered like the cadence of a hundred soldiers marching through the street. *Say it.*

"Monica Wichfeld, death."

Despite the constant banging of the gavel, the packed room erupted with protests and cries of distress that gave voice to their shock. "She's a woman," someone cried out. And from another corner, "For God's sake, show some mercy!"

It was as if the windows had been opened and the room filled with the whoosh of a sudden wind. As the courtroom protest gained momentum, the judge stood and shouted for order while the soldiers repositioned their weapons to ensure his command was heeded.

Behind her she heard Viggo gasp. She needed to do something – anything – that might calm him. Some distraction that would take his mind off her sentence and the terror he must feel, not just for her but for himself. Surely his sentence would not be so harsh. Reaching into her jacket pocket, she pulled out the enameled gold compact Kurt had given her years earlier. It was one of the personal items Viggo had thought to include with the clothing he'd brought her months earlier. She opened it and positioned it so that the mirror reflected Viggo. She caught his eye as she removed the puff and calmly powdered her nose. She smiled at her reflection, and that accomplished her purpose. Viggo looked confused, but her action had managed to momentarily distract him, giving him the moment he needed to compose himself. She saw him find his courage as he straightened and faced the panel of judges. Next to her, the three men condemned to die also stood a bit straighter.

The pronouncement of sentences continued: Thor and Hans received life at hard labor, while Pia was given six years at hard labor. Miraculously Viggo was set free for lack of evidence. Monica was so relieved she was not sure her legs would hold her upright, but she locked her knees to maintain her balance. Following protocol, such as it was, the judges allowed each of those condemned to death to make a closing statement. The three men next to Monica each delivered patriotic discourses in their native language, calling on their Danish countrymen and women to remain strong and stay the course of resistance. The judges turned to Monica. At first she remained silent, but then she gazed at them as if they were no more than hired hands she had agreed to meet with. "Will there be anything else, gentlemen?" she asked.

The prosecuting attorney stepped forward. "This is your opportunity to plead for mercy, Frau Wichfeld."

That is what they want, she realized. *It adds to the drama they have created here.*

"And does that opportunity also apply to my friends here?" She indicated the three condemned men still standing next to her.

"No," the attorney replied.

Monica quirked an eyebrow. "Then it is of no interest to me." She turned her back on the attorney and judges as she took hold of Viggo's hand. She was done with this charade.

There was a moment of silence, and then the presiding judge declared court adjourned, before following his cohorts from the room. Immediately the soldiers moved forward to surround the prisoners, and together they walked from the courtroom, down the corridor and stairs, to the waiting trucks that would deliver them back to the cells they had called home for months now. Having been freed, Viggo was left standing as once again the soldiers herded the others onto the lorries. Viggo was sobbing, and it broke Monica's heart that she could do nothing to console him except blow him a kiss as the trucks pulled away.

West Prison – Spring 1944

By the time the trucks arrived at the prison late that afternoon, reality had set in. Monica was exhausted, and the strain of what lay ahead filled every fiber of her being. She stumbled exiting the truck, and her entire body ached with exhaustion. She was aware that her shoulders were stooped and she looked every day of her forty-nine years. Her mind was muddled, and she seemed incapable of coherent thought.

Ten years had seemed bearable, but death?

What a fool she had been to think she was ready.

The young guard who had once called her a queen took her arm – gently, as if helping an old lady cross the street – and she couldn't help but compare the kindness of their Danish prison guards against the callousness of the Germans transporting them to and from Dagmar House. He led her through the heavy iron gates, the sound of them banging shut behind her hitting her like the gunshots of a firing squad.

Back in her cell she ignored the evening meal left for her, the coded taps on the wall, and Claire's soft calls to her through the hole in the wall. Instead she lay on her cot, her forearm over her eyes, and prayed for the oblivion of sleep. She was awakened by the distant chiming of a city clock.

One...two...three...four.

Then all was silent.

Later she heard the unmistakable rasp of keys turning in locks somewhere above or below her cell block, followed by the stamp of booted feet marching in formation. Minutes passed, and from outside her narrow window, which she had figured out overlooked the exercise yard, she heard voices raised in singing the Danish national anthem. Her heart swelled with pride at the courage of these prisoners, whoever they were, and then plummeted as the last chorus of the anthem faded away.

Had her friends been taken from their cells for transfer to Ry-vangen on the north side of the city – the place where prisoners condemned to die went to face their end – and if so, how long before they would come for her?

The waiting was its own form of torture.

Dr. Rostling called on her later that week, bringing news that people were deeply upset by the harsh sentence she'd been given. "Pulpits throughout the land are said to reverberate with calls for prayers on your behalf. The idea of a woman being put before a firing squad..." Perhaps realizing *she* would be that woman, he looked away. "After all, your husband's family is well respected – has been for generations. And you as well, of course. People seem to admire you despite your being British."

"Ah, but I am no longer a Brit, you see. The day I married Jorgen, I surrendered any claim to that identity along with my passport. So, they have not condemned a British woman – an enemy – they have condemned a Dane."

Rostling hesitated, then turned back to her. "Are they treating you well?"

She shrugged and lit a second cigarette from the one she was just finishing. "As well as you might expect them to treat someone they view as a traitor." She would not speak to him of the torture that came with not knowing what might be next for her. "Thank you for coming," she added, hoping he would go.

Once he did, she pulled out the supply of paper and pencils Rostling had brought. He had not needed to suggest she might want to use her time for writing final letters to Jorgen and the children. But she found that quite impossible. What to say... how to explain. Varinka would understand and so would Viggo, although both would be inconsolable. But Ivan? Jorgen?

She decided to begin with someone less invested in the life she had led, and Claire Schlichting came to mind. Yes, Claire was perfect. In the weeks they had occupied neighboring cells, it had been Claire who had kept her spirits from crashing. Her humor as well as her outrage had stoked the fire of Monica's passion for the cause she would never abandon. If Claire could survive, she would be able to see Jorgen and the children through it, help them understand, once it was done.

My dearest friend...Thank you for everything. I shall not forget. I have one more favor to ask of you. It is not just for me, but for those I hold dear. Viggo brought me to the brink of tears when we parted after the trial. Ivan and my daughter are stronger, but my husband might never understand why I chose to act as I did.

She paused and stared at the page. The truth was that in many ways she had achieved what she'd set out to do. Those she loved most were safe and, when this horrid war ended, would be free to get on with their lives. But she regretted not being able to do anything for her friends who even now were suffering as they awaited the fulfillment of their sentences.

In the courtroom she had seen Thor on the verge of breaking

down, and she was afraid that would set off others. Any show of weakness would only assure their accusers of the rightness of their case. She'd known she needed to do something to bring her fellow prisoners strength. Powdering her nose had been a silly act of defiance that she hoped had worked not only for Viggo, but for the others as well.

I am determined, dear Claire – whatever the personal cost – to maintain my sense of humor. From childhood on, I have always done as I chose, even if others found my choices unsuitable.

Once again she hesitated, her thoughts drifting to the past. She had always preferred solitude, even as a child. In those early years at her family's estate, she had often sat by the lake daydreaming of a time when she would travel and meet other people from other cultures and live life to its fullest. And had she not realized those childhood dreams? Through her marriage to Jorgen and her own determination, she had dined with aristocrats, known poets and writers and artists, all while forming solid friendships with laborers, farmers, and shopkeepers. She had waltzed with Jorgen in grand ballrooms, wearing designer gowns and precious jewels. She had pawned both to pay for a future for her children.

Returning to the letter, she wrote:

I have come to believe that there is no such thing as black or white, only gray. No one is born evil through and through. It depends on how one is raised and reacts to life's difficulties. I have done my best. Dearest Claire, when this war finally comes to its end, please go to my family and tell them what you know of me, help them understand why. And when they protest that I chose the war over them, assure them that I was choosing them and their future.

Rostling returned a few days later, arriving in the evening, which was unusual. On top of that he entered her cell with an air of excitement that stirred Monica's curiosity.

"I have just come from speaking with Doctor Best," he announced.

Werner Best was Reich commissioner for Occupied Denmark – Hitler's man in charge. From what Monica had observed the one time she had seen him addressing a gathering of Danish aristocrats, she had not especially trusted him. But later she learned that he had managed to divert orders from Germany to rid the country of its Jewish population by passing along that information and turning a blind eye as hundreds of Jews slipped away to the safety of Sweden.

"And how is Herr Doctor Best?" Monica sat on the side of her cot, her legs crossed, as she picked at a thread on her sleeve. The door to her cell had been left open, with a guard posted outside. It was a small gesture by those who daily escorted her to and from her cell for exercise – the Danish prison guards she knew had come to respect her.

Rostling knelt next to her so that she felt forced to face him. "Monica, he has the power to pardon you and has decided to do just that." His smile was triumphant. "You only need submit a petition for mercy and I am sure it will be granted."

"And what of the others?" Although she had heard rumors of prisoners being transferred to Ryvangen to face a firing squad, she had no confirmation that those sentenced with her had yet been shot. For one brief second, she allowed herself to hope she might have the power to help them as well as herself.

"Only you," Rostling replied.

Monica snapped the loose thread on her sleeve free and balled it between her thumb and forefinger.

"Monica?"

"What's the use then?" She stood and paced the cell. "Better to leave things as they are."

"But – " Rostling got to his feet.

She stopped pacing and looked directly at him. "I am tired and it is late, so if you wouldn't mind…" She glanced toward the cell door.

"Yes. I see," he muttered as he backed away from her, stopping in the open doorway. "Think about it, Monica."

"Thank you for coming." She followed him to the door, going so far as to step into the corridor. "Goodnight, Helmer," she said, turning away and waiting for the door to close, the key to turn, and the footsteps to retreat before letting the tears come.

Claire's frantic taps came within minutes of Rostling's departure. Of course, with the door left open, her friend in the next cell would have heard enough of what Rostling had said to be curious. The man had practically shouted the news. Monica sat on her cot and translated Claire's one-word message.

Why?

Too weary to answer in code, Monica tore a slip of paper and wrote out her reply, rolled it, and poked it through the slender hole.

Several minutes passed. She imagined Claire writing furiously, objecting to her disjointed response. *Not fair,* she had written, then added, *Others still will suffer. Why me?*

Grains of mortar toppled to the floor. She knelt and retrieved Claire's reply. Two words:

Yard tomorrow.

Claire was relentless. Earlier in her imprisonment, she had developed the habit of constantly muttering gibberish whenever a guard or person of authority was around. She had discovered it helped during interrogations, sometimes causing her examiners to give up and send her back to her cell. In the yard, she interspersed her ramblings with carefully placed comments on Hitler and his thugs – comments that clearly helped brighten the day for others near enough to overhear.

But on this morning, contrary to what others might have thought, Claire's mutterings were for Monica's ears only, and she was making perfect sense.

"Think of your family," was her opening.

"They will understand."

"And if they don't? Do you really want their last memory of you to be that they were angry and hurt by your selfishness?"

Monica bristled and quickened her step. She thought of the letter she had not yet given her friend, and wondered if Claire would be the right person to console her family.

Claire kept pace. "All right, that was harsh. But then what of Denmark? Do you not understand the work that will be needed once this horror is over? Do you not appreciate all you have to give toward that rebuilding? Do you not – "

"Enough!" Monica realized she'd uttered the response in a normal tone that caught the attention of other prisoners as well as the lone guard watching them. While inside the walls, they were watched over by Danish guards; here in the courtyard, their keeper was a German soldier. He straightened and readied his rifle, scanning the yard for the source of this outburst, cigarette dangling from his lips.

All was silent save for the shuffle of feet as the prisoners continued circling, heads down, fists clenched, steeling themselves for a random shot that might or might not come. To Monica's left, Claire was muttering gibberish, and every few seconds, she would raise her voice, shouting out some nonsensical word followed by a cackle of hysterical laughter, her eyes on the guard as his were on her.

After what seemed like minutes but was only seconds, he shook his head in a gesture that made clear his view that Claire was insane, lowered his rifle, and resumed his bored stance with his back and one foot braced against the prison wall as he drew on his cigarette.

"I will think about what you've said," Monica whispered. "Now stop talking before you get us both shot and this conversation is moot."

She did not miss the sliver of a satisfied smile Claire gave her as they continued their walk, shuffling along to the rhythm of her dear friend's mutterings.

Claire's accusation that Monica was being somehow selfish resonated. For two days – and long nights – she wrestled with that charge even though Claire had admitted it was harsh. Was Claire right? Would her family understand why she had refused to be singled out for reprieve? Was there work to be done once the war ended? And how much longer could it go on? The tide was turning. Rostling had told her this himself, and as a German, he would never make such a statement unless he believed it to be true – and verifiable.

If she could just hold on.

She reached for a sheet of paper, then decided against that in favor of the thin newsprint they were given as toilet paper. She scrawled a brief request for clemency that included her version of a defense, then signed her full name and the date. Rostling was due to visit later. She would give him the request to deliver to Dr. Best.

A week passed, then two. Finally, Rostling returned, bearing not only the letter announcing her reprieve from a death sentence to one of life imprisonment, but also a copy of an underground newspaper celebrating the news.

"It would appear your countrymen are beside themselves with relief," he told her. "There have even been articles applauding the decision in approved publications as well. It seems everyone is pleased."

"Well, perhaps, not everyone," she replied with a wry smile, thinking of her interrogator, the tribunal judges, and Hitler himself.

Still, it was good news. As Claire had reminded her on numerous occasions, life in prison did not mean exactly that. Once the war ended – and perhaps even before – the Allies would secure the release of those like her and her fellow prisoners. And once they were free, there was work to be done. She slept soundly that night.

The following morning she received the news that the three men given death sentences with her had been taken from their cells and executed.

She understood the cruel message being sent: you live; they die. *Quid pro quo.*

West Prison, Copenhagen – Summer 1944

Monica smoothed the original blanket that had been her only cover when she arrived months earlier. She had packed all her things and was fully dressed and groomed. She was waiting – had been waiting since midnight. The public clock on some building blocks away had just chimed five o'clock, although the sun had yet to find its way fully above the horizon.

Today was the day. She was to be taken across the border into Germany, where she would serve out her sentence in a German prison. It had not escaped her notice that even the usually loquacious Claire could find no words of encouragement to offer her. The excuse given was that there was no suitable prison for a woman in Denmark – ironic, since had she not been housed in just such a prison for the last several months? Even after Ivan had pleaded with the authorities – gone himself to see Dr. Best and pointed out her age – the answer had not changed. The Reich had shown Monica "great mercy" according to Best, implying she, as well as her family, had failed to show the slightest appreciation for that gift.

And once she was out of Denmark and in Germany? Removed from anyone who might advocate on her behalf? What then?

She glanced at the suitcase she had packed earlier. She supposed she should be grateful for the fact they had allowed her to have her own things – her own clothes, even the accessories. Her lighter and wristwatch, the single remaining precious comb Jorgen had given her all those years earlier. Rostling had brought her a small bottle of red nail polish, and she had done her nails the night before, asking the night guard to make sure Claire got the rest of the polish along with the letter she'd penned when she thought her fate would be death. None of her family had been allowed to visit, and since granting the reprieve, the Germans had moved quickly to have her transferred. She had been able to write to each of the children and Jorgen, and hoped her letters struck the right note of hope to ease their worries.

Hearing the outer door opening and the boot steps moving closer, she put on her hat and checked her image in the mirror of her enameled compact before turning to face the door. The warden – a German like the two soldiers with him – opened the door to her cell. "Monica Emily Wichfeld," he intoned in Danish as he read from an official looking document, "you are to come with us now for immediate transfer to the women's prison in Kiel, Germany."

She had traveled through Kiel on a trip to Berlin, but had never spent time there. She recalled it as a bustling seaport town on the shores of the Baltic. It was known for hosting the international sailing events that Jorgen and Heini had attended on occasion. She very much doubted she would have the opportunity to take in any of the town's culture or beauty on this journey. Picking up her pocketbook, she dropped the compact inside and snapped it closed. Then she drew in a breath and straightened to her full height before facing the warden. Their eyes met. He looked away and stepped aside to give her room to pass. As she did, she saw him gesture to one of the soldiers, who took her suitcase and followed her down the corridor, past cells that had been empty when she'd first arrived but now were filled with people like her – men as well as women who had tried to do what they could. A supportive chorus of tin cups banging against the metal doors provided a percussive escort.

She hesitated only once on her way to yet another canvas-covered truck waiting at the end of the long tunnel. It was when the warden handed her a folded piece of paper that, when she opened it, revealed a hastily scribbled message of farewell from Claire.

"Tak," she said, her voice shaking as her eyes met those of her jailer. He could as easily have refused to deliver the message. Clutching the note from her friend, she turned and walked to the truck. As the young soldier helped her climb aboard, he murmured, "You should understand that you are much admired, Frau Wichfeld." She glanced at him, expecting to see one of her Danish guards. The young man wore a German uniform and snapped to attention so quickly she wondered if she had only imagined his comment.

A moment later two guards escorted Pia Baastrup-Thomsen and Greta Jensen, a young woman Monica had met in the yard, to the truck, and they climbed aboard, smiling as they clasped hands with Monica. Their reunion was short-lived, as a half dozen heavily armed Germans clamored aboard, pushing the women toward the cab of the truck before taking their positions at the opening. In addition, Monica heard the rev of motorcycles coming alongside the vehicle.

"So, we are to have an official escort," she remarked to her companions. "Lovely."

The truck jolted forward, and all three women grabbed for something to hold onto. Apparently their journey – at least through the streets of Copenhagen – was to be a sprint rather than a stroll. Monica thought of the day she and Jorgen had walked in London's Hyde Park – the day she had teased him about the pace he'd set. The day he had proposed.

A lifetime ago.

As they cleared the gates of West Prison, Monica saw the guard, Heinz, touch two fingers to his uniform cap in a salute. She had thought of leaving a note for him, thanking him for his many kindnesses, but then realized such a note could do him more harm than good. She moved as close to the opening as possible, hoping he might see her.

One of the German soldiers shoved her back, while his companions refocused their attention on the passing scenery, nervously fingering their weapons.

"They expect an ambush from the Resistance," Pia whispered.

"*Nicht sprechen!*" the soldier who seemed to be in charge bellowed as he raised the butt of his rifle threateningly.

Pia shrank back. Monica grasped her friend's hand and held tight, her eyes locked on those of the soldier. He muttered something foul and turned away.

As they left the city, Monica saw the more familiar landscape of woods and fields and deserted roads. Small tenant farms with livestock grazing in the fields that stretched toward the main road, their neat thatched-roof cottages in the background. What lay beyond those idyllic scenes were more stately homes like Engestofte. The truck rumbled past a field of poppies, and she thought of her husband and hoped he was finding solace in his beloved gardens. She closed her eyes to block out the sheer beauty of her surroundings. At least for the foreseeable future, beauty would no longer be part of her world.

The convoy turned onto the highway that ran for miles along the seashore, and she thought of the days – those carefree days – when she and Kurt had raced their cars along this straight section of road. He in his yellow Hudson, his handsome face intent on winning. She in the white convertible Jorgen had bought for her, its top down and her hair free of its bonds, being whipped playfully about her face by the wind. She would grip the steering wheel and press the accelerator all the way to the floor, waving as she passed Kurt.

Kurt, who had turned out to be such a disappointment in the choice he'd made to sit the war out in America – and yet, she had loved him.

When she felt something land in her lap, Monica's eyes shot open. The soldier was back, doling out food and cigarettes to the three of them. The other soldiers had relaxed, and were now seated on the side benches, their weapons at their sides, as they feasted on bread, cheese, and sausage.

"You should eat and smoke," the commander said. "There will be no smoking once we reach our destination."

Will there be food?

Monica decided not to ask. Instead she smiled up at the soldier. "*Danke*," she murmured and helped herself to a chunk of rye bread. "Is there water?" While she had spoken only Danish or English to him up to this moment, she decided perhaps she might gain more information if she switched to German.

His eyes widened with something she hoped was not just surprise, but also respect.

"*Wasser*," he bellowed, and one of his men hurried to pass him a thermos. He took a long swallow, then handed the container to Monica without bothering to wipe the opening.

She saw that he expected she would refuse to drink after him, or that at the very least, she would wipe away his saliva. By its weight, she judged the thermos was still more than half full, and she did not hesitate before taking a long swallow. Wiping the opening with her handkerchief, she passed the water on to Pia and smiled at the soldier. "I don't suppose there's a chance of some vodka?"

He laughed and his men laughed, and when they did, Monica saw them for the true men they were – farmhands or perhaps shopkeepers, not soldiers. Monica realized she was probably twice their age or more. To her, they were boys playing with grown-up weapons in a war they probably didn't understand, but could do nothing about. Boys who, when this was all over, would have what kind of future?

"You are old," their leader said bluntly.

She did not consider forty-nine old, but understood to these young men, she must seem ancient. "And you are wondering how an old lady got herself in a situation like this," she replied as she lit the first of what she had decided would be a chain of cigarettes until they were taken from her. She blew out the smoke slowly, savoring the taste of the tobacco. "I might ask each of you the same."

"We serve the Führer," the one in charge said, stopping short of the one-armed salute.

But behind him Monica saw the wistful and exhausted faces of the others. What did they know of cattle cars filled with humans, and concentration camps, and property pillaged and redistributed?

Her sympathy was short-lived. After all, she reminded herself, two of her children had stood against the regime – Viggo barely escaping a prison sentence, and Varinka in great danger even now. No, in times like these everyone had a choice – and a responsibility to understand who they were electing to follow regardless of their age. She glanced at Pia and Greta. Both, like her, had chosen to hide British paratroopers, distribute information, and take part in other Resistance activities at great risk to themselves and their families. It occurred to her that no one ever questioned a man abandoning his family to fight for freedom and justice, and yet a woman was judged.

Monica once again turned her attention to the scene outside. They were coming to the bridge that led into Falster. The truck slowed, and immediately the soldiers assumed their positions, weapons poised, faces stern. There was a flurry of shouted conversation before the truck started forward again and made a turn.

"What's happening?" Greta asked nervously. "Are we turning back?"

Both women looked to Monica for an explanation. She would not tell them what she feared most – that they were not going to Germany at all, but rather at some point, the truck would be diverted to a backroad and after awhile would stop, and they would be ordered out and told to run. And then they would be shot as prisoners trying to escape. It would not be the first time the Germans had disposed of captives in this way. By some reports there were mass graves across Germany and Poland holding dozens and sometimes hundreds of so-called escapees. Through her work with Muus and others, she had even heard of cases where the condemned were made to dig the grave themselves.

She signaled Pia and Greta to be quiet so she could hear what the soldiers were saying. After a moment, the lead soldier turned to them. "A convoy blocking the way," he said. "We must take a different route."

Could they trust anything he told them?

Her pulse racing, she leaned forward for a better view of their change in direction. She saw the other stalled convoy, but was still suspicious. After several minutes of woods to either side of them with no sign that the truck was about to slow, Monica let out a breath, then gasped again – this time with pleasure. They were within sight of the lake – her lake. And as the truck made a turn, Kurt's farmhouse came into view, with his family's fairy-tale castle visible in the distance. Of course, she realized she was peering out at these landmarks of a far happier time in her life through the grit of a military transport on its way to deliver its cargo to a prison in Germany.

Oh, the things in life we take for granted.

Once the convoy reached the ferry that would take them from Denmark to Germany, the journey took on a more ominous ambiance. The crossing brought back more memories – of the night they had left Italy and the kindness of the captain as well as a meal that included all the things they'd been unable to obtain as they made their way to meet the ferry. Now, standing at the railing as the vessel approached the dock, Monica saw that since that night, the German town of Warnemunde had been even more heavily bombed. While she thought of the tavernkeeper and his wife who had sheltered them and hoped they were safe, Monica could not help taking some satisfaction from the devastation.

After docking, they were marched to the train station, where she saw a dozen or more other women waiting. The guards took control of a third-class cabin, forcing passengers already there to find other accommodation and ordering the women to board. Monica took a seat next to one of the windows. The bench was hard wood and backless, but she was glad to see the windows had been recently cleaned and offered a clear view of the German landscape. It was midafternoon when the train pulled out of the station, and they'd been told the prison in Kiel was only a couple hours away.

"You'll be there in time for supper," one of the guards had said, and then he'd laughed.

Monica took that to mean there would be no supper for them, and thought more kindly of the soldiers who had shared their food and cigarettes on the military truck.

The train inched along, once again having to move to a side track to allow others filled with troops to pass. Twice they were delayed while the crew inspected tracks that had been damaged and hastily repaired. After hours of delay and no food, she could just make out the outline of Kiel's buildings when suddenly the train pulled to a stop in a field that was mostly marshland as air-raid sirens wailed. Monica and the others huddled together on the floor, hoping the heavy benches might protect them from flying glass should the bombs strike.

Finally the all clear sounded, and those passengers who had left their more comfortable accommodations seeking shelter in a ditch or just moving away from the tracks – a natural target – scrambled to reboard. It was after midnight when they finally pulled into the Kiel Anhalter Bahnhof. Monica had been there before, but on this night she exited the train and looked up to see the impressive domed roof she had admired on previous visits had been reduced to a skeletal web of girders.

Carrying their luggage, the three women marched with the other prisoners from the station to the prison under the constant harassment of the soldiers surrounding them. Outside the prison gates they were received by the head matron, who made no secret of her disdain for these new arrivals. In a stream of rapid German, she let them know they had kept her waiting, as if the air raid had been something they had orchestrated to inconvenience her. She separated them immediately, locking each woman in a small separate cell. Monica looked back once to signal her younger companions to maintain their strength, but they had already been led away.

The cell was even more spartan than the one she'd occupied in West Prison – half the size, with whitewashed walls, a narrow bunk attached to the wall, and a cracked white china pot with a lid that Monica assumed was the toilet. She had been awake for over twenty-four hours by this time. All she could manage was to lie down with no concern for what vermin might have taken up residence in the mattress. But sleep was short-lived. Sometime before dawn, she was awakened by a sullen female guard and given a tin cup of coffee made from beets along with a thin slice of stale rye bread. She closed her eyes and chewed the tough bread, trying hard to ignore the shot of pain that coursed through her mouth. She could no longer ignore the tooth she'd been dealing with since she'd lost a temporary filling earlier that spring. It was getting worse, a constant throbbing in her mouth, salved only by her tongue anchored to fill the hole or the warmth of any hot liquid – always in short supply.

The bad tooth was but one sign of her struggle to maintain her energy and physical strength. The long hours without sleep, the lack of anything approaching proper nutrition, were beginning to take their toll. She had to face facts. She could no longer count on the vibrancy of her youth. And depending on how long the war continued, she might not see it to the end – might not ever return to her beloved family and home again. She swallowed the wad of self-pity filling her throat and stood. She would do her best. If nothing else she would be, as she had always tried to be, an example for the others. She would not allow these horrid Nazis to defeat her. If she died before the end came, then at the very least she would leave behind a legacy of strong-willed, spirited women who would stand and fight for freedom and justice wherever the call came.

Along with Pia, Greta, and the other new prisoners, she crossed the courtyard in predawn darkness to a room where they were ordered to strip and watch as their clothing was inventoried, packed, and taken away. They were then issued wooden clogs, gray woolen stockings, bloomers with an opening at the rear, and a black sack-like dress with the yellow armband that indicated their status as political prisoners.

Monica accepted the paper receipt she was handed, knowing it was worthless, and was glad she'd had the foresight to secrete three of the cigarettes the soldier on the truck had given them, plus matches and a small bar of chocolate, in the container meant to be used as her toilet. While she guessed guards were removing any personal items from their cells while they were receiving their new wardrobes, she very much doubted any of them would drag the bowl from under the cot to inspect it. Once they were dressed, she and the others were given menial tasks to perform – scrubbing floors, cleaning toilets.

"Allow me to show you how this is done," she teased Greta as they worked their way down a row of cracked and chipped urinals half filled with rusty water. "I was quite the expert back in the first war when I worked in a London canteen." She made a show of holding her nose and turning her head away as she swabbed the bowl, and was relieved to see Greta smile. The girl was so very young – both she and Pia. Monica felt a maternal stirring and was heartened when that evening they were told they would need to share a single cell because the prison was filling up. Two mattresses had been added to Monica's already cramped space. Pia and Greta insisted Monica take the cot, and once all went quiet on the other side of their cell door, Monica produced her bounty.

"How did you – "

"Where did you – "

She took such solace in her young companions' excitement. Their youth and vitality would sustain her, and in return, she would do whatever she could to keep their spirits raised and hope alive.

To her surprise, they were summoned once again just over a week after arriving at the Kiel prison. There had been rumors they would be transferred, but Monica was surprised when their clothes were returned along with a toothbrush, comb, and small piece of soap. With true German efficiency, they had to sign for each item. Monica waited in the line for her turn, clutching her bundle of clothing.

A middle-aged male guard seated at the desk reached over and thumbed through her bundle, then thrust a paper toward her. "*Hier unterschreiben*," he said, and as Monica bent to sign, he added in a soft undertone, "The attack on Europe has begun – the Allies came on land in the north of France yesterday."

Monica could hardly believe what she was hearing. She looked up at the guard, but he took the signed document and turned away, motioning the next person to step forward. She was not delusional, and she was fluent in German. She had heard him correctly. This was the best possible news. This meant the war was finally – after five years – moving into its final stages. This meant they might all make it home by year's end. She bit her lip to hide her smile.

That night, just after they had settled into what passed for sleep, the guards rousted them from their cells and ordered them into the yard.

The Allies? Impossible they could have advanced this far so quickly.

There was no time to gather the personal belongings they'd been given earlier. Without explanation the guards marched them from the prison to the Kiel railway station, where chaos reigned. Surrounded by the devastation inflicted over the past several weeks by Allied bombers, entire platoons of German soldiers in full combat garb crowded the platform and, as each train rolled into the station, pushed their way aboard. Regular passengers – those not dressed in the uniform of soldier or prisoner – stood in small groups, peering up and down the tracks as trains came and went, and hours passed. The guards grew increasingly annoyed, but Monica enjoyed the warm clear night, gazing up at the stars. She thought of her brother Jack as she focused on the sliver of a new moon that forecast yet another change in her life's journey.

The Allies have landed, Jack. They may still be miles away, but they are here – on the continent.

A train pulled away, and for a time, the platform was quieter. Murmured conversations, rumors then confirmation they were headed for Hamburg, skittered from prisoner to prisoner. Then in the distance she heard the unmistakable cadence of marching feet and singing. Monica could not help but hum along to the familiar melody made popular by the German actress Marlene Dietrich. As the soldiers came closer, Monica and her companions joined in singing the second verse of the wartime love ballad as popular with the Allies as it was here in Dietrich's native land:

When we are marching in the mud and cold,
And when my pack seems more than I can hold,
My love for you renews my might.
I'm warm again, my pack is light,
It's you, Lilli Marlene, it's you, Lilli Marlene.

As they trooped past, Monica no longer saw German soldiers. She closed her eyes and imagined row after row of British and American infantrymen making their way across Europe, setting the world to rights again.

Finally, a train whistle sounded and the transport for Hamburg arrived. Their guards hustled them past boarding passengers to a special car at the back of the train outfitted with cages. Each featured a wooden bench that would seat two.

"We three will stay together," Monica told the guard. "We can make do."

The guard smirked. "You will make do all right," he muttered as she along with Pia and Greta were shoved into a cage already occupied by two others – two women who had laid claim to the bench. He slammed the door, leaving them with no choice but to stand pressed against one another.

In the dim light cast by a single bulb above the door leading to the next car, Monica noticed writing on the walls of their cell. Leaning in closer, she made out names and dates, sometimes a country or message for those who came after. Using the stub of a pencil she'd found and secreted in the pocket of her prison uniform days earlier, Monica scribbled a note of hope in Danish, then signed and dated it. Pia and Greta did the same, while the two strangers eagerly waited their turn. Their bond formed, the five women alternated sitting and then standing as the train rolled on.

As had become usual, the trip to Hamburg took three times as long as it would have in normal times, and when they arrived, it was already midmorning. The summer day was clear and warm, and a blue sky dotted with marshmallow clouds was in direct conflict with the ruins of the city. The guards hustled them to a transport for the ride to the prison – a ride that took them through a wasteland of half-fallen mansions, blocks of closed shops with shattered windows, and churches with decapitated spires. The streets were mostly deserted, but the few people out looked haggard and exhausted, and they hurried along as if being chased, their mouths drawn into hard, thin lines, their eyes lifeless.

Accommodations at the Hamburg jail were a considerable step above what they'd known in Kiel. Running cold water, a lavatory, and enough space to move around, but their reprieve was short-lived, as just a few days later they once again boarded a train – this time one headed for Hanover. Monica realized they were moving ever deeper into Germany, heading east – toward Russia. And with each clack of metal wheels on metal tracks, Monica realized they had traveled hundreds of miles from home.

Perhaps it would not be the Americans and Brits who would save them, but the Russians. She thought of Jorgen's grandmother – the beautiful Varinka – of the legacy of light and beauty she had instilled in Engestofte. The truth was Monica hardly cared what nationality their saviors might claim, as long as they came soon.

Three weeks after leaving Copenhagen – with stays at two German prisons along the way – they finally arrived at Cottbus Prison, a hundred miles northeast of Dresden.

"*Willkommen zu Hause, meine Damen,*" the prison matron announced sarcastically as she ushered Monica, Pia, and Greta into their cell. Blessedly the three of them would be together in a space furnished with a stacked bunk bed plus one other that could be folded against the wall. They had a scarred, rectangular wooden table and two benches, as well as the now-familiar chamber pot. The table, they were told, was their work station where they would perform whatever piecework deemed most necessary for the brave soldiers of the Reich.

That night Monica lay awake long after her cellmates had fallen asleep, nursing her tooth by biting down on a piece of fabric she had wadded into a ball. She passed the time by recalling a sunny day in Rapallo when she, Jorgen, the children, and her mother had been lounging on the terrace of Alice's villa. They had been blissfully unaware of what lay ahead for any of them, but Varinka had raised a question.

"What would you say is the purpose and meaning of life?"

Ivan and Viggo had rolled their eyes, dismissing their sister's penchant for raising such philosophical discussions. But Monica recalled having given her daughter's query serious consideration, perhaps because, over the course of her life, it was one she had pondered often. On that occasion she remembered saying that for her, life was a bit like being onstage and getting caught unaware in the spotlight. "Your entire life might have been but a rehearsal for this one brief moment in the spotlight," she had told her children that day.

She had thought she was giving her children advice for their futures. Little had she known her moment would come that January morning when the Gestapo agents invaded their home and arrested her. From that moment to this, like it or not, a spotlight had followed her every move. Even now, she stood out, for certainly her age was a factor that made her fellow prisoners, as well as the guards, regard her with curiosity. Lulled by the steady breathing of her cellmates and trying to swallow the coughing that was a byproduct of the virus she had developed over the course of their travels, she considered her latest circumstances.

There was no question of escape, for the prison was a labyrinth of thick-walled and multistoried brick buildings with barred windows. Wire fencing capped with coiled barbed wire and anchored by guard towers where armed guards kept watch, their automatic rifles always at the ready, completed the compound. Inside, the place was a maze of stairways and heavy iron gates. Mostly political prisoners, all had been sentenced to hard labor or to serve out their days working in the various prison factories turning out goods to support the Reich. On top of that, eventually winter would set in, and besides the monotony and the inadequate food, they would have to deal with the cold.

But if the Allies were now on the march from both east and west, how long before the prison gates swung open and they would be free to return to their families? It was nice to dream, but Monica had already noticed signs of fatigue and depression among her cellmates. If she could just find a way they might continue to feel useful and keep their spirits up while they waited for release.

The answer came the next day. The Wachmeisterin set them to work unraveling the knots in literally miles of twine that had been used in the fields baling hay, then rewinding it so it could be used again. It was Pia who came up with the idea that maybe not every single knot needed to be untied.

"Oh, but we must take great care. If we miss one or two, that might cause the harvesting equipment to break down," Monica said with mock concern.

Greta and Pia looked up, and when Monica winked, they giggled with delight and bent to their work with renewed vigor.

To cut through the monotony of hours spent unraveling tiny knots, Monica came up with the idea of a sort of prison university, with Monica teaching the younger women history and languages and geography. Her ability to speak several languages fluently gained her widespread respect.

It seemed that every day more prisoners had been crowded into the wing of the prison reserved for women. Well into the night they heard a chorus of languages from French to Polish to Dutch. There were even German prisoners, sentenced for anti-Nazi crimes. Groups were placed in cell blocks by nationality. And while Cottbus also housed male prisoners, the two genders were kept separated, rarely even catching sight of each other, except on those rare occasions when the female prisoners were allowed to use the exercise yard, and the males serenaded them with whistles and shouted invitations from their cell windows.

The women were managed by a squadron of blonde, blue-eyed, hefty women who took their orders from the prison's Direktorin, a woman not much younger than Monica named Gertrude Schaubel. Monica eyed her with suspicion. For, despite the times Monica had observed the woman hugging her husband and children at the gate that led to their private home on the prison grounds, there was an underlying vindictiveness in the air of vanity she presented when going about her job. The prisoners learned soon after arriving that Frau Sauchel was capable of unspeakable cruelty when defied or disobeyed – even if such an infraction were only in her mind. She and her squadron of wardresses had sworn their allegiance to their Führer and saw no reason to show empathy to even the most dire cases of suffering among those they clearly deemed the enemy.

Monica found their blind loyalty frustrating. Did they not see that the culture they had embraced viewed them as second-class citizens whose primary function was to birth children who would populate the ranks of the so-called "master race"? These were mothers and daughters – women who would surely be horrified if their children were imprisoned. She simply did not understand how they could be so unmoved by the sheer numbers of dead and dying.

Why do they not question? After nearly five years, why do they not see?

The days and weeks passed. Monica was determined to lift her own spirits by keeping her cellmates, and the other women who crowded into their cell to complete the daily work, looking forward, preparing for the future they would have once they were free. As possibly the oldest woman in the prison, she assumed a maternal role, nurturing her younger companions in any way she could. When they were given the new task of weaving corn leaves into mats, which she assumed were meant for sleeping on in the fields, Monica collected the scraps and at night plaited them into gifts – slippers and belts for their guards. The activity helped her deal with the withdrawal she was experiencing from having no access to cigarettes after a lifetime of smoking several packs a day. The guards repaid her by allowing her to see the prison dentist, who pulled the abscessed tooth and gave her a tonic for her persistent cough.

In mid-August two new prisoners were added to their cell. Maria Boucher and her sister had been transferred to Cottbus from a prison in Halle where they had managed to see a newspaper and speak to Allied prisoners. They brought news of the Allied advances through France, to the West, and to the Vistula River on the Russian-Polish border, to the East. That night Monica used a chunk of mortar she found on the floor to scratch out from memory a map of the region. She wanted to show the others how close they were to liberation. Of course, they had no way of knowing how fast the Allied troops would progress. Each morning they were roused before sunup to choke down their meager rations, stand at attention for roll call, sometimes for an hour or more, and then rush to their posts to meet the daily quota of work they'd been assigned. Frau Sauchel took a good deal of pride in having decided to have them work in their cells. No reason to waste time having them move to and from some other place. They kept track of the passing days by marking them off on a calendar they had scratched into a corner of the floor.

One night in late August, while the others were already sleeping, Monica took her usual position near the window, where she could catch a bit of air. She was just dozing off when she was startled by sounds of a commotion. From across the compound she heard the unmistakable sounds of voices raised in cheers, followed by singing. In the courtyard, guards were racing around as if trying to figure out what to do, while inside the prison, the word spread like wildfire from one cell to the next. Paris had been liberated and the Germans were on the run. Monica could hardly believe it.

She imagined Jorgen hearing the news. Varinka, by now surely married to Flemming and safely in hiding in Sweden, must be beside herself with relief and joy. Ivan and Viggo could truly move forward with their lives. She woke her cellmates and laughed at their sleepy disbelief, even as she urged them closer to the window, where strains of "La Marseillaise" echoed from building to building. Beside themselves with joy, the five women clasped hands and danced in a circle as they joined in the singing.

They had made it this far – they would hold on until they, like Paris, could be liberated.

Cottbus Prison – Autumn 1944

Their jubilation was short-lived.

Two days later, Frau Schaubel and her counterpart in the men's prison rounded up all the French prisoners, as well as Maria and her sister, and shipped them off to the Ravensbruck concentration camp – a detail the director seemed to take a great deal of delight in announcing. Everyone knew that it was retribution for the audacity of the French prisoners to celebrate the Allied entry into Paris. Everyone knew conditions at Ravensbruck were far worse than those at Cottbus.

As air raids came nearly every day, approaching ever closer to the prison walls, the guards were issued special uniforms and helmets and stationed near the fire escapes, presumably to stop prisoners from escaping should a blast from a bomb blow open cell doors. Trying to ease fears, Monica made a game of the air raids, having her cellmates rate the presumed level of destruction as they heard the bombs hit.

September became October, with every day the same. In November, two new prisoners joined them – both Danish. Tulle Fiil and Alice Bergman-Jensen had both been in Denmark during the national uprising that had occurred in June, and Monica eagerly questioned them to learn the details.

"You'll be pleased to know that since the Allied invasion at Normandy, all executions have ceased," Alice said.

"The Germans are scrambling to shore up support wherever they can," Tulle added.

Their news lifted Monica's spirits and gave her the energy to keep moving forward, day after day, despite her deteriorating health. Yes, her cough was much worse, her breathing more difficult, and her hair had gotten so brittle and thin, she could no longer manage to arrange it properly. Still, she might just be able to see this through. She might just be able to return to Jorgen and their home. She might just live long enough to see that everything she had done and given – insignificant as it might be in the larger scheme of things – had not been in vain.

I shall do more once the war ends.

But as the cold air of winter found its way through the walls and floors of cell number twelve, Monica could no longer pretend that her health was not declining. She had used up the tonic, and her cough was even more persistent. Aside from her physical health, it was becoming increasingly difficult to maintain her emotional well-being. In the nearly six months since she had left Copenhagen, she had received only a single piece of mail – Viggo's scrawled words on the back of a Red Cross postcard assuring her all was well.

And then in early December she received a visit from a Red Cross representative and was presented with letters from Jorgen and Ivan, as well as two thick parcels containing woolen stockings, a handknit scarf, toiletries that included small bars of scented soap – and cigarettes.

"It's like Christmas morning," she exclaimed to the Red Cross worker, and before the guards could discover and confiscate her treasures, she buried the loot in the piles of corn stalks that filled the cell, knowing if the guards searched the cell, they would be unlikely to rifle through those. Besides, with the threat of the

Allies on the march, the guards had other things to worry about. As she flattened and folded even the wrappings that had covered her loot, she had an idea. She would do whatever she could to give her cellmates a proper Danish Christmas.

A week before Christmas, she saw her chance. One morning two guards escorted all four of her younger cellmates to a factory making gas masks. When Monica protested staying behind, they told her she was too old for the work and should continue plaiting corn stalks into mats. As soon as they were gone, she set to work, first thoroughly cleaning the cell, doing her best to freshen everything. Later in the afternoon, she moved the wooden work table to the center of the room and, taking several of the white flour sacks her family had used to pad the goods in the parcels they'd sent, fashioned a covering for the table. Then she took a few twigs of evergreen she'd found during her exercise period and arranged them on the table.

In addition to the few pinecones still nestled among the needled twigs, she tore the foil wrappers from the cigarette packages and the red paper that had lined the bottom of the boxes she'd received to create stars to add to the decoration. Food was another issue altogether. Her younger friends spent much of their time talking about what they would eat once the prison was liberated. They spoke lovingly of favorite bakeries and cafes in Copenhagen, naming the items they would order as if reading off the menu. Monica wanted this party to be special, and that meant having more than the usual stale bread and ersatz coffee they were commonly served.

Occasionally they were given a small chunk of hard cheese, and Monica had saved her last three helpings, wrapping them in a handkerchief and slipping that under her mattress. But she so wanted to give them more.

From the corridor she heard the squeal of a serving cart passing, rushed to the cell door, and peered through the slit.

Frieda.

She smiled. The guard had been charged with the daily task of collecting produce from the root cellar. Not that the prisoners would ever see any of it. These vegetables were for the staff. The prisoners might get a taste of the scraps in the watery broth they were given when they woke each morning. The important thing was that Frieda was someone Monica could bribe. She'd done it before, trading a pair of corn leaf slippers for a small bottle of paregoric to keep her abscessed gums from throbbing quite so badly. She pulled a cigarette from the pack and slid it halfway through the slit.

"*Ich habe Zigaretten*, Frieda," she said in a low voice.

The cart stopped and the corridor went still. She could hear Frieda breathing, her face close to the door, her fingers reaching for the precious cigarette Monica held out to her and then snatched away.

Frieda let out a weary sigh. "*Wie viel?*"

"I'll trade you six for six pieces of produce from your cart."

She did not expect the deal to be accepted. After all, it was known throughout the prison that even supplies for the guards were running low. But as children, whenever they wanted something from their parents, Jack had always advised, "Shoot for the moon and perhaps you'll land a star." Four pieces of produce would be a major victory.

The key turned in the lock.

"Show me the six," Frieda hissed.

Monica fanned out the precious goods like a poker hand. "Show me the produce," she retorted.

Frieda selected a small onion, two stunted carrots, a beet, and two small potatoes, lining them up for Monica to approve. It was a veritable feast, given what they had subsisted on for months now. She passed Frieda the cigarettes and collected her bounty. "*Danke*," she whispered as Frieda closed the cell door and locked it.

Monica spread the meager assortment out on the table and stood back to look at it. "A Danish smorgasbord," she said aloud and clapped her hands.

Now for the gifts.

It was dark by the time Monica heard the others return. Their slow shuffling footsteps and the lack of their usual chattiness told her how exhausted they were. Their suppers had been delivered hours earlier, and if there had been any warmth to the food, it was long past. Monica had divided the cheese she'd saved and placed a slice on each piece of tasteless rye bread. She'd used the outer brown-paper wrapping and twine from the parcels she'd received to wrap the gifts she'd made for each of them since first coming up with the idea of a party. At the center of each bow, she'd tied one of the precious cigarettes and placed the gifts around the tree twigs.

She heard the key in the lock and waited for the door to open, knowing the guard would be eager to be on her way back to somewhere warm. As always the cell was frigid – a fact that seemed to bother the others a great deal less than it bothered Monica. Greta, Alice, Tulle, and Pia stumbled in, so weary they could barely stand. It took a moment before they noticed the table.

"What's all this?" Pia asked, her lovely blue eyes widening with surprise.

"I've no idea," Monica replied from where she sat plaiting corn stalks. "I've been here all day working, and when I looked up, here it all was. I suppose we may as well enjoy. I mean, it is almost Christmas." She set aside the work, and gave them a wink.

All four young women squealed with delight and took turns giving Monica hugs.

"Wait," Tulle announced. "We must prepare."

"Prepare how?" Greta scowled. "It would appear Monica or her elves have done everything."

"No. We must clean ourselves up – at least comb our hair and do what we can to look our best. We would not go to a party the way we look now, would we?"

Monica watched as her friends collected snow that had blown in through the gaps in the high windows. They used it, along with the precious soap Monica had received in her parcels and shared with them right away, to wash themselves. They took turns brushing each other's hair while telling stories of their own family celebrations. And once they were ready, they gathered around the table, giving Monica the honor of doling out their meager feast while they sat cross-legged on mats each had made before being reassigned to the factory.

Even savoring the food, it did not take long for them to finish. Monica stretched her hands out to Pia and Greta to either side of her, and they completed the circle, holding hands with Alice and Tulle. Monica hummed the tune to the treasured Danish carol "Glade Jul," and the others joined in. Then, in a sweet soprano as fresh as the cold December air threading its way through the window cracks and gaps in the walls and floor, Greta sang the verse in her native Danish.

Glade jul, dejlige jul,
engle daler ned i skjul!
Hid de flyver med paradis grønt,
hvor de ser, hvad for Gud er kønt,
lønlig iblandt os de gaar
lønlig iblandt os de gaar.

They all joined in, trying to recall a second verse, and surrendering to humming the melody. Then Monica sang the words in her native English, tears filling her eyes as she thought of holidays shared with her family in Ireland and later at Engestofte.

Happy Christmas, lovely Christmas,
angels slowly fall into hiding!
They fly here with that which is paradise green
where they see what is pretty to God
they walk among us in secret
they walk among us in secret!

Her voice died away, and silence filled the spartan cell, each of them lost in memories of other times. Not wanting the evening to end on such a somber note, Monica stood and clapped her hands. "There seem to be gifts," she announced as she handed out the packages. She watched with delight as each of her friends tried to guess what might be inside.

"Wait!" Tulle held up her hand, and the others rolled their eyes. Tulle was well known for wanting to do things a certain way – her way. "We should take turns so we can all appreciate each gift. After all, Monica – I mean, the elves – went to a great deal of trouble for us. I'll go first." She carefully plucked the cigarette from the bow and held it up. "A priceless treasure!"

"I have one as well," Alice noted.

"We all do," Pia said with a sigh. "So dear Tulle, please do not tell us we must smoke them individually so we can 'appreciate' them?"

Monica collected the cigarettes and laid them in a line on the table. "I thought perhaps once lights are out…"

"Yes," Greta agreed. "After lights out, so we can enjoy the glow of each in the dark."

With that bit of business decided, they all turned their attention back to Tulle. She smoothed back the wrapping on her gift to reveal a pair of woven corn-husk slippers and a tiny tube of MacLean's toothpaste.

"I'm all set head to toe," she crowed with delight as she kicked aside her hated ill-fitting wooden clogs and stuffed her toes slowly into the slippers. "Heaven," she proclaimed, and they all laughed.

Greta and Alice took the next turns, opening their parcels to discover necklaces Monica had fashioned from saved dried kernels of corn and the silks of the occasional cob. It had taken her most of the afternoon to make them. Poking holes in the kernels came far easier than threading each kernel onto the silks. Even though the day had been sunny, she had to admit her eyesight was not what it once had been.

"Well, clearly you haven't lost your touch as a designer of fine jewelry," Greta said as she helped Alice try hers on, and then turned so Alice could do the same for her. They linked arms and posed as if they were Parisian fashion models.

"There's more," Tulle exclaimed as she held up a miniature deck of playing cards hidden in the folds of the wrapping in Alice's package.

Greta hurried to check her discarded paper and squealed when she found a length of ribbon for her hair.

"I'm next," Pia said as she untied the string on her gift to reveal a small basket – one that would easily fit in the pocket of her prison dress. She lifted the lid.

"It's empty," Tulle announced for benefit of all.

"A place to hold all those dreams you have for after," Monica told Pia.

"It's perfect," Pia whispered, her voice hoarse with emotion. "*Mange tak*, Monica."

The others chorused their thanks, giving Monica hugs. She blushed at their effusive praise, even as she savored the thrill of having made them so happy.

Moments later, cell twelve went dark as the main switch was thrown, and only the searchlights outside swept across the room. They quickly cleared away all evidence of their celebration, took turns using the chamber pot and preparing for bed, then stood in a huddle as Monica lit their cigarettes for them.

"Goodnight, my friends," she said as each woman lay on her cot, the glow of her cigarette like a candle on a proper Christmas tree. They smoked in silence. One after another the embers died, and the scent of tobacco faded.

Monica thought she must be dreaming, because at first, she could not believe the sounds of singing wafting over the compound could be real. But when she roused herself, she realized what she was hearing was no dream. From every part of the prison came the beautiful strains of *Silent Night*, sung in the languages of the inmates – Dutch, Norwegian, Russian, Polish, and even German. The last word lingered in the air and, Monica had to believe, in the minds and hearts of all who heard it.

Peace.

Let it be so, she silently prayed and understood that, although she had convinced herself – and others – that she would die with no regrets, it was difficult not to hope for one more Christmas with her beloved family.

March to Waldheim – Winter 1945

Snow filled the courtyard and thick icicles lined the ledges outside
the barred windows of the prison. Pia reported there seemed to
be fewer guards around, and the meals they had thought sparse
before sometimes never arrived at all. Nightly they heard the
distant rumble of airplanes and explosions of bombs. As January
waned, the sounds of heavy gunfire told them the Russians were
coming ever closer. Inside the compound there were signs of panic.

One morning as the women stood in the cold for roll call waiting for Frau Sauchel, Monica saw a canvas-covered truck parked
outside the Sauchel home. Several men hurried back and forth,
loading furniture onto the truck, and she saw the warden hustle
her children into a car that drove away as soon as the doors closed.
Frau Sauchel stood a moment looking after the departing car, her
hands at her side, her body stiff, before she pivoted and marched
down to the compound, where the prisoners stood shivering in
their thin cotton uniforms while the guards walked among them,
snapping at any perceived infraction of the warden's protocol.
This prisoner was not standing up straight; that one was coughing
too much; and Gretae was declared guilty of looking at the guard
with insolence and made to kneel in the snow.

Monica stood next to Pia, who seemed about to intercede, but
Monica brushed her friend's hand in warning, and thankfully, Pia
understood. Monica was so cold she could not feel her fingers or
toes. She briefly wondered if she might lose them to frostbite, and
to keep from giving in to the desire to simply sink to the ground,

she turned her thoughts to what tasks might be affected. Putting on lipstick and arranging her hair would certainly be a trial. Of course, that assumed her hair, which was so thin it barely covered her scalp, revived.

"This one," she heard someone say, and she looked up to see Frau Sauchel standing in front of her. "She will take her place in the factory with the others." Her lips twisted upward into what passed for a smile. "Unless, of course, Frau Wichfeld is too old to do the work, in which case..."

Monica's chest felt as if the cold had lodged there, an iceberg filling her, preventing her from drawing a breath, but she would not allow this woman to intimidate her. "I hope your children are on their way to a safe place, Direktorin."

For a moment, Monica thought the other woman might attack her physically and knew she was in no condition to endure a beating. Instead, Frau Sauchel turned on her heel and walked away.

Monica and the others arrived at the gas-mask factory in the dark of predawn and left well after dark had set in for the night. There were only a few narrow windows near the factory ceiling, and the electric lights were inadequate for the close work involved in constructing even one mask, much less dozens. Monica's job was to glue the eye pieces into the cloth of the mask – a two-step process that involved applying the glue and then positioning and securing by pressing down the lever of a machine. She sat shoulder to shoulder between Pia and Greta and was grateful for their help as her fingers stuck to the fabric, making the assembly difficult.

There was no talking allowed, and the hours passed to the symphony of pressing and sewing machines as each mask made its way down the table. At night they were so exhausted, they could barely manage to eat the meager rations left for them before collapsing onto their cots. Often the lights throughout the prison were already extinguished by the time they were led back to their cell. Day after day, the same, as it became nearly impossible for Monica to find the energy to keep up the spirits of her friends. Instead, they cared for her – making sure her quotas were met, even on those days when she could not stop coughing.

And then, one bitterly cold morning, the guards descended on their cells with shouts of "*Schnell!*" Assuming they were being roused for the morning roll call, they trudged out to the court-yard wearing only their prison dresses and wooden clogs. While standing in deep snow, they were told they were leaving at once for a transfer from Cottbus to a prison in Waldheim – over one hundred miles west.

"It is for your safety," Frau Sauchel announced, and then gave the signal for the guards to start marching them out of the pris-on gates and on to the railway station. The guards wore heavy coats, hats, gloves, and boots that allowed them to move briskly through the deep snow covering the road. The prisoners had had no time to grab even the threadbare blankets they huddled under through the night. Their clogs slipped on the icy path as they slogged through sometimes calf-deep snow trying to match the pace set by their escort.

They had barely started the forced march when Tulle fell, and Greta and Alice quickly helped her to her feet, hoping a guard had not seen. The weak would not be tolerated. Monica leaned heavily on Pia, her feet so cold, she could barely put one in front of the other, but she was certain this was their chance. Not a march to death, but a march to freedom. Once they reached the station, Monica saw that a train was already waiting, the engine huffing impatiently. As they were led to cattle cars, she saw the prison matrons, including Frau Sauchel, boarding passenger cars, their luggage being piled on with them.

They had known. They had had time to prepare.

The air filled with the bedlam of soldiers yelling, dogs snarling, and women screaming in protest as they were forced onto cattle cars hooked to the passenger cars – the guards counting off sixty women crammed in each before the door was slammed shut and sealed with a heavy lock. Inside the car, there was no straw or hay to insulate the floor, and the walls were covered in a thick moldy frost so that even being inside, out of the driving snow and wind, they were freezing. The train lurched forward, sending the contents of a bucket used as a toilet by previous occupants spilling over the floor and the feet of those nearby. Pia helped Monica to a spot near an opening in the slatted walls, holding her upright between the wall and the crush of bodies around her. Instinctively she found her balance as the train settled into a rhythm, clicking off the miles.

This trip was no different from those they had endured before. Sometimes the train slowed or came to a complete stop and sat on a sidetrack for hours waiting for a troop train to arrive and go on its way. Sometimes that train never came, and without warning, they started forward again. Hours passed. There was no food and no water, and they were not allowed off the train even when it was stopped for long periods of time.

Monica continued to find the strength to lift the spirits of her friends – as well as her own. "March in place," she advised, her voice so weak that Pia had to repeat the instructions for the others. "And flex your fingers." But such actions were impossible in the crowded conditions while trying to maintain one's balance as the train rocked and swayed. Eventually Monica slid to the floor, while her cellmates formed a protective guard around her.

Night came and went.

On the second day, during one of their stops, the women nearest the doors found their voices and demanded water. To their shock, the door to their car was wrenched open as one of the matrons was helped aboard and then handed a bucket of water. Monica saw the others press closer, but something in the way the guard looked at them told her this was a trick.

"*Wasser!*" The female guard dumped the contents of her bucket over those prisoners closest to her and then, to a chorus of laughter from her fellow guards who had gathered round to watch, she jumped back to the ground and walked with them back to the warm car. Once again, the door slammed shut, and other than sporadic sobs from some corner of the car, all was quiet.

Day two passed, and darkness brought an even deeper cold. Although she felt the need to somehow come up with a plan for getting through this horror, Monica's thinking was jumbled, careening from one thought to another, from one time in her life to another. She lost consciousness and came to, not knowing where she was or why these women around her were there. She tried to speak but could not find her voice. Her breath came in shallow gasps.

By day three, she was barely aware of the passing of time or, indeed, who she was. The woman closest to her kept calling her Monica and urging her to suck on a bit of ice chipped from the dirty wall. She did not recognize this young woman. Was it her daughter? Did she have a daughter? Unable to work out the mysteries, she sank back into the oblivion of unconsciousness.

She dreamed of other times and awoke only when the train

came to a stop, but instead of the usual silence of deserted fields and countryside, she heard the stamp of marching feet, the snap of rifles being positioned at the ready. The doors slid open and armed soldiers shouted at them to jump from the fetid car to the station platform below. Two women lifted Monica to her feet and half carried her from the train. Prodded by the butts of the soldiers' weapons and the barely constrained lunges of large dogs, they shuffled their way out of the station and down a street. When Monica stumbled over an ice-encrusted rut in the street, a soldier gave her a shove.

"*Sterben!*" Spittle puddled at the corner of his full lips as he repeatedly shouted at her to die.

With the support of the other women, Monica slowly found her footing, straightened, and looked him in the eye.

"*Du zerst,*" she replied as she allowed the close quarters of the throng of her fellow prisoners to move her along. *You first* would probably earn her a bullet in the back, but she no longer cared. She might be confused about who and where she was, but she had no doubt anyone wearing that uniform was her enemy.

Ahead she saw the first of the prisoners entering a church. She fixed her eye on the steeple and forced herself to keep moving forward, grateful for the strong support of the young woman from the train who had never left her side.

When she woke, she was lying on a wooden pew, covered by a rough but thick wool blanket. A man sitting next to her – a minister by his garb – was holding a cup.

"*Guten Tag,*" he said. "I am Pastor Emil Viereck, and you are – for the moment – sheltered here in the church. Do you think you might be able to swallow a bit of broth?"

A coughing jag made any response impossible.

"Monica!" A smiling face appeared from the pew behind where she was lying. The young woman was familiar, but Monica struggled to find the name. In spite of the days and nights of unbearable cold, now she felt as if she were on fire.

"She has a fever," she heard the minister say.

"She was ill before we began our journey here," the young woman replied. "It's a miracle she made it, but Monica is the strongest, most courageous woman I have ever known."

Pia!

Over the next days they were moved to the Waldheim prison, where once again they were under the guard of Frau Sauchel and her matrons. But Monica was so weak that she was barely aware of anyone or anything. Once again, they were in separate cells, and because she could scarcely stand, much less take a turn in the exercise yard, she saw none of her fellow prisoners. Pastor Viereck visited and tried without success to intercede on her behalf. And then in late February, when the guards suspected Monica might have contracted typhus, they had her moved to the prison's sick ward and isolated there, with the pastor as her only visitor.

She drifted in and out of consciousness, her mind playing a loop of memories like the silent films she had seen as a young girl.

Dancing with Jorgen...walking the streets of Paris with Kurt...playing with her children on the terraced green lawn of Engestofte...long walks with her mother in Rapallo...the garret room in Paris...the kindness of Heinz at West Prison...the meetings with Flemming...and then, more distant childhood memories of adventures with Jack....

At such times she saw herself as the young, vital woman she'd once been. At other times she fought for the strength it would take to hang on just a little longer. *So, this was what it was like to die.*

Pastor Viereck continued to visit, bringing her updates he obviously hoped would inspire her to continue that fight, but Monica could not make sense of his words, only his tone. She found comfort in his presence and his hand holding hers, even as she felt as if she were slowly drowning from within.

Behind him, through the lone window in the room, Monica caught sight of the brightness of the moon in the blackness of the night.

She roused herself enough to pull her hand free of his and point. "Open?"

"Of course." He hurried to do as she asked.

Monica closed her eyes as the freshness of the cold air filled the room, overpowering the stench of illness. Prison walls and bars obstructing her view faded. In a moment of rare clarity, she understood this was likely her final hour – her final moments. How appropriate that it should be the moon lighting her way. All her life she'd had a fascination with the moon, and now the silent movie scenes came with the dizzying speed of a flip book she had once created for Viggo.

Walking with Jack at night on the cliffs of Donegal, planning their futures...slipping from the house at Engestofte to retrieve the arms and supplies...sitting near the window of a prison cell while her friends slept....

She thought of Jorgen and the marriage they had created from nothing more than a contract.

And she thought of Kurt – of his passion and his weakness – and decided to forgive him that weakness and wish him well.

As she reluctantly let go of the last vestiges of consciousness, she thought of Ivan, Varinka, and Viggo – for it had all been for them.

She surrendered at last to the peace and calm that came over her like a blanket. She had lived life on her terms – without regret.

She had won her war.

AFTERWORD

ON THE TENTH OF APRIL, 1945, one of the matrons unlocked Pia's cell. The matron was smiling, and Pia realized that her smile was a bit shy and there was a nervous catch in her voice as she told Pia she should gather her belongings and come with her.

Belongings? The only thing she had managed to hold onto was the basket Monica had made for her. She placed her hands in her pockets and faced the guard. "I have nothing to gather."

Once out in the corridor of the prison, they stopped to collect Greta, Alice, and Tulle. The guard kept up a friendly chatter as they followed her across the compound toward the gates of the prison – and then on beyond the gates, where a blue-and-white bus, its sides emblazoned with a Danish flag, waited. The driver hopped down from his seat.

"*Velkommen, mine damer!*" He stepped aside and indicated they should board the bus.

The four women could not contain their happiness. They were free. They were going home. They joined arms and danced in a circle as they laughed and cried out with jubilation.

But once they had boarded and had feasted on the box lunches the driver gave them, Pia could not help but think of Monica. Her dear friend had died just six weeks earlier, and Pastor Viereck had seen to her burial in the church's cemetery. He had assured Pia that his letter had reached Jorgen Wichfeld and given him the details of Monica's final hour.

Once the news reached the family, Jorgen, along with Ivan, Varinka, Viggo, Hanne, and Flemming, traveled to London to attend a memorial service organized by Alice Beresford. So much time had passed since they had all been together in Italy, the reunion was one filled with tears and laughter. The church was crowded with friends and family and those to whom Monica's work had meant so much. Afterward the family returned to Engestofte, while eventually Alice went home to Rapallo.

Less than a month later, as Pia sat in her apartment listening to the BBC, a news bulletin interrupted the regular programming with the announcement that the Germans had surrendered. Denmark was free. Along with her neighbors, Pia rushed to tear down the blackout curtains from her windows and replace them with lighted candles. Across the land, church bells rang, and by morning, it seemed every home flew the Danish flag.

Perhaps at long last, we can bring Monica home, she thought.

But peace does not come without complications. Once Waldheim became part of the Russian zone following the war, Pia and the family lost contact with Pastor Viereck. Word reached them that the cemetery had been overrun by Russian soldiers and the church had been badly damaged in the days following the surrender. Viggo and his siblings worked tirelessly with the authorities to arrange for returning Monica's remains for reburial in the family graveyard next to the chapel at Engestofte. But when, after months of negotiation, a Danish commission was finally granted access to the cemetery in Waldheim, they found the grave empty.

Monica's remains have never been found.

AUTHOR'S NOTE

This is a work of fiction based on the life of the remarkable Monica Beresford Wichfeld. While I am grateful for the research others have provided regarding the events of her life, I have also found it necessary to try and imagine details such as conversations and the internal thoughts and emotions Monica might have experienced. That said, the timeline and events of the story are well documented, and I have endeavored to remain true to those factual details. After my planned trip to Denmark had to be canceled due to the COVID pandemic, the manuscript was vetted for historical accuracy by Caspar Jetlex, curator at the National Museum of Copenhagen and formerly curator at the Museum of Danish Resistance (also in Copenhagen). Sections of it have been reviewed in workshops with readers in Wisconsin and Florida. I am indebted to Caspar and to my Sarasota workshop friends – all gifted writers in their own right – to whom this novel is dedicated. Nate Voellm's striking cover design adds to the stark reality of Monica's difficult life, and

Elizabeth Lotito went above and beyond in her role as editor. It does indeed take a village.

In answer to the question of what happened to other key players in the story, there was little to discover. Monica's mother, Alice, lived out her life in Rapallo, Italy, dying in 1948. Jorgen remained at his beloved Engestofte, where he died in 1966. Ivan and Hanne divorced shortly after the war ended, and Ivan remarried. He died in 1959. Varinka and Flemming Muus were married in 1944; she died in 2002. Viggo married late in life and died in 1994. None of Monica's three children had children. And Kurt Reventlow remained in America, where he died in 1969.

In building this story, I have found much to admire – and even love – about Monica. Whenever we encounter a person of such courage and conviction, the question we must ask ourselves is: What would I have done in similar circumstances – and what would I do today? Monica Beresford Wichfeld was not perfect, but she was a woman who faced dark times and made decisions that led to a real difference in the world she left her children. I hope you come to admire her strength and character as much as I have.

Thank you for choosing this book. Please let me know your thoughts at JOHORNEAUTHOR.COM/CONTACT.